TRACKING THE TEMPEST

The barghest crouched in front of me, ready to fight. We raised our shields almost simultaneously and then seamlessly blended them together, my water flowing through his combined air and earth to create a wall of elemental force that was virtually impenetrable.

Which was lucky, as right then a blast of fire streaked across the pasture toward Anyan. It was red and angry, and it was backed up by a pummeling wave of power so fierce that even behind our übershield I staggered under its onslaught.

I went to one knee but no farther, for Anyan was there, bracing me with his massive shoulder. Engulfed in fire, we barely kept it at bay with our shields. We were as yet unharmed, but fire and snapping energy were everywhere.

Only then did my dazzled brain put together what had just happened.

I may have fled Boston for my own safety, but all I'd accomplished was bringing danger directly to Rockabill and the people I loved.

BY NICOLE PEELER

Jane True novels
Tempest Rising
Tracking the Tempest
Tempest's Legacy

TRACKING THE TEMPEST

Book Two of the Jane True novels

NICOLE PEELER

orbit

www.orbitbooks.net

ORBIT

First published in the United States in 2010 by Orbit
First published in Great Britain in 2010 by Orbit

A CIP catalogue record for this book
is available from the British Library.

ISBN 978-1-84149-967-3

Typeset in Times by Palimpsest Book Production Limited, Falkirk, Stirlingshire
Printed and bound in Great Britain by CPI Mackays, Chatham ME5 8TD

Papers used by Orbit are natural, renewable and recyclable
products sourced from well-managed forests and certified
in accordance with the rules of the Forest Stewardship Council.

Mixed Sources
Product group from well-managed
forests and other controlled sources
www.fsc.org Cert no. SGS-COC-004081
© 1996 Forest Stewardship Council

Orbit
An imprint of
Little, Brown Book Group
100 Victoria Embankment
London EC4Y 0DY

An Hachette UK Company
www.hachette.co.uk

www.orbitbooks.net

To Janis and Saul Bellow,
for opening my world

CHAPTER ONE

This time was for real. Nothing could stop me. I *would* crack this lesson. I *would* create this damned mage light. I *would not* burn off another eyebrow . . .

Keeping up my flow of positive thinking, I watched as a tiny sphere of blue light flickered to life in my palm. It began to grow as I fed it with my power, trying to keep myself calm. But my stomach strummed happily as a wave of triumph washed through me. I fed the bright orb just a tiny bit more . . .

And with a terrific bang it exploded, knocking me back on my ass and the breath out of my lungs.

When my vision cleared, I made out a pair of muddy-brown eyes staring into mine. The eyes were attached to Trill, the kelpie, who lived most of the time in the sea surrounding my village of Rockabill, Maine. As a kelpie, she had two forms: the weird little sea-pony form she was in now and a humanoid form that would *never* pass as normal, even with tequila goggles.

'She still has both eyebrows,' the pony reported, her voice oil-slick slippery.

'Good,' came Nell's deceptively grandmotherly tones. 'She looked hideous with just the one.'

The kelpie nodded sagely, and I gave her my most

baleful glare. 'Thanks for caring, Trill,' I told her as I grabbed a hank of her seaweed forelock to help haul myself up.

'No problem, Jane.' She winced, shaking free of my hold on her mane. Without which I thumped back onto the grass, my head spinning. Magic hurts when it goes kablooey.

I groaned pathetically as Nell's little face loomed over mine. 'Come on, Jane. Get up. Now is not the time for resting.'

I took a deep breath, blinking my eyes to clear my vision. Finally, I struggled upright, still a little woozy. Nell the gnome smiled at me, but I wasn't fooled. Behind those rustic clothes and that pleasant expression lurked the disposition of the gunnery sergeant from *Full Metal Jacket*.

'Come now, Jane. Stand up and do it again.'

Do or do not. There is no try, my weary brain chittered at the tiny but implacable old lady currently staring at me with her wee fists balled at her hips. If I didn't know she could drop me in a heartbeat, I would have picked her up by her giant silver bun to discus throw her into the trees. Instead, I laboriously clambered to my feet and then took a second to reclip my bangs off my face. I was growing them out, and they were officially at the stage where they were driving me crazy.

When finished, I slowly, painstakingly, cleared my mind, trying to picture my head as an empty room, painted all in white, that held no sound. I then pictured myself sitting cross-legged in the middle of that colorless, silent room – eyes shut and perfectly in control of both my body and my mind. I felt my breathing grow shallow as I tried to withdraw even further inward, to where the power lay within me.

'Concentrate, Jane, and pull from within,' came Nell's soothing voice. 'Now, this time, create the light without focusing *on* the light. The light is the natural result of your manipulating your powers. Don't let the light itself distract you from control.'

I held my palm out in front of me. Technically, I didn't need to use my hand to create the light. But it helped to solidify my visualization of what I wanted, and I'd seen that a lot of supernatural folk, including my lover, Ryu, used their hands in creative ways when making mage lights.

And Ryu has very creative hands, chimed in my ever-irrepressible libido, as if on cue.

'Jane!' Nell barked as my attention veered to Ryu, and the little shell of power I'd begun building around myself began to fizzle. I pulled my hormones up sharply and went back to my clean bright room, keeping it conspicuously absent of a certain handsome man and his big beautiful fangs—

'Jane!' This time Nell's voice was decidedly miffed.

I sighed and focused, firmly banishing all stray thoughts. When I was finally centered, I pictured the mage light as a spark flaring up in my palm. I fed the spark, keeping my emotions at bay, and watched as it grew into a little golf ball-sized globe of light. I held it steady, maintaining it in my palm.

'Good,' said Nell. 'Now, try making it bigger.'

'Bigger' was where things usually went wrong. I focused, again, doing my best to keep calm as I started feeding energy into the small sphere. As I did so, I visualized it expanding. The shape in my palm trembled, and I forced myself to continue my slow, deep breaths. And then it grew, its pulsing skin stretching until it was about the size of a baseball.

'Excellent, Jane. Now disperse it, but remember to recycle your energy.'

This part I was good at. I focused my will and gently siphoned the energy out of my mage light, being careful to bring as much of it back into me as I could. Technically, I could let the power just flow back into the environment, but Nell was a firm believer in 'waste not, want not'.

The light wavered, stilled for a split second, and then winked out of existence. I couldn't help but close my hand with a little flourish. Now that I couldn't blow anything up, I was allowed to be pleased with myself. That was the first time I'd managed to create and disperse a mage light start to finish.

'Who's your daddy?' I demanded rhetorically, doing a little happy dance.

'He died centuries ago; you wouldn't know him,' Nell replied, coming toward me. 'Stop hopping about and shields up.'

Aye aye, Captain, I thought, even as I dutifully raised my defenses.

Almost immediately, the gnome let loose a fierce barrage of tiny mage balls straight at me.

'Shit!' I swore, reflexively throwing up an arm to shield my face. Despite my momentary lapse of control, however, my defenses held. I watched, still flinching every time, as each little blast of Nell's power struck the invisible barriers I'd erected about arm's length in front of me. Nell's little mage balls weren't enough to do any real damage, but I knew all too well that the little fuckers stung like hell. This time, however, they all fizzled out on my shields in bright bursts of light. After a moment, I realized it was quite pretty, like being trapped in an inverse snow globe.

Finally, the gnome grunted happily and ceased her attack.

'Excellent, Jane. Your defenses are strong.'

I squirmed with pride at Nell's words, for having strong defenses brought me even more pleasure than creating the mage light. After all, while mage lights did make finding my underwear easier in the dark, having strong shields would save my life.

'You've never had any trouble seeing through glamours,

so I think you're ready to start creating them,' Nell continued, gathering tighter the shawl she wore about her shoulders. 'But we'll leave that for next time. For now, go eat. And don't forget to swim tonight. You'll need more power than you expect for glamours.' She came toward me to pat my thigh with one of her tiny hands in the gnome version of a pat on the back. 'You're beginning to make real progress.'

'Thanks, Nell,' I said, meaning it from the bottom of my heart. Although I knew I had tons to learn, at least I wasn't as entirely helpless as I had been.

My introduction to the supernatural world I now inhabited had been brutally swift. Four months ago I'd been boring old Jane – bookstore clerk and secret night swimmer. Till one night I'd found a dead body and suddenly I was Jane True, half selkie and heir to a very nonboring magical heritage. The dead body had turned out to be one of a series of murders being investigated by Ryu, the guy I was currently seeing, and I'd gotten embroiled – big-time – in the investigation. During which I'd nearly been killed twice: once in a physical attack by Jarl, the closet Hitler, and once by Jarl's lackey, the now-deceased Jimmu, who'd frozen me with his magical snaky stare. I'd been a sitting duck to Jimmu's naga glamour, which is why, four months back when I started training with Nell, Anyan Barghest's sole command to my new teacher had been that Nell teach me to make my shields secure before anything else. I think Anyan was just tired of playing hero, considering he'd been obliged to rescue me both times I had nearly lost my head.

That said, and despite how chaotic the last months had been, I had no complaints. My life was a constant cycle of work, train, take care of my dad, and swim, but I loved every minute. And, while things had been too crazy for me to make it to Boston yet, about once a fortnight I would meet Ryu in a bed-and-breakfast in Eastport for our patented weekend marathons of sex and eating. In other words, I was happier now than I'd been since Jason had died so many years ago. I felt . . . whole again. I did stay up late, sometimes, worrying about what had happened with Jimmu, unable to understand the true motivations behind the murders he'd committed. Ryu had assured me that the investigation they'd done into the nagas' murders, after the fact, had been extensive and thorough and hadn't uncovered anything for me to be worried about. But I did worry . . . and I knew there was more to those murders than just the nagas' racist hatred of halflings urging them to homicide.

That said, I couldn't spend my life worrying about Jimmu. Especially not when everything had fallen into place for me. It's like I'd finally discovered the Jane True I'd always been meant to be. I still had a lot to learn, but I was really, really excited to grow into the woman I glimpsed lurking on the horizon.

She is pretty fucking fierce, I thought, laughing at myself for my little burst of sheer narcissism.

The gnome ignored my random giggling but did acknowledge my thanks with a nod. Then she took her leave, waddling toward the forest surrounding our training pasture. Trill gave me a horrible pony grin – her eerie gray skin stretched taut over her bony skull – before she turned tail to follow Nell into the woods.

I stretched, long and leisurely, before wandering off toward the cabin that butted up to the pasture we used for training. The door was locked, so my bag was lying on the stairs of the cabin's wide, wraparound porch.

I eyed the little house, wishing I could get in there. I had to pee, first of all, but I also loved snooping around Nell's cabin. It was full of amazing art, and it had this awesome kitchen I would kill to cook in. It also smelled deliciously of lemon wax and cardamom, a combination of scents I'd come to crave. But it was closed up, and the gnome had gone off to do whatever it is gnomes do, so I dragged my battered old messenger bag off the stairs and started down the path that led to my house.

Feeling my oats, I gave my bag a jaunty swing. It twirled, obligingly, around my arm and I laughed. So I gave it another swing, harder this time. Which resulted in me dumping its contents onto the rough path beneath my feet.

Sighing, I knelt down to pick it all up, wondering, for about the fifth time that month, whether Nell had a spell to make me less of a spaz.

'I saw it and knew it was for you. Happy early Valentine's Day!'

I held the T-shirt up to admire it as Iris's honeydew voice washed over me. That said, I had to tear my eyes from her, resplendent in an aquamarine wool sheath dress that accentuated her golden skin and hair, to appreciate my gift. The shirt was white, with huge dark gray and silvery angelic wings etched on the back and a small heart with wings and a halo emblazoned on the front. It was adorable and I loved it.

'Thank you *sooo* much, Iris,' I said before passing the gift I'd gotten her over the table.

We were at the Trough, our local diner. Many of Rockabill's businesses had pig-related names in honor of our whirlpool, the Old Sow, which was a tourist attraction as well as my favorite place to swim. Not intending to seduce the good people of Rockabill, Iris was dampening down her natural mojo, but I could still feel it brushing against my carefully constructed shields. And despite her efforts, the succubus's effect on the other diners was very evident. Everyone in the Trough was turned toward Iris, their own postures reflecting each of her movements, just a little, like flowers tracking the path of the sun through the sky.

She pawed aside the gift bag's decorative tissue to find the first three books of my new favorite paranormal romance series. They featured the antics of extraordinarily boink-able demon men, and since Iris *was* a succubus, after all, I thought they were an entirely appropriate Valentine's Day gift.

'Ooo, covers,' Iris cooed, stroking a French-manicured nail over the lusciously muscular tattooed back of the first novel's cover model. I nodded my agreement. I normally didn't like the whole 'brooding man' choice of cover, but these totally rose my biscuits. They focused on the body and the tats – rather than the usually disappointing pretty-boy face that most covers sported – and I was happy to follow their lead.

'I know.' I grinned, partially happy that Iris liked my gift but also happy that I could even have a conversation like this with her. A few months ago I had no chance of keeping my shit together around an aroused incubus or succubus. And they were *always* aroused. But now, while I felt the waves of Iris's sexual juju against my protected mind, I was totally capable of keeping on my underpants.

'Sexy?' she asked, arching an eyebrow at me.

'Incredibly,' I answered. 'Slightly bizarre caveman-style monosyllabic dialogue in some of the sex scenes, but other than that, they are *hot*.'

'Mmmm. Sex scenes,' Iris purred, her eyes glowing gently in that trademark succubus manner. I laughed as Amy, our local nahual waitress, came to take our orders.

'What can I get you fine ladies this evening?' she asked.

'The usual,' I said, which meant a lemonade and a tuna melt.

'Can I have this?' Iris asked in her honeydew voice, holding up one of the novels I'd bought her so that Amy could see the cover.

'Sorry, hot man is all out at the moment. We have some corpulent taxi driver and a slice of crazy cat-lady left, but we ran out of hot man hours ago.'

Iris tsked, her luscious lips pouting adorably. 'Then I'll have a Diet Coke and the chef's salad. Dressing on the side.'

'You got it,' Amy said as she ambled off.

'Now, Jane,' Iris said, her brilliant blue eyes fixing on mine like spotlights. 'Tell me what you and Ryu have planned for Valentine's Day. Maybe a ménage à trois?'

'Why?' I asked suspiciously. 'Has Ryu said something to you?'

'No,' Iris laughed. 'I was trying to make a joke.'

'Never joke about Ryu and sexual experimentation. Ever. My heart can't take it.'

Iris grinned a particularly feral little smirk. 'If he weren't a waste of my time, I'd take him for a spin. Share trade secrets and whatnot.' Iris wasn't calling Ryu a waste of time because she didn't like him but because, for whatever reason, only humans and some halflings created the right type of magical essence that succubi, incubi, and baobhan sith needed to feed.

I shook my head at Iris. 'The thought of you two together terrifies me. You'd burn through the floor. You'd probably smash your way to China. The friction would start a cold-fusion reaction.'

Iris laughed. 'Unfortunately, he's like celery to me. I'd burn more energy eating him than I would get from digesting.' I cocked my head at her metaphor, trying to decide if it was sexy or just bizarre as she continued, 'And besides, except for feeding, he's got eyes only for you, Jane.'

At her words, my whole body froze. The thing is, the situation between Ryu and me was really complicated. I liked him, a lot. But he lived in Boston, where he was based. He was kind of like a supernatural detective, and it was a big deal to be in charge of a city so large and important. Meanwhile, my life was here, in backwater Rockabill. My dad would never move, as he was convinced my mother would someday reappear. He also had a bad heart, so I had to be around to help take care of him. I wasn't about to abandon my father, and Ryu wasn't about to abandon his career. So, even though we'd been dating since we met, we were still in this delicious honeymoon stage. We had our heady weekend flings, and we never had to deal with real life.

But I still knew damned well that 'real life' meant Ryu's being with other women. He was a baobhan sith, the beings that had inspired our vampire mythologies. He drank blood, but not much. He only needed essence, not food. Nevertheless, Ryu couldn't do his job without expending a lot of energy. Therefore, he couldn't do his job without consuming a lot of essence from human veins. As my veins were in absentia, in this scenario, two plus two equaled him getting a little nookie on the side. He couldn't just find any old neck and sink in his fangs, or rob a blood bank, or drink synthetic blood like vampires did in the movies. After all, it wasn't the actual blood Ryu fed on, but the emotions. So he had either to scare the shit out of someone or arouse them. He had either to become a creature of nightmares, the kind of creature I wouldn't *want* to date, or stick with arousal and do what, in human terms, would be considered cheating.

But just because I could do the math didn't mean I wanted to. Ever. As Iris kept pouring lemon juice in my wounds, my face went all blank and weird, and I knew my friend could sense how uncomfortable she'd made me by bringing up Ryu's sanguinary infidelities.

'Oh, gods, Jane, I'm so sorry. That was so stupid of me to say. I'm really sorry. I know Ryu cares for you . . . I shouldn't have mentioned the feeding . . . I'm sure he'd just feed off you if he could. And I can tell you from experience that the sex really doesn't mean anything . . .'

I tried to take deep breaths as Iris plied her shovel, digging herself deeper.

'I mean, he probably doesn't have to feed *that* often anyway, and you do see each other quite a bit, so it's probably only a few times a week that he needs to go off on his own . . .'

Before Iris could apologize any more, I forced my throat to work. 'No, Iris, it's stupid of me to get upset. It's just all so *fucking complicated*.' My stressed, already overly loud voice rose on those last two words, causing old Mrs Patterson of the randy Yorkies to glare at me from over her bowl of clam chowder before she went back to staring in rapture at Iris. 'Let's just change the subject,' I begged. 'Tell me about *your* plans for Valentine's Day.'

The good thing about succubi was that they were wonderfully easy to distract. Wiping away her sad expression, Iris started telling me about the marathon of debauchery she had planned for the weekend. I let my mind start to wander when she got to the part about her intended visit to Eastport's fire station.

'. . . so the good part is they can just hose me off at the station and I won't have to worry about showering. Get it? Hose me off? Since it's a fire station? Jane, are you listening?'

Iris's syrupy French-toast voice finally interrupted my inner critique and I snapped to attention.

'I'm sorry, Iris. I'm here. And you're talking about hosing. Again.'

Right then, Amy came with our food and I managed to veer Iris toward more innocuous subjects as we ate. We talked about her boutique and some new stock she wanted me to try. When we were finally finished, I insisted on picking up the check, so she insisted on paying the tip.

'Should we head out to the Sty?' Iris asked when we were in the parking lot. I shuddered. Not because I didn't love the Pig Sty, our local bar that was owned by a pair of nahuals whom I adored. It was just that the Sty was also usually home to Stuart Gray, Jason's cousin and Rockabill's self-appointed made-for-TV bully. Stu hated me, and I hated him right back.

'Sorry, Iris, but I'm gonna pass. I don't want to deal with Stuart.' Not tonight, with my self-control just about shot. One word out of Stu's obnoxious mouth and I'd probably zap him with a lightning bolt. If I could zap lightning bolts, that is.

'How about a ride home?' she asked.

'Make it the beach and you got a deal.'

She nodded and we ambled over to her little pink hybrid. 'I don't see your wet suit,' she said, casually, as we got in her car.

I ignored her as I buckled my seat belt.

'Are you just going to leave your clothes in the sand?' she asked, trying a different angle. 'Don't they get dirty?'

I blinked at her, and she started up her car.

'I could hold them, you know. For you. Make sure they stay dry.'

I fiddled with her car's stereo.

'Just a little sex? Please?' Iris's voice was like caramel apples. I burst out laughing.

She laughed with me. 'I'm sorry. I can't help it.'

'I know, Iris. I know,' I said, still giggling as I patted her hand affectionately. 'But those lines do put the *suck* in "succubus".'

CHAPTER TWO

After work the next day, I went home before going to train with Nell. The screen door on our little house creaked alarmingly when I opened it, and I made a mental note to oil the hinges. My key stuck, as usual, and I jiggled it the way I knew it liked to be jiggled until I was allowed inside. My dad was sitting in our little living room to the right of the door, watching poker.

'Hey, Dad!' I said, surreptitiously checking on his condition before I hung up my coat.

'Hey, honey,' he answered. He sounded, and looked, really tired.

'How you feeling? Can I get you anything?' I knew he'd hate that I fussed, but I couldn't help it. I was good at fussing.

'Oh, I'm fine. Just tired.'

I ignored him, walking over to give him a good once-over. Despite his obvious fatigue, he didn't look too bad, and whatever new medicine the doctor had prescribed seemed to be helping. He'd looked decidedly rosier recently, and he was sleeping better.

'Really, I'm fine. I just stayed up too late watching that stupid movie.'

I grinned at him. 'I hope you didn't tell the guys you stayed awake to watch *Steel Magnolias*,' I chided.

He groaned. 'Are you kidding me? I'd never hear the end of it. I'd have to go out and chop down a tree or change a tire to prove my masculinity. But I do love that damned movie,' he confessed finally.

'And that's why I love you, Dad,' I said, leaning down to kiss him on his stubbly cheek.

'I love you too, honey. And I don't want you to worry so much. I really feel good. That new treatment seems to be helping.'

'You do look better,' I said, as much to myself as to him.

He nodded, closing the subject. 'So, what's for supper?'

'I thought I'd make that ginger fish and some rice and salad.'

'Sounds good, honey. And there *might* be something in the kitchen waiting for you.'

I narrowed my eyes. 'What kind of something?'

'Oh, just something,' my dad answered casually.

Well, it couldn't be a naked vampire or my dad wouldn't be so calm. But I still crept into the kitchen warily, knowing my lover's penchant for taking the Hallmark holiday to a whole new level of gratuity. I was terrified fireworks would explode or the naked vampire would jump out of a massive cake.

My mouth started watering suddenly, although I wasn't sure if it was over the thought of Ryu naked or the idea of cake.

Mmmmm . . . cake . . .

My cake-and-sex fantasies were foiled, however, for neither lurked in my kitchen. Instead, there sat on our counter a perfectly normal bouquet of red roses. All right, there were a *lot* of roses – at least three dozen – but they were just roses. I checked to make sure the vase was a standard-issue florist vase and not diamond encrusted. It had taken Ryu a while to understand that I just wanted him, not his money. Where was *I* going to wear designer clothes or jewelry? In the Old Sow? So I was happy to see the roses, as he knew how much I loved flowers. Hopefully, Ryu would follow up his gift with a visit – Valentine's Day wasn't until tomorrow – but the roses were an excellent start . . .

 . . . *and quite a finish*, I thought as I finally found the card attached to the flowers. Which was no card at all, but an open-ended ticket to Boston. For the next day.

I giggled, just as the heavens cued our phone to ring.

'Hello?' I answered, knowing damned well who it was.

'Hey, baby,' purred out the voice that, no matter how familiar it had become, still sent shivers down my spine.

'You,' I said. 'You . . .' I continued, unsure whether to thank him or just give in to temptation and lick the mouthpiece.

'Are amazing? Extraordinary? Sexy? Yours? I can continue—'

'Ryu,' I interrupted.

'Jane,' he breathed, as my womb did something involving a roundoff and jazz hands. 'Do you like your gift?'

'The flowers are beautiful, babe. Thank you.'

'Not nearly as lovely as you, my sweet. But they aren't the real gift. Can you come?'

I smiled at how he drew out that last word, feeling my bosoms commence their familiar Ryu-related heaving. If I hadn't been excited to see him before, he'd just catapulted me to positively gleeful.

'Yeah, I can come. I'll still have to check with Grizzie and Tracy, but I'm sure it will be okay. The store is dead right now, with the holiday. I'll also have to make sure the boys check up on my dad. But that shouldn't be a problem. I'll just make a few calls and then I'm all yours.'

'*All* mine, baby?' he purred. 'Because you know I'll take you up on that offer . . .'

I laughed. 'Easy, killer. If you make me self-combust, I won't make it to Boston. But I *am* really excited to see you. I've missed you.'

'I've missed you, too, honey. I always miss you. I've talked to you about this . . .'

I fell silent. Ryu had been intimating we move our relationship up to the next level since the last time we saw each other. But I just didn't see how that was possible. So I handled the situation with my usual, very mature tactic of ignoring him completely.

'Well, you're lucky; you had good timing,' I said. 'This is a perfect time to visit. But next time, you might want to check with me first. What if I *had* been busy?'

Ryu chortled his funny trademark laugh, and the lust in my belly spread through my limbs like Greek fire. 'You're never too busy for me, baby. I *know* you.' Before I could protest that claim, he moved on. 'And you're going to love it. I've got an amazing weekend planned. You'll never want to leave.'

'You always have amazing things planned,' I said gratefully. 'You're Ryu.'

'And you're Jane. For Jane, I'll move mountains.'

I laughed. 'I'll be happy with dinner, darling.'

'Then I'll just move your legs. Around my waist, while you're up against the wall and I'm standing. After I've removed every last stitch of your clothing . . .'

I blushed, as my nearly immortal beloved attempted to engage me in phone sex while I stood in my well-lit kitchen, my dad in the next room watching poker in his battered recliner.

'Ryu.' I gulped, my voice husky. 'I'm in my *kitchen*—'

'Then you can spread yourself out on the table while you listen to me. You know what we like to do on tables—'

'*Ryu*,' I interrupted desperately. I couldn't take it. Maybe *I* had the bad ticker. 'Tomorrow. I'll see you tomorrow. Then we can—'

'Yes.' It was his turn to interrupt me. 'Then we can. And we will. I've missed you, Jane. It's been, what, two weeks?'

'Yes.'

'Too long. I hate missing you.'

'I do too, Ryu.'

'Well, tomorrow you'll be all mine. For the entire weekend, and longer if you like. The return ticket can be used whenever.' He knew I was going to tell him I had to come back, so he didn't let me break in this time. 'But this weekend, for certain, you're mine.'

'All yours,' I agreed.

'Think about me tonight, Jane. When you go to bed.'

There was no chance of me *not* thinking of him, not after this evening's phone performance. 'I will, Ryu. Believe me.'

'Good. And tomorrow you'll be in *my* bed.'

I shivered, silent.

'Bye, baby.'

'Bye, Ryu. See you tomorrow.'

He was wrong, of course. It felt like an eternity till I was in his arms.

But then, just like that, I was.

One minute I was craning my head trying to figure out which carousel my luggage was on and the next my feet were dangling as I was swept up into a tight embrace.

'Jane,' Ryu purred into my ear. 'Gods, it's good to see you.'

Pressed that tight against him, I could feel just how good it was.

I rubbed my cheek against his short-cropped chestnut hair and then pulled back slightly so that my skin dragged across the slightly rougher texture of his smooth-shaven jaw. Wrapped up in his arms, I was blanketed in his signature scent of warm skin and balsam soap, with that hint of cumin that made my mouth water. As I inhaled, I continued on my mission until I found what I'd been searching for and my lips met his. The heat that had been pooling in my gut exploded through my body with palpable force.

We stood, necking like teenagers, as my fellow passengers claimed their luggage. They were oblivious to us; Ryu unconsciously sent out various glamours either repulsing or attracting attention, depending on the situation. Despite knowing we were unseen, I would normally have been uncomfortable with the bustle around us. But it *had* been two weeks, and I was losing myself in Ryu's clever mouth. Our kiss deepened and I pulled my legs up to wrap around his waist, until I gasped as Ryu's now well-extended fangs cut my lip deeply. I tasted blood, for just a second, before my lover's mouth found the pain. He sucked gently at the wound – making me moan – before his tongue swept across the gash once, twice, and then a third time, finally healing me.

We were both breathing heavily and I could feel him tremble. I unwound my legs, allowing myself to slide down the hard length of his body. Leaning back in his arms, I let my eyes scan up over his broad shoulders in their crisp white button-up to the strong column of his neck, to his handsome face, finally meeting his beautiful, golden-green gaze. I'd never get enough of Ryu's eyes. They were really hazel, but with only the barest flecks of green that gathered together right near his pupils, leaving the rest of his eyes a nearly unadulterated amber-gold. A surge of pure lust washed through my system. When I was away from him, I forgot just how gorgeous Ryu was, and the effect he had on me.

I knew my lover could read every sign of my arousal – my dilated pupils, my rapidly beating heart, my blood rushing through my veins – as if it were written on a billboard. But, just in case he had any doubts, I moved my hips in a firm little shimmy against his already straining trousers. He closed those lovely eyes and groaned, pulling me tighter against him before pushing me away.

'Unless you entertain a secret sexual fantasy involving Logan Airport, I suggest you quit torturing me,' Ryu said, his normally smooth voice delightfully lust-gruff.

I grinned at him. 'You deserve torture after last night. I had to swim an extra hour to expunge the horny from my system.'

'Well, I hope you didn't swim off *all* your horny,' he said, running a hand over my backside to guide me toward the luggage carousel.

'I'm sure I'll manage to dredge something up,' I said drily as I made a grab for my heavy suitcase. Ryu pulled it easily off the belt, grinning at its size.

'Planning on staying for a while?' he queried, his voice hopeful.

'No, I've definitely got to get back on Monday, at the latest. But I made the mistake of asking Iris to help me pack.'

The succubus had driven over that night with a month's worth of stuff already packed in the massive suitcase. She'd taken one look at the little carry-on rollerboard Ryu had given me and burst out laughing. The carry-on had disappeared, the few things it already contained stowed into the last remaining corners of the behemoth sitting at our feet.

'Really?' Ryu asked slyly as he took the suitcase's

retractable handle with one hand and my fingers with the other. He raised my palm to his lips in his signature gigolo gesture before leading me toward the exits. 'And what, exactly, did Iris suggest you pack?'

I blushed. If my case sprang open at that moment, spilling its contents for Logan International Airport to see, most people would assume that Boston was hosting some sort of adult entertainment convention and that I worked for one of the big names.

'Socks. Vitamins. The usual,' I squeaked. I knew the succubus had gotten into my dirty drawer, where I kept all of Grizzie's presents. Grizzie gave dirty gifts for *every* occasion, and as I'd known her a long time now, the drawer in which I stored my unmentionables was a veritable cornucopia of fetish-tastic smut. I couldn't begin to guess at the intended usage of some of the vaguely phallic bits and bobs Grizzie had given me, and so they'd remained unopened, safely tucked away. But I'd come back from digging out my old toiletries bag from the hall closet to find the dirty drawer open and Iris patting my suitcase, her eyes glowing like high beams.

'Mmm-hmm,' Ryu drawled, arching one of his achingly expressive brows at me. The man had developed a form of communication akin to that used with fans by women in the nineteenth century; he could converse eloquently and at great length using just his eyebrows. Right now, the otherwise very sophisticated vampire by my side had a mouth saying, 'I'm so glad you're here, Miss True.' But what his *eyebrows* were saying was 'I'ma rock yo' shit, shorty'. I liked what both his mouth and eyebrows had to say, so I strained up on my tippy-toes to kiss them each in their turn. Ryu obliged me by stooping into kiss range.

'I'm glad I'm here, too,' I told him, trying to get my own

eyebrows to say 'I'ma rock you right back, boo', but I managed only to look constipated.

'Although, we may have to leave this suitcase here. I don't know how it'll fit in my car...' Ryu had every right to be concerned. The suitcase was enormous, and he drove a Porsche Boxster.

Or at least he used to.

Because he was either stealing the itsy-bitsy black BMW we were walking toward in Logan's parking garage or he'd bought a new car. This time my eyebrows did manage to speak volumes.

Ryu grinned. 'I got bored,' he said, his voice arch.

'What *is* that thing?' I asked. The little car *was* beautiful. But it stank of overcompensation, midlife crisis, or general skankiness. Ryu had nothing to compensate for, and he was too pimp to be skank. That left midlife crisis. He *was* a few decades short of three hundred years old and probably due for some sort of nervous breakdown.

'A Z4 M Roadster,' he answered me, running a hand over the car's hood.

'What happened to the Porsche?'

Ryu smiled innocently at me. I knew that smile well. It was the smile he gave me right before he did something unspeakably filthy. 'I had an accident,' was all he said as he opened the trunk and began stuffing it full of my suitcase.

'Do I want to know?' I asked when he'd finally wrestled the trunk closed.

'No,' he replied as he came around to open my door.

I let myself be herded into the car, buckling myself in and then twice checking to make sure I was securely fastened. I pulled the belt sharply to be certain that it worked.

'You probably learned an important lesson about safe driving from the accident I'm not supposed to ask about, right?' I inquired of my vampire as he settled into his own seat. Ryu gave me his most angelic smile, the one he used when I was *really* in trouble.

'And you don't want to wreck this nice, new car, do you?' I continued, praying he didn't want to wreck this nice, new car. The vampire ignored me.

'Ryu, you have all this lovely fresh upholstery. You don't want me to wet myself with fear, do you? Ryu? Ryu?'

Once belted in, Ryu adjusted his rearview mirror and then deigned to turn to me.

'Honey, why do you worry? You know I'm always safe.'

'No,' I said. 'You are not "safe". You drive like a fucking lunatic.'

'Jane, don't worry.' Ryu chuckled as he started the engine. It growled like a rabid dingo. 'This is Boston.' I thought about that. He wouldn't have to be so aggressive on his home turf, right? And Boston was famous for its tight squeezes and tiny roads. *Boston never burned!* I reminded myself. How nuts could you drive in a veritable labyrinth?

He whipped out of the parking space so fast my stomach was left sitting there, burbling in surprise. He aggressively shouldered in front of one of those faux-military SUV wank machines that could have steamrolled us flat as a Fruit Roll-Up. He braked just long enough to fling money at the bored parking attendant in her little booth. She didn't even flinch when he gunned the evil little car so sharply that we barely missed crashing through the slowly lifting barrier.

'What happened to "This is Boston, Jane"?' I asked my demon lover through clenched teeth.

'It *is* Boston, Jane,' Ryu began as he embarked upon a complicated maneuver that involved seven lane changes, two milk trucks, an old VW van with every inch covered in SUPPORT OUR TROOPS stickers, and a few choice expletives.

My heart was in my throat. My stomach had retreated to my shoes.

'. . . and *everyone* in Boston drives like a fucking lunatic,' Ryu finally finished, just as he slammed on the brakes to avoid hitting the car that had totally just cut us off while going about ninety miles per hour.

It was a black-and-white Boston Police squad car, lights off, just making the rounds.

I'd never been a very spiritual person, but at that moment, I learned to pray.

CHAPTER THREE

It wasn't until Ryu told me we were home that I opened my eyes. I'd shut them when we'd reached Storrow Drive and Ryu had bypassed Ridiculous and gone directly to Ludicrous Speed.

'Jane, darling, you all right?' The little shit leered at me.

'Smoke if you got 'em,' I mumbled as Ryu helped me out of the car.

'Huh?'

I shook my head. '*Spaceballs*. Never mind.'

'Ah. Anyway, welcome to my home.'

We were in Bay Village, looking at an adorable brick town-house with a navy-blue front door and navy blue shutters. It looked like a miniature version of one of the grand town-houses we'd seen on Beacon Hill.

'Ryu,' I breathed. 'It's lovely.' And it was. The whole street was lovely. Small, tree-lined sidewalks meandered alongside other townhouses, all of which had doors and shutters painted different colors. Many had window boxes that I'm sure would be full of flowers come spring. Everything was small and perfect and neat; Bay Village offered a little oasis of order tucked into the middle of downtown Boston right up against the glorious chaos of Chinatown.

'I like it here,' he acceded, looking pleased. *And preda-tory*, I thought as he took my hand to lead me forward. 'I'll get your suitcase later, unless you need it now.' I shook my head. After all, we couldn't fornicate until we'd gotten past that stately front door, and I was as eager to get inside as Ryu.

As we crossed the threshold it suddenly struck me that I was finally in Ryu's Boston. I couldn't believe that after having known my lover for months now on such an intimate basis, I had no idea how he lived.

Warm sunlight flooded into the townhouse: the wall opposite the door was made up entirely of floor-to-ceiling windows, interrupted only by glass French doors that led out into a courtyard shared by the neighboring townhouses. The walls of Ryu's home were a soft white, although I could see various accent walls in darker shades of dun or taupe. I could also see lots of leather and chrome, and tons o' technology. A flat-screen television took up almost an entire wall across from the Bauhaus-inspired sofa and chairs that dominated the sitting area to our left. In front of us was the dining area. Its glass-and-chrome dining table winked at me in the soft light. To our right was a gorgeous open-plan kitchen: all dark granite, shiny black-lacquer cabinets, and gleaming appliances. An enormous island of granite helped to divide the living space from the kitchen. All the warm sunlight made Ryu's home even more like that of a Hollywood movie set. Everything was perfect – tasteful, polished, and coord-inated – with an overall effect that screamed *money* and *masculine*.

Ryu wrapped himself around me from behind, his lips finding my earlobe. He suckled gently, making me melt back against him, before he finally spoke.

'Do you like, Miss True?'

'It's gorgeous, Ryu,' I answered, tilting my head and raising my cheek a bit so that my ear brushed against his lips again. He obliged me with another little suckle and a nip of his teeth.

'Come in, make yourself at home,' he said, as he pulled away to walk toward his kitchen. I followed him, running a hand over the beautifully aged leather of the sofa. I realized it was probably not Bauhaus-inspired but Bauhaus-for-real.

Ryu pulled a bottle of champagne out of a built-in wine refrigerator next to the actual refrigerator. I excused myself to use the washroom that I could see lurking off the kitchen, tucked underneath the stairs that led upstairs. It was all marble and chrome, of course, with an unbelievably artsy toilet that made me giggle until it took me forever to figure out how to flush the damned thing.

I heard the pop of a cork as I washed my hands and I opened the bathroom door just as Ryu finished topping off two champagne flutes. A bowl of sex-red strawberries beckoned me from the island.

'To you, Jane, and to Valentine's Day. That most romantic of massacres,' Ryu said, after he'd passed me my flute. I raised my glass to his and we clinked.

'And to you, Ryu. Thank you for everything,' I added.

We drank, Ryu never taking his eyes off mine. The second we put our glasses down, he had me in his arms.

'I've imagined you here so many times,' he whispered as he kissed my cheek, my forehead, my eyelids. I relaxed into his hold, let him find my lips with his. Our kiss was slow, gentle, and – unlike the greedy need of our airport PDA session – it was a kiss of promise, a kiss that said we *did* have the whole weekend and that we needn't rush things.

A promise I blatantly ignored as I raised my hand between us to run my fingertips down the expensive fabric of his shirt

to the slick steel of his belt buckle. But before I could get in
a good crotch fondle, Ryu's phone blared out a ringtone that
sounded like a siren.

'Shit,' Ryu said, pulling away. He looked down to where
my hand hovered above his groin. 'Fuck, and damn,' he added
for good measure. 'I have to take that; it's one of my deputies.'

I shrugged and let go of his belt. Ryu was the supernatural equivalent of a police detective, and I knew he had to
do what he had to do.

'Yes?' Ryu demanded of his cell phone as he strode toward
the door that led out of the kitchen. I got a brief glimpse of
a cluttered office before the door shut firmly on my curiosity.

I quaffed the rest of my bubbly, which fizzled its way
directly to my brain. While it was up there, the champagne
reminded me that Ryu's inopportune phone call had given
me the chance to do the *other* thing I really wanted to do the
moment I saw Ryu's front door. I wanted to snoop. And so
snoop I did, starting with the kitchen. Which was *hilarious*.
Not because it wasn't as impressive as it had appeared from
the front door. Everything *was* state of the art, but the reason
it shone so was that it was almost entirely unused – he still
had plastic coverings on the racks inside the oven. The wine
refrigerator was full, but the actual refrigerator was empty
except for beer, bananas, bacon, and bread.

B *is for 'bachelor'!* my brain chortled as I started in on
the kitchen drawers.

Again, everything was state of the art, expensive, and
entirely unused. Really fancy knives sat in an expensive
butcher's block, all but the largest still with their handles
wrapped. A salad spinner sat in a box and a Le Creuset
Dutch oven was fresh from the factory, still taped shut. Ryu
did have a well-used microwave, espresso maker, blender,
and toaster oven on the counter, but there were no other

appliances. And except for dishes and glasses, the cupboards were practically empty, as were the drawers. One held cutlery, another dish towels, and a final drawer held about one hundred takeout menus.

I could hear Ryu arguing in a low, heated voice with someone. I couldn't make out what he was saying, but I didn't think the conversation was going to wrap up any time soon, so I went right ahead and made my way upstairs.

To the left of the landing, I found what had to be a guest bedroom. It looked like a luxurious hotel room – both inviting and impersonal. Then there was a guest bathroom that was small but, again, luxurious. Which left the last door, the closed one, to be Ryu's bedroom. I turned the handle slowly and let the door swing open.

There were no sex swings or stripper poles or mirrors on the ceiling. And yet, just like the man who made his home here, the room reeked of sensuality. The bed was *huge*, first of all. It was like a playing field, dominating the room. And, except for two nightstands, a low bureau, and a small armchair, there was nothing else in the bedroom. No television for late-night talk-show viewing or bookcase full of late-night reading. The furniture arrangement clearly stated that this room was about the bed and everything that occurred there.

Maybe the sex swing's in the closet, my libido hummed optimistically as I stuck my head between the two doors that led off the bedroom. The ridiculously organized walk-in closet served as a showcase for Ryu's impeccable taste, but there was no sex swing, much to my libido's disappointment. Meanwhile, the other door led into an amazing en suite wet room. Sex swing forgotten, the libido purred with anticipation at the granite shower with its plethora of spigots and jets and seating upon which to lounge. I wasn't all that surprised that in Ryu's world, even bathrooms became conducive for sex.

I shut the door on the wet room and returned to the bed. Standing before it, I giggled, for the bedding was all black satin. In A.S. Byatt's novel *Possession*, when the slightly repressed English heroine thinks of her louche former lover, Fergus Wolfe, she sees an unmade bed with sheets like 'whipped egg-whites'. Inspired by Byatt, whenever I'd thought of Ryu, I'd thought of black satin sheets. And here they were, in all their playboy glory.

I kicked off my old green Converse and stretched out on the bed, resting after my long day of travel and the stress of Ryu's kamikaze driving. But the call to snoop still rang in my ears and – after listening for a moment to make sure Ryu wasn't sneaking up on me – I opened the drawer of the right-hand nightstand. Which contained four long silk scarves and a silk blindfold, still sporting their store tags. I snorted in glee as the sight of the black silk both tickled my funny bone *and* tinkled my ivories. The vampire had a thing about tying me up, and while I definitely wasn't complaining, I did keep threatening to go Freud on him. After all, I wasn't entirely sure he was kidding when he said that one day he wasn't going to let me go.

But so far, every time I got him on the couch, we ended up having sex. It didn't take a doctorate in psychology to diagnose the both of us with impulse-control issues. We were still like kids in a candy store with one another, and I loved it.

Beside the lamp on the other table was one of those electronic picture frames that showed digital images. I flicked it on, and to my astonishment, there I was: sticking my tongue out at the camera from the steps of the Notre-Dame de Québec basilica cathedral. The next picture was of Ryu and me, heads nestled together, grinning. Then there was a beautiful black-and-white photo of a woman sleeping, her naked back to the camera, a sheet draped over her hips to protect her modesty. After a second I realized it was me, and I reached out to turn off the frame. I felt uncomfortable for some reason, even though they were pictures of me that – with the exception of the one where I was asleep – I knew had been taken. I blinked at the frame for a second before reaching for the drawer of the second nightstand.

The other drawer was empty except for random detritus, like a broken watch. Seeing Ryu's junk drawer was the first indication that a real person lived here and not just a rogue gigolo.

I eased the drawer shut and lay back on the pillows, smiling. It felt good to be here, to see how Ryu lived when I wasn't around. Turning my head to nuzzle into the pillow beneath me, which smelled deliciously of Ryu, I rolled over to lie on my side. Then I reached toward the nightstand to angle the clock so I could see what time it was. In doing so, I jostled the old-fashioned rotary telephone standing bulky and proud on the table, revealing a nondescript address book hidden beneath it.

It was black. I told myself that this scenario was way too fucking clichéd. There was no way that thing was Ryu's 'little black book'.

My heart sinking, and my hands suddenly trembling, I reached for it.

Don't do it, Jane, my brain warned me sagely. *You're not going to like what you see.*

But I could no more not look at what was in that book than I could resist rubbernecking at a car accident.

The contents the book were laid out in Ryu's neat, professional handwriting. There were names and phone numbers, as I knew there would be. And there was even a vampire version of the sort of sexual rating system a human male might use. Instead of a gal's abilities in the sack, however, Ryu's system for evaluating a woman involved her vulnerability to glamour (some humans were more resistant than others), the amount of elemental essence in her blood (low, medium, or high), and her blood type.

I closed my eyes, letting the book flop forward onto my chest.

Dear gods, I thought. *Am I in here?*

I once again raised the book and, with trembling fingers, searched back toward *T*. While there were quite a few entries, there was no Jane True listed. Just to be on the safe side, I searched under *J* as well. I wasn't listed there, either.

I shut the book and stuck it back under Ryu's phone. Suddenly cold, I burrowed under Ryu's black satin duvet, curling up in a fetal position.

There hadn't been anything I didn't know in that book, but seeing it all laid out like that made Ryu's existence so much more real than it had been. I was just thankful I hadn't found my own name among all the others.

That list of names is no different from that drawer of takeout menus in his kitchen, I realized. I didn't know if that idea made me feel better or worse.

I could still hear the murmur of Ryu's voice downstairs. Keeping my eyes closed, I let the warmth from Ryu's bed seep into my skin, even though my heart still felt chilled. I wished I could just pass out, but I wasn't a napper. I was tired from traveling all day and getting up so early and having swum so late. Not to mention that, at that moment, I would give anything for the sweet oblivion of sleep to take me away from my frenzied thoughts.

Ironically, the last thing I remembered thinking was that

I really wished I was someone who could sleep in the day time . . .

I tried to swat away the mouse climbing my stomach, but it persevered. And then the mouse began to take my shirt with it, and I suddenly realized that I was no longer in Rockabill, in my childhood bed of white wood and pristine cotton sheets, but in a black silk boudoir of vampiric possibilities.

And said vampire was looming over me, running his finger up the soft curve of my sleeping belly, pulling my T-shirt up over my breasts. His warm tongue found my navel, and then traced its way north, dragging me with it into full awareness. My nipples waved hello at him as he pulled down the cups of my bra. Graciously, Ryu returned their salutation by suckling each in its turn, leaving me gasping.

'. . . so much better than an alarm clock,' I mumbled, as my brain struggled to keep pace with my body.

Ryu's mouth released my suddenly heaving bosoms and he snuggled close, his lips against my ear.

'Did you have a nice nap?' he purred.

'Mmm,' was all I could think to say in response, burrowing sideways into his hard chest. 'How long was I asleep?'

'Two hours,' he said. 'You were too sweet to wake.'

'Wow, sorry. I never nap like that. You should have gotten me up.'

He did his best to chuckle, but because it was Ryu, he sounded a bit like a braying donkey. I instantly melted – my lover's laugh was the only nonsuave thing about him and I adored it. Then I thought of the little black book, waiting like a time bomb beneath the phone next to me, and my stomach sank.

'I want you well rested for this evening, Miss True,' Ryu said archly. I focused my gaze on his lovely mouth, reminding myself that I knew what he was, I was pretty sure I knew what we were, and I knew that it wasn't fair of me to freak out for him feeding. It would be like freaking out on a diabetic for injecting himself with insulin.

Except insulin doesn't talk back, my inner cynic reminded me in her driest voice.

I shushed my passive-aggressive streak, reminding myself that I had two choices: I could either confront Ryu and have a talk I wasn't sure I wanted to have, or I could save that conversation for another time. Preferably a time that wasn't Valentine's Day.

Suck it up, buttercup! my libido commanded. It clearly didn't want anything interfering with its romantic weekend.

'And besides, watching you sleep always gets *me* up . . .' Ryu said, as if he'd heard my libido's demands. So I tried to pacify both parties by wiggling my hip closer to his groin, just to test, and was not disappointed.

'. . . although we do have dinner reservations and we both have to get ready. So quit yer wriggling, aargh,' he said, using his pirate voice for the last bit. Ryu gave great pirate and it always made me giggle.

'We can't push the reservations back?' I asked, refusing to cease wiggling. Having Ryu teasing me, being sexy and silly, made me forget everything else, even that damned book.

'No, sorry . . .' Ryu looked pained. 'I managed to get us a table at the one restaurant in Boston that even I am intimidated by. It's not only *the* place to be seen at the moment but it's also run by a gorgon, who, quite frankly, scares the shit out of me. So cease and desist, woman.' I neither ceased nor desisted. When Ryu finally realized I was not going to give him a break, he pinned my hip down with his hand using but a fraction of his preternatural strength. I shivered; I loved it when he went all alpha on me.

The minute he felt me shiver, his eyes went dark, staring into mine with a new intensity. His fangs were out and I knew what he needed.

'Maybe a little aperitif?' I whispered, my voice soft even to my own ears.

Ryu smiled, but it never reached his eyes. He pulled me to him, his mouth meeting mine as his hand again found my breast. His fingers stroked my nipple, then pinched, and my whole body tightened in response.

'Minx . . .' Ryu purred, as his lips nuzzled into my neck and his hand roved down my belly until he was at the waistband of my jeans. He unbuttoned them slowly, laving my pulse point with his hot tongue. I knew he was 'laving' because I'd been reading all about various forms of vampiric 'laving' – definitely the word of the day – in my paranormal romance books.

My breath hissed out of my lungs as his hand slipped into my panties to find me already slick with need. He sighed his approval as he made a fist in my underwear, loosening the restraining fabric of my clothing to give him enough room to work.

The man is an artist, I thought, just as he slipped two fingers inside of me and all coherent brain waves ceased.

I was so hot and so ready and Ryu was playing for keeps. Within minutes, I was panting his name, and when he brought his thumb into play, directly on my sweet spot, my back was arching and I was practically screaming and he was biting and then the pleasure was just too much. It was all I could do to ride the waves of sensation that threatened to carry me up out of my body and off to Orgasm Central.

When I came back to Earth, Ryu's fingers were still inside of me, enjoying the feel of the aftershocks racking my muscles as his tongue healed the wounds at my neck.

'You?' I mumbled, barely coherent. But Ryu understood.

'Later,' he answered. 'This was more than enough for now.'

He kissed me gently, and I tasted the coppery sheen of my blood on his lips.

'Go shower; I'll get your suitcase,' he said, finally withdrawing his hand.

'You don't want to come, too?' I asked, enjoying my pun.

He frowned. 'Quit it, Jane. Seriously. She's a *gorgon*. She refused a state senator *and* pushed back the reservation of a pregnant teenaged starlet to give me this table. If we're not exactly on time, she will destroy me.'

I sighed.

'Please, if you sigh like that, I'll fuck you. And if I fuck you, I won't stop, and then we will be late, and then the gorgon will *destroy* me. Did I mention the part where she destroys me? And then we won't ever fuck again, and *then* you'll have something to sigh about.'

Ryu knew damned well that humor could overcome any emotion in my world, even lust. I couldn't help but laugh as he helped me to my feet and pushed me toward the wet room.

Meanwhile, I began strategizing all the various ways in which *I* would destroy him, later. *And he's afraid of a little gorgon*, I thought as I wondered what, exactly, Iris had packed from my dirty drawer. *Game on, Vlad*, I thought, waggling my own eyebrows at my vampire's back as he went to get my suitcase.

I'll show you an 'Impaler' . . .

CHAPTER FOUR

I breathed out a sigh of pure pleasure as we gazed off over Boston's city lights. Ryu's arms were tight around me, and he whispered in my ear as he pointed out various points of interest. After my eyes had had their fill, we returned to our little table by the window to enjoy our cocktails.

We were at the Top of the Hub, a restaurant and bar perched high atop Boston's Prudential Tower. We'd had dinner earlier, at a different restaurant, and I got the feeling that Ryu considered the Top of the Hub a little too touristy to be cool. He'd brought me anyway, however, because he knew I'd love the views.

We'd had dinner at a place so chic its name was simply its address. It was an extremely small and intimate restaurant, where we were treated like royalty. And apparently the table next to us, all men dressed like sheiks, really *were* Saudi royalty, so I had a direct comparison. We'd ordered the chef's seven-course tasting menu, paired with seven different wines, and Ryu had worked some metabolic mojo on me to keep me from being completely schlitzed. I found myself, once again, in that physical state I'd come to associate with my time with Ryu: stuffed to the gills, slightly drunk on both wine and barely sated lust, and feeling utterly, totally pampered. A girl could do worse.

'Nell said you're having no trouble erecting your shields, although you're still not erecting them quite as reflexively as you should be.'

'Exactly,' I said, honing back in on Ryu and resisting the temptation to point out that he'd said 'erect'. Twice.

'Well, your reflexes will develop with time and experience. You need to be around your own kind more, besides Nell and that lot. You're living in a bubble out in Rockabill.' I frowned, and he rolled his eyes. 'I'm just saying, Rockabill isn't the real world. But, in the meantime, I can show you a few things while you're here. Nell said you were ready for glamours, so we can go ahead and start working on them if you'd like.'

I grinned. 'Excellent.'

'I think you'll be good at it. You're creative, and when you focus, you have a tremendous amount of concentration behind your power. It's just getting you to focus.'

'Hmm?' I asked, too busy attempting to engage him in a round of footsie to hear what he was saying.

'Exactly,' Ryu laughed smugly. 'Although I do appreciate your choice of distractions.'

Ryu stood up and moved his chair next to mine, pulling me to him. He kissed the tip of my nose and then found my mouth, sucking gently on my bottom lip.

'You have no idea how good it is to have you here, baby,' he murmured between kisses.

'I like being here, too. I like seeing how you live.'

'In most ways, I live really well,' he acceded, smiling. Humility wasn't Ryu's strong point. 'But having you here makes it even sweeter.'

His tongue swept over the pulse throbbing in my throat

and I shivered. I wanted to say something sexually empowered that would curl his toes with lust. Instead, to my horror, I blurted out, 'I saw the book under your phone.'

Ryu withdrew, his eyes narrowed.

'Sorry?'

'I was trying to see what time it was and I bumped your phone. And I saw your address book.'

'And you looked inside.'

I nodded, glumly, although I didn't really feel all that apologetic. After all, Ryu's life here was something we needed to discuss, eventually. But I was also well aware I wasn't going to win any houseguest awards.

'Well, Suzy Snoopsalot, we obviously have to talk.' Ryu scrubbed a strong hand over his face, his typical gesture of worry. 'I'm sorry you saw that, but it's the truth. And I know you know that. Are you okay, first of all?'

'Of course,' I said, my voice surprisingly firm. 'I think I understand, as much as I can. And I think I'm okay with everything. Sort of. But it is strange. And I think I feel like I shouldn't be okay with everything, even though I do feel okay . . .' I trailed off, losing momentum. 'It's complicated,' was my lame conclusion.

Ryu looked grim. 'It is complicated. And, to be honest, I hate it; hate the whole thing. I'm so tired of . . . Shit, Jane, I'm just tired. Can we get out of here? And really talk?'

That drained voice, coming from the man I associated only with vitality, cut to my core, and I folded like a glove. I reached over and took his hand, raising *his* palm to *my* lips. I kissed him gently and closed my eyes as he moved his fingers to cup my jaw.

I let the heat of his hand sink into my skin, finally meeting his eyes with my own.

'Please?' he asked.

'Anything you want, Ryu.' And I meant it.

'C'mon, baby. I have one last surprise for you.'

Ryu paid for our drinks and we left. He wouldn't give me any indication of his plans, so we strolled, arm in arm, down Boylston Street until we got to the Boston Public Gardens, all shut up and dark for the evening. Stopping at the locked gate, Ryu stooped down, making a stirrup with his two hands.

'Alley-oop, my darling,' Ryu said, grinning.

'Um, really?' I asked. 'You're the master of "opening things",' I reminded him. 'Can't you just unlock the gate?'

'I could. But this is much more fun.'

Sighing, I placed my foot in his cupped hands and he lofted me like a cheerleader. I squeaked a protest, fumbling for the heavy iron gates to steady myself. I carefully maneuvered my feet into the most secure-looking crevices I could spot, which were part of the fancifully curlicued top of the gate, and then shifted my weight from Ryu's hands onto my chosen footholds. Ryu waited until I was clinging to the fence before he grabbed a hold of the iron bars and launched himself smoothly up and over in a single burst of strength. I grumbled something unforgivably rude about his family heritage and began arduously stepping over the very top of the ornamental gate, setting my feet back into their little crevices on the opposite side so I was facing back out toward Boylston.

'Go ahead and drop, Jane. I'll catch you.'

I looked at the vampire beneath me. If I hadn't damn well known I'd be stuck clinging to the fence, I would have attempted to beam death rays at him through my eyes.

'C'mon, baby. You can trust me.'

I didn't remind him that the last time he'd said those words to me, I walked funny for two days. I just gathered courage, took a deep breath, and pushed myself away from the fence.

Ryu caught me effortlessly, laughing.

'I said *drop* down, Jane, not launch yourself like a rocket.'

'I'll give you a rocket,' I mumbled.

'Sorry?'

'Nothing. Just put me down.'

'No,' he murmured, cuddling me closer to his chest.

I considered protesting but being in his arms felt good. So I let him carry me. When we got to the bridge that crossed the little lake where the swan boats were, he set me down on my feet.

He waved a hand and the lights came on, illuminating the river and the boats and the bridge. Well, he didn't actually light *the* lights, he just made his own.

I looked out over the dark water, feeling it murmur to me. Where my ocean roared, this man-made reservoir whispered. The lights of the city glittered off its surface, helping Ryu's own lights illuminate the graceful lines of the swan boats floating at their moorings, each tucked into its place like horses in a stable.

'It's lovely, Ryu.'

'I thought you'd like it,' he replied, resting back against the bridge's balustrade. 'You said you remember it from your childhood?'

I smiled. Only the second time he'd come to Rockabill, right after all the drama at the Alfar Compound so many months ago, I'd told Ryu about a family trip we'd taken years and years ago when my mother was still with us. A conversation Ryu had not only remembered but also included in his plans for my visit. It was unbelievably sweet, but part of me wanted to curse at such sensitivity. This was the kind of shit that made me want to fall in love with the vampire, and *that* was too complicated for words.

'Yeah, I was only, like, five, so the memories aren't very clear. And maybe they're not even my memories, but just me remembering looking at the pictures. We came to Boston the year before my mom went away. I like to think I remember it.'

I walked over to where he stood, leaning over the bridge to look out at the water and the pavilion where the boats sat moored.

He watched me in silence as I tried to place myself, even shorter than I was now, on this same bridge, holding the hands of both a man and a woman. The woman would soon leave, and my life would never be the same, but for that moment I must have been happy.

Ryu brushed my hair behind my ear, turning his body so that we were hip to hip, facing the same direction, looking out over the water.

'Jane,' he said. 'I want to ask you something. You don't have to answer now, and we don't have to do anything about it yet. It's just something I want you to think about.'

I turned toward him, looking up into his face. I'd never seen him so serious.

'It's just that I like us together. I like *us,* period. I like being with you, having you near me . . .' Ryu's voice trailed off nervously, and he reached up to fidget with the strap of my top. He ran his fingers down to trace my bicep. 'You feel right. We feel right. I know you don't like to talk about this stuff . . .' His finger continued its featherlight trail down my forearm, but when he went to take my hand, Ryu accidentally hooked my bracelet in his finger. When he pulled down, it came off.

'Shit, sorry,' he said, as we both bent down at the same time to pick it up and knocked noggins. We laughed ruefully, rubbing our foreheads.

'I'll get it, hold on,' I said. The bracelet had been my mother's; I didn't want to lose it.

Which is what saved my life. Just as I knelt to scrabble around at my feet for the bracelet, a wall of flame came blasting out of the darkness from our left, straight toward our heads.

Ryu hadn't been kidding about magical reflexes. His shields were up the moment the first tingle of magic hit us, a split second before the fire came. Unfortunately, his reflexes had yet to include me, and I had missed that lecture altogether. So when the blast hit, I was barely covered by the edges of his shield. Which stopped the majority of the fire; otherwise I would have been well cooked. But his shields didn't stop the sheer force of the power behind the flames.

I'd just managed to grab hold of the bracelet when I was launched into the air. I don't remember hitting the cement light pole that stopped me from hurtling into the pond, nor do I remember falling to the concrete ground of the bridge. But I do remember pain and I do remember smoke.

I also remember thinking I'd better learn me some reflexes, pronto.

CHAPTER FIVE

When I swam back to consciousness, Ryu's polished Gucci ankle boots were planted on either side of my waist as he protected me with his shields. Blast after blast of power hit us, but he held the flames at bay. He was barking orders into his cell phone and seemed in control. But he shook with every fresh barrage of that deadly combination of fire and raw force.

I reached out my hand – the one not clutching my bracelet – to touch his calf through the black wool of his trousers. But with my focus distracted by pain, I needed skin-to-skin contact, so I wiggled my hand under the hem of his pants' leg in order to wrap my fingers around his ankle.

I wasn't trying to get frisky; not even I am that licentious. I knew Ryu's shields were sucking the strength out of him. So I added my strength to his, visualizing my own power arcing down my arm, out of my palm, and into his body.

The moment my power hit him, he jerked. I was tied to the element water; as a baobhan sith, Ryu cultivated essence, which was elementless. So he couldn't 'absorb' my power to strengthen himself, but he could funnel that force directly into his shields. In a flash, he'd built his defenses till they were more like stable walls surrounding us than a shield held out in front. Ryu glanced down at me to give me a tight smile of thanks. I nodded, continuing to pulse power down the thread connecting us.

My little bit of shared power allowed Ryu to go on the offensive. From behind our walls, he began to launch arrays of little blue energy balls out into the darkness toward where the fire was emanating from. They weren't meant to hurt; they were more like probes. Ryu was trying to determine *exactly* where our attacker was located.

He was still shouting into his phone, but when I heard a note of triumph in his voice, I knew he'd found his mark. He was immediately yelling directions, and this time he was sending out larger bursts of energy that were tinged with red. They *were* meant to hurt.

Suddenly, feet pounded past us on the bridge, and I heard shouts and thumps coming from somewhere far off. Voices were yelling in the distance, but I tuned them out and focused on sending my little tendril of power up through Ryu.

It wasn't until he bent down and pulled my hand from his ankle that I stopped. He crouched over me, running his hands over my body.

'Jane, are you all right? Where are you hurt?'

I was exhausted, having given him, magically, just about everything I had in me. In my confusion and pain, I hadn't controlled my output very well.

'. . . back . . .' I mumbled, trying to struggle upright.

Ryu held me down, shouting for someone named Julian.

A tall young man wearing small wire-framed glasses knelt next to me. He looked kind and very young.

'She's drained herself. She needs a boost,' Ryu barked.

'Water, right?' asked the boy.

'Yes. Hurry.'

Julian put a cool hand on my forehead and suddenly power arced into me. Not only was it power, but it was also *my* power – the force of the sea roared through my system as if I were roiling about in the Old Sow rather than lying on the dirty concrete of the Public Garden's footpath.

Julian's power boost chased away the exhaustion, making me realize just how much my back hurt. I hissed, going pale, and Ryu's hand tightened on mine.

'Caleb!' he barked.

The kind-faced boy backed away, giving me a sweetly crooked smile. I closed my eyes as the pain intensified, and when I opened them again, I was staring at a pair of huge hooves.

My gaze swept upward over powerful, shaggy goat haunches, past what could only be described as a 'prodigious manhood', to a powerful torso and finally to a handsome, craggy face replete with mussy blond hair and an impressive set of ram's horns.

The goat haunches crouched down, putting me uncomfortably close to the goat man's naked haunches. The satyr – for this had to be a satyr – ran his hands lightly under my neck. I felt healing warmth flow through me and I closed my eyes. Both to block out Caleb's dangly bits but also because the healing really hurt. I felt bones knitting and muscles restitching, and I gritted my teeth against the pain.

I felt Ryu's warm lips on my fingers as he kissed my knuckles and crooned comforting nonsense.

The powerful hands on my neck gently began to push me over until I was on my stomach. Ryu lay down next to me, his hand cushioning my cheek from the dirty pavement. The satyr started on my back again, unzipping my corset-style tank top so that he could have full access to my spine. But this time, the healing didn't hurt. It just soothed and relaxed.

'There were a few cracked ribs, a chipped vertebra, and torn muscles.' The satyr's smooth, deep voice reverberated down into my body through his hands on my back. 'Everything's fine now, although she'll need another few healings or she'll be sore tomorrow. But just some basic work, nothing you can't handle, sir.'

The satyr put my clothing back to rights, and Ryu helped me roll over and sit up before he gathered me into his arms. His eyes searched my face as he ran a trembling finger over my lips.

I wanted to ask him what had happened, now that I had a chance, but as I opened my mouth, exhaustion flooded through my system. Ryu saw the look on my face and nodded.

'I'll explain everything when we get home, I promise. You rest now,' he whispered, kissing my forehead gently before turning toward the small knot of people suddenly surrounding us. If I was honest, I wanted answers *now*, not later, but I still wasn't entirely sure I was capable of keeping conscious. So I had little choice but to take Ryu's advice and listen as I rested my head against his chest.

'What the fuck happened out there?' demanded a dark-haired, swarthily handsome man pushing his way to the front of the little crowd.

'Conleth is back,' Ryu replied, his voice dark. 'He caught us unawares.'

'Damn. How do you know it was Con?'

Ryu looked up, his eyes hard. 'Fire, Daoud. Shit loads of fire.'

The handsome man nodded ruefully. 'Ah, right. Of course.'

'We should have known it would never be that easy,' the satyr said sadly as he met my eyes. His were bright green and beautiful. 'Any pain?' he mouthed at me, and I shook my head, keeping my eyes firmly on his so I didn't gawk at his nakedness.

'How did he find you and your bedmate?' interjected Swarthy.

I pursed my lips at the word 'bedmate'. I'd been called that before by one of Ryu's friends back when we were at their Territory's Compound. I hated that word.

The very edges of Ryu's mouth twitched at my reaction, although the smile did not reach his eyes. 'I have no idea. But everyone's back on high alert. If anything, he's gotten even stronger since we last saw him.'

At that moment, a slender, elegant, slightly flappery woman with bright red hair cut in a precise bob came and stood beside the tall, gawky youth. She put a hand on his shoulder before turning to Ryu.

'Is your bedmate all right?' the woman inquired politely. My pursed lips evolved into an *ick* face.

'Her name is Jane, and, yes, I think she's okay,' he said, gathering me closer so that he could stand.

When Ryu was on his feet, I peered around at the group gathered about us. They were all looking at me with equal curiosity. I wished I wasn't being held like a doll but was unsure whether my legs would hold if Ryu put me down. I was shivering, although I didn't feel cold.

'Hi,' I said, gritting my teeth against the shakes wracking me. 'I'm Jane.'

One by one they introduced themselves. The tall boy was Julian, whose crooked grin propelled him from cute to absolutely adorable. Next to him stood Swarthy, who told me he was Daoud as he gave me the sort of smile that could remove a girl's panties at fifteen feet. Caleb the satyr was next, prodigious manhood and all. I was very grateful to him for healing me, but I couldn't deal with his oh-so-full monty. I suppose the goat haunches made wearing pants virtually impossible, but that's why the gods created ponchos. Next was the elegant woman, who was named Camille. She watched me intently, as if I might have some answer she'd been waiting for. Ryu told me that these were his personal deputies. Finally, there was a big burly man with a short blond crew cut who comported himself with a military bearing. His name was Stefan, and Ryu said that Stefan was like their police chief. Other creatures milled about, but they seemed to be the supernatural version of beat cops. Occasionally, one would approach the burly blond with questions.

Speaking of questions, I had about a million. But with all the hustle and bustle, I couldn't get Ryu's attention.

'Caleb, Daoud, get us home,' Ryu said. 'Camille, my car's parked at the Pru. Will you collect it for me, please? The rest of you, finish up here and we'll talk tomorrow. I want reports ASAP. Stefan, the scene is yours.' The blond man bowed slightly, already moving off toward his people.

Camille and Julian also inclined their heads. Julian gave me a friendly wave that I returned with a tired smile before Camille turned on her heel and strode off, Julian pacing loose-boned behind her.

We followed Daoud and Caleb toward an SUV parked right outside the garden. As Ryu settled me into the backseat, Caleb got into the driver's seat. He barely fit, and I noticed that his horns had shredded the material on the top of the car. Suddenly, Daoud was leaning toward me from the front seat. With a wink, he passed me a lollipop that I could have sworn he pulled directly out of his pants.

'Get well soon.' He grinned, winking at me as Ryu gave him the gimlet eye. I buckled myself in as Ryu closed my door and joined me from the other side. I settled back into my seat as I felt my lower back start to ache.

When we got home and I dredged up the energy to speak, my vampire, much like Lucy, would have a lot of 'splainin'' to do.

I didn't wake up till the voices were saying good night. We were at Ryu's door, and I was once more cradled in his arms. I must have fallen asleep *again*.

'I *never* nap,' I blearily informed Caleb and Daoud. Daoud looked confused and Caleb gave me a tolerant smile before they both walked away.

'Two naps in one day,' I continued to marvel as Ryu carried me inside and up to his bedroom. His face was set in a grim mask, granting me my first glimpse of the Ryu that other people called 'sir'.

'I'm sorry our romantic holiday was a bust,' I said, as we entered Ryu's room. For some reason, I wasn't that freaked out about the attack. Don't get me wrong, I knew it would hit eventually. But for right now, post-shock and post-nap, I felt strangely calm about the whole thing.

Ryu shook his head, remaining silent.

He sat me down on the edge of the bed before pulling off his boots. Then he knelt to remove my own over-the-knee, black, high-heeled, piratey sex boots, gifts from Iris. I loved these boots even more than I loved my Converse, not least because I felt like some sort of swashbuckling slattern while wearing them. When he'd managed to wrestle them off, Ryu stood me up to undo my tight, stretchy black trousers, sliding them down my legs. My black lace panties followed. Finally, he lowered me back to the bed to remove my red corset-style top and the black lace basque I wore underneath. He still hadn't spoken a word to me, and although his hands were gentle, his eyes were hard.

When I was naked, Ryu slid both of us to the middle of the bed, his arms scooped under mine and viselike against my still-aching ribs.

Then he draped himself over me, fully clothed, his cheek pressed to mine. I nuzzled at his neck, trying to inhale his warm balsam scent. He was so heavy that I struggled to breathe, but Ryu needed this, whatever 'this' was, so I lay still. After a full minute, I felt his lips trace the curve of my ear and then brush downward over my cheek to my neck. He raised himself up, straddling my thighs, and he finally spoke.

'Turn over. Onto your stomach,' he commanded.

I met and held his gaze for a moment before I raised my hand to his cheek. He turned his face slightly so that he could kiss my palm, and as he did so, he closed his eyes. For that split second, I saw the pain on his face: all the fear, guilt, and rage he'd felt for me radiated from him in a white-hot blaze of agony. I stroked my fingers down his jaw and then did as he'd asked.

When I was settled on my stomach, Ryu traced his hands down my spine, trailing that telltale healing warmth, and then followed them with his lips. He painstakingly stroked his hands over my sides and up my ribs, before indicating to me he wanted me to turn over. Once I was settled on my back, he continued to heal me, concentrating on my ribs and sides. I touched his hands with my own, trying to reach through his guilt and anger to find *my* Ryu beneath this unsmiling mask. He answered my touch with his lips, meeting first my own mouth and then my breasts.

I started in on the buttons of his shirt, suddenly wanting to feel him pressed against me in the same way he'd obviously needed to feel me just moments ago. Ryu was still working on my ribs, but he released his hands for a moment when I went to pull his shirt off his arms.

I undid his belt buckle and trousers, trying to push them down over his hips before I realized they were going nowhere while he was still straddling my legs. At my gently touching his knee, he scooted down my body and moved his thighs between mine. I pushed his trousers down and opened myself to him, wrapping my legs around his hips to draw him inside of me. Ryu never ceased healing me as he surged into my body.

I raised my hips to him as I pressed my heels into the small of his back. I wanted Ryu to meet me where I was: wild and a little frightened still, but mostly happy to be whole and healthy and feeling the warm rasp of my lover's skin against mine. Answering my body's none-too-subtle demands, Ryu braced his palms on the bed as his passion betrayed his own adrenaline-roughened emotions. All gentleness ceased as his hips pounded into mine relentlessly. He held himself above me, staring into my face. I felt like Ryu was imprinting me with his gaze and I raised both hands to trace my fingertips over the hard set of his mouth.

As if activated by my touch, Ryu spoke.

'Don't you ever scare me like that again,' he said, his voice nearly breaking.

It wasn't often that Ryu let his guard down to show me how much he truly cared about me. I knew he did care, but he was so slick, so sure of himself, that sometimes it was hard to figure out what was really him and what was just his public persona. So seeing him like this made my heart feel heavy and full, and I wanted to tell him I'd been scared, too. That he'd saved my life tonight, and I was grateful to him for so many things. But he knew exactly how to touch that place deep inside of me that turned my body on even as it turned my brain off. So I only managed a throaty whimper.

My whimper turned into a moan as he upped the pace. We

were both close, propelled by passion and fear and our greedy need to prove ourselves still alive and still able to feel, and when I felt the steady rhythm of his hips grow erratic, I reached my fingers down between us as I tightened myself around him, precipitating my own nearly catastrophic release.

I knew I was practically screaming my pleasure, but the crescendo of blood pulsing in my ears was so loud it blocked out almost all sound.

But I did hear Ryu repeating, 'Never lose you, Jane . . . never,' until he buried his fangs in my throat and his own orgasm overtook him.

Afterward, we lay quietly for some time as I again supported his weight without complaint. I knew we *both* needed this closeness.

Nuzzling at my neck, he asked the question I couldn't really answer.

'Are you all right?'

I thought about it. I should have been completely wigged out, but everything had happened so fast. It felt like one minute we were talking, and the next Caleb was healing me. The healing had hurt, as had hitting that light pole, but now I was good as new. So, physically and emotionally, I felt all right . . . It was my mind that was going a hundred miles an hour as I tried to sort through the implications of our having been attacked.

'I'm fine, but I need to know what happened. Who is Conleth? He was so *strong*. He's an Alfar, isn't he?'

I assumed that the attack upon us must have been orchestrated by Jarl, working through one of his underlings. Whoever this being was, he had to be incredibly powerful, so he could only be Alfar. And the Alfar stuck together, so, unless I'd made an enemy I wasn't aware of, that meant whoever had attacked us had to be associated with Jarl.

And if Jarl is randomly attacking you and Ryu, you'll never be safe in Rockabill again . . . My brain's dire warning made my body flush with fear, and I fisted the sheets convulsively to fight off a wave of panic.

Ryu remained silent while he shifted to lie beside me, obviously considering his response. When he finally spoke, his voice was low and serious.

'Conleth isn't Alfar, Jane,' Ryu said, brushing my hair away from my face before continuing.

'He's a halfling. Like you.'

CHAPTER SIX

I stared at Ryu as if he'd just told me Boston was being terrorized by a rabid guinea pig with very sharp, pointy teeth.

'A halfling?' I asked, confused.

Ryu merely nodded, sitting up to unwind his trousers from around his ankles and pull off his socks. I realized then just how upset Ryu must have been about the attack. He never made love in his socks.

'An Alfar halfling?' My mind had leapt gracefully to the conclusion that Jarl the racial purist was also Jarl the hypocrite and had himself a halfling son.

'No, not Alfar. Conleth is half ifrit,' Ryu clarified, lying back to gather me up in his arms.

'*Ifrit?*' I demanded, thinking of the fire elemental I had met at the Alfar Compound so many months ago. He'd been entirely engulfed in flames and I'd nearly barbecued myself trying to touch him. 'How the hell does a human boff an *ifrit*?'

'Just like the apocryphal porcupines.' Ryu shrugged. 'Very carefully.'

I stared at him, nonplussed.

'They can control their fire when they wish, honey. But it's still a risky endeavor for the human,' my lover clarified.

'Wow,' I breathed, as Ryu's words finally sank in. I found it hard to believe that Jarl wasn't behind the attack on Ryu and me. It's just that I'd gotten so used to equating 'murderous attacks' and 'Jarl' that my mind had immediately hopped right on top of that assumption.

So I had to adjust to the idea that somebody *other* than Jarl wanted to kill us.

Plus, that someone was a *halfling*. One who had made Ryu tremble at the sheer force of the magic hurled at us tonight, and Ryu was no pushover. I'd seen Ryu face off the power of the naga prince, Jimmu, *while swordfighting*.

I couldn't wrap my brain around the idea that a halfling could have that much power.

'How?' was all I asked, but Ryu understood my variety of implications.

'Just because someone, like you, is part human doesn't mean they're "halved" in anything other than blood. Remember way back when we first met, when we talked with Iris about Peter Jakes? She told you how halflings have a tendency to surprise their parents?'

I nodded. 'But Jakes could barely do anything and I blew my eyebrow off—'

'First of all,' Ryu interrupted, 'the eyebrow was an accident. We've all blown something off at some point. Second, Peter Jakes *is* important, but not because he was "weak". You're correct that he couldn't do anything the rest of us can. He was essentially mortal if your criteria consist of things like mage lights, or glamours, or whatever. But' – Ryu paused for effect – 'Jakes could do something that none of us could. He could *sense* power, even when it wasn't being used, and – given enough time – he could follow it through to its potential. None of us can do that. None. Unless we're dealing with a satyr, like Caleb, or a goblin or some other distinctive physical type, we can't begin to identify one another unless we're actively using our magic. If I saw you on the street, I would see a young woman. Nothing more. Now, if you tried to glamour me, I'd know you had power. But I still couldn't connect you to selkies, or know exactly how much power you had, or any of the other things that, for some bizarre reason, Jakes could just by spending some time with you.'

I felt my brow furrow and Ryu reached up between us to smooth it out with his fingers. 'And tonight,' he asked, 'what did Julian do for you?'

'He recharged me,' I replied, automatically, before I realized just how impossible that was. 'But how did he do it?' I asked rhetorically, for Ryu's benefit. I had the whole sidekick's 'ask questions so the boss can explain' shtick down pretty well by now.

'Exactly.' Ryu nodded. 'Julian is Camille's son with a human. She's of my faction, baobhan sith. And Julian, for all intents and purposes, is exactly like us. He needs to gather essence the way we do, and he exhibits all of the same capabilities that the rest of us do. Except for one. For some reason, Julian's human heritage changed his abilities enough so that not only can he absorb essence, but he can also convert that essence into various elemental forces and recharge others. I've never heard of a power similar to Julian's. There's nothing in our history, nor anyone living at this time whom we know of, that has the same power. And yet there's Julian: the walking, talking, portable charger.'

'Julian's a halfling,' I murmured, pleased. I liked Julian before; now I liked him even better. It also explained his mother's interest in me.

'Yes, he is. Now stop mooning or you'll make me jealous.'

Speaking of jealousy, I'd had another thought. 'So, why can't Julian charge you up, too? Instead of . . . ?'

I could tell by the look on Ryu's face that what seemed too good to be true was exactly that.

Ryu shrugged, obviously uncomfortable. 'For some reason, Julian can only do elements. Essence he gets like his mother. Like me . . .' He trailed off awkwardly. Which meant that Julian had to run around either frightening or seducing people.

Why are vampires so complicated? my brain whined, in my daily dose of 'holy shit, how my life has changed'. In the meantime, Ryu had steered the conversation to safer waters.

'Now, Julian and Jakes also make good examples because both of them were raised within our society. Jakes because he had a responsible father who took care of him when his human mother died shortly after his birth, and Julian because mothers are usually more involved with their halfling children.'

My studiously blank expression morphed into a frown. My mother hadn't taken care of me.

Ryu stroked a hand down my side gently. 'I'm sorry, that was insensitive. I just meant that the females of our kind are more likely to integrate their halfling children into our society. In your mother's case, when you couldn't join her in the sea, she was forced to leave. But she did ensure that Nell and the others were keeping an eye on you.'

I shrugged noncommittally. A gnome babysitter wasn't the same as a mother.

'What about the fathers?' I asked to change the subject.

Ryu frowned. 'Not so responsible,' he answered abruptly. 'C'mon, Jane. You know your human mythology – faerie changelings, supernatural creatures and gods always knocking up human women. Where there's smoke, there's fire.'

'So, like, Zeus was just some great big preternatural baby-daddy?'

Ryu ignored me. 'There is a certain mentality among some of our males that it's okay to father children on human women without taking responsibility for their issue *unless* the child turns out to have power. If the child does have power, they assume they will have the opportunity to take over the raising of that child when the time comes. In other words, they assume nothing will happen to them before the child exhibits his or her power, and they ignore the fact that halfling children with latent powers have, on occasion, gone supernova at puberty. Now, if the child is integrated into the community, a late or chaotic revelation of power will be controlled and the damage to the child and to the community will be minimal. But if it's out there on its own, the results are guaranteed to be messy.'

I shuddered, thinking about the damage someone as powerful as this Conleth person could do in that sort of situation.

'So there are tons of potentially rogue halflings running around and waiting to come into their power, and Conleth represents why this is such a bad thing?'

Ryu frowned. 'Actually, no,' he said. 'There are relatively few halflings on our radar, at the moment. Which is more than a mystery, but one that has nothing to do with Conleth. And Conleth is too old to be hitting his power now. He's probably around your age, but we don't know very much about him.'

'What do you know?'

'There was a laboratory blown up in Dorchester, killing a bunch of humans, shortly after our trip to the Compound. It appeared to be an entirely nonsupernatural affair, so we left it alone. Not least because I was still dealing with the fallout from what happened with Jimmu. But then a bunch of supes, starting with an ifrit male, were murdered by someone with a hell of a lot of power. Eventually, we put together that it had something to do with that human laboratory.'

'Why would Conleth just show up and attack a laboratory?'

'No,' Ryu said, his expression dark. 'He didn't attack it. He *escaped* the laboratory.'

'Escaped?' I blanched.

'Yes.'

'So, he was . . . what? A test subject?'

'Yes.'

'Holy shit,' I breathed. 'No wonder he's pissed off.'

'"Pissed off" is an understatement, even for you.'

'How long was he in there?' I asked, horrified by what I was hearing.

'We think for his entire life. We're almost certain that the ifrit – the one who was murdered – fathered a child with a human woman. He wasn't around when the child was born, and the baby must have come to the attention of human authorities under circumstances that were probably unpleasant. Conleth ended up in that laboratory.'

'How could a baby just disappear like that?' I couldn't imagine what Conleth's life must have been like. I still felt betrayed by my mother's abandonment of my father and me. But contemplating a life spent as some guinea pig . . .

'Who knows?' Ryu shrugged. 'If the baby was born with his powers intact, shooting flames, a human woman would think she'd given birth to the Antichrist. And the father probably wasn't even aware he had a child. But, you're right, somebody should have known of the existence of this laboratory. We have people at every level of human government. We are part of their medical community, their military, their university system. How a research lab with connections to *all* of these institutions could have existed without our knowledge is mind-boggling.'

'The military and the government? Really?' I wasn't surprised that supes were part of the university system. Some of my more eccentric professors now made perfect sense. But I couldn't quite picture any of my supernatural buddies in either fatigues or the Oval Office.

'Of course, Jane. And now we have people in the private sector. Ever since the Roswell debacle, the military has made it policy to contract out government involvement with the "paranormal" to private companies, like the one running the laboratory from which Conleth escaped.'

'Roswell?' I squeaked. Tonight I was getting a heady dose of 'too much information'.

Ryu's eyebrow shot toward the ceiling. 'Yeah, Roswell. That was one of us, obviously. You don't believe in *aliens*, do you?'

'I didn't believe in vampires until a few months ago, either, Ryu. You can cut me some slack. So you've got people spying on humans from, like, everywhere?'

'Yes.'

'And who do these spies report to?'

Ryu paused, looking away from me. 'Traditionally, the monarch's second-in-command performs the duty of spymaster.'

I blinked, cursing Alfar traditions. 'So you're telling me that *Jarl* is in charge of all the information that is passed on to the Alfar.'

'Yes. But before you get all crazy with conspiracy theories—'

'Ryu, come on! Seriously? They've got *Jarl* in charge of spying. So everything they know is filtered through him.

He can keep to himself, or exaggerate, or even make up whatever he wants.'

'Yes, any spymaster could do those things, Jane. But that doesn't mean Jarl does. Remember, he *is* one of us. He needs to keep us all safe for his *own* benefit, as much as ours.'

'You're assuming he has the same priorities that you have. What if he doesn't? I still think we don't know everything about why Jimmu murdered those halflings, and I still think the real reason, whatever it is, involves Jarl.'

'Jane, I'm not going to argue about this again. No, I don't trust Jarl. But you take it too far. You'd have him be this ultimate bad guy from some human blockbuster, twirling his mustache and ordering the destruction of the entire planet. My team and I went over every single crime the nagas committed and couldn't pin a single thing on anyone except Jimmu and his nestmates. They were acting on their own.'

I wanted to argue, but to harp on why I distrusted Jarl so much would only lead toward the one secret I had kept from Ryu: that Jarl had nearly choked the life out of me four months ago at the Alfar Compound. After Anyan had saved me, he convinced me to keep Jarl's actions a secret for Ryu's own sake. Although I agreed with the decision we had made that night, I knew Ryu would freak right the hell out when he found out that I had kept something from him . . . especially something that involved Anyan Barghest.

'Fine,' I said, changing the subject. 'So, Conleth was in a laboratory that you should have known about. But couldn't it just have been the one private lab that you guys missed somehow?'

'Maybe. I suppose. Still . . .' Ryu's face darkened in thought, till he sighed. 'Anyway, what matters is that Conleth is back, again, and he has to be stopped.'

The way Ryu said 'stopped' gave me pause.

'So what do you do with people who commit crimes?' I asked. 'I mean, do you have prisons, like we do?'

Ryu gave me a long look, the look he always gave me when he was about to tell me something about the supernatural world he knew I wouldn't like.

'We do have methods of incarceration, yes. And sometimes we use them, usually for those of high status who've done something that can't be ignored but also can't be treated . . . normally.'

'And the "normal" treatment?'

Ryu pursed his lips, and I knew what he was going to say. So I said it for him.

'You just kill them, don't you?' The leap to execution wasn't a long one; after all, I'd seen Orin and Morrigan, Ryu's king and queen, condemn Jimmu to death in front of me without even consulting one another.

Ryu shrugged.

'I'd think the fact that Conleth was abandoned and raised in a laboratory would serve as "mitigating factors" in your decision as to whether or not you just kill the guy—'

'Jane, he's vicious. Yeah, he's suffered. But it's made him an animal. There's nothing there to be saved, Florence.'

'That could have been *me*, Ryu. What if I'd been caught in the Sow as a child and ended up in a lab? Would I just be one more loose end?'

Ryu snorted. 'You're nothing like Conleth, babe. The comparison isn't even close to accurate.'

'Yeah, but I had a loving father who took care of me. Who knows what I'd be like if I'd had Conleth's life. I mean, can you imagine what he must have gone through . . .'

Ryu's strong hands stilled at my words.

'Jane, you do realize you're defending the guy who just tried to kill both of us. Conleth is a monster.'

'Maybe he is, Ryu, but he was *made* a monster.'

Ryu shifted me over and then drew me out of bed. 'Come with me,' he said.

I pulled on my underpants and his discarded dress shirt before following him out of the bedroom and down the stairs.

Ryu was already in his office waiting for me with a file folder. My breath whooshed out of my body as he used a central table to spread out pictures of various crime scenes. I withdrew my eyes from the gruesome montage of twisted, blackened bodies.

'Conleth killed nine people when he escaped from his laboratory. Under such circumstances, however, extreme actions could, perhaps, be excused. Then he went after various employees of the laboratory. Again, revenge might have been understandable. But he was killing *anyone* associated with the lab. Not just the scientists, but a janitor. A secretary. A parking lot attendant. Their *families*, if they were in the house with the victim. At some point during this spree, he discovered the identity of his true parents. That's when he killed his human mother, her human husband, and their three teenaged children. His half siblings. Burned the house down while they slept.' Ryu pointed to a photo. I glanced at it only long enough to see the huddled, blackened figures before I had to look away or be sick.

'Then he went after his ifrit father. And then he just started killing any supernatural being he could get his hands on. Three beings, total. He did all of this in two weeks, Jane. Two. Then he disappeared. We figured he'd gotten his revenge and had hightailed it. That he'd disappeared into the Borderlands or had become some other Territory's problem. We were wrong.'

I steeled myself to look at the photos. There were prone figures everywhere. Conleth wasn't a serial killer; he was a massacre on legs.

I walked out of the office and into Ryu's kitchen, where I pulled a glass down and filled it with water from the tap. I drank half of it and then placed the glass in the sink. When I turned around, Ryu was leaning back against his granite island, watching me.

'One of those pictures looked suspiciously like an exploded Porsche.'

He gave me a wry smile. 'I told you I had an accident.'

'When did Conleth try to kill you?'

'Right before he disappeared. That's why I didn't say anything. I figured the threat was gone, no reason to frighten you.'

I frowned. I hated when Ryu coddled me. I knew I was half human and ignorant of many things in Ryu's world, but I wasn't a child.

'How close did you get to capturing him?'

'Not very. He's extraordinarily powerful. And he can do things I've never seen before. The way he travels, it's like a fucking comet. I've never seen anything like him.'

I fell silent, as I finally began to put together everything that had happened tonight and what it meant for me and for Ryu.

'He obviously still wants you dead,' I said to my lover. He only nodded.

'That's not what I'm worried about, though. I'm worried that Conleth saw *you*.'

'He wouldn't come after me, would he?'

Ryu frowned. 'I don't know, baby. But there's a good chance he would if he could, either to get to me or because he thinks you're a pureblood.'

I mulled over the implications of Ryu's words before speaking. 'What are our options, then?'

'Well, you could stay here. I could protect you, but you're

also guaranteed to be a target. Or we smuggle you back to Rockabill, but set Nell to watch over you.' Ryu shrugged ruefully. 'I hate to say it, but you're safest with her.'

He read the doubt on my face before it could be articulated.

'I know you find it difficult to take Nell seriously, but you should. I've told you about how powerful a gnome is, and I know you've felt her strength. And that's just her doing her daily thing. Imagine her pissed off.'

'It's not Nell, Ryu. I don't like the idea of leaving you like this, knowing there's some loony tune out to get you.'

'I know, Jane. And I appreciate that. But, really, what can you do?'

'I'm not completely inept,' I said drily. 'I came in quite handy the last time we were being stalked by a killer, remember.'

'I know, babe. But this is different. We didn't understand the threat to you when we went to the Compound before. Had I known Jimmu was behind everything, I wouldn't have delivered you right to him, believe me.'

'But what if Conleth does follow me back to Rockabill? I'm not as worried about myself as I am about my family, my friends.'

'Nell will understand how serious it is. I'll make sure she has everything covered.'

My frown grew. Nell might be strong, but she was only one person. Er, gnome.

'Plus, there's Trill—' My face went deadpan at Ryu's suggestion. I loved the kelpie, and she was an awesome swimming partner, but really? Sitting ducks were tougher.

'Ryu, my dad and my human friends are totally vulnerable . . .'

'Okay, fine. I'll call Anyan. Will that make you happy?'

I blinked at the edge in his voice. 'Ryu, this isn't about me getting my jollies. This is about me protecting the people I love. I don't like the idea of leaving you here alone, to start with. And I really don't like the idea that I may be bringing some fiery harbinger of death back to Rockabill. So yeah, I would feel better if I knew Nell had some backup and I would appreciate if you did call Anyan, or whoever else you think could do the job.'

I could tell that Ryu still wasn't pleased, but he forced his face into a neutral expression.

'I know, Jane. And I'm sorry you got dragged into this. Con doesn't have any way of finding you, that I can think of, once you're out of Boston. So you should be safe. In the meantime, I'll make sure you're protected. No matter what.'

I went to him and wrapped my arms around his waist. 'I know, baby. And I'm sorry we have to cut our visit short.'

'Not as sorry as I am, honey,' he said, as he lowered his face to mine and kissed me soundly. And I knew he meant it. It sucked that I had to leave. But I couldn't be ticked off at the fact that we were attacked, or ticked off that our time together had been short. That was unfair to Ryu. I wasn't dating an accountant, after all. I knew what Ryu did for a living; hell, we'd met because Ryu did what he did and I'd seen, firsthand and from the get-go, that what he did was dangerous. So I couldn't turn around now and wish he drove a cab or sat in some cubicle somewhere.

So I squished down my disappointment and put on my happy face. Okay, I really put on my horny face but, with Ryu, those were pretty much one and the same.

'I wouldn't bet on that,' I purred. 'I've been dying to try this thing Iris told me about, but we would need one of those bouncy castles, at least fifteen feet of aluminum siding, and lots of canola oil. So we'd need time to source the raw materials . . .'

Ryu's elegantly expressive eyebrows arched and my already frisky libido perked up in Pavlovian response.

'Funnily enough, I just happen to have a bouncy castle in my spare bedroom,' he said. Then I squealed as he picked me up in a fireman's carry. He started off toward the stairs and then stopped and walked back to the kitchen, turning around so I was facing one of his cupboards.

'Do you really have a bouncy castle?' I wheezed, my diaphragm rather compressed by Ryu's shoulder.

'No. But I'm sure we can think of something . . . because you know what they say, right?'

'No, what?'

'The couple that bounces together, stays together.'

'Is that scientific fact?' I giggled, wheezily.

'I dunno. But we can certainly experiment. Now reach out and grab the canola oil from that cupboard, will ya?' I blinked, then extended my arm.

If this was Ryu's version of scientific experimentation, I was perfectly willing to be the control.

CHAPTER SEVEN

'So Linda Allen comes in with her dad and is being absolutely awful,' Tracy told Grizzie as I sat there blushing. Grizzie had been off on one of her mystery jaunts when I got back from Boston, and she'd just returned that morning. So Tracy was filling Griz in on what she'd missed while I quashed down my desire to ask where the fuck she'd gone.

'As usual,' Grizzie chimed in, giving me a conspiratorial wink as she settled down in the seat next to me with her coffee. Traffic through the store was dead that day, so we were all sitting at one of the café tables, enjoying a little three o'clock latte action.

'Linda's ignoring Jane, even though I'm making the coffee. She's just standing there, clutching her book and staring over Jane's head. Even Mr Allen is looking at Linda like "What the hell?"

'Jane reaches for the book, cool as a cucumber, and says, "I can help you." Linda *still* tries to ignore Jane, until Mr Allen yells at her.

'Jane rings her up and Linda's futzing with that silly Prada bag she's been showing off like she gave birth to the Messiah and he's contained within—'

At that, Grizzie had to interrupt. 'If that thing is real Prada, I'm a goddamned virgin . . .'

Tracy laughed. 'Just wait! You're stealing Jane's thunder!'

'Sorry, passion flower,' Grizzie apologized to her lover. 'And sorry, Jane,' she said, wrapping a long arm around me.

'So she's huffing and pawing through that enormous purse, saying to the people behind her, and I quote, "My Prada is just soooooooooo big!"' Grizzie snorted out a laugh and I couldn't help but giggle at Tracy's impression.

'First time Linda's said *that*; otherwise she wouldn't be such a cunt,' Grizzie murmured, causing me to choke on my coffee as Tracy got to the punchline.

'So she finally comes up with her wallet and pays for her book. As she's putting her stuff away, Jane says, "By the way, Linda. The people at Prada are not 'mad in China'," pointing at the label inside that damned purse. Which, sure enough, says MAD IN CHINA. I nearly died. Then Jane goes for the kill with, "They're perfectly content in Italy."'

'I *knew* it was a knockoff!' Grizzie crowed, leaning over to kiss my cheek.

'It was amazing. I nearly applauded.' Tracy sighed happily before she nodded toward me. 'And she's growing out her bangs,' she added.

I fidgeted as Grizzie smiled at Tracy knowingly.

'Our little Jane is growing up,' Grizzie said, reaching both hands over the table toward her partner's. 'Next thing we know, she'll be barefoot and pregnant.'

I gave my best friends two friendly middle fingers, and then, embarrassed by the attention, I nervously pulled out my ponytail in order to fix it up tighter. When Grizzie hissed, I cursed as I realized my mistake.

'What the hell did you do to your hair?' she demanded. 'Some of it's . . . *missing*.'

I sighed. I may have emerged from Conleth's Boston attack unscathed, but my hair hadn't. The first time I went to brush it out after the attack, I'd realized that my brush strokes were shorter in the very back. I really needed to get it fixed, but I was afraid a hairdresser would cut *all* of it off, and I'd always had long hair.

That said, I did look like I had an inverse mullet. Plus, my hair was a constant reminder of the awful week I'd just had. When I'd first gotten back to Rockabill, I'd been *terrified* every minute of every day that I was going to get a phone call while at work that my dad had been barbecued, or a phone call at home that Grizzie and Tracy had been torched in their beds. I wasn't big on getting attacked myself, but I was more frightened about my family and friends.

Nell, however, had been a constant presence, popping up in the most unlikely places to give me a little wave of her chubby hand and a reassurance that she'd just checked on everyone. Also, when Ryu hadn't been able to get hold of Anyan, he'd sent Daoud and Caleb back with me. Introduced as friends from college, and glamoured to hell so my dad wouldn't notice Caleb's goatier half, they'd immediately started playing poker with my father and had only stopped to sleep and eat since. Luckily, they played for pennies or I think both supes would have been wiped out financially. They'd assumed a mere human would be easy pickings, until my poker-god father beat them at nearly every hand.

Thankfully, however, there hadn't even been a wisp of smoke to indicate that Conleth was in any way aware of who I was or where I lived. He was definitely still in Boston, taking potshots at Ryu, Stefan, and their deputies whenever he got the chance. But he seemed distracted, or at least not as intent on killing everyone and anyone as he had been the first round. Which made me wonder if he wasn't just trying to come home and going about it in the only ass-backward, violent way he knew how.

Caleb and Daoud were scheduled to stay another few days, and I did finally feel safe again. So even though I still hated the idea of leaving Ryu behind with a very powerful and very murderous halfling, I felt we'd done the right thing. Ryu didn't have to worry about me, I didn't have to worry about Conleth, and we could get back to 'normal' life. For me, that meant training, and for Ryu, that meant chasing down baddies.

And for Grizzie, it meant freaking out about my hair.

'Seriously, what the *fuck* did you do to it? It looks like it's been *burned*. It looks like *shit . . .*'

'Grizzie!' Tracy barked.

'What?' my ever-so-honest friend whined. 'It *does*. I mean, look at it!'

I buried my face in my hands as Grizzie picked up the sizzled bit at my nape and held it up for Tracy to see. Even Tracy was flummoxed.

'We are getting this *fixed*, missy,' Grizzie threatened.

'Griz, no . . . I'm just going to let it grow out,' I gasped, panicked.

'Hell no. You can't just let that shit grow out. It's *awful*.'

'I know, but I know a hairdresser will just cut it all, and I don't want short hair! So I'm just going to let it grow—'

'Nonsense,' Grizzie snapped, pulling out her cell phone. When I made to protest again, she silenced me with a stern purple look. And a kick to the shins.

'Salim?' she cooed. 'I know this is last minute, but I have an emergency. And I mean an E. Merge. En. See. Like of biblical proportions . . . No, not me. A friend. Thank God! . . . I know, right? But, yeah, she looks absolutely craptastic . . . If I get her there in one hour, can you work your magic? . . . All righty, see you soon . . . Mwah,' she finished, kissing into the phone.

'C'mon, Jane. Get your coat. We've got to go now to make it to Eastport in time,' Grizzie said as she stood.

I glared up at her mutinously. 'I don't want my hair chopped off!'

'Salim will *fix* it, not chop it off. He's a genius. And you look like a mental patient, Jane. Even more than you did when you *were* a mental patient.'

'Grizzie!' Tracy gasped, throwing me an apologetic look. But I was already giggling.

'You are such a bitch, Griz.' Then I remembered I had a trump card. 'Okay, fine,' I said, my voice gone crafty. 'I'll go with you to see this Salim person *if* . . . you tell me where it is you go when you disappear.' I figured I had her there. That was her biggest secret, the thing no one knew besides Tracy. She'd never agree to tell me. . . .

Grizzie eyed me appraisingly, her lips pursed. Tracy appeared to be holding her breath. Finally Grizzie nodded sharply.

'Fine, Jane. I owe you the truth after all these years. And I've been wanting to talk to you, anyway. We'll kill two birds with one stone. So get your coat.'

Shocked, I did as she told me, trailing behind her to her car. I couldn't believe, after all these years, Grizzie was going to tell me her secrets. The question was . . .

Could I handle the truth?

The hairy man eyeballed me lasciviously, his full lips slowly pursing into what I think was supposed to be a 'come hither' smile. I backed away a step.

'Salim, this is Jane. Her hair is horrifying. Fix her.'

Salim let his eyes rove over Grizzie. Then I watched as

they roved over another passing customer. Then they roved over his own image in the mirror, at which time he noticeably sucked in his paunch. Finally, he deigned to return his attention to us.

'Darling. Of course. I will fix your friend.' His gaze again raked over me. 'Oh, yes. An hour with Salim and she will be beautiful.' Salim's throaty accent spoke of desert heat, sweet tea poured by soft women, and sex. Tons and tons of insanely raunchy sex. Which was no small feat, considering he was only about three inches taller than my five-foot-one and about as wide across. Masses of chest hair sprang from his half-unbuttoned shirt, flowing up his neck to blend seamlessly with his longish stubble and then spraying out of the top of his head in a thick wave of carefully coiffured jet-black curls.

'Darling. This hair. It is . . . unfortunate. But Salim make it beautiful. Oh, yes. Do you know Salim's method?'

I shook my head. I hadn't known there'd be a 'method' involved.

'First I cut you wet. Then I cut you dry,' Salim said, finally looking me in the eyes. 'Have you ever been cut dry before?'

I had no idea what he meant, but I had a funny feeling he wasn't just talking about hair. I responded by doing an ambiguously circular 'maybe it's a nod, maybe it's a shake' motion with my head.

Salim clapped his hands sharply and I jumped. 'Today. I cut you dry. ALFRED!' he bellowed, nearly making me jump out of my skin.

A large man with a doughy face shuffled over, clearly terrified of the hirsute tyrant standing before me.

'Alfred. Take Jane. Prepare her for me.'

I swear Alfred actually bowed before turning to me with a kind, if harried, expression and nodded toward a row of sinks in the back of the salon. I followed, grateful that my 'preparation' only involved a shampoo. At this point, I wasn't sure if Salim had misunderstood my desire for a haircut and was, instead, treating me to a sampling of his patented sexual-harassment treatment.

I was profoundly grateful I wasn't there for a facial.

Alfred's huge hands were clumsy, if gentle, on my head, and he managed to get water all down my back. Scared that Salim would actually beat Alfred in front of me, I vowed to go to my grave keeping my damp skin a secret. Finally, I was returned to where Salim waited for me, standing behind an empty chair. Grizzie sprawled in the chair next to him, her kinky purple catsuit clinging to her surgically enhanced frame.

Upon delivering me, Salim barked something at Alfred in a foreign language and the huge man skittered off.

'My cousin. From Lebanon,' Salim informed me, as he draped me in plastic and began furiously jacking up my chair, his fat little leg pumping like a scratching rabbit. 'He's an idiot. But family. Did he get you wet?'

'No,' I replied, reminding myself not to squirm as my soaked shirt pressed against the back of the chair.

'Good. Only I get you wet. Ha!'

Grizzie shrugged her shoulders at me, apologetically, as Salim began moving about my head, peering and poking and pulling. I met her eyes in the mirror, trying to remind her that it was her turn to spill. She smiled.

'Jane wants to know my secret, Salim.'

I pulled a face, unable to believe Grizzie's *hairdresser* knew her secret when I, one of her best friends, did not. But I guess what they say about hairdressers and gynecologists knowing everything about their clients is true.

'Ha!' Salim barked again as he began furiously stroking the right side of my head with both hands.

'Should I tell her?'

'Hmm.' The hairy little man shrugged, starting in on my left side.

'Where do I begin?'

'With the money,' he said cryptically, as he pressed my hair down on either side of my face and peered at the both of us in the mirror before backing away to grab his scissors.

'Then the sex,' he continued, making ominous chopping gestures in the empty air.

'Then the love,' he finished, as he dove toward my head and I nearly fainted.

Sheets, torrents, *floods* of hair began to circulate in the air around me as Grizzie began talking.

'The money *is* a good place to start,' Grizzie conceded, obviously gathering herself to embark upon a grand narrative.

'I was not born as any of the women you know, Jane. Neither Grizzie, nor Dusty. I was born Amelia Vanderbilt Bathgate. The Amelia is my grandmother's name on my mother's side, as is my middle name.'

My eyes boggled, because of what Grizzie was telling me of her heritage and because I was literally sitting in a sea of my own hair. It was beginning to appear as if 'cutting me dry' would end in making me bald.

'Yes, those Vanderbilts. But my Bathgate relations secretly considered them vulgar. Nouveau riche and not all *that* wealthy. After all, the Bathgates put the "pure" in "Puritan". They were at the helm of the *Mayflower*. They supplied the coal that blackened the faces at the Boston Tea Party. The ink that signed the Declaration of Independence. The lamp oil that lit Paul Revere's ride.'

I knew my jaw was hanging open. I'd been waiting for all sorts of shocking things to pop out of Grizzie's usually shocking mouth . . . but I wasn't ready to find out she was a Daughter of the American Revolution.

Grizzie ignored my reaction and kept talking. 'When Boston society became too impure, my family moved to Chicago in order to start afresh in a city whose social milieu they could hand select. They did, and they controlled it with an iron fist until the city grew to a size even they couldn't manage. But by then the Bathgates *were* Chicago, at least behind the scenes.'

'How?' I asked simply. What I meant was, *how* had she left? *Why* had she left? Especially when she'd been born into a family so famous in both Chicago society and politics that even I, who lived in the farthest corner of the East Coast, had heard of them?

'It's easy, Jane. Being born a Bathgate wasn't all it was cracked up to be. I was born into a world of pure privilege. And total ignorance. Don't get me wrong; I had the best schools, the best tutors, all of that.' Grizzie grinned, but the smile was sarcastic, bitter. 'But I took everything for granted. I never questioned the way I was raised – the benefits I enjoyed – versus the way other people lived. If I thought about the fact that others had less than I, it was merely as a way to determine whether or not they were present to serve me or play with me. "Friends" were people whose mothers and fathers inhabited the same tax bracket as mine; everyone else was there to do something for me.'

Beads of sweat were forming on Salim's forehead as he pranced around me, his plump hands darting through the air like corpulent hummingbirds.

'That's how I lived for the first sixteen years of my life,' Grizzie continued, tucking her long legs up under her so she didn't trip the whirling dervish currently shearing me like a sheep.

'I firmly believed, if I thought about it at all, that I deserved everything I had and that people who didn't have everything I did *deserved* to have less. Which is called, what? Classism? And then there's the racism, sexism, and homophobia. Oh, and the hypocrisy. My peers found it perfectly acceptable to bugger their poor, black, or Hispanic gay lovers, but God forbid someone attempt to come out of the closet or say they agreed with affirmative action or suggest that maybe, just *maybe,* people from underprivileged backgrounds deserved access to some of the opportunities to which our silver-bespooned births gave *us* access.'

'So what happened when you were sixteen?' I asked, my voice muffled by Salim's gut as he leaned over me to do something to the back of my head that involved a seriously scary number of snips.

'I fell in love with a girl. Which, as you can imagine, went down *really* well with the establishment.'

'Ha!' Salim ejaculated, as he whirled my chair around to face Grizzie. 'Went down!'

Grizzie shot him with an imaginary pistol. 'Anyway, I fell in love with a girl who was also merely middle class. I don't know which was worse in my parents' eyes.' She grinned. 'They banned us from seeing one another, of course. Put me into therapy for "inversion", since in my parents' world it's still the mid-1800s. But of course I rebelled, and eventually my girlfriend and I did what any star-crossed lovers worth their salt do. We emptied my bank account, stole a bunch of my mom's jewelry, and ran away.'

I was literally on the edge of my seat at this point, partly because I was wrapped up in Grizzie's story but also because my body was being dragged forward as my hair self-consciously attempted to escape the Lebanese lunatic assaulting it. I nearly died when Salim cut Grizzie off by starting up the blow-dryer. I blanched as I realized that now was the time on 'Sprockets' when I got 'cut dry.'

When he was finally finished, Salim picked up a different set of scissors and a comb. I closed my eyes, unable to watch. All courage had failed me.

'And?' I squeaked, prompting Grizzie.

'Obviously, the money that seemed to be *so much* when we stole it lasted about six months. And then the girlfriend went back home. Her parents had joined PFLAG, decorated their house with rainbows, and welcomed her back with open arms. But in running away, I saw the world for what it really was. I was scared, way too young, and in way over my head, but going back home would have required me volunteering for a lobotomy. I literally couldn't conceive of going back to a place that was so . . . pointless. I realized that all we did, as a social class, was circulate money. And I wanted to *live*.'

Salim's motions were slowing, his snips growing more considered. I knew he was finishing up. But I refused to open my eyes until the bitter end. Then, when I discovered I looked like Vin Diesel, I could burst dramatically into tears and make him feel at least a little guilty.

'So I did a lot of crazy shit to survive. You know where it all ended up: with Dusty Nethers committing unspeakable, if rather titillating, acts of depravity for money. There are a million things that I wish I had done differently, and a thousand things I regret. But I never regret breaking with Amelia's world. Never. Although "Amelia" does go back, sometimes, to monitor her trust fund and to pay homage to the womb that bore her.'

'How were you not disowned, Grizzie? Your family can't have accepted who you are now, let alone who you've been?'

Grizzie laughed, but it was a bitter sound. 'First of all, you have to understand that my world thrives on appearances and runs on toadying. So who is going to tell my mother a truth she wouldn't want to hear? She'd be more than happy to shoot the messenger. As for my disappearances, she doesn't want to know the truth any more than I want to tell her. So she accepts my lies about doing degrees in Paris, or volunteer work in Africa, and doesn't ask questions. Plus, I am a totally different person when I'm Amelia. A person I don't know if even you, Jane, would recognize. I doubt many people have made the connection between Dusty and Amelia. And, while I'd love for my mother to know Grizelda Montague and her loving wife, Tracy, I also know that's not going to happen. Anyway, I'm glad "Dusty" has been shelved. I won't even get into "Crystal" or "Tyler"; they were just disasters. But now, for most of the time, I get to be me: I get to be Grizzie.'

I opened my eyes to find myself still facing her. She smiled at me, and for a split second I saw all the women Grizzie had been layered over each other in a complex tapestry of experience. Then they resolved themselves into the woman I knew, sprawled in a salon chair and practically glowing with a sense of place and self-contentment. I blinked back tears.

Granted, it was partly because I'd caught a glimpse of just how much black hair was currently drifting around my feet.

'How?' I asked, keeping my mind off my imminent hair horror. 'How did you find Grizzie?'

My friend smiled. 'Easy, kid. I found Tracy. I met her when I was really down. I was in that talk-show jargon "bad place". I really wanted out of the industry, but didn't know how. I didn't know how to live as "Amelia". but all my constructs were nearly as disastrous, just in different ways. Then I met Tracy. And she *saw* me. I mean, really *saw* me. I know I sound totally full of bullshit, but it's the truth.' Grizzie blushed, looking down. 'I looked in her eyes, and there I was.'

I'd just started to ask a question when Salim tilted my head up to peer at me and then grunted hard. He whisked my chair around so I was facing the mirror, placing another mirror in my hand so I could see three hundred and sixty degrees.

I gasped, awestruck. My hair was *amazing*. It was still long, well past my shoulders, the burned patch camouflaged by the clever cut. Salim had even integrated my mostly grown-out bangs so that my hair was seamless and healthy and lovely. If I hadn't damned well known that he'd dry hump me in response, I would have thrown my arms around my perverted little saviour.

'Salim,' I breathed. 'It's beautiful.'

He merely grunted. 'Of course. You had doubts? Salim is a genius.' He mopped his brow with a purple silk handker-chief. 'I am exhausted. You refresh me?' he inquired, waving his singular, and singularly impressive, eyebrow at me.

'Easy,' Grizzie commanded, unfolding her long frame to stand behind me and play with my new hair. Her eyes met mine in the mirror and she frowned.

'Now we talk about you. And Ryu.'

I blanched, setting the mirror down in my lap.

'Don't worry, hon. You know I don't give advice,' she said. 'I've made enough mistakes for four hundred women, and I have no business telling anyone how to live their life.' She paused, thinking. When she started speaking again, her voice was soft. Hesitant. As if she wasn't sure how I'd react.

'You keep saying that things with Ryu are complicated. But I know you really like him. And I know you need time to figure shit out, especially after Jason and everything you've been through. But I don't want you to be afraid to take risks. If it's worth it . . . if the person in his eyes is the person you want to be, the person you know you could be . . . then don't be scared. That's all.' She tugged my hair roughly, her deep voice roughening as her confidence reasserted itself.

I thought about what she said. I knew it was good advice, even if I didn't know exactly what to make of it. I had come a huge way since that night in the cove, so many months ago, when I'd made peace with Jason's death. But I also knew a body didn't recover from something like that overnight. Grizzie was also spot on in calling me out on the fact that my constant reply to questions about Ryu was, 'It's complicated.' I sounded like Facebook. But our relationship *was* bloody complicated . . .

'You okay?' she asked, tugging again on a thick lock of my hair.

'Yeah, Griz. I am. I'm just thinking about what you said. And it makes sense. Thank you.' I leaned my head back so that it nestled in her soft belly, looking up to meet her eyes with my own. 'And thank you for telling me your secret. I'll keep it close.'

'I know you will, hon. And you're welcome.' She leaned down to kiss me on the forehead. I closed my eyes, so glad of Grizzie's friendship and the trust she'd just shown in me. She left her lips pressed to my forehead for a few seconds until she rounded out the action with a typical Grizzie gesture. As she stood, she swiped her tongue over my forehead, causing me to squirm.

'Ewwww, Griz!'

She snickered, high-fiving Salim. 'Quit yer whinin'. And let's go so we can take you to the Sty and show off your new hair, you sassy minx . . .'

I rubbed my sleeve over my damp forehead, laughing as Grizzie pulled me from the chair. I paid Salim, who gave me the 'Grizzie discount', thank the gods, since the prices on the chart behind him were ridiculous. Then Griz and I headed out the door. It was a beautiful night in Eastport: the sun had set an hour ago, but it still tinged the sky so that around us shone a swathe of sapphire blue. I could hear the sea beckoning, and I promised to join her soon for our nightly frolic. I sighed contentedly. My family was safe; my friends were safe; I was training and growing my magic and working. All was well with the world and, now, with my hair.

What more could a girl ask for?

CHAPTER EIGHT

After work the next day, I went to Nell's to train, as usual. Caleb and Daoud were with my dad. Scheduled to leave tomorrow, they were furiously trying to fit in as many hands of poker as they could to try to recoup their losses, alongside their wounded pride.

Despite, or maybe because of, the threat of Conleth, Nell and I had not stopped our daily meetings. For that first week, while the threat had loomed, we'd worked on beefing up my shields even more, but now that caution had abated, we'd moved to glamours for the last few days. Unfortunately, I'd discovered I sucked at creating them. My brain just couldn't make the connection between forming an image and then projecting that image. Nell told me it was because I was thinking in terms of physical, rather than magical, laws, but I had no idea what the hell she meant.

That said, I may not have been looking forward to training, but I was very much looking forward to getting to the cabin. I'd sucked down a coffee before leaving work, and I was seriously about to pee in my pants. The gnome was going to have to open her house for me, or suffer the consequences.

I hotfooted it through the growing dusk of the evening, up

the rocky driveway toward the main door of the cabin. As I mounted the stairs, I noticed that the front door was open, although the screen door was shut. Nell almost never left the doors open, so I didn't try to enter, but walked around the wraparound porch to the back door, as usual. Unusually, however, it was open as well.

'Hello? Nell?' I called, placing a hand on the screen door's handle but not pulling. I could see the bathroom beckoning me, but after what had happened in Boston, I wasn't taking anything for granted.

I peered around the dim interior of the cabin until I thought I saw someone: a large, man-shaped shadow upstairs on the wall of the open loft that was the cabin's only bedroom. I backed away from the door, raising my shields cautiously.

'Nell? Are you there?' I called, suddenly nervous. 'Are you okay?'

'Easy, Jane. It's me,' came a growling voice as the dark shadow melted down the loft's stairs and toward the door.

'Anyan.' I grinned, relief flooding through me.

A huge dog padded into the glare of the porch light, his red-tinged black coat as thick and shaggy as I remembered. His tail wagged and his mouth was split in a doggy grin, tongue lolling.

Anyan Barghest lived in the cabin with Nell when he was around, which wasn't often. He would pop in every three weeks or so, stay for a day or two, and then be off again. I think he used to live there full-time, but after what had happened at the Compound last November, Anyan had been mostly MIA.

He pushed open the screen door with his broad head. 'C'mon in. Nell will be here soon.'

I walked inside, eagerly inhaling the cabin's delicious scent of lemon wax and cardamom. I hadn't been inside in a while, but everything was the same. A huge kitchen dominated one half of the cabin, replete with a gorgeous Wolf restaurant range and equally impressive Sub-Zero fridge and freezer. The rest of the cabin contained a rectangular trestle table that would probably seat twenty and a seating area full of comfy, overstuffed furniture covered in battered brown leather.

I jumped when Anyan nuzzled his cold nose into my fingers, and then laughed as he maneuvered his head under my hand. Obligingly, I scratched the base of his fuzzy, erect ears, the tips of which were just about level with my breasts. I might be a small woman, but he was one giant dog. For a second, I considered throwing my leg over him and riding him like a pony. Then I thought better of that idea.

'How have you been?' he asked.

'Oh, fine. Busy. How about you?'

'Fine,' he chuckled. 'Busy. I got back as soon as I could, when I got Ryu's messages. But all seems quiet?'

I nodded, scratching downward from his ear, down the ticklish crevice where his cheek met his neck, and then underneath to his chin.

'It's good to be home,' he panted, helping my quest by tilting his head, obligingly.

'When did you get back?' I asked, just as I hit a sensitive spot and he closed his eyes and growled in doggy pleasure. He did love a good scratching.

'Just a few hours ago. I was napping.'

I thought of the big shape upstairs. The big man shape.

'Oh,' I said, withdrawing my hand, feeling my face flush. Anyan was a barghest, a two-formed like my mother. Only he could shape-shift between a dog and a man. And by dog, I meant the hellhound whose ears I'd just been scratching. And by man, I meant a huge, very muscular, rugby-thighed, gorgeously gadonked, throw-you-over-his-shoulder male. And

I know this because I had been thrown over his shoulder, while he was naked, where I got a good gander of the whole thighs-slash-gadonk combo.

We'd never talked about what happened at the Compound, and I'd dealt with everything by convincing myself that man-Anyan and dog-Anyan were two entirely different entities. Which I knew was inaccurate, but it was also an easy delusion to maintain, as I never saw man-Anyan. I'd met Anyan when he was furry, and I had only seen him furry since, except for that time he'd saved my life at the Compound. Because of this, I had no trouble forgetting there was a man inside the gargantuan puppy that played frisbee and liked his belly rubbed. Every once in a while, however, I was reminded of the truth, which made things decidedly weird.

'Are you all right?' he rumbled, scanning my black eyes with his gray ones, until he leaned down to nuzzle my fingers again. 'You look tired.'

I smiled. 'Just busy. And I hate glamours, by the way.'

He chuckled, a gravelly sound that should have sounded abrasive but didn't. 'They're tough. You'll get it.'

I sighed. 'I hope so. 'Cause they're killing me right now.' Suddenly, a stabbing pain emitted from my bladder as it reminded me, brutally, of its existence. 'But I really need to pee. I mean, I need to use the ladies' room. Excuse me.'

Mortified, I waddled off, practically cross-legged. I placed my messenger bag on the granite worktop of the kitchen's island before leaping toward the bathroom off the kitchen.

While washing my hands, I admired the huge piece of ironwork that I could see reflected in the mirror from the opposite wall. I loved all the art with which Nell had decorated her cabin – the gnome had oodles of good taste crammed into her tiny body. Most of the work had, I think, been done by the same artist, as many of the pieces showed consistent use of color, and there was something about the way the artist drew those big, liquid eyes that made me think it was all done by the same person. That said, the styles were very different, ranging from stuff that seemed really classical and old to really new stuff that looked almost like Japanese manga. But my favorite piece was this one, hanging in the bathroom. It was like an iron version of a graphic novel: full of strange little caricatures doing fantastical things. I didn't recognize any of the characters, but from what I could tell, it told the story of one group of odd beasties and people getting the better of another group of odd beasties and people – sometimes through trickery, sometimes in battle, and sometimes apparently by accident. It was massive, taking up the entire space of the large wall it hung on, and I loved how it was like the fine-art version of a magazine rack next to the toilet.

When I'd finished up in the bathroom, I went back into the kitchen. I was standing there, contemplating how the hell tiny little Nell could reach any of the massive appliances, when Anyan called from the porch that he and the gnome were ready.

I walked outside warily, afraid Nell would pull one of her favorite tricks and ambush me with her tiny mage balls. She was on her best behavior, however, sitting on her little rocker in the circumference of the porch's light and chatting with Anyan and Trill while the last dregs of dusk filtered out from the night sky.

When they were finished, we started working. And just like the past three days, I kept fucking it up. I would have what I wanted to do in my mind, but it just wouldn't translate into effect. I was trying to make myself unseen, which was the most common type of glamour. I wasn't supposed to make myself invisible, but to make myself . . . unnoticeable. No matter how many times I tried, however, I remained utterly tangible, totally visible, and increasingly hacked off.

'Fuck! Fuck fuck fuck!' I shouted, finally, as I felt the little bubble of power I'd accumulated burst within me, creating a little sparkle in the air around me, but nothing more.

Nell sighed, and even she looked pissed. The damned gnome had a perpetual smile plastered on her face, so for *her* to lose patience told me just how crappy I was at glamouring.

She looked like she was about to give me a dressing down when Anyan interrupted.

'Nell, may I?'

The gnome nodded, giving Anyan a look that clearly said, 'Good luck, sucker.'

'Sit down, Jane,' the big dog instructed. I did so, cross-legged, happy to take a load off. I'd been standing there *not glamouring* for well over an hour.

Anyan sauntered over and then sat directly in front of me, so close that the tips of his paws brushed the front of my shins. His intense gray eyes stared into mine, and I forced myself not to look away.

'You're focusing too much on what you want to see. This isn't about sight; it's about perception.'

My brow furrowed, but before I could protest that I had no idea what the hell he was talking about, he asked me to shut my eyes.

'And keep them shut. Don't try to see; don't think in terms of sight. Just open yourself and feel me. Feel what I do.'

So I did, and I *did*. Anyan's strong magic pulled me inward, and I felt what he was doing. With my eyelids shutting out my reflexive reliance on visual imagery, it suddenly all made sense. His magic didn't make an image; it didn't try to do some *Predator* chameleon thing, or Kevin Bacon's *Invisible Man* watery silhouette, both movie images I'd had in mind when I thought 'unnoticeable'. Anyan didn't try to look like anything at all. Instead, he just deflected interest. He had a type of barrier, built just like a defensive shield, but this one wasn't about deflecting weapons. Instead, it emanated a bored whisper of *bland, boring, nothing to see here*.

I shifted my own power, imitating his. It took me a while, and knowing what I was supposed to do was never the same as actually doing it. Eventually, however, I felt it. I felt myself blanketed in a power that wearily insisted on my status as a nonentity. I opened my eyes, slowly, to find the barghest still watching me, his tongue lolling as he smiled, doggy-style. I smiled back, my heart filled with that fierce joy that comes when something formidable has finally been conquered.

Anyan and I were so wrapped up in our little moment that we didn't hear the first scream. But we heard the second. Trill's shriek of pain cut through our reverie, and suddenly I noticed she was on fire. Then she was rolling, putting herself out, and above her Nell was floating in midair, power crackling around her tiny form like she was one of those static-energy balls they have in science museums.

The barghest crouched in front of me, ready to fight. We raised our shields almost simultaneously and then seamlessly blended them together, my water flowing through his combined air and earth to create a wall of elemental force that was virtually impenetrable.

Which was lucky, as right then a blast of fire streaked across the pasture toward Anyan. It was red and angry, and it was backed up by a pummeling wave of power so fierce that, even behind our übershield, I staggered under its onslaught.

I went to one knee but no farther, for Anyan was there, bracing me with his massive shoulder. Engulfed in fire, we barely kept it at bay with our shields. We were as yet unharmed, but fire and snapping energy were everywhere.

Only then did my dazzled brain put together what had just happened.

I may have fled Boston for my own safety, but all I'd accomplished was to bring danger directly to Rockabill and the people I loved.

CHAPTER NINE

Just as quickly as it hit, the fire ceased its barrage. I staggered to my feet, pushing up off Anyan's broad back. The pasture was still full of smoke and flames and noise as I peered around, trying to see if Nell and Trill were okay.

'Are you all right?' the barghest roared over the cacophony. I nodded.

'Can you see Nell?' I shouted, and then abruptly had my question answered. A fierce wind blew outward from where the gnome had been hovering over Trill. It pushed away the smoke, clearing the pasture and revealing all.

Yes, I'd been told countless times that gnomes were fierce, that in their own territory, they could take on pretty much anyone or anything that came gunning for them, even Alfar. But no, to be honest, I hadn't really believed it. I mean, c'mon, Nell really did look like a supersized garden gnome. At just over two feet tall, she looked like a kindly miniature grandma.

And, oh, dear gods, was I wrong to underestimate her. Still hovering above Trill, protecting her friend with shields that would make Fort Knox envious, Nell had gone full-on Yoda. Check that: Nell had gone Yoda if he were on PCP, had been saving up his force for about six months, and had some serious anger-management issues.

Her hair, pulled from its bun, whipped around her in long gray tendrils as Nell pulled so much elemental power out of the earth that a mini-tornado of wind and energy spun in the center of the pasture. Only, this tornado shot what looked like lightning bolts but were actually blasts of pure elemental force.

Her target was standing at the end of the field farthest from the cabin: a pillar of flame that was far brighter and fiercer than the ifrit I'd met so many months ago. Conleth's – for it had to be the halfling – fire glowed so bright it was almost blue in the center. Even so, he was kept more than a little busy by the gnome. They were lobbing power at one another so fast and so furiously it was like watching a tennis match between Serena and Venus Williams.

Nell was obviously fine and perfectly capable of taking care of herself, but Trill lay crumpled on the ground, unmoving.

'Trill's hurt!' I shouted, pointing toward her still, little figure.

Anyan ignored me, his attention fully on the action as he growled nonstop, his hackles raised. I knew the only reason he wasn't on the offensive was that he was protecting me. But I wasn't helpless, goddammit.

'Trill's hurt!' I repeated, giving the barghest's ear a hard tug. He looked at me sharply, obviously less pleased about tugs than he was by scratches. 'We have to go help her!' He nodded as his eyes found Trill's huddled form.

'If she'll let us through her shields,' he shouted, clearly referring to Nell. 'Hold on to me!'

I grabbed a firm hold on his ruff, where he would have had a collar if he were that kind of dog. I clung to him for dear life as we forged our way forward, buffeted by the gnome's and ifrit's competing forces.

At the edge of Nell's insanely large and strong shield, we ground to a halt. A magical tank wasn't going to get through that bad boy. I felt Anyan's force gather even as he did the magical equivalent of a polite knock on Nell's shields.

'If she lets us through, we need to meld the edges of our power,' he commanded. I nodded, understanding that otherwise there'd be a weak spot Conleth could take advantage of.

Keeping my eyes on Trill's still form, I waited impatiently for Nell to let us in. Finally her shields opened, just a bit. Anyan inserted a wedge of his own power, seamlessly integrating our combined force into Nell's so that our little orb of shield grew out of Nell's larger orb, just as sometimes happens when children blow bubbles and two of them combine.

We moved forward, the two bubbles integrating seamlessly, until we were entirely within the circle of Nell's power.

Inside the gnome's shields, all was eerily quiet. Only Nell's enraged shouts echoed as, to my utter disbelief, she swore a blue streak. I am well aware of my own penchant for the potty mouth, but I could only stare at Nell in awe at the expletives streaming out of her mouth.

She had just started in on Conleth's sexual affinity for ground squirrels when Anyan barked my name, reminding me what we were there for.

I went to him, shuddering at the sight of Trill. The kelpie looked awful. Her little pony shape was blistered and blackened, and it took me a second to see that she was, indeed, still breathing. I tamped down a wave of nausea at the sight of her oozing wounds as I knelt down to where Anyan was already hard at work healing her.

The barghest had created a bubble of power around her, keeping the air off her wounds to decrease the risk of infection. Slowly, painstakingly, he was healing her from the inside out. I sent him a thread of my own power, this time careful to monitor my power expenditure. With all of his attention focused on Trill, Anyan pushed what I gave him into his little infection-shield without comment or acknowledgment.

I kept pumping him energy, but other than that, I didn't know what to do. In this shape, Trill had no hand to hold and I couldn't see a patch of untouched skin to stroke and try to comfort her. There was nothing I could do to help her besides feed Anyan my strength.

Nell hovered above us, still shrieking insults and threats as she hurled bolts of power at Conleth. I shifted around, trying to get a better look at the ifrit halfling, but Anyan was in the way.

So, still feeding the barghest my energy, I walked around him toward the outer edge of Nell's shield where I could get a better look.

Conleth was starting to falter under Nell's onslaught, and his fire had become less bright, which meant I could finally discern a human shape. Tall and slender, his focus seemed to be on Nell. Until suddenly, I saw eyes, startlingly blue in all that fire, shift from the gnome to my own face.

The halfling's attacks ceased as we stared at one another. It only lasted a few seconds, but his intense gaze was enough to raise the hairs on my arm. To my amazement and horror, he raised a hand to me in a manner that appeared . . . beseeching.

Before I could react, Nell had taken advantage of our attacker's momentary lapse of concentration. She hit him with a double-barreled blast of power – one from each hand – that made him stagger. He sent me one last searching look as she gathered herself for another hit, and then suddenly he was engulfed in even more flame than before.

And that's when he blasted off, like a motherfucking rocket ship. One moment he was there, the next he was gone, arcing away from the pasture to the gods only know where.

'Well, *well*,' Nell breathed, obviously impressed.

We were both still standing there, blinking in shock, when Anyan called to Nell.

'Gnome! Here!'

Nell was instantly at Trill's side, taking over for Anyan.

I switched my power feed from Anyan to Nell as the big dog stood and shook himself.

His fierce, iron gaze met mine. 'Stay with Nell,' he commanded before turning to the gnome.

'Protect her,' he rumbled, causing me to shiver.

With that, the barghest was off, streaking away to follow the trail of fire that Conleth had left blazing behind him in the night sky.

My shivering increasing, I finally realized just how very fucked I was as I plopped down next to the nearly healed kelpie.

Then I dug my cell phone out of my pocket to call Caleb.

The next morning, at 8:00 A.M. sharp, my ride rolled in. I recognized Caleb's SUV as it pulled in the drive, and Daoud climbed out to collect me. I was expecting Ryu, but I wasn't about to kick up a fuss, considering my audience.

I turned to say one last good-bye to my very confuzzled father.

'Okay, Dad. I'll see you soon. As soon as I can. I know this is out of the blue, but Ryu needs my help with something important. In the meantime, Nurse Ratched here is going to help around the house.'

My words were backed up by a gentle compulsion from Nell, whom I'd called Nurse Ratched in a moment of complete and utter retardation. Luckily, she didn't get the allusion, so it was fine. Because, as I had learned last night, she could kick my ass from here to Montreal without breaking a sweat.

'Okay, honey. Call me when you get there,' my dad replied foggily. I hated all the magic we'd worked on my dad for the past week, but we had to keep him happy so I could lure Conleth away from him and the rest of Rockabill. My dad also had to be amenable to having a gnome bodyguard. Ideally without him realizing she was, indeed, a gnome. Or a bodyguard.

So I had my father's welfare covered, and Amy was covering for me at work. Now that Valentine's Day had passed, Sarah from the Sty, could also take a few shifts. And there was always Miss Carol, although I shuddered at the thought. Miss Carol, Nell's niece, was an immature gnome with a penchant for debauchery. She special-ordered books so filthy we had to keep them wrapped behind the counter. Miss Carol was also constantly insinuating she'd like to work at the bookstore, for kicks, but the woman had a major edit-button malfunction. She said everything and anything that popped in her head. 'It's just the truth,' she would always say in her own defense, and I'd grown tired of trying to explain that the truth did not make for easy listening.

I hadn't yet told Grizzie and Tracy, as I figured I'd call them on the seven-and-a-half-hour-drive to Boston from Rockabill. And because I was a coward. At least I'd sorted everything out, schedule-wise, so I didn't feel quite so bad leaving Grizzie and Tracy in the lurch the second week running. Plus, at the end of the day, I'd rather they fire me than have them barbecued because Con had attacked me at the store.

I gave my dad a fierce little hug, careful not to linger and make him worry. Then I wheeled Iris's big ole suitcase outside and passed it on to Daoud. I hadn't yet unpacked it except to take out my dirty clothes and my toiletries, since I'd been rather distracted the last week, and most of it was Iris's contributions, anyway. So I'd just shoved some more practical clothing on top of all of Iris's impracticalities and called it a day.

Daoud loaded my bags as I climbed into the backseat. Caleb smiled at me from the front.

'Hello, Jane.'

'Hi there, Caleb.'

'Ryu's at the scene. We'll deliver him to you and then we'll all leave for Boston.'

'Okay,' I said, as Daoud got in the car, and we drove off toward Nell's. We'd all had a long night, so we didn't bother chitchatting.

When we got to the cabin, Ryu's little car was parked rakishly in front of the wide front steps. He was around back, with Trill, examining the destroyed pasture with an extremely irate expression on his face. The kelpie looked almost normal, except that her mane was pretty much burned off. When I walked toward the pair, a look of pure relief came over Ryu's face. He trotted over to me, picking me up in a fierce hug.

'Thank the gods you're unhurt, baby,' he murmured, holding me tight. But I wasn't paying any attention to the vampire.

For over Ryu's shoulder, I could see the remains of the once-lush pasture. It had been dark when Con had attacked last night, and seeing all the damage in the light of day freaked me right the fuck out. It was one thing to be attacked in Boston, but this was Rockabill. This was my *home*. And it was devastated. Trees were uprooted around the edges of the field and partially burned. The grass was gone, and huge gouts of earth were upturned like divots from a giant's polo match. My face was grim as Ryu walked me to the cabin's back stairs.

He sat me down gently, turning my chin till I met his eyes.

'Are you okay, baby?'

'He came to where I *live*,' I said, anger infusing my tone. Ryu leaned in to kiss me, stroking my hair soothingly.

'I'm sorry,' I said. 'I just didn't realize . . . Shit, I didn't realize.'

'Yeah, Con does pack a punch,' Ryu said dryly, stroking his thumb over my cheek.

I shuddered, looking out again toward the ravaged pasture.

'I'm sorry, baby. I'm so sorry this happened.' Ryu's voice had lost the sarcastic edge. He sounded very sad.

'It's not your fault,' I said. 'I'm just lucky Conleth was dumb enough to attack when he did. If he'd come for me at home, or at the bookstore, things would have been different.' By 'different'. I meant I'd be very, very dead. And so would a few other members of Rockabill's human population, most probably.

'Yeah. He probably hasn't come across any gnomes and thought she'd be easy pickings. Thank the gods she was here.'

'And Anyan,' I agreed. 'He's the one who saved me.'

Ryu's mouth tightened. 'Yes. Anyan. Where did he run off to, by the way?'

'He took off after Con,' I replied, leaning back on the stairs and wearily shutting my eyes. 'Okay, I need to swim. Recharge. Then we leave. Sound good?'

'We don't have to leave, honey. We can stay here, draw Conleth out, fight him here. We'll protect you.'

I cracked open one incredulous eye at Ryu.

'Are you serious? Hell no. Look at this fucking place, Ryu. I'm not sticking around, leaving the people I love vulnerable.

What could a human do against Conleth? Even Iris wouldn't have lasted two minutes against him, and she, at least, has some power. Gods, if he'd come after Grizzie and Tracy, or my dad . . .' I shuddered, nauseated by the thought of what he'd do to my human friends and family.

'We're going back to Boston,' I concluded, using my 'final answer' voice.

'Jane . . .'

'No, Ryu. We're leaving. And we're not coming back here till Conleth is found. I will *not* risk everyone by staying here.'

Ryu was silent, frowning at me as he thought through the logistics.

'You're probably right, Jane. You are safest with me,' Ryu said after giving it some thought. 'And I have to admit, I like the idea of you coming home with me again. Although I hate that it's because of this attack. I never wanted you wrapped up with Conleth.'

I shrugged. 'I know you didn't. But how the fuck did he find me?'

'When you left, we tore the city apart looking for Con, and we even found him a few times. Although he persisted on escaping. Then, a couple of days ago, Julian, he's our resident techie as well as our portable charger, went to put some new software on my computer. He discovered it had been hacked soon after that night in the Commons. I don't use it much, and never for work, so we didn't panic. Hell, we thought we could use it to our advantage. Use it to trap him, or something.' Ryu scrubbed a hand over his face before guiltily meeting my eyes. 'But that's how he must have found your information and figured out who you were. E-mails and pictures and stuff.'

'Shit. He read our e-mails?'

Ryu nodded and I frowned, really uncomfortable. If Con

had read my e-mails to Ryu, he would know pretty much everything about me. Ryu and I wrote each other a lot, and I told him everything about my life as it was at that moment. All of my friends were sort of divided: the humans knew nothing about the supes, and the supes didn't really care too much about my human life. Iris did, to be fair, but she was so scatterbrained. Only Ryu bridged that gap between my new supernatural existence and my more mundane, human life. I could tell Ryu about my father's health and about my training with Nell, and he seemed equally interested in both. Now I felt really vulnerable knowing Conleth knew so much about me.

'So,' Ryu said, 'we figure he came out here thinking he'd get to me through you, not expecting to find you so well protected. But he got a nasty surprise instead. Too bad we never e-mailed each other about how Nell is secretly the Terminator in a tiny gnome shell.'

My frown deepened as I remembered Conleth reaching his hand out toward me. The more I thought of what had happened last night, the more questions I had. After all, if Con had just attacked from the other side of the field, closer to the house, he would have hit me first and I'd have been a goner.

I knew Ryu was right; Con would never have guessed how fierce was our resident gnome, and he'd thought I'd be easy pickings. But there was something about the way things had played out, and about the look in his eyes when he'd reached out to me, that caused my skin to prickle with unease.

I pushed away the feeling, standing up as I did so. I was just skeeved out, tired, and stressed. I needed a swim and some rest, and then everything would seem less portentous, less dire.

'Take me to the ocean, Ryu. Then take me home,' I commanded. 'Your home,' I amended hastily when he cocked an eyebrow at me. His would have to do, for now, as I'd made my own unsafe.

A thought that made me sad, I realized, as Ryu slipped his arm around my waist and led me off to his car and away from the field of battle.

Very, very sad, indeed.

CHAPTER TEN

Ryu's tongue swiped over the pinpricks in my wrist as my orgasm subsided, sending one last, gentle spasm through my system. He pulled me down to his chest from where I straddled his hips, cuddling me close and tucking my head under his chin.

'Gods, it's nice to have you here, Jane,' he murmured, stroking idle fingers down my spine.

'Always happy to oblige, my sweet,' I drawled, kissing him with a loud smack on the neck. The part of me that continually gnawed at things it had no business gnawing at wondered whether he was referring to my company or my blood. For a second, I wondered whether, for Ryu, there was much of a difference. Not letting myself dwell, however, I nudged him aside so I could get up to take a shower.

It was late, around nine. After leaving Nell's cabin, I'd gone for a quick swim to recharge and then we'd driven straight back to Boston. It should have been about a seven-and-a-half-hour drive, but Ryu the Rocket did it in six. I was still seeing flashbacks of my life spinning before me.

After we'd cleaned up and had a quick dinner of bacon

sandwiches and bananas, Ryu's deputies arrived to talk strategy.

We were in the office, with Camille, Julian, Daoud, Caleb, and Ryu crowded around the table with a map spread out before them. I was curled up in Ryu's desk chair, listening closely to everything that was said while trying to stay out of the way. Julian, whose position as tech guru made him the one everyone seemed to communicate with, was relaying everything he'd culled from their various sources.

'We have reports of a firefight between Conleth and Anyan four hours ago, near Lebanon, Vermont. Barghest nearly got him, but Con escaped. And we have what sounds like a positive ID for Conleth, just about an hour ago, in Concord, New Hampshire.' I breathed a sigh of relief at Caleb's words. Con was moving away from Maine and toward Massachusetts. I wasn't entirely thrilled with the latter bit of information, but I was very happy about the former.

'He's coming home,' Ryu said. 'We need to be ready. Have you made any headway in finding his base, Daoud?'

'No, I've got nothing. We thought he might have been holed up in a squat in JP, but that was a dead end.' From the corner of my eye, I saw Daoud pull out gum and offer it around the table. I could have sworn he pulled it from his pants, but I must have been seeing things. That said, everyone did decline the gum.

Ryu sighed, scrubbing his hands through his hair. 'Well, the good thing is that he's not subtle, so we'll know when he hits town. The bad news is, he'll probably announce himself with death. In the meantime, we need to go back to the beginning. There has to be something we're missing, and as it stands all we've got is that damned lab.'

Everyone straightened, so I stood up as well. I hated to admit it, but I was morbidly curious to see the place in which

Conleth had been imprisoned. Everyone started to file out of the office, and Caleb ushered me in front of him with a gentlemanly nod.

I had just walked into the living room when I heard Ryu say, 'Caleb, Julian, you're with me. Camille, Daoud, you stay here with Jane.'

I stopped dead in my tracks, causing Caleb to bump into me. Well, causing a specific part of Caleb to bump into me. *Loincloth!* I thought, even as my mouth said, 'Um, Ryu?' I turned around to see the vampire staring at me, his mouth set in a determined little moue.

'Honey,' he said, affecting patience. 'I know you don't want to hear it, but you should stay here.'

I stepped aside to walk back toward my lover. Who, by the way, was so not getting any later.

'Why should I stay here? That's dividing up your forces, which is silly. Plus, maybe I can help.'

Ryu's smile turned patronizing, at which my blood started to simmer.

'Honey, be realistic. How can you help?'

Okay, if I were honest, that wasn't an entirely illegitimate question. But it wasn't *what* Ryu asked; it was the *way* he asked. Like me helping him was the craziest, most preposterous thing he'd ever heard.

The simmer became a boil as I struggled to keep my voice under control.

'Well, first of all, I'm a halfling. Maybe I can understand Conleth a little better than you can.'

Ryu's patronizing smile shifted into full-on condescension and he actually snorted.

Oh, hell no, I thought as my anger-pot boiled right the fuck over.

'Second, *honey*,' I said, through gritted teeth, 'it appears to me like you need *something* to help you, since you don't have jack on Conleth after all this time. Maybe a fresh set of eyes is exactly what you need. And maybe you shouldn't underestimate me.'

Ryu's eyes snapped with irritation, but I already had that emotion monopolized, thanks.

'Jane, c'mon. You need to be kept safe. Just stay here, make yourself at home . . .'

Oh no, he didn't.

'Unfortunately, Ryu,' I snapped, 'this is not my *home*. I had to leave my home because I was made a target because I visited you. And now I've had to leave my home, and my responsibilities, and my friends and family, so that they don't get killed by the insane firestarter who wants to use me to get to you. So can we quit acting like I'm not involved? Because I am *really* fucking involved.'

'Jane, don't be selfish. I have to focus. I can't be worrying about you getting hurt—'

'Selfish?' I interjected. 'Seriously? How is my wanting to help catch the person who nearly fried me, twice, selfish? And I can take care of myself, Ryu. I'm not a weakling.'

'Honey, I know you're not a weakling,' he soothed, as if I were a preschooler throwing a tantrum. 'But Con is very strong, and you're just not there yet. So stay here, like a good girl.'

My jaw plummeted, and I saw, from the corner of my eye, Julian and Caleb shake their heads as Camille winced. Daoud dropped his face in his hands.

'Like a good girl?' I wheezed. 'Like a *good girl*?' Ryu stared at me, clearly at a loss for why I was suddenly so pissed.

'All right, that's it. Hit me.'

Ryu blinked.

'I'm serious, Fangs. Hit me.'

'Jane, come *on*. I'm not going to *hit* you, fercrissakes.'

'Not with your fist, numpty. With your power. Hit me. I can take it. *Hit me*.'

Ryu rolled his eyes. 'I'm not hitting you.'

'Hit me!' I roared.

Ryu shrugged, lifting his hand and petulantly throwing a little mage ball at me. It was the magical equivalent of a shuttlecock.

I narrowed my eyes at him. Despite everything I'd gone through in my twenty-six years, I knew I looked young, small, and vulnerable. I'd dealt with people judging me because of that fact all of my life, and it would have been one thing for Caleb or Daoud or Camille not to take me seriously. I wasn't fucking them. But this was *Ryu*: the man who kept giving me anxiety attacks by hinting he wanted me to be a bigger part of his life. For *him* to treat me like a child was *infuriating*.

So I did what I'd been told a thousand times not to do and reached into my power with all that fury. I built up a shield wall so strong even I was a bit surprised, as I let my emotions take over what happened next. I'd never consciously built a mage ball, but I poured my strength and ire into four big-ass mage lights that I sent arcing out, knocking over a lamp and forcing Julian to dive out of the way, where I let them hover for a moment. I met Ryu's eyes with mine, hoping he couldn't see that I was as shocked at the power of my performance as he was.

'If you ever treat me like less than an equal again, Ryu Baobhan Sith, you can find yourself another bedmate. I *will* help you in this investigation. I may not be much, offensively, but I can certainly protect myself.'

And with that I let the power-filled mage lights fly

toward me. One clipped Ryu's ear and he yelped, before reaching up a hand to heal himself. As they hit my shields, they fizzled out harmlessly. Then I dropped my defenses, glaring at Ryu and daring him to argue.

'Fine, Jane,' he said, obviously ticked off. 'I don't have time for games. But at least have the good sense to stay close to one of us at all times.'

Then he stalked toward the door. I allowed a small smile of triumph to cross my face before a wave of weakness swept through me and I felt my knees nearly buckle. In a flash, Julian was at my side, supporting me by my elbow but using his own body to keep that fact from anyone else.

He grinned at me, as I felt a flood of elemental water energy surge into me.

'Way to stick it to the man,' he said, clearly thrilled at what he'd just seen. 'That *rocked*.'

I tried to be pleased, but I was still mostly angry that I'd had to create such a scene in the first place. I nodded toward Julian's hand on my elbow. 'Yeah, well, thanks for the top-up.'

'No problem. Seeing everyone's face when you did that was *awesome*. I'm so tired of everyone assuming halflings are weak.'

'Well, I think I overdid it a bit,' I admitted.

'Nah.' He shook his head. 'It was spot on. You've got to prove yourself in our society. And power is the only thing that's respected. Just try not to let your emotions trick you into using too much juice.'

I nodded glumly. Damned feelings . . . At times I envied the Alfar their preternatural calm. Not least when my boyfriend was being a complete dickhead.

'Are you ladies ready?' Ryu griped from the front door, shooting Julian a vicious glare. My fellow halfling dropped my elbow, turning toward where the others waited.

'Yes, sir,' Julian replied, agreeably, as I resisted the temptation to give Ryu the finger.

Once outside and walking to our cars, I wondered if I'd finally gotten a taste of the 'real' Ryu.

Which left me a little worried at how much I preferred the fantasy.

Caleb parked the SUV on a quiet side street lined by slightly shabby apartment buildings. Bits of family detritus – half-inflated soccer balls, rickety-looking picnic tables, brightly colored plastic toys, and the like – were washed up on the front lawns like litter on a beach. It seemed a strange place to have a secret laboratory devoted to studying the supernatural, and I said so.

'Good camouflage, cheap rent,' Ryu suggested, shrugging. It was the first time he'd spoken to me since we'd left the house, and he still wasn't meeting my eyes. 'Who knows why they picked this location.'

Waiting for us on the corner, underneath a streetlight, stood Camille and Julian. Together, we all walked toward Conleth's former prison. The building was large and might once have looked impressive. It was hard to tell with all the damage. One side of the glass doors had been shattered, but the other side was intact. That door was emblazoned with a sign: FOCUS ON FAMILY: SPECIALISTS IN IN-VITRO, GIFT, AND ZIFT. I stared at the sign, narrowing my eyes as my brain started to fire off possible connections.

'The laboratory was a fertility clinic?'

'Well, it operated under the auspices of a fertility clinic,' Ryu said. 'And it seems to have been a real fertility clinic at one time.'

I gave him a pointed look, which he finally returned. He shrugged, again, knowing I was suggesting a link between this clinic's stated purpose, Conleth's identity as a halfling, and the fertility problems facing the supernatural community.

Basically, as it had been explained to me, the supes had trouble making babies with each other. They could do it, but it took tremendous amounts of concentration and resources. I had my own theories about why this trouble existed, although I hadn't shared them with anyone. But I knew contact with magic kept us healthy and relatively immortal. Since I'd started my training, I hadn't had a cold or a hangover or even a pimple. Which was great, but I couldn't help but think that the purgative qualities of our magic – cleansing us of all irregularities – had something to do with the supernatural fertility problems.

Wrapped up in my thoughts, I followed the others as they made their way into the building. When it was my turn, Ryu stopped me. He gently wrapped his hands around my waist and carefully lifted me over the jagged glass still lining the bottom of the door. When he put me down, he kissed me on the forehead, his way of attempting to mitigate the tension between us. After a moment, I leaned into his lips, accepting the gesture.

The front of the building wasn't too badly damaged considering what had happened there. Besides the broken front door, and water damage from putting out the fire, the entry room to the facility must have missed the brunt of Conleth's attack. The only significant Conleth-related damage were the doors that led to the rest of the lab, which had been blown entirely off their hinges, and what must have been the receptionist's station, which looked like it had been blasted with blow-torches at five paces.

'The receptionist survived the initial attack by hiding, but Conleth took quite a bit of time firing away at her station, as if to scare her, before making his escape. And he caught up with her a few days later – killed her and her boyfriend.' Ryu dug around in the file he was carrying, snapping toward Daoud at the same time. The hawk-nosed man walked forward, and this time I definitely wasn't seeing things: Daoud reached into the front of his tight black jeans and pulled out a large flashlight. He handed the flashlight to Ryu, who nodded appreciatively. Daoud then pulled three more large flashlights out of his pants: one he passed to Caleb, one he stuck under his own arm for safekeeping, and one he passed to me. I accepted it without thinking, too shocked to do otherwise, until I remembered where it had come from and scootched my shirt sleeve down to cover my hand. I shook my head, about to ask Ryu why Daoud had a general store in his underwear, when I was cut to the chase by Ryu's showing me two photos: one of a young couple smiling behind a birthday cake and the other of two crispified corpses. *The receptionist and her boyfriend*, my brain reminded me as my body responded with a wave of nausea. I told my stomach, quite firmly, to *settle*. It obeyed with a petulant rumble.

We kept walking forward, through the blasted doorways and into the rest of the laboratory. There were still thick stalactites of melted steel warping off where the doorframes would have been, the resulting Daliesque shapes testimony both to Conleth's enormous power and to this laboratory having been a prison. As we progressed farther toward the back of the facility, the damage increased, as did the body count. The first rooms were relatively body-free, except for the nurse's break room, which had been broken into. In the pictures Ryu had shown me, the two 'nurses' who were killed in that room looked more like the type of bouncers who are fired from motorcycle bars for being too violent. In their 'after' pictures, both had been roasted like chestnuts.

By the time we got to the last two layers of the complex,

the fire damage made almost everything unidentifiable. The roof was entirely missing, walls were crumbling, and everything was sooty and blackened. The smell was horrible: ash and smoke compounded by the smell of mold and rot. I did my best to breathe out of my mouth.

The majority of people killed that night had died in these last few rooms. On duty the evening Conleth escaped were two 'scientists', although I wondered what kind of doctor would participate in this sort of experiment. Both had bit the big one, courtesy of their lab rat. Besides the two nurses killed in their break room, another two had died in front of the room in which Conleth had been kept. Just like the other two nurses, these were also bulky and unpleasant and most assuredly *not* people I would trust with inserting catheters or IVs.

'Conleth's motivation for killing his nurses and doctors is obvious; they were his keepers, his torturers, his enemies. And we see from where some of the bodies were found – the scientist holed up in the john, the nurses in their station – that he went looking for them to kill. But he seems to have done the same thing with the janitor and the parking lot security guard.'

I stared down at the pictures Ryu held in his hand. I could understand why Conleth would blast his way out of the place that had held him. I could even understand his desire for revenge. I hadn't shed any tears when Ryu told me he'd killed Jimmu, who had murdered so many and would gladly have added Ryu and me to his list had he gotten the chance. But a lust for vengeance so strong as to send Conleth out of his way to kill someone hiding, someone difficult to get to, despite the fact that he wasn't yet free himself . . . that I couldn't understand.

We continued, entering a final, blasted doorway. It stood

at the very back of the compound and was where Ryu and the others believed Conleth had actually been held. But it was so blackened that I couldn't make out anything of the layout. All I could see was more evidence of Conleth's strength and rage.

'We keep finding people too late; they get linked to the investigation because they're already dead. Which makes them useless to question, obviously. We can't link this lab to anyone or anything bigger, even though it had to have a network of funding, etcetera. It's like this place didn't exist. Hell, I would doubt its reality if we weren't standing here in the middle of it.'

'Do you have anything at all?' I asked.

Ryu grunted. 'We've only got one real lead. There'd been a head scientist in charge of everything, a Dr Silver, who signed all the bills and had been in charge from the beginning, when this clinic was probably legit. He'd gotten fired about two years ago, though, for reasons unknown. Luckily for us, Silver was on vacation when the attack occurred. He must have recognized the threat, and he went into hiding. He hasn't been seen or heard from since. Julian had a trace on him moving across Europe, but we promptly lost him before we could mobilize an extraction unit. He's been MIA ever since. For all we know, Conleth has already gotten to him.'

'So you've got nothing,' I said, indulging in a moment of brutal honesty.

'Pretty much,' Ryu conceded, staring down at the photos in his hand as if he'd like to tear them in half. I moved closer to him, wanting to comfort him even though I was, admittedly, still a little pissed. I put a hand on the small of his back.

'You'll find him, Ryu,' I said. 'I know you will.'

'Thanks, baby.' Hesitantly, he leaned forward to kiss me,

letting his lips linger when I didn't pull away. 'I'm glad you're here. I shouldn't be, but I am.' He swore lightly under his breath, and then closed and tucked the file under his arm. Turning to me, Ryu put his hands on my hips to draw me close.

'Jane,' he began. 'I know it's selfish, but I miss you. More than you seem to realize. Having you here, it's like—'

But before he could conclude his speech, the stinking air around us began to swirl. From where they'd been scattered at various ends of the huge room, Ryu's deputies sprang into action. They all moved in toward us as Camille moved protectively closer to her son, shielding him with her body, even as Julian joined Daoud and Caleb to flank Ryu in front of me.

Two dark shapes swooped overhead, veiled by the shadows thrown off the city-lit night sky, as powerful wings sent dirt and grime skittering through the air into our faces. Ryu and I threw up our shields, but not before I got an eyeful of grit. Blinking my tearing eyes, I watched as the dark shapes made their descent. Talons scraped loudly against blackened concrete as two sets of brown-and-gray-mottled legs thudded to the ground. As my vision cleared, I got quite an eyeful. From their thighs down, the beings' skin was the scaly texture of birds' legs, but the strange gray-brown flesh morphed into a normal human hue that covered the rest of their bodies. Except for their arms, which were elongated into sweeping, elegant wings covered in feathers that shaded from dark brown to light gray at the tips. They wore no clothes, but they were so slender as to be almost sexless. Only their lack of visible male plumbing told me they were female. From above their small, sharp noses, two sets of eerie, jet-black eyes peered with the concentration of raptors searching for prey. I shivered as their beady gaze raked over me.

'Kaya. Kaori,' Ryu said, stiffly, in acknowledgment. 'To what do we owe this honor?'

'Your own ineptitude, Investigator,' said a cold voice from behind me.

Ryu and Daoud whirled around, the former pulling me behind him as Caleb stayed in position, keeping the bird women in sight and guarding our backs.

Before us stood a tiny woman – as short as me – with olive skin and a bald pate. If she hadn't been dressed in black leather and carrying dozens of visible weapons, she would have looked like a child in a commercial for a cancer charity. Her huge eyes were shadowed, but they stared at Ryu with a cold intensity that made me shudder. *Alfar*, my brain whispered, recognizing her curious stillness and the power that, even now, I could feel crackling around her.

She stepped forward from where she was partially concealed in the blasted doorway, followed by two more beings.

One was obviously a spriggan. He was huge, towering well above Caleb, his gray skin covering muscles so massive they would have made the bodybuilders on Venice Beach give up and go home to take up scrapbooking. But otherwise he had exactly the same aura as the 'nurses' who had guarded Conleth; he radiated stupidity, viciousness, and cruelty in equal measure.

The final being, however, surprised me. He looked like an angel, an Apollo. Long, elegantly muscled limbs were topped off by a perfectly symmetrical face that was an ideal melding of cherubic and masculine. Huge blue eyes blinked in the darkness, brushed by the soft golden curls that crowned his perfect features. Ryu's hand enveloped mine an instant before the beautiful man stopped looking over Camille, clearly undressing her with his eyes, and then turned to me.

A wave of incubus juju crashed against my shields but it felt *wrong*. Instead of that heady mixture of lust and the promise of pleasure that I was so used to from my time spent with Iris, this being's magic promised something altogether darker. Something based on pain, on cruelty, on bodies being taken to the edge of control and then thrown over that edge. I shivered as beautiful blue eyes latched onto my tits and the being leered.

Evil and *a tit starer*, I thought. *Quite the combination . . .*

'Phaedra.' Ryu said the word as if he were spitting. 'You're keeping interesting company these days. I hadn't realized you'd been released, Graeme.'

The beautiful blond man wrenched his gaze away from my breasts to meet Ryu's cold stare with a smirk.

'All a misunderstanding, Ryu. Nothing more. You know how fragile humans are. I didn't mean to hurt that girl and I certainly didn't do anything to her she didn't ask for.' The incubus's eyes found my boobs again. 'She wanted pain . . . I graciously obliged.'

I blanched as I finally put together one plus one regarding Graeme's having been 'released', realizing that he must have been one of the Alfar's exceptions to execution. Which meant he was protected by someone powerful.

'And the others?' Ryu asked, his voice furious.

'What others?' the incubus replied, his voice as light and innocent as whipped cream, but the eyes he raised to meet mine were charged with a promise so cruel I clutched Ryu's hand convulsively.

'Enough,' the Alfar, Phaedra, announced, putting an end to Ryu and the rapist incubus's pissing contest. 'You've gone back to the beginning, Ryu, which means you are lost. Still, months have passed since you were assigned to this investigation. And yet, here you are, at the beginning.'

The small woman strode forward, all squeaking leather and clinking weaponry. She skirted our little group to join the two bird women. Graeme and the spriggan followed.

'Harpies,' Daoud leaned over to whisper in my ear. My eyes widened; they weren't what I would have expected. 'Kaya and Kaori. The spriggan is Fugwat; he's a brute. Avoid Graeme at all costs—'

'Quiet, djinn,' Phaedra commanded. 'Do not speak in my presence unless granted permission to do so.'

Daoud's jaw clenched as he straightened up to glare at the Alfar.

A *djinn*, I thought, his cornucopia groin suddenly making sense. Months ago, at the Alfar Compound, I'd watched another djinn, named Wally, pull a series of very large and very edged weapons out of his pantaloons. Yes, pantaloons. Oh, and he'd also pulled out a mace. In other words, Wally put the 'hammer' in 'Hammer pants'.

I really should have figured out Daoud's faction sooner, but Wally and Daoud looked so dissimilar, and used their powers so differently, that it was like they came from different centuries.

They probably do *come from different centuries, moron*, I realized before turning back to the argument unfolding before me.

'You do *not* command my deputies, Phaedra,' Ryu shot back, barely in control of his temper. I'd never seen Ryu so ruffled.

The Alfar female eyed Ryu speculatively, making her point by not reacting to his outburst.

'Perhaps not *yet*, baobhan sith. But soon. When you have failed in this assignment, as is guaranteed by your incompetence, I will take over, find your halfling abomination, and wipe him off the face of this earth.'

At the words 'halfling abomination', Phaedra sent me a rather pointed stare. Ryu hissed and I squeezed his hand, reminding him that he was not to lose his temper over me.

'And this must be Jane True,' the little woman sneered.

I nodded, refusing to fall to her intimidation tactics.

'I have been looking forward to meeting you. Indeed, we all have.' In my peripheral vision, I noticed Graeme's cruel smile grow crueler still.

I raised my chin defiantly, keeping silent. So the little Alfar upped the ante.

'Especially Graeme. He loves vulnerable little humans, do you not, Graeme?'

The incubus smiled at me, focusing a beam of his creepy rage-tinged lust at me.

Fuck bravery, I thought, moving closer to Ryu as he angrily interrupted the Alfar's little game.

'Why are you here, Phaedra? This investigation does not concern you. Or your master.'

'Of course it does. You know how much of an interest Jarl takes in the *welfare* of halflings.'

My heart dropped into my shoes when Phaedra said the name 'Jarl'.

I should have known, I thought, glancing toward Graeme. *Only Jarl would protect such a monster.*

'Jarl expressed his concern over recent events to our king and queen, and Orin and Morrigan granted him permission to send my team . . .' here Phaedra smiled, a small and unpleasant expression that made my stomach twist, '. . . to *assist* your investigation. While the king made it clear that our role is one of support, *Jarl* made it clear that he expects you to be replaced if this situation is not soon resolved.

'And considering that all you have managed to do is lose

nearly a dozen lives under your watch while nearly getting yourself killed at least twice, I expect that my orders to replace you will come shortly. Unless your mongrel bedmate has some clue hidden in her fragile little body that would explain her presence here.'

Ryu's face was white with rage as his hand gripped mine so hard it hurt. I thought he might actually crush it when the rapist incubus piped up with his own creepy two cents.

'If she does have anything hidden on her, I'd be happy to get it out for you,' Graeme said, letting his gaze wander over my body with an expression in which lust and malice rivaled one another for dominance.

'I swear to the gods that if you touch her . . .' Ryu started forward, as I grabbed his wrist and both Caleb and Daoud put restraining hands on his shoulder.

'I won't just touch her,' the incubus said, stepping forward to goad Ryu. 'I am going to fuck her sideways – stretch her little cunt so far you can crawl inside it and retire, you pathetic excuse for a—'

'Enough!' Phaedra boomed, shooting a beam of hot white light between the incubus and Ryu.

I knew that only the threat of Phaedra's Alfar power kept the situation from turning into a full-on brawl, with me smack dab in the center. Ryu was literally glowing he was so angry, and all of his deputies looked equally pissed. Daoud was practically gnashing his teeth and Caleb was tossing his horns at the mountain of spriggan in a goaty challenge. Camille was eyeing the harpies like they might make a decent snack; the harpies, in turn, had their beady eyes focused on Julian and his mother like hawks that had just spotted two fluffy bunnies.

'This is neither the time nor the place,' Phaedra warned her evil entourage. 'We are here on *official* business.'

While the tension didn't ease, everyone did take a step back. Except for Graeme, who kept himself forward, staring at me and daring Ryu to do something about it.

'Just stay out of our way, Phaedra. And keep your minions out of my sight.' Ryu's voice was tight, his control barely in place.

'Sorry, Investigator, but I have strict instructions to aid you in any way I can. And I *will* aid you.' The Alfar smiled. 'Get used to us. I am sure we will get used to you. Until then!' she called, walking back toward the door to the lab.

The harpies crouched low and then heaved themselves in the air, wings flapping furiously. We were again besieged by filth and dust, only this time Ryu's shields were in place well before anything could hit us. Behind the dirt swirling against our protective barrier, I saw Graeme mouth something at me. I'm no lip-reader, but even I could make out 'See you soon.' I trembled, pressing myself into Ryu's side.

Finally, the dirt settled and we were alone in the laboratory. Daoud groaned and stretched. Caleb shuffled his hooves in the dirt, as if he were considering chasing after Phaedra's gang at ramming speed. Camille watched Julian worriedly as her son took off his glasses, breathed fog onto them, and then wiped them with his flannel shirt. His eyes, a beautiful sea green, met mine as he gave me a grin even more crooked than usual. Julian's kind expression helped to wipe away the smudge of Graeme's interest.

Ryu, meanwhile, looked apoplectic. He was gripping my hand like a vise, and I pulled, gently, to free myself. My fingers, when he eventually let go, were mottled red and white.

We all stood there in silence for a few minutes till, finally, Ryu put into words what we were all thinking.

'Shit.'

We nodded.

'Fuck.'

We nodded again.

'And damn.'

Then he strode angrily toward the door as we scrambled to keep up.

CHAPTER ELEVEN

My fingers scrabbled at the smooth leather interior of Ryu's BMW as he missed the exit we needed, causing him to drop a few more F-bombs and slam on the brakes. He then opened up what I assume was a rift in the space-time continuum in order to hurtle his German-made steel cage of doom through said continuum, only just managing to avoid two Jesus truckers with their grill crosses glowing brightly in the night.

Ryu was decidedly cranky.

We were on our way to the head scientist's, Dr Silver's, family home. It was about two in the morning, so we were officially on baobhan sith time. When we'd gotten back to the cars, Ryu had hurled poor Julian's laptop at him and said, 'Find something. Now.' Much to everyone's surprise, and especially Julian's, he had. In the month since they'd officially canned the investigation, there'd been a few pings on the good doctor's 'secret' accounts, and from somewhere in the States. So we'd split into pairs to investigate whether he'd made it back to his home turf. Camille and Julian had shot over to Silver's Boston pied-à-terre, Daoud and Caleb headed out to his summer home in Cape Cod, and Ryu and I drove out to the family manse in a ritzy suburb of Boston.

'This is probably a wild-goose chase, but it's all we've got. And at least we know Silver is alive, and hopefully back in the country.' Ryu frowned, again. 'Plus there's something about this house in particular that I don't get. I'm glad I'm going back.'

'Whaddya mean, you "don't get"?'

'I can't put a finger on it. Something with the layout,' he said, as we pulled up in front of an enormous, gorgeous old home that bordered on being a mansion.

'Wow.' I breathed. *I guess there's a good living in running evil laboratories.*

We walked up to the house and Ryu murmured something to the door, which opened up as if in welcome. The house was warm, but unaired. From the foyer, I could see that it had been carefully shut up for the Silvers' holiday to the south of France: furniture covered, plants fitted with complicated watering devices, electronics unplugged.

I stuck close to Ryu as we walked toward the grand staircase dominating the foyer.

'Pay attention to the upstairs layout, and then think about it when we come back down,' he told me.

'Okeydokey, smokey,' I said, solemnly.

The house was professionally perfect; there had very obviously been a decorator involved. Even the family photos had been chosen for maximum effect. Tons of pictures covered the walls of the stairway, all full of healthy, wealthy people doing healthy, wealthy things. A baby-boomer couple, who I assumed to be Silver and his wife, dominated the action. In one photo, dressed in black tie and holding champagne, they flanked a famous politician. Another picture showed the same couple, this time wearing tennis gear and clutching rackets, sandwiching a famous tennis player. In others, they wore equestrian gear, or picnic-wear, or fancy dress, or business attire. Inevitably they were accompanied by someone either famous or who exuded a similar air of wealth and status.

I stopped at a picture of Dr Silver at a ribbon-cutting ceremony for a children's hospital in Chicago, and I tried to figure out how somebody who looked so respectable could be, for all intents and purposes, a kidnapper. I stared at the picture, looking for clues, until I saw something in the background that made me gasp.

'What is it, Jane?' Ryu asked, as he stepped up the stair next to me to peer at the photo.

I pointed at the woman behind Silver. He looked closer.

'Oh, that's Amelia Bathgate, of the Chicago Bathgates. Why are you interested in her?' For a second, I nearly told him to look closer. Then I remembered I'd promised Grizzie I wouldn't share her secret.

'Um, I was just wondering how Silver could be so good in some ways, and so evil in others.'

'Yeah, it's hard to believe the guy who owns this house is the same guy who ran that lab,' he said, stroking a hand down my back to comfort me. 'Come upstairs when you're ready?' he asked.

'Sure,' I said, turning back to the photo. 'Just give me a minute.'

I stared at the woman in the picture for one last moment. I could understand why Ryu didn't recognize her, and why Grizzie claimed few people had made the connection between Grizzie, Dusty Nethers, and Amelia Bathgate. As if by magic, she was the *complete opposite* of everything Grizzie represented. Whereas Grizzie oozed sexuality and strength and a kind of chaotic joy that bordered on the anarchical, the woman in the photo could have been a Nazarene minister's spinster aunt. She was wearing a conservative suit in dull taupe and her hair was slicked back in a tight bun. But it was her facial expression that I found most fascinating. She had an expression that was like the human, nonmagical version of what Anyan had taught me about glamouring. Her whole demeanor – the set of her shoulders, the way she pulled in her height as if she were ashamed, the downcast eyes – all said, 'Nothing to see here. Pay me no mind.'

Unable to believe that Grizzie had lived like that for so many years of her life, I wondered, sadly, whether I'd ever meet Amelia Bathgate. Finally, I turned to join Ryu.

On the second floor, beds were stripped and covered and everything was unplugged. Except, I noticed, the security cameras set up in strategic locations throughout the house. Ryu's power was swirling away, making us invisible to them, but they still made me uncomfortable. Not least because they were our first sign that the man who made this his home was not all that his wholesome exterior claimed.

I tried to keep a mental map of the upstairs in my head, as Ryu had asked, and when we finished and made our way through the downstairs, I understood why. My spatial perception was excellent, and I'd always been good with floorplans. But the mental plan of the upstairs that I'd drawn as we explored did not match my mental plan of the downstairs.

'There should be an extra room down here,' I said, as we stood in the living room.

After pondering the issue for a few seconds, I walked out of the living room, through the kitchen, and into the large office. I paced it again, to be sure, and then looked up at Ryu. 'This room is short,' I said. 'There should be more office to this office.'

Ryu grinned at me. 'Exactly. But there's less. So where's the rest?'

I looked around, and then started walking along the walls,

followed by Ryu's eyes. The red lights on the cameras settled in either corner, however, blinked blindly at me, unable to see past Ryu's mojo. I leaned against Silver's desk, staring at them.

'Why two cameras, Ryu? You said you didn't find anything of interest in here?'

'No. Nothing that revealed anything about the lab, at least. It was all personal – taxes and shit. Nothing related to any sort of business dealings whatsoever. Silver obviously didn't work from home.'

'So why have two cameras in this room? And where do these cameras go?'

'They're internal,' Ryu replied. 'They can be accessed by the TVs in each room. But we don't know where they're actually controlled from. There should be a control room, or something, somewhere, but we can't find it.'

We both fell silent, staring at the cameras and thinking. This scenario – the cameras inside the house, the foreshortened room – reminded me of a movie I'd seen a few years ago. Okay, so a movie wasn't the most professional thing to go on, but films – like the mythological monsters I now ran with – had to have some basis in reality, right?

'Quit your glamour for a second, Ryu,' I suggested.

'Why?' he asked.

'Just a hunch. I've seen too many action flicks, probably, but it's worth a shot.'

He frowned at me and then shrugged. 'Fine, but it'll mean that Julian will have to hack into the security system to erase the tapes. Are you sure this is worth it?'

'Nope,' I said, honestly. 'Just a hunch.'

Ryu frowned at me, and for a second he looked like he might refuse. But then I felt the tickling little wind of Ryu's strong glamour ease up around me, and I knew we could be seen. I walked away from Ryu and toward the wall to my left.

After a moment, the camera tracked my movements.

'Bingo,' I breathed. 'Panic room. And someone is in there.' I turned to my vampire in triumph. He was staring at me in surprise.

'Jane, you're a genius.' Ryu grinned, as he got out his cell to call in the reinforcements.

'You'll be like Bob Dylan in "Subterranean Homesick Blues". Only cute,' Daoud said, as he capped his marker.

'Thanks,' I said, as I put my own marker away.

Ryu and I had torn the office apart, trying to find the entrance to Silver's hidey-hole. We'd gotten nowhere when we'd been joined by the others, first Camille and Julian and finally by Daoud and Caleb. Then we'd all proceeded to get nowhere together.

That's when Julian had suggested signs. The cameras didn't have microphones, so talking was out. If we weren't getting to Silver, we had to get him to come out to us. Explaining to him that we weren't there to kill him, and could actually help him, would probably be a good start toward achieving our goal.

So we got crafty. Silver had paper; the genie's Underoos provided the markers; all we had to do was make sure the message was readable. So I'd written, one word per page, 'Tracking Conleth, must find him. Need help. Won't hurt you.' I'd been elected to show the signs because I was the only one who didn't look at all dangerous.

When my big moment came, I felt like a jackass standing there with the signs. I shuffled through them slowly, and then started over. Daoud helped out by humming an off-tune version of the Dylan song.

I'd just started my fourth shuffle through when we heard a hissing sound. I dropped the signs at my feet.

A large section of bookcases swung outward to reveal a stubble-cheeked elderly man with wild hair wearing pajamas and a bathrobe. He was holding a shotgun and his hands were trembling. Not a good combination.

Ryu tensed, but I stayed him with a hand on his elbow. I'd started this. Silver had come out at my behest; I would be the one to finish it.

'I'm sorry to break in like this, sir,' I said, as I stepped forward. 'My name is Jane True. We're tracking Conleth. We know the damage he's done, and he's going to continue killing until he's found. We have to stop him.'

The old man eyed me warily. He looked far less healthy and wealthy now than the man in the photos.

'Knew he'd be back,' Silver grunted, finally. 'Told my family he was gone, but I knew he'd be back.'

I nodded. 'He is back, sir.'

He nodded, as if to himself, and said, 'My family's hidden. And I'm here. He may come for me, but they'll be safe.' Then he looked up at me sharply. 'How do I know you're not working with him?'

I shrugged. 'You don't. But if we were, we'd have attacked you already.'

He stared at me hard. I tried to look as innocent and small as possible.

'Besides,' I added, 'how could Conleth be working with anyone? He's been trapped in a lab all his life, as you know.' For a second the man's face hardened. I cursed myself, thinking I'd made a mistake in pointing out Silver's role in Conleth's tragic life. I blundered on quickly. 'We're not working with him. But we know what he did to the people you worked with and to his own family. He needs to be found.'

Silver's eyes bored into mine as if trying to read my soul. I hoped mine was shinier than his must be.

'Who do you work for?' he asked. 'Who are you?'

'Can you put the gun away?' I countered. Silver's hands hadn't ceased trembling and I wasn't sure whether any amount of magic could heal a shotgun blast at short range.

'First, tell me who you work for.'

I gestured toward my vampire. 'This is Ryu. He's an investigator who works for . . . some very powerful people. They want Conleth stopped.' I figured that answered Silver's question without raising any more. 'Everybody else works for Ryu.'

'And you?' Silver asked.

'I'm Ryu's . . . girlfriend.'

'You're his girlfriend?' Silver asked, his voice clearly indicating that he thought tracking mass murderers was not the proper place for people's 'girlfriends'.

I ignored him. 'Now will you put the gun away?'

Silver thought for a minute and then shrugged. He turned back to the room behind the bookcase – which I could see had a toilet and sink, an army cot, a control deck for the security system, tons of leather-bound books, and a big box of files – in order to put the gun down. He also picked up the box and then walked past us, toward the living room, as the door to the panic room slid shut.

'I was dead when I opened that door,' he said, over his shoulder. 'So I might as well have a brandy.'

In single file, we shuffled after Silver's disheveled, wild-haired form as if we were in some bizarre pantomime performance of the Pied Piper. Silver put his huge box down in order to pour himself a stiff belt of booze, and the rest of us all joined him when he offered. It had been a long night, and it was just beginning.

'Here's what you came for,' Silver said, kicking the box over to Ryu. 'Everything is in there. Well, everything from my time, so I don't know how much it'll help.' The old man's face grew grim. 'I'm not responsible for what happened after I left . . . But there's Conleth's childhood, the records of the testing we did, and records about everyone who worked with me at the laboratory. What's not on paper is on the data sticks at the bottom.'

Ryu contemplated the box like he'd just been given a great big gift horse, one he now had to look in the mouth. He finally bent over and started rummaging.

Camille came over to Silver, and I could feel her glamour reaching out to him, trying to soothe and relax him, magically buttering him up. She sat down on the ottoman next to him.

'You were in charge of everything until a few years ago,' Camille said gently, staring Silver in the eyes. 'Why did that change? Who took over the lab once you left?'

Silver shrugged, blinking slowly. 'I don't really know. Until a few years ago, we were basically functioning as Conleth's guards. With his powers, he couldn't be released into the general population. So even though we weren't experimenting on him anymore, the government paid us to keep him. We knew how to handle him. We were the only thing he knew. I think he considered us family. But then we got word from our corporate offices in Chicago that we'd been bought out by a new company and that we had a new sponsor. A private sponsor. That's when everything changed.'

'Changed how?'

'It started small. New nurses. Who weren't really nurses in my estimation. Then new technicians. They were rough and they started doing their own "experiments" when I wasn't there. Things that could not really be called . . . science.'

'Such as?'

'Strange things. Invasive. And that couldn't have been pleasant for Con. I started looking into it and voicing my opposition, and was I summarily fired. They replaced me with the worst of the new technicians. He was . . . off. I don't know what his deal was, but he wasn't right. On any level. I don't know what they did to Con for the last few years, but it must have been horrifying. The boy I left wouldn't have done those things. He wasn't really a prisoner to us. And I think he loved us, and we cared for him, in our own ways. But now . . . Whatever they did to him changed him, completely.'

Silver took a deep pull from his drink as we fell silent, each wrapped up in our own thoughts, until Camille spoke again.

'Do you have any idea who this company, or this sponsor, was?' she prompted, trying to tease his memory with both her questioning and her glamour. I could sense her magic probe, but every time she did so, Silver's face went slack. I realized his mind had already been messed with, and not by us.

The old man's jaw worked, as if he were forcing himself to speak. 'The company's information is in one of those files. Well, what I could find, which wasn't much. It seems to be a shell organization, hiding God only knows what. As for the new sponsor, when we first got the news, there was a liaison sent to look everything over. She spent a lot of time with Conleth.' Silver frowned, his gaze losing focus. 'It's . . . fuzzy. She's . . . hard to remember. I know I met her, but . . .' He fell silent as his face went blank. 'What were you asking?' he said suddenly, looking at Camille as if he wasn't sure when she'd sat down.

Oh yeah, he'd been fucked with, all right. His memory was shot full of holes so big Ryu could have driven through them.

I'm surprised he even remembered she was a woman. At least that's something.

'Did you ever meet the actual sponsor?' Camille asked, knowing that Silver would never remember anything about the female liaison.

Silver shook his head. 'Only the higher-ups, the money people, ever met him. Which is why Con must be working with someone,' he insisted. 'Someone who knows the power structure.'

'We haven't found any evidence that Conleth *is* working with anyone,' Ryu said, soothingly. 'Everyone from the laboratory he's attacked, he's attacked on his own.'

'Well, then, who's killing the others?' Silver demanded, his voice rough with fear and grief.

'Others?' we all asked together.

Silver stood, slowly and stiffly, and walked to the box. He took out a sheaf of papers.

'These are from a woman named Dr Donovan, who went between Boston and Chicago. She worked for the old company that owned us, as the person who approved the testing. And she's the only person I know who stayed on after corporate changed hands. For the few years I worked for the new company, she's the only one I ever dealt with. Everything came down to me, to our lab, through her.'

Ryu took the papers. 'And?'

'Brenda and I worked for years together. She was always in and out of Boston on business, and we spent a lot of time together. We . . . we had an affair, briefly. But even after the affair, we stayed friends. We trusted each other, and she had my private e-mail, my addresses, everything. But we had a falling out over the new administration after I was fired. I wanted her to tell me what they were doing to Conleth and she refused. She was ambitious . . . Anyway, we lost touch.

Which is why I was so surprised to get that first e-mail, there.' Silver pointed to the paper on top of the stack. 'She sounded so scared. That came about a week after Conleth escaped.'

'Is that why you went into hiding?' Ryu asked.

'I didn't know what Con would do when I knew he'd escaped. So yes, I hid from Con at first. But he only killed people from *after* my time. There are tons of employee files I have there, in that box. The people who were with Conleth from the beginning, but who were fired by the new admin- istration, are still alive. I've checked up on them. So at first I hid from Conleth, yes. But then I hid because of what Brenda told me in those e-mails.'

'Which is?' Ryu prompted.

'She starts off by telling me that something isn't right, asking me questions about who and what Conleth could have known about people in corporate. I tell her that he couldn't have known anything, unless things had changed that much since I was in charge. Hell, I didn't even know anything about who had taken over, and I was at the top in Boston. She e-mails me back saying she was wrong to get in touch, nothing was happening, and she'd just been overtired. Then she starts writing me letters . . .'

I watched as Ryu flipped through the papers, nodding at Silver's words.

'Brenda writes to tell me that her e-mail is monitored and so are her phones. Hence the letters. She tells me that the people above her are disappearing. That they're showing up dead. Burned. She asks me how Conleth could have known about the people in Chicago, who worked with her in cor- porate.

'But he *couldn't* have,' Silver insisted. 'Everything was set up so it went through Brenda and me, or whoever replaced me. We were as high as anything could be traced, and Brenda was the buffer keeping even *me* from knowing anything. I know because I tried like hell to find out more about that company even before I was fired, and I've got some pretty impressive contacts. Nothing could be discovered. Nothing.'

'But you'd been replaced,' Ryu interjected, gently. 'Maybe things had changed.'

'Bullshit,' Silver swore. 'There's no way a company puts that much effort, money, and influence into remaining invisible just to rip off the veil one day.'

'What happened to Donovan?' Ryu asked.

'Last page,' Silver said. 'The photo.'

The photo showed a picture very similar to the ones Ryu had shown me at the laboratory. Dr Donovan was dead, her body burned.

'You're sure it's her?' Ryu asked.

'Dental records,' was the only response.

'When was this? And where?'

'Right after Conleth killed his family here. But Brenda was killed in Chicago.'

'It looks like one of Conleth's kills,' Camille said from behind us. She had moved to peer at the picture from over Ryu's shoulder.

'It *looks* like one of Conleth's kills, but it isn't,' the old man insisted, shaking his white head adamantly.

Ryu crooked his eyebrow. He didn't believe Silver.

'Damn it, boy,' Silver said, and I almost smiled. Ryu might look about forty years Silver's junior, but he was actually around two hundred years older than the human in front of us. Silver stood up, painfully, to go stand in front of Ryu. Taking the sheaf of papers away from him, Silver flipped through till he found what looked like a report.

'That's Donovan's autopsy. Her body was obviously very badly burned, but they still found evidence that she hadn't just been killed and then set on fire. She was abused first. Brutally.' Silver pointed to one line buried in the middle of the report. One word had been highlighted.

The word was 'tortured'.

I shuddered, as Ryu read the report.

'How did you get all this, sir?' I asked, giving Ryu time to read and trying to keep my overactive imagination from dwelling on that single, horrible word.

'I had a contact in the police I pumped for information when I hadn't heard from Brenda in a while. Her letters just stopped and I knew she was in trouble. So I came back to the States.' The gray-haired head bent as Silver stared at his hands. When he finally spoke again, his voice was dark with competing emotions. 'She was an ambitious bitch in a lot of ways. But she didn't deserve to die. Especially not like that.'

Ryu finished reading, and he put the autopsy report at the back of the sheaf of papers as if to get it out of sight.

'Conleth's changed his MO,' he said. 'He's even more dangerous than he was before. He needs to be caught *now*.'

Silver peered at Ryu as if he'd just claimed that cream cheese was made of moon spooge.

'Have you listened to a word I've said, boy? Whoever killed Donovan made it look like Conleth, but there's no way Conleth did that. Whoever killed that woman was something else entirely. Con's a murderer but he's not, yet, a monster.'

'Sir, you said yourself that Conleth had changed.'

'Not that much, damn it. And none of the murders in Boston are like this. He kills, but he doesn't torture!' Silver was getting increasingly irate and I, for one, was glad he no longer had his shotgun.

'And how did he get to Chicago, anyway? And then back to Boston?' Silver looked like he'd played his trump card, but I'd seen Conleth go rocket blaster. I wasn't sure how far he could sustain such power, but his getting to Chicago wicked fast wasn't an impossibility.

'Conleth has ways of traveling great distances.' Ryu's voice was still gentle, but it was also obvious that he didn't believe a word Silver had said. And the old man knew it.

'If you won't listen, you won't listen,' Silver said. 'But I'm warning you: you're making a mistake not looking beyond Conleth for something more. I'm not saying he's an innocent; God knows he's committed crimes. But this isn't one of them. And I have no doubt that once you begin digging, you'll find other bodies, other murders. And they won't have been Conleth, either.'

The old man poured himself another brandy and then settled himself on his sofa. His white head bowed and he stared down at his hands. He looked defeated, but his voice was strong when he finally spoke.

'Now get out of my house and let them come for me.'

Of course, we hadn't just let them come for Silver. We'd left a pair of Stefan's most powerful deputies to watch him. He was, after all, a well-baited trap as well as an innocent in need of protection.

Well, relatively innocent, I thought as I remembered everything that had been in those files.

We'd gone from knowing virtually nothing about Conleth to knowing *everything* – down to his preference for boxers – in one evening. We should have been euphoric at the break in the case. But the 'break' had just led to a billion more questions.

We finally discovered exactly how Conleth had ended up in that lab. He'd been abandoned at a convent when he was a baby, which he proceeded to burn down, killing everyone inside. Rescue services had found the baby – perfectly unharmed – sitting in the smoking ruins, still burping fire.

Which is how he'd ended up in a laboratory. One reason he'd never come to the attention of the supes is that the FBI labeled him a different code word than the one they usually used for their brushes with the supernaturals. They'd genuinely thought he was some Rosemary's baby devil-child and had code named him 'Firecrotch', a stonkingly inappropriate name for a being one supposes is the Antichrist. Any supe in the Bureau at the time probably thought it was a dirty joke involving a redhead.

So, through a series of accidents, Conleth had gotten swept away in bureaucracy, to be forgotten about until he'd come to the attention of this mysterious donor. The records petered out then and stopped with Silver's having been fired. But, from what the old doctor had said, that's when things had really gotten bad for Conleth.

Unfortunately, we had no easy way of investigating Silver's claims about the murders in Chicago. The supes were all very territorial, and both Nell and Ryu had drilled into me their supernatural geography. Most of what humans considered to be northern Illinois was firmly entrenched in an area the supes knew as the Borderlands. Much like the mountainous regions between Pakistan and Afghanistan, the Borderlands between neighboring territories were lawless places, ungoverned by the Alfar. Chicago, however, was an extreme case. The city and its surrounding suburbs were a sort of black hole for the Alfar: they sent spies in, but no spies ever emerged. This huge urban area that everyone knew was there, and functioning, and even Google Mappable, was invisible to the Alfar and their pure-blooded subjects.

I imagined it must drive the Alfar crazy, but apparently there was nothing they could do about it. With the fertility issues and their already low numbers, compounded by the nagas' treachery – Orin and Morrigan's territory had lost a lot of people fighting Jimmu and his nestmates – they simply didn't have the manpower to charge into the Borderlands willy-nilly.

So we were at an impasse, in terms of that aspect of the investigation. Ryu had no contacts in the Borderlands. There was no supernatural power structure that he knew of to call and question. So he'd set Camille to calling the human police. But with only a very limited ability to glamour them over the phone, they were unlikely to give up any sensitive information. Ryu had also set Julian to hacking into the Chicago PD's computer system. He'd search for bodies that had been burned, hopefully giving us a place to start.

Silver's files had, however, yielded some extra clues for our Boston investigation. After Ryu took me for a quick swim off a pier near the New England Aquarium to recharge my batteries, we'd pored over Silver's files all night, trying to get a bead on Conleth.

Unfortunately, there were only two people left alive who'd worked at the laboratory during the years the new sponsor had been in charge. One was a receptionist who had straddled Silver's reign and the new sponsor's regime. Conleth had developed a rather serious crush on her; one she hadn't reciprocated. Eventually, he'd turned violent against the scientist that he was convinced she fancied. She'd either quit or been asked to leave and was replaced with the woman who Con toasted with her boyfriend. If Con was that mean to somebody who merely worked the front desk, I shuddered to imagine what he'd do to someone who'd also rejected him.

That's what had brought us to Allston, and the apartment where Tally Bender, the former receptionist, had moved. She'd been tough to track down, as she'd been living with an ex and had been in the process of moving out when she had quit. Not to mention, Allston was populated almost entirely by students from either Boston University or Boston College, so a lot of renting was done through sublets, or moving in as a roommate on somebody else's lease. But once we had a Social Security number from Silver's files, Julian was able to get a fix on her.

I was perched on the hood of Ryu's car, parked a few

houses down, as the others made their way to Tally's. Julian was with me, and we'd been tasked with making sure our friends weren't followed into the apartment. Worried for the girl's safety, Ryu and his team were going in hard and fast, so they really meant 'stay out of the way'. It sucked, but I had to agree. I'd gotten good at defense, as Ryu's leaving me with Julian acknowledged, but offense was still not my strong suit.

'Sorry you have to babysit,' I said to my fellow halfling, as he cleaned his glasses on his shirt.

He grinned at me, the ridiculously long lashes framing his sea-green eyes waving a friendly 'hello' as he blinked.

'No problem. I'm not really all that big on the action,' he said. 'If this were a human movie, I'd be the hacker. The one bent over the keyboard, sweat dripping down my face, the music crescendoing behind me to disguise the fact that all I'm really doing is typing.' He finished wiping his specs and put them back on. 'Of course, the hacker usually dies in those films, so I hope I buck that trend.'

I laughed. 'What is it with you people and pop culture? Don't you have your own stuff to quote?'

'I'm a halfling, too, remember. So I'm curious about my human side. But the purebloods all love human stuff. Humans know how to live. I'd get philosophical and say it's because they know they're going to die, but someone already wrote that book.'

'*The Human Stain*, among others.'

'Interesting choice. Wouldn't figure you for a Philip Roth fan.'

'I know, women are supposed to hate him. But I love me some Roth. He's brutal, but he's honest.'

'You read a lot, don't you?'

'That's how I lived, for a long time,' I said, as I pulled my sleeves down lower over my scarred wrists, my thoughts turning to Jason and the years I'd grieved for him. The pain would always be there, but now it was manageable. 'Anyway, yeah, I read. A lot.'

Julian used his elbow to poke me in the ribs, kindly if awkwardly. 'Well, now you're living enough for three people.' I snorted in agreement.

We sat in companionable silence till I broke it with a question I knew was probably inappropriate but I was dying to ask.

'Can I ask you a rather invasive personal question, Julian?'

'Probably. Depends. What is it?'

'Did you know your human father?'

Julian met my eyes, and for a second I thought he was going to plead the fifth. But then he took off his glasses for another round of his nervous-cleaning gesture.

'No, I didn't know him at all. I don't think my mother really knew him, to be honest. He was basically a human sperm donor.'

Julian's voice wasn't bitter exactly, but there was an edge to his normally warm tone.

'I'm sorry, I shouldn't have asked.'

'No, it's fine. We halflings all have our stories—'

Julian's words were cut short by a shout from Ryu.

'Back!' my lover roared, just as holy hell broke loose.

A burning figure was launched from the second floor of Tally's apartment house. It hit the floor with a disgusting squelching sound as, a second later, her apartment blew heavens to Betsy.

Julian's slim body covered mine, shielding us with his power. We were two houses down from the blast, and yet, when he dropped his barriers, we could still feel the heat on our faces.

'Holy shit,' I breathed. Julian's face was as white as mine in the orange glow.

'Stay here,' he murmured, darting toward the blaze. The others were kicking down the front door of the building, with Daoud frantically pulling fire extinguishers out of his jeans and passing them around. Tally's building had at least five other apartments in it, and it was dinnertime on a Monday night. People would be home.

I started forward but fell back as I heard the wail of sirens in the background. A second later, the first of Stefan's supernatural police arrived in an inconspicuous black sedan. Then the humans arrived: both fire crews and police. The supernatural and human emergency services blended together seamlessly, the one controlling the other like master puppeteers while the other was totally oblivious to any intervention. I retreated to sit on the hood of Ryu's car as I watched the orchestrated chaos unfold, surrounded by neighbors drawn out by the explosion.

'What happened?' said a voice to my left. The question was repeated, and I realized the voice was aimed at me.

'An explosion. Probably a gas leak,' I improvised, not bothering to turn around.

'A gas leak? Wow.'

I was trying to wrap my brain around Conleth. Even as I stared in horror at the paramedics surrounding the ifrit halfling's victim, I felt such terrible pity for him – a pity only exacerbated by everything we'd read in the files yesterday. There was one file of crayon drawings in which he'd drawn pictures of a small stick figure – shaded with orange scribbles – holding hands with two larger stick figures dressed in white uniforms. A terrible parody of the 'My Family' portraits I'd drawn in kindergarten.

The man next to me continued to speak, though I was very obviously not listening.

'. . . old buildings often have things wrong with them,' he was yammering.

I hunkered lower in my jacket, as if cold, but really because I wanted to play turtle and take refuge in my shell. There'd been letters to Santa covered in a scientist's notes on the psychological implications of Conleth's asking for a basketball and a Transformers figure.

'But that's quite an explosion for a gas leak.'

I sighed and finally looked at the man talking to me. He was tall and slender and, except for his height, entirely unprepossessing. His hair glowed very red in the light of the fire.

'Well, gas is highly flammable,' I answered, curtly.

He grinned at me as if I'd made the funniest joke he'd ever heard.

'Would you like to go get an ice cream?' he asked, causing me to start.

'Excuse me?' It was February. I was a stranger. There was a body on the sidewalk.

'Would you like to get an ice cream?' he repeated, as if we were the best of friends.

I stared at him, feeling my temper rise. What was wrong with this guy?

'There's a place around the corner in Brookline that has great ice cream. I love ice cream.'

'Thanks, but no thanks. I'm here with my boyfriend, there's a woman burned to a crisp over there, and it's way too late for ice cream, anyway.'

'C'mon, Jane. You'll love this place. They make this great mint chocolate chip, your favorite . . .'

I recoiled at the sound of my name. *What the fuck?* I thought, as I inched away from him.

He responded by grabbing my arm. His grip was tight and hot, even through the leather of my jacket.

'Come with me, Jane,' he repeated as I wrenched my arm away.

My fears were confirmed when I felt something burning. Looking down at my sleeve, I saw the charred imprint of a hand. My jacket, where the man had touched it, was smoldering.

'Ryu!' I shrieked, depending on my lover's preternatural hearing to save me.

Standing in front of me, the man's face shifted from one of easygoing neutrality to confusion and then to venomous anger.

'Why'd you call *him*?' he asked. 'He's just getting in the way.'

I scrabbled farther back on the car hood, enforcing my shields as I attempted to put more distance between me and the no-longer-mysterious stranger.

'Jane? What's going on?' Ryu asked behind me, his voice calm but edged with danger.

'Ryu, meet Conleth,' I squeaked. 'Conleth, Ryu.'

I felt my lover's hand on the waistband of my jeans as he tugged me backward off the car and to his side and then pushed me behind him.

'Conleth,' Ryu said, grimly. 'I'm glad you're here. That we get a chance to talk. We know what's been done to you—'

Before Ryu could embark fully on his 'why don't you come with us?' speech, the amiable, skinny everyman who'd asked me to go for ice cream was gone. In his place was a being sheathed in flames, his fiery hair whipping about in the maelstrom of power emanating from his wraithlike figure.

The human neighbors surrounding us all backpedalled furiously, only to be herded away and immediately glamoured by a handful of Stefan's deputies. Another few deputies threw up a thickly woven visual shield around us, deflecting any more attention from unwitting human eyes. Despite my influx of emotions at being confronted like this by Conleth, there was still part of me that couldn't help but marvel at the supes' efficiency in dealing with unwanted witnesses.

Conleth, however, didn't seem to be all that impressed.

'Don't give me that crap,' he was shouting at Ryu. 'I trusted everyone, and everyone lied.'

'I understand that,' Ryu said, his voice exuding reason and calm. 'I understand why you wouldn't trust us. But we can help you.'

'I help myself,' Conleth snarled. 'That's what none of you get. You have your little society, your little world, all set up. But you're weak and I know it. You're old, and you're weak, and you're done. Your time is done.'

Conleth was practically spitting with rage, his face deformed into a horrible grimacing mask. Ryu's power swirled around us as he fortified his barriers. I touched my lover's fingers, splayed on my hip, adding my strength to his shields.

'Jane and I are the future. We're not weak like you.' Conleth turned his head to smile at me, and suddenly his expression was beatific. 'She's beautiful, inside and out, and she's powerful. Just like me. *We* are the pure ones. Not you. Us. Our humanity makes us pure.'

Great, I thought, as soon as the word 'pure' entered Conleth's speech. *It's the halfling version of Jarl. What is it with lunatics and purity?*

Personally, I liked things nice and corrupt.

Ryu was nodding along to everything Conleth said, as if he were really, really interested. Which I knew was standard negotiator procedure, as I'd also seen that movie. Unfortunately, Conleth must have seen it as well.

'Stop nodding, you idiot,' he shrieked at Ryu. 'You don't

believe me. You don't agree with me. You're just like all the others. You're a liar and you're complacent and slow and weak. And you're being replaced. Don't think I don't know what's going on. I know about them, even if they won't come to me. But soon I will lead them, and do away with all of you!' Conleth turned to me again. 'Will you join me, Jane?'

I knew better than to inform him I liked talk of me being at his side even less than I did delusional murmurings about 'them'. Did he mean Phaedra and her lot replacing Ryu in the investigation? Why would he think he could lead *that* bunch? Anyone associated with Jarl would hate halflings, even if they hadn't taken executing Conleth as their most recent assignment.

Ryu kept trying to shove me farther behind him, but I didn't let him. He would need my extra swirl of power if he wanted to go on the offensive, and Con was up to something. He was shifting around as if he were trying to position himself for an attack.

'Stop touching her,' Conleth demanded, staring at where Ryu's hand was stretched behind me to grab my hip. 'She wants to come to me and you won't let her.'

Conleth said this with such adamancy that, for a second, I almost believed it myself.

'Conleth, this isn't about Jane,' Ryu said, reasonably. 'We'd all like a chance to talk to you, hear your story, but if you want that to happen, you're going to have to come with us . . .'

Ryu had stretched a hand out to Conleth, opening his frame and exuding warmth and understanding. He was staring the ifrit halfling in the eyes with such noble intensity that I would have bet money Conleth was a goner and would be ours in minutes.

I would have, if I hadn't seen the flash of the knife come

out of Conleth's sleeve, at his wrist, and into his hand. It was rather ineptly done, if truth be told. The point to this story *is*, after all, that I'm a jackass.

When I was a little girl, about four, we had a really old grandfather clock. It was very unstable, but we kept it propped up against a back wall. It had been in my father's family for ages, so there was no way we were getting rid of it. I was playing on the hall floor one day, in front of it, when it started to topple over. My dad – my human parent – was at the other end of the hall going through all the old boots in our front closet, deciding which to keep and which to donate.

My mother, and then Nick and Nan – our neighbors who learned the story from my mom – would say that he was bent over a stack of shoes one minute and the next he was there, holding me away from the clock as it smashed to pieces right where I'd been sitting. My dad was big at that time, all muscle and limbs and not exactly known for his speed and grace. But he'd moved like a panther, my mom had said, to get to me.

I couldn't really remember the event, except for all the noise when the clock broke and being in my dad's arms. I couldn't remember where he'd come from or how he got to me so quickly. To be honest, I don't think I'd ever entirely believed that story to be true.

Until I, Jane True of the anti-athleticism, moved like a striking adder. One minute I was slightly behind Ryu's hip, Conleth about six paces in front of us, and the next I was hurtling myself in front of my lover.

Who was, by that point, standing about five feet away. No fool, Ryu had also known Conleth would try something, and he was a fuck of a lot quicker than I. Too bad I hadn't figured that out before I decided to save his damned life.

Ryu's shocked eyes met mine in what was a regrettably

brief out-of-body experience. I looked from Ryu's face to Con's, seeing his expression shift from rage to a confusion that mirrored Ryu's and finally to horror. Because at that point the blade had already sunk deep.

Into my hand. I stood there, gaping at the steel sunk straight through my palm, Conleth still holding the hilt as if he were about to serve up some sort of bizarre cannibalistic kebab.

I didn't stay out of body for long.

'Mother*fucker*,' I breathed, staring up into Conleth's wide eyes as he let go of the knife. 'You *stabbed* me.'

And that's when the pain hit. I'd never felt anything like it before – it was like getting hit, so there was an impact kind of pain that was sort of bone-deep and involved lots of achey bruised tissues. And probably the breaking of some delicate little hand bones. On top of that, obviously, there was the slicing – which was searing and hot and agonizing. I knew, finally, why people writhed when they were wounded. It's because pain was like a thousand millipedes with burning feet running up and down your nervous system. My legs gave way and I sat down.

Ryu was there, of course, his face white as a sheet. Caleb was also there in a flash, and they were both staring at my hand as if strategizing how best to proceed. Conleth buggered off in a fiery blaze, doing his little rocket-ship trick and flying away. Various people gave chase in the direction of his comet's tail, while the glamour police got to work on the surrounding humans. I would wonder later about what they told the bewildered populace of Allston. Comet sightings? Falling stars? Bad acid?

At the time, however, I didn't give it much thought. I was too busy, what with the knife through my palm.

'Get it *out*,' I whined through gritted teeth, extending my hand to the satyr. Caleb nodded, as Ryu knelt behind me. His arms went across my chest and I thought he was hugging me. I realized he was keeping me immobile only when Caleb moved forward and, with one swift movement, pulled the knife from my hand. I shrieked incoherent, made-up swear words as the pain stopped messing around, bent me over, and made me its bitch.

Ironically, I still didn't fucking faint. I fainted all the damned time, except when I really wanted to. How shitty is that?

The second the knife was out, Caleb started healing. I ground my jaw together, wondering whether it was possible to pulverize your own molars. There must have been a lot of damage done to my hand for Caleb's ministrations to hurt like that. But looking at the knife lying on the ground in front of me, it made sense. It was huge, as in Crocodile Dundee 'Now that's a knoife' *huge*.

'Motherfucker stabbed me,' I repeated, as Ryu kissed my cheek and then used a finger to turn my face toward his.

'What were you doing, baby?' he asked, gently.

'Saving your life,' I informed him, my voice an interesting admixture of humiliation and sarcasm.

He chuckled. 'Oh, Jane. What were you thinking?'

'That I was Robo-Jane?' I responded, wincing as Caleb's healing magics wrenched a few more tiny bones together.

Ryu kissed me gently, his lips staying against mine as he murmured what I'd known was coming.

'You took a knife for me, baby. Thank you.'

I blanched, pulling my face away to watch Caleb play doctor. I knew Ryu was interpreting my actions as some ultimate declaration of my affection, something I wasn't entirely comfortable with.

You did just take a fucking 'knoife' for him, my brain chipped in drily.

And now Ryu totally owes you, my libido added, making lewd suggestions about how he could pay me back.

I ignored both my brain and my libido and instead concentrated on not snatching my hand back from the satyr and running back to Rockabill where everything was simple.

Ryu's hand stroked my hair. He was clearly waiting for a response.

'Yeah, well, stabbing *hurts*, Ryu. A lot. I never want to do that again.' It wasn't subtle, but it made him clam up. He chuckled, and I glanced up at him from the corner of my eye. He was still very white. Normally my vampire had a nice healthy glow about him. I think he used sun beds, but I didn't have the heart to ask. The men I'd grown up with didn't go tanning.

'Pity that,' Ryu murmured, as Caleb took one last look at my hand. The big goat-man eyed my palm professionally, until he declared me healed.

I thanked him, withdrawing my hand. Before I could inspect it properly, however, Ryu had already snatched it into his own.

With long strokes of his tongue, he cleaned the blood away, causing my breath to catch in my throat. Caleb coughed and walked away as my vampire sucked each of my fingers into his mouth, swirling his tongue along the length of each. Then Ryu carefully licked the creases between my fingers, until my hand was entirely free of blood. That's when he drew me to him for a kiss.

And I surreptitiously wiped my wet hand on the seat of my jeans.

Trailing kisses from my mouth to my ear, Ryu's voice came low as his breath sent shivers down my spine. I was seriously incorrigible; I'd just been stabbed and there I was all horny. I should be drinking soup. Not vampire.

'Pity that,' he repeated. 'Since I was planning on taking you home and then bathing you.'

I gasped again as Ryu swept me up in his arms.

'First in my shower and then with my tongue.'

I cooed, cuddling closer to his chest as he carried me off to his car.

'And then . . . *I'll* give you a stabbing. Only the good kind.'

He does owe us, my libido primly reminded me.

And I gotta admit, my still-aching hand heartily agreed that some sort of payback was *definitely* in order.

CHAPTER THIRTEEN

While staring at Ryu's ceiling, I flexed my hand, trying to work the stiffness out of my fingers and wrap my head around the fact that I'd been stabbed last night. And not Ryu's euphemistic stabbing, but stabbed. For real. With a knife.

In fact, there had been no euphemistic stabbing. Halfway to Ryu's, I'd gone a bit shocky and blue. Two big healings in as many weeks had sapped me physically. While Caleb's magic orchestrated everything, it was my own body's energies and tissues being eaten up.

Plus, I had seen a knife sticking through my hand, never a pleasant experience. So when he got me home, Ryu sat me in his wet room, under hot water, till I'd stopped with the shivering and the blue-face routine. Then he'd made me drink lots of fluids, and he put me to bed with a large dose of valium. I'd slept like a baby.

I was out for about fourteen hours, and when I woke up – for the first time – Ryu was doing his death sleep next to me. Except for the fangs and the little sips of blood, there was nothing 'vampirish' about my vampire. Human stories had gotten most things wrong. But while he wasn't a dead man, he did sleep so hard that I could understand why the legends claimed his kind must be corpses.

So I got up, ate every last thing I could find in Ryu's apartment, and drank an entire liter of orange juice, while avoiding thinking about how I'd been stabbed. Then I crawled back in bed to sleep some more. I was really going to need a swim soon, but nap first.

When I woke up the second time, it was evening and the bed was mine alone. I heard Ryu talking to someone, and after a moment I realized it must have been the Peapod guy delivering the groceries we'd ordered yesterday. I could eat only so much restaurant and takeout food, no matter how good it was. Knowing I should join the land of the living, I eventually got up, went to the bathroom to brush my teeth and wash my face, and tried to muster the will to shower. I finally just gave up and went back again to lie in Ryu's massive bed, stare at the ceiling, and finally address the fact that I'd been stabbed.

After he put away the groceries, Ryu joined me. He pulled off his T-shirt and his black lounging pants before sliding between the sheets. I held out my arms and he pulled me close.

'How are you feeling?' he asked.

'Fine,' I said after a few seconds.

'You're sure? You sound not so fine.'

'I am fine, really. It's just weird to think about.'

'Yeah,' he murmured, kissing my cheek. 'It is.'

'Thanks for not making fun of me.' If I'd been in his shoes, I totally would have taken a moment to point and laugh by now.

'Baby, you tried to save my life. Yeah, you got yourself stabbed for no reason, but do you realize how it feels to know you did that for me?'

I blinked in the darkness. It had all happened so fast; I can't even remember what I was thinking when I did it. Was I thinking I loved Ryu and had to rescue him? Or was it just reflex? Would my father have moved that fast for any child, or just for his daughter?

Shut up, you, the libido butted in, silencing my thoughts. *He still owes us nookie*.

As usual, my libido won and my only answer to Ryu's unspoken questions was my mouth on his.

We made love slowly and gently. I didn't want him to know my hand was still aching. Anything athletic was out of the question, but it was not what either of us wanted, anyway.

Then we showered and he left to go investigate another of the two leads, besides poor Tally Bender, that we'd gotten from Silver. The old doctor had known where we could find Pat Hampton, who'd been the medical coordinator brought in by the new sponsor for all of Conleth's 'testing'. Hampton had led a double life: married with kids in one and gay as a bird in the other. Which had saved his life, although his family hadn't been so lucky. While he was holed up in hiding with his secret lover, his wife and young sons were burned in their beds by Conleth. But Silver had told us where to go, and Ryu had coordinated a team to retrieve Hampton while I'd slept the previous evening.

Ryu kissed me good-bye, promised to be back in a few hours, made *me* promise not to open the door to anybody but him or his deputies, and left me to my own devices. I was still exhausted, and getting stabbed had put the kibosh on my investigative gusto.

The first thing I did was call home. My dad was fine, but worried about me. He was also wondering why he could never remember the midget nurse's name. I told him I loved him and I'd be back soon, which was true, hopefully. Then I called the bookstore. They were about to close, and Tracy was being super cagey and had gotten off the phone pretty quickly. I could have sworn I heard Miss Carol yelling at someone in the background.

Oh gods. Is Miss Carol covering for me at work?

I prayed that I still had a job and that Tracy wasn't going to kill me, as I slipped on undies and one of Ryu's dress shirts. Then I went downstairs to prepare dinner, rooting happily through the refrigerator, then the cupboards, humming to myself as I surveyed my spoils. Before executing my culinary genius, I first poked at Ryu's iPod, set in his state-of-the-art sound dock thingie, until I found the Killers and put them on shuffle. I was officially obsessed with the Killers, not least because of the lead singer's slightly-spastic-yet-strangely-sexy dance moves. I did a little dancing of my own, until my tummy grumbled a hungry protest. I gave one last shimmy before I started pulling out ingredients. I was going to make puy lentils, Provençal style, with two beautiful filet mignon steaks, cooked very rare. Also on the menu was a green salad, heavy on the spinach, with this super-garlicky dressing I'd gotten from a Barefoot Contessa cookbook. It was a family favorite and went well with the spinach. Lots of iron was required when one was dating a vampire.

Favoring my sore hand, I slowly chopped onion, leeks, and carrot, and then did a fine dice on the celery. After unwrapping Ryu's Le Creuset pot, I gave it a quick wash and set it on the stove to melt a little butter with olive oil. When it was just starting to bubble, I added the vegetables and then turned down the heat to let them soften. I washed the fresh herbs I was using in my bouquet garni, tying them into a little bundle using a string of sliced leek. I then started finely dicing the garlic, a few cloves for the lentils and a few cloves for the dressing, which got an additional mashing. It was lucky the garlic thing was untrue about vampires, because no garlic would have been a deal breaker. If Ryu couldn't live with garlic, there's no way I could live with him.

When I finished chopping the garlic, I set the knife down to stir the veggies. I was just pulling the lentils and a package of chicken stock out of the cupboard when there was a loud knock at the door.

I froze, then stood like that for about thirty seconds before the knock was repeated.

I figured it had to be one of Ryu's deputies, or Stefan's people wouldn't have let whomever it was through to the door. But just in case Conleth had killed my guards and was standing outside bearing chocolates and death, I scraped the last of the garlic off Ryu's massive Santuko knife and took it with me.

I'll show that halfling a 'knoife', I thought as I stood on my tippy-toes to peer out of Ryu's peephole. All I could see was warped man chest. So I made like a granny and called out, 'Who is it?' in a tremulous voice.

'Jane?' came the growling response. I knew only one talking dog-man who growled like that.

'Anyan?' I asked, just to be sure.

'Jane.' He sounded pissed.

As I started in on the locks, my suspicions were confirmed. Before I'd even finished with the dead bolt, I heard his rough voice again.

'Shit, I should have known you'd be here.'

'Nice to see you, too,' I replied as the door finally swung open.

Anyan, in human form, responded by glowering at me, so I glowered right back. Or at least I tried to. But his iron-gray gaze was too intense, and I broke, focusing on his frown instead.

'Catch Conleth?' I asked, grasping at conversational straws.

'No,' he said. 'Fucker's quick. Are you going to let me in?'

I moved aside so he could squeeze past. As he did so, I finally broke down and ogled.

He was just as big as I remembered, maybe even larger with clothes. My eyes swept up his big black boots, up his worn jeans, and over a thick leather motorcycle jacket. There was a saddlebag thing over one broad shoulder, and he held a helmet in his hand. I smiled at the sight; I'd always wondered how he got around. He couldn't run everywhere, could he?

When my eyes finally met his again, he was still frowning. I also noticed that his longish hair was suffering a bad case of helmet head.

'I didn't know you'd be here,' he said, 'or I would have changed.'

I was about to tell him that he certainly didn't have to dress up for me, when I realized he didn't mean his clothes. Anyan meant his shape. I was about to ask him why he always came to me as a dog, when he saw the knife.

'Expecting someone?' he asked, nodding toward the gleaming Santuko.

'Oh, I'm feeling vengeful. Got stabbed yesterday.'

His eyes nearly bulged out of his head, and his frown deepened so much that, with his big nose twitching at me and his hair flattened, he looked like Sam the Eagle from the Muppets.

'What?'

'I got stabbed,' I repeated, as I remembered that I hadn't locked the door. So I turned around to do so, and when I turned back, I caught him staring at my legs. I went red as I realized I was only wearing Ryu's shirt.

'Lemme change,' I squeaked, running up the stairs to my right.

I dug out a pair of black stretch yoga pants and a tank top before I remembered I needed a bra. Then I still felt a little naked and was about to put Ryu's shirt back on when I changed my mind and dug out my own purple cardigan. I took a moment to compose myself and brush my hair and my teeth before I realized with a little aria of swearing that I'd left the vegetables on the burner.

I raced downstairs and into the kitchen, expecting to find a conflagration of burned onion. Instead, Anyan was stirring the vegetables with one hand as he stretched his long arm out toward the sink to rinse the lentils.

I stared at his back, unsure of what to do, as he used the colander to flick off the tap and then dumped the lentils into the pot. Then he stirred it all around a bit, just as I would have done, before adding the carton of chicken stock. Then he rummaged around in the cupboards till he found another, dumping that one in, too.

I took a seat across from him at the island to watch, my brow furrowing, as he raised the heat and stirred everything. He brought my bouquet garni up to his long nose and sniffed it before adding it to the pot. He ground a bunch of pepper into the mix, added some salt, and gave it one last stir before he turned to face me. He placed his palms on the cool granite of the island and leaned over to stare into my eyes.

He'd taken off his jacket, and I noticed that his black T-shirt sported an advertisement for Milk-Bones. If he hadn't been staring at me so sternly, I would have laughed at that.

'What in the hell are you doing here? And what do you mean, you got stabbed?'

I eyed him warily. 'You usurped my lentils.'

'The stabbing, Jane,' he replied, not batting an eyelash.

'Did you add the garlic?'

'Yes. Tell me how you got hurt.'

'I usually cut the stock with water.'

'I don't. Now what happened to you?'

'That's kind of a waste of stock.' I noticed that the very tip of his nose was starting to twitch.

'I swear to the gods that if you change the subject one more time, I'm going to put *you* in the lentils.'

'The pot's about to boil over.'

Anyan swore and wheeled about to lower the heat and stir the broth into submission. He also took a moment to visibly gather himself before turning to face me. I took the opportunity to compose myself as well. It's not just that I was trying to be difficult; it was also that I didn't know how to act around Anyan the man. The dog Anyan was no problem, but the man was a whole different kettle of fish. Kettle of man. Kettle of supernatural shapeshifting man-dog. Whatever.

And he *had* usurped my lentils.

Anyan picked up the wooden spoon again to dredge up a bit of broth. He turned around, blowing on it to cool it, before holding it out for me to taste.

'Check the seasoning for yourself,' he demanded, so I did. 'Is it fine?' I nodded. 'Good, now forget the lentils and tell me what happened to you.'

I glared at him, but did as he asked in as few words as possible. As I told him, I unconsciously rubbed at the aching spot on my palm where the knife had gone in.

When I was finished, he stood there, staring at me. Then he walked around to where I was sitting. His large hand gripped mine, and he held it gently, probing at it with magic.

I shivered at the touch of his power and pulled my hand from his.

'Anyan, it's fine—' I began to protest, but he silenced me with a thumb over my lips. The barghest cradled my jaw with his hand, forcing me to meet his gray eyes with my black.

I could smell cardamom and leather and man. And maybe the faintest whiff of clean doggy.

'Shush, you. You're still hurting. Let me see it.'

I *was* still hurting, damn him. So I pushed my curled fist back into his palm.

He gently spread my fingers open with both hands, stroking his thumbs over my palm. I didn't know which was hotter: Anyan's own skin or the healing magics he sent through me. I felt like a child, dwarfed by his imposing frame as he loomed over me, his attention turned inward as he fixed whatever was still wrong with me.

'You took a knife to save Ryu?' he asked, making me start. His voice had gone quiet, if still rough. His fingers tracing over my skin were ridiculously gentle.

'Yeah,' I said, blushing. 'And it was a *Crocodile Dundee* "knoife",' I clarified. Then I hung my head. 'But Ryu had already jumped clear. So I saved a patch of empty air.'

'It's not what you did, Jane. It's what you intended.'

I frowned. *But I don't know what I intended*, I suddenly wanted to tell Anyan, even though I couldn't for the life of me figure out why it was so important he know that.

I was distracted, however, as another warm surge of power went into my hand and I felt – and heard – something pop. The ache was gone finally, and I suddenly really wanted to stretch my fingers.

'You were very brave,' Anyan told me, his rough voice dark.

I blushed, stretching my hand out underneath his calloused palm.

'Never do something like that again,' he concluded, as he ran his rough thumb one last time over my palm before he turned back to the stove to stir the lentils.

Suddenly too warm, I took my cardigan off as I watched

him fiddle with the fire until he got the lentils to simmer just so. My eyes widened as, suddenly, everything fell into place. I was such a moron.

'The cabin,' I breathed. 'It's yours, isn't it? Not Nell's.'

He snorted, still facing the stove.

'You thought it was Nell's?'

I glared at his broad back. 'Dude, you were a dog when I met you and I thought that's *all* you were. Dogs don't usually own property.'

'Okay, but how did you think Nell reached anything? Levitation?' he asked, as he finally turned back around to face me.

'Stepladders,' I replied automatically.

'Stepladders?'

'Yes, stepladders. Like I have.'

Anyan's big face opened up in a huge smile, and I couldn't help but smile back; it was that infectious. It transformed him.

'Poor little Jane. Your life must be one giant stepladder. When we get back to Rockabill, I'll make you stilts.'

I laughed, looking down at his hands. I'd felt how rough the skin was on them, even if his touch had been gentle. They were scarred and tough and calloused. A working man's hands.

Or an artist who, among other things, sculpted metal.

'Did you make all the stuff in there?' I asked. 'The art?'

He nodded, looking a little embarrassed. 'Yeah, most of it. It's what I do. I'm not really good at the human money stuff, like the others, so I do what I've always done. I stick to art. Luckily, I have a few lifetimes' worth of international reputation, so the money's decent.'

'It's beautiful. I love the one in the bathroom,' I admitted before I had time to reflect that that probably sounded a little weird.

He laughed, a big, rich sound that filled the kitchen.

'I knew you would. That you'd get why it was in there.'

I thought about it. 'It's one of the stories you told me when I was in the hospital, isn't it?'

He nodded again. I leaned forward on my stool. 'And those stories about the fighting dog who saved his people, those were really your stories, weren't they?'

I think he actually blushed. 'I didn't know any other stories,' he admitted.

'They were good stories,' I told him gently. 'I appreciated them very much.'

His big hands clenched into fists and he turned back to the stove to stir the lentils.

'So you saved your people, and you made an iron cartoon about it, and then you hung it in your bathroom.'

He shrugged, silently, in assent.

'How very postmodern of you.' I grinned.

He chuckled and then went to open the refrigerator door.

'I'm assuming the mashed garlic was for something different?'

'Yup. Salad. The stuff's in the crisper. I'll help.'

I sliced tomatoes and olives while Anyan grated a carrot and washed lettuce. We worked in companionable silence, only talking when I made the dressing and he wanted to see what went in it. I pointed at where the steaks sat, still wrapped, warming up to room temperature while waiting to be cooked.

'Sorry, we only have two steaks. But you can share mine.'

Anyan smiled at me. 'No worries, Jane. I usually don't eat meat unless I catch it myself.'

I frowned at him. 'Why?'

'Because,' he said, poking at the steak with one finger as it sat – packaged in cellophane – on its little Styrofoam plate. 'This is just not sporting.'

I snorted. 'You're a strange man, Anyan. Or dog. Dog-man?'

'Barghest,' he clarified, giving the filet mignon one last contemptuous poke.

'Barghest,' I repeated, as he smiled into my eyes and I was suddenly glad I'd taken my cardigan off. What with all the cooking, it had gotten really warm in the kitchen.

'So what do you eat?' I asked.

'Well, I hunt. There's great hunting around our area. And there are a few people I'll buy meat from around Rockabill. But otherwise, I'll just not eat meat. With two exceptions I can't resist.'

'What are the exceptions?'

'Haggis and White Castle.'

'What is haggis?'

'It's the Scottish national dish. The pluck of a sheep – meaning the heart, liver, and lungs – all diced up with oatmeal and spices and then baked in the sheep's stomach.'

I thought about that. I had but one question.

'How the hell can you eat White Castle?'

He chuckled. 'Sliders are little pellets of greasy love, Jane. Don't knock 'em.'

I shuddered just as the door to the apartment swung open.

'Honey,' Ryu called. 'I'm home!'

Anyan and I turned toward the door. Ryu stood, arms outstretched, holding the largest bouquet of flowers I'd ever seen. He was staring at Anyan. The vampire didn't look at all happy.

I put on my cardigan.

CHAPTER FOURTEEN

Dinner was very, very awkward, although the lentils were delicious. When we'd finished eating and had cleared away the plates, we returned to Ryu's dining table to get down to business.

'What exactly are you doing here, Anyan?'

'I was sent. After everything that happened with Jimmu, I decided I'd been out of the game too long. So for the past few months I've been working for the Alfar, sniffing out leads, keeping an eye on the powers that be,' Anyan said, not looking at me. I knew how much he'd valued his secret life in Rockabill, and I regretted that he'd lost his hard-won independence. 'Something's cropped up at the Compound, and I was sent to assist you. And by Morrigan herself.'

Ryu and I exchanged glances. 'You're not the only one who's been sent as "assistance",' Ryu replied.

'An Alfar named Phaedra is here,' I interrupted. 'Sent by Jarl.'

Anyan's eyes met mine, and he nodded. He knew I was touching on our little secret. Ryu didn't entirely understand the implications of Jarl's involvement, as he didn't know about Jarl's attack on me at the Compound. Ryu knew that Jarl was bad news, but not quite *how* bad. He didn't know Jarl definitely blamed me for the loss of his foster son, or that he'd tried to kill me, and that, due to his failure, there were two witnesses to his attack. I had the feeling Anyan and I were going to have to tell Ryu the truth very soon, and I wasn't looking forward to that conversation. Those two had enough alpha-male issues as it was, without Ryu thinking I was keeping secrets. Secrets I shared with the other top dog, no less.

'I know. That's partially why I'm here. But who did Phaedra bring?' Anyan asked Ryu.

'Kaya and Kaori. Fugwat. And Graeme.'

Anyan's frown transformed him back to Sam the Eagle. 'Graeme?'

Ryu only nodded as Anyan stared at him.

'I know,' my lover said quietly. 'I'll keep her away from him.'

I shivered, knowing that they were talking about Graeme's unhealthy interest in my breakability. Uncomfortable, I muscled through the moment with my usual delicacy.

'And it gets worse. There's the possibility of more murders, in the Borderlands, that may or may not have been done by Conleth,' I informed Anyan.

'Of course they were done by Conleth,' Ryu said, rolling his eyes. I shrugged. I wasn't going to argue with Ryu about this issue but, like Silver, I wasn't convinced it was Con who committed the other crimes. He'd been so clumsy with that knife, for one thing. And I could have sworn he was genuinely horrified when he saw it sticking through my hand. He was somebody who blasted at people, who roasted them from afar or who set their house on fire while they slept. Conleth didn't walk up to people and carve them up, or at least he hadn't until last night.

And there'd been no pleasure in his eyes when his knife had sunk deep.

'Actually,' Anyan said, shifting his long legs, 'those "other" murders are the reason I'm here.' The big man stretched, sitting a bit sideways in his chair so he could extend his legs. 'One of Nyx's pals is a baobhan sith, a famous surgeon in both the human and supernatural worlds. His lover was a human, another doctor, from Chicago, who spent half her time in Boston. Name was Brenda Donovan.'

Ryu and I blinked in surprise. 'That's Silver's contact with the corporation that funded his lab,' I told Anyan, and then I explained to him who Silver was.

'Well, Silver's not the only one she told about her concerns. Right before Donovan died, she called her boyfriend, told him she was sending him a package. There was a list of names and an audiotape with her story. Said she was afraid someone was after her. If she disappeared, he should go to the police with the list. She thought he was human, obviously. When she vanished, he knew she was dead. He sat on the information for a week or two, but when he finally laid hands on the autopsy, he discovered she was killed so viciously that he went to Nyx. Nyx eventually went to Morrigan. Morrigan made the connection to Conleth and came to me.'

We chewed on that information for a bit.

'But didn't she know that Jarl had already sent someone to investigate Conleth?' I asked.

'Of course she did,' Anyan replied. 'I was there when he volunteered his team. He made a big deal about how he knew a half-human would rise one day to become a problem, and he'd prepared Phaedra to take them out.'

'But Morrigan sent her own people in, too. She didn't trust him? Am I sensing a rift?'

Anyan nodded and Ryu smiled grimly at me. 'Orin may be in Jarl's pocket, but Morrigan is in Nyx's. Nyx and Jarl believe it or not, hate each other.'

'Really?' I asked, genuinely surprised. Nyx was one of the more obnoxious creatures I'd had the displeasure of meeting and I would have pegged her and Jarl as made for each other.

Ryu shrugged. 'I know, it's weird. But they've always loathed one another. I think that Nyx recognizes that Jarl will only ever see her as a lesser being, since she's not Alfar. And now Nyx has the ear of the queen.'

'So Morrigan doesn't trust Jarl?' I asked. This was the second time, including the investigation four months ago when I met Ryu, that Morrigan had sent out her own people to investigate.

'Who knows what Morrigan thinks or doesn't think. She's Alfar,' Anyan growled. Ryu arched an eyebrow and smiled at that, making me smile. I liked it when we all got along.

'So what exactly do the Alfar know about this investigation?' Ryu asked.

It was Anyan's turn to shrug. 'I've no idea,' he said. 'They know what you've reported about the murders here in Boston, and what the deceased doctor said about the deaths of others in Chicago.'

'And what do you know about those murders?' Ryu asked.

'Very little. Donovan didn't have any concrete information, and she wrote down only a few names. She just knew that some of her colleagues had died and others were missing. I found obituaries for all of the people on her list, so she wasn't crazy. But that was as far as I'd gotten before Conleth attacked us in Rockabill. I was home to check on Jane and then I was going to start investigating Donovan's claims.'

Ryu and Anyan stared at each other for a bit until Ryu got up to get the files Silver had given us. He passed Anyan the file with the 'other' murders.

'Where'd you get these?' Anyan grunted as he flipped through the contents.

'Silver had them. I don't know how he compiled everything, but he's obviously got a lot of connections. And he's a smart old buzzard.'

'This one – that's Brenda Donovan,' Anyan said, pointing at one of the photos. 'The baobhan sith's lover.' He continued flipping until he got to the autopsy. He studied it carefully.

'Do you have the autopsies from the Boston murders?' Anyan asked.

Ryu nodded and then dug them out for the barghest. Anyan flipped through them quickly. There wasn't a lot on them to read, after all. Everyone had been burned up from afar. End of story.

'So we have two groups of murders. We know Conleth is doing one, but the jury's out on the other. I don't understand why he'd alternate between MOs like this. Plus, I chased him. He's fast, and that rocket trick he does is good for a quick getaway. Not least because we have to spend hours glamouring any human witnesses. But he can't sustain it for very long, and it weakens the hell out of him. I don't know if he could get to Chicago and back this quickly. Some of these murders in Chicago overlap with murders in Boston by just a few days.' While he talked, Anyan had made an impromptu time line with some of the police reports. We three, sporting similar looks of frustration, sat staring at the papers in Anyan's hands.

Finally, the barghest broke the silence. 'Have you uncovered any recent leads on your murders?'

Ryu sighed. 'We had a lead but Conleth beat us to it.'

I blanched. 'Is Hampton dead?'

Ryu nodded. 'He was still smoldering when we got there.'

'How the hell did Conleth find him?'

Ryu shrugged. 'Silver's missing,' he added. 'As are the people we had watching his house.'

I looked down at my hands, shocked. Everyone so far who Conleth had killed had been just pieces of paper or photos for me. I'd had a drink with Silver. He'd seemed like a nice man. Well, except for the bit where he kept children prisoner for the government.

'And where the murders in Chicago are concerned, we're fucked as far as getting info on them. Julian's working on finding recent fire-related deaths in their police records, but . . . There's only so much info we can get from the Borderlands.'

Anyan gave Ryu a long look, as if weighing his options. Finally, he spoke.

'You get me some names and I'll see what I can do.'

His eyes narrowing as his lips pursed, Ryu stared at the barghest. 'Are you telling me you have contacts *inside* the Borderlands?'

Anyan merely shrugged.

'Do our king and queen know of this?' Ryu demanded angrily. 'If you know things we don't—'

'Cool your britches, baobhan sith,' the barghest replied. 'I haven't kept anything that needs to be known from anyone. My life is my own,' he growled, clearly ending Ryu's line of inquiry.

Amen to having our own lives, I thought, thinking about how I kept getting uprooted. Ryu, however, was far less pleased with Anyan's response than I was, and he glowered at the barghest from the other side of the table.

Always eager to ease tension, I asked Anyan about chasing Conleth. For my efforts, I got a strangely sad smile and then everything that happened after Conleth attacked us in Rockabill. There'd been lots of chasing, a few fights, and finally Anyan had tracked the ifrit halfling down to a squat here in the Boston area. Con had fled, not to return. But at least we now knew where he'd been living.

After Anyan finished, he and Ryu built up how they thought Con had ended up in Maine in the first place.

They figured he'd attacked us in the garden, assuming I was just another human 'dinner companion' of Ryu's. Might I add that I managed to keep my face beautifully reposed at this hypothesis. Anyway, when I helped Ryu with his shields and Con saw I was a supe, he'd become interested and hacked Ryu's computer. Apparently, Ryu had downloaded a junk mail game called Elf Bowling, which had contained a malware virus thingy that had eaten into his computer and left a bunch of hardware that spied. Or spyware. Or something. Ryu's explanation, probably originally explained by Julian, was garbled, but I tuned out the minute he started with the jargon, anyway. In my defense, when I'd looked over at Anyan, he was staring out the window like a math major in freshman composition.

A few days after Con had discovered where I lived, he'd set off for Rockabill.

'He must really want to get to me,' Ryu said ruefully, 'to attack you like that. I'm sorry, baby.' He raised my hands to his lips to kiss my palm, but was interrupted by a contemptuous grunt from the barghest.

'Oh, he's not interested in you, baobhan sith.'

Ryu frowned. 'What do you mean by that?'

'You never asked what I found in the squat.'

My lover's eyes narrowed. 'Don't be cryptic. What did you find?'

The barghest stood up. 'You'll have to see it to believe it. We might as well get this out of the way.' Anyan turned to me, his face gentling. 'Jane, this is going to freak you right the hell out. But I'd rather you see it yourself, see how serious it is. And you'll be safe. I'll be there, and Ryu's team's already there. I called Caleb earlier.' Ryu frowned, clearly ticked off at Anyan's intervention with his own men, but the barghest paid no mind.

'Ready?' he asked, standing up.

'No,' I answered, very honestly. 'But let's get this over with.'

For, while I wasn't sure what 'this' was exactly, I knew it couldn't be good.

The squat was in Southie, in an abandoned tenement. Anyan was behind us, on a beautifully refurbished Indian motorcycle that I really wanted to get a closer look at.

I was peering back at the barghest in my side mirror when Ryu suddenly lurched the car forward, then backward, and then I swear he made it go directly sideways into a parking spot that would have given a kindergartner on a tricycle trouble. I considered barfing on him to clarify my opinion of his driving. But just then my door was opened, and I was confronted by an enormous penis.

Eventually, the penis moved aside and a large hand descended to help me out of the car.

Caleb, I thought.

'Pants,' I muttered.

'Hmmm?' the being connected to the schlong asked politely.

'Nothing,' I replied, telling myself that if he was comfortable with the Platonic ideal of going commando, then it was his genitalia and I could get over my human prudishness. So I took the goat-man's hand and let him help me out of the car.

He smiled at me benevolently and I decided I liked him. Until I slipped on a patch of ice, reached out to steady myself, and put my hand directly on his crotch. Horrified at making contact with bare flesh, I let go before I could steady myself . . . and promptly fell forward, planting my face directly into the concrete sidewalk.

'Jane!' Ryu barked, as four strong sets of hands lifted me off the ground.

My nose was bleeding and I was seeing stars. They wound their way around the concerned faces of Ryu, Anyan, and Caleb, who reached out to grab my nose with a warm burst of healing magic. The fourth set of hands must have belonged to Daoud, who was grinning at me like a jack-o'-lantern and pressing a clean, white handkerchief to my chin to catch the blood streaming down my face. I didn't want to know where the handkerchief had come from.

'Are you all right? What happened?' I peered at Ryu over Caleb's fingers.

'Apron,' I mumbled, my mouth partially covered by the satyr's palm. 'Or a loincloth . . .'

Daoud was openly laughing now, but Ryu still looked confused. I realized he'd been on the other side of the car and hadn't seen what happened.

'What?'

Daoud clapped a hand on Ryu's back. 'She's fine, sir. She got distracted by the size of Caleb's . . . horns. That's all.'

Ryu gave me a funny look as I shot Daoud an eyeball so hairy it would make a chinchilla envious.

'All better,' Caleb interrupted.

I muttered an embarrassed, 'Thank you,' unable to meet his eyes.

'Well, then, let's get going, shall we?' Ryu suggested, putting a strong arm around my waist. 'On both feet this time, Jane?' he murmured in my ear, earning himself an elbow in the ribs.

We walked up to the main door, where Anyan waited. Then we all walked upstairs. The barghest led us to an apartment on the third floor and then put a hand on my shoulder.

'Remember, Jane,' Anyan said, 'we're all here. And that all of this is in Con's head. You haven't done anything.'

I nodded, my stomach falling. I really didn't want to go in there.

But I did; we did. Anyan first, then Daoud, then Ryu and I, his arm wrapped protectively around my waist. For once, I was glad of the possessiveness that often irked me. Caleb followed, and I was happy to have him at my back.

What greeted me wasn't as bad as I'd thought it would be. Partly, I was distracted by how sad Con's life was. I now understood why they called squats 'squats'. There was a filthy mattress in a corner, and a battered lawn chair, but that was it for furniture. Whatever clothes Con owned must have been with him, for there were only a few old T-shirts and a pair of discarded, very unclean-looking boxers. From the litter on the floor, it appeared that Con lived on cheap junk food, probably stolen.

That said, I should probably have been more freaked out. For decorating the walls were pictures of me. They'd been printed on a shitty printer, on regular paper, but they were clear enough. I saw, among them, the same photos from Ryu's digital picture frame, only none of the ones with him were present. Taped to the wall above the dirty mattress were the pictures I'd seen of me sleeping and me sticking my tongue out while sitting on the cathedral steps.

'It's not Ryu he wants. It's you,' Anyan said from the side of me unclaimed by a very perturbed vampire. 'You okay?'

I looked up at him. 'Yeah,' I said. 'It's not as bad as it could be. I thought things would be . . . stickier. Photos just hanging there I can handle.'

Anyan smiled at me and his hand raised as if to stroke my hair, but he stopped. Not least because Ryu had tugged me closer and away.

I pulled myself out of the clutches of Mr Jealous Pants and turned back toward Anyan.

'But I don't get it. Why me?'

The barghest reached into his leather jacket and pulled out a thick sheaf of battered, well-thumbed pages.

'I haven't read these. They were by the bed.'

I hesitated before taking them. 'Are they *sticky*?'

Anyan rumbled his growly laugh. 'No. Just . . . well-read.'

They were all my e-mails to Ryu, printed off and bundled together. Daoud wandered over, and although he was trying to act nonchalant, I could see he was trying to get a gander at what they said. I realized that everyone in the room, except for Ryu and me, probably figured they were sexy, that Ryu and I had been talking dirty over e-mail, and that explained Con's interest.

Ryu rolled his eyes at his deputy and set everyone to searching the apartment again, Daoud included. I settled down in a corner to flip through my e-mails. I knew what they contained, obviously, but I was hoping there was a way I could tell what it was about me that Conleth saw. What it was about me he liked, or felt an affinity toward. Because maybe we could exploit his weaknesses.

The e-mails were arranged chronologically, which was a bummer, as I'd hoped Con would have picked out his favorites and left them on top. Maybe labeled them. But nothing's ever that easy, is it?

That said, some did seem more well-read than others. Sadly, the most battered appeared to be the ones in which I talked about my home life and my dad's health. Those e-mails were testaments to my love for my family, and Con's interest in those particular e-mails suggested, at least to me, how shattered he was by his lack of such love.

I kept shuffling, trying to find more clues, occasionally looking up as one or another of Ryu's deputies found something they thought might be interesting and called out. I was so distracted by Daoud's – and of course it was Daoud – having found Con's porn stash that I almost missed the note card stuck in among the much larger sheets of my e-mails.

It was a handwritten note that read simply:

Felicia Wethersby
She Knew

The script was large, loopy, and old-fashioned. It certainly wasn't Con's cramped, all-caps print that I'd gotten so familiar with from his case files.

'Ryu! Anyan!' I called, snapping out of my reverie as I realized that, unlike Daoud's find of *Hometown Hotties*, I might really have found something.

I held out the note, which Anyan took as Ryu helped me to my feet. The two men shared it between them.

'It's not his handwriting,' Ryu said. I nodded my head in agreement.

'Definitely not his handwriting.'

'Who is Felicia Wethersby?' Anyan asked.

'No idea. Julian!' Ryu barked, and a second later, Julian's lean, bespectacled frame was peering at the note.

'On it, sir,' he said, as he walked to where his backpack, containing his laptop, sat on top of the grungy lawn chair.

'Who the hell wrote this note?' I asked.

'No idea,' replied Ryu. 'Add that to the list of things we need to figure out.' I shook my head, giving the note a baleful stare. How could something so helpful be so entirely confusing?

A few minutes later, Julian had our answer. 'I think I've got her. There's a Felicia Wethersby on LinkedIn. She lists herself as an administrative assistant. For a private practice, run by a Dr B. L. Donovan. And we have an address.'

Ryu gave me a joyous high five, then pulled me to him for a kiss.

'Told you I was useful,' I murmured in his ear, quite pleased with myself over my find.

'And I should never have doubted you,' he replied.

Damn straight, vampire, I thought as I turned to find Anyan frowning at us. I blushed and ducked my head, going over to where Julian was still scanning his computer screen.

But too bad you did.

CHAPTER FIFTEEN

Phaedra's gang was waiting for us on the street. I tucked the file folder with its secret note into my jacket so that the Alfar wouldn't see. I didn't want her reading my e-mails to Ryu, first of all, and I also didn't want her knowing about that note. It seemed like too much of a coincidence already that Jarl would be showing so much interest in a matter that didn't directly involve him. That we'd found some mystery note clueing Conleth in to a potential victim seemed even sketchier.

Standing in front of a giant Escalade, the little Alfar polished a knife as casually as if she were filing her nails. Her leather-clad body absorbed the street's light, and – for the first time – I noticed that her eyes were red. Not red as in bloodshot – but genuinely red. Her pupils were the color of drying blood.

Her little intimidation act ceased, however, when she caught sight of our newest compatriot. I'd never seen an Alfar furious until I saw how Phaedra stared at Anyan. Of course, as she was Alfar, it wasn't normal anger. It didn't rage and seethe. But standing there, even this far away, I felt like that little Dutch boy with his thumb in the dyke. The power thundering behind the walls of her otherwise-placid face screamed for total annihilation. Nothing less would suffice. And all that ire was centered on the barghest.

Anyan merely yawned, stretching his big limbs nonchalantly.

I couldn't see the harpies. I looked up, imagining them hovering above me, claws extended. At least the spriggan and the rapist incubus were accounted for. The former was standing in front of the Escalade, dwarfing the enormous vehicle with his knobbly gray bulk. As for the latter, Graeme was also staring at Anyan. But he wasn't radiating anything but shock and more than a little nervousness.

'Anyan Barghest. Tell me what you are doing here,' Phaedra commanded. Anyan ignored her, reaching into his leather jacket's inner pocket. The Alfar tensed, but the big man only pulled out a piece of gum. He unwrapped it slowly before popping it in his mouth. Phaedra hissed.

'What are *you* doing here, Phaedra?' Ryu interrupted, advancing a few paces as Daoud and Caleb moved in to flank me.

The Alfar pulled herself up with a visible effort. 'We're working together, no?' she asked, her childlike voice toeing that sandy line between rhetorical and insolent.

'I can handle this investigation, Alfar,' Ryu hissed. Phaedra sheathed her knife, striding forward to confront him. Once again, I was struck by how tiny she was. Unlike me, however, hers was a terrifying form of tiny: the tiny of poisonous spiders, plastic explosives, or the Olsen twins.

'Can you, baobhan sith? You've not even been able to elude *us*. We've been following your "investigation" despite your attempts to hide. And we have borne witness to your further failures. The body count mounting up on your watch is alarming, really.' Phaedra's eerily large eyes stared at Ryu, her bald pate gleaming in the soft light of the surrounding streetlamps.

I saw movement on top of the SUV, and with a start I realized that the two harpies were huddled together on top of Phaedra's Escalade. About their legs were folded their dun wings, from which their faces emerged like eerie white globes.

'All precautions taken have been routine,' Ryu replied to the Alfar's insinuations. 'I wasn't trying to avoid your lot.' Phaedra didn't look like she believed him, a suspicion I also, admittedly, held.

'Well,' the Alfar said, an unpleasant smile splitting her little face. 'We are all here now, so let us commence with this evening's plans. Where are you going, Investigator? Off to collect the body of another human you could not protect?'

Ryu's jaw clenched and I reached out a hand to rest it on the small of his back. We were here, with him, and we believed in him.

Phaedra chuckled, an unpleasant, sneering sound. 'Whatever it is, you will take Graeme and Fugwat with you. They will assist you tonight and report back to me on your progress.'

Ryu looked like he was about to protest, but Phaedra silenced him with a dazzling little display of fireworks. Sparks of power erupted from her hand, bathing her evil little face in a sickly blue glow.

'I outrank you, baobhan sith. Do not question my authority or I will charge you with insubordination and forcibly remove you from this case. And then it will be mine, by rights,' Phaedra purred, challenging all of us to protest. When we kept silent, she sighed.

'Graeme, Fugwat, you know what to do.'

Phaedra walked back to her Escalade, and we watched as she opened the door to scramble up into the high seat. She had to back up a few steps and then hop in with the aid of the armrest. She looked gloriously undignified and I smiled.

She deserved undignified for driving that awful wank machine. And for being an evil, evil bitch.

As she started the massive car, the harpies stood, spreading their long wings. I felt a burst of elemental power swirl around me as they launched themselves up into the air. I had a funny feeling they'd also be going our way, rather than with their mistress.

Ryu walked back to me and took my hand, leading me toward his own car. Once I was safely in Ryu's possession, Caleb and Daoud strode forward to collect the spriggan and Graeme. The latter looked positively relieved to get away from Anyan, who was staring down at the incubus like he was fresh meat. Or, in Anyan's case, perhaps a White Castle slider might be more accurate.

When we got into Ryu's car, he started swearing. My vampire was a master swearer, and I listened in awe as he took his art to a whole new level of formal experimentation. I had no idea that anyone could invent such varied and stimulating usages for cocktail forks, a trampoline, 'tiny fucking Alfars', and gasoline.

When he was finished, he scrubbed his hands through his hair and slumped backward in his seat. Everyone else was waiting on us, and soon enough, there was a knock on the window.

It was Anyan, in full commander mode. He was very intimidating. As soon as Ryu had the window down, he was barking orders.

'I'm not having Jane around Graeme unless she's at full strength. You take her swimming. Now.'

'Anyan, this is my investigation,' Ryu snapped, but the barghest wasn't having any.

'Fine. Then I'll take her. Get out. We'll reconvene at the Wethersby house, two hours.'

Ryu glared, clearly torn. Eventually, he replied by rolling up his window and starting the car.

I put my hand on his sleeve. I did *really* need a swim, but I hated feeling like I was a burden.

'Ryu, we don't have to—'

He shook his head angrily. 'No,' he interrupted. 'Anyan's right.'

I dropped my hand into my lap, knowing there was nothing I could say.

'He's always fucking right,' Ryu added, and I wondered, once again, what had happened to make him resent the barghest so much.

Since we were already in Southie, Ryu took me to Carson Beach. After a brief but fierce swim, I was whizz-banging with power once again. I was also very salty, but I had no time to go home for a shower before we left to catch up with the others.

Our impatience on the drive over to Felicia Wethersby's apartment was palpable. This was our first real lead in a while, the first new connection. It would also, hopefully, link what was going on in Chicago and the murders that had taken place here in Boston. After all, if her boss, Dr Donovan, had straddled both worlds, Felicia might have, too.

Felicia lived in Davis Square, on the other side of the Charles River, in a little walk-up apartment eerily similar to Tally Bender's. I fervently hoped there was no launching of partially cremated cadavers involved in tonight's activities.

'Stay close, Jane,' Ryu admonished, as he popped the locks of the BMW. For obvious reasons, there was no longer any talk of me staying with the car.

Ryu and I walked up the steps to Felicia's apartment building. Power swirled about us – all sorts of magical probes and shields were whirling around my lover while I held our fortifications steady. I could feel our combined power along my skin, raising the hairs on my arms as it blew in a cool gust around us.

He passed his hands over the door's dead bolts and they clicked open. I shook my head, reminded once again that what humans called 'security', the supernatural beings around me called 'just give me a second'. Our big doors and big locks barely slowed them down.

As we entered the building, Caleb pulled up down the street with the SUV. Obviously, with my swim break, they should totally have been able to beat us to Felicia's. Being considerate of his out-of-town guests, however, the satyr must have taken them on the scenic tour. He was a clever goat-man, and now Ryu and I would be the first people in the apartment, in the unlikely case that Felicia *was* at home.

'Stick close,' Ryu murmured, as we went up the stairs.

Felicia's apartment was on the third floor. The door was painted a crisp, clean white and it was firmly locked. When no one came to the door, Ryu went right ahead and jimmied it with his magic. It swung open only a tiny bit, though, before it got stuck on something behind it and stopped moving.

Ryu and I gave each other a dark look as I put the strongest shield I could around us. For his part, the vampire cupped a swirling ball of light-blue power in his hand as we stepped toward the door. Then he nudged it open with his foot.

The good news was that the door didn't catch on a body, as I'd expected. The bad news was that the apartment was *trashed*. Not just searched, but systematically destroyed. Everything that could be broken had been, including some of the walls.

I was standing in the middle of the kitchen, right off the

front door. The dishes and glasses were smashed on the kitchen floor. Felicia's sofa and chair were shredded in the little living room to my left. I could see an overturned bookcase and broken plant pots. Her bedroom revealed a similar level of destruction. The mattress was ripped apart. Bedding and clothes were strewn everywhere. The floor-length mirror had been smashed.

And seven years bad luck to you, dude, I mentally cursed whoever had done this.

Ryu and I picked our way back through the mess to the main rooms as Caleb, Daoud, Graeme, and Fugwat entered. Anyan brought up the rear, filling the doorway with leather and denim. I was keeping an eye on them as they entered, and what I saw surprised me. Graeme blinked, innocently, at the chaos of the room. But I would have sworn Fugwat smirked, until he caught Graeme staring at him. With a visible effort, he wiped the smug expression from his face.

He'd be the type to get off on mindless destruction, I told myself. But there was another part of my brain that wasn't accepting such excuses.

Whatever, that was a look of pride. Like he did all this himself. But that was ridiculous. Fugwat hadn't even known where we were going tonight till Caleb drove up.

I shivered, watching Fugwat's mean, stupid face, and then I turned around to look at the wall behind me that had once housed Felicia's pictures and diplomas. Unlike the spriggan, she was a bright cookie, with a bachelor's degree from Duke and a master's degree from Harvard, both in English literature. I didn't even think to make any snide jokes about what an English degree bought you in today's job market. Considering the circumstances, my heart wasn't in it.

I felt a pang; I really hoped Felicia was still alive, but I already knew to expect the worst. So finding out all these things that made her more real to me just made the danger she was in more difficult to bear.

We stood there, silently surveying the chaos. Caleb bent down to a pile of smashed crockery, but before he could start sifting through it, Daoud stopped him. The djinn pulled a bunch of workmen's gloves out of his waistband and passed them around to the others. I accepted mine gingerly, still uncomfortable with wearing things that had started life in another person's pants.

'No evidence of the girl,' said Ryu. 'But obviously this place has been visited before.'

'Only recently, though,' I said. Ryu and the rest turned to me. Graeme leered at my tits until Anyan caught him doing it and thwapped him on the back of the head with an open palm.

'The smashed plants are alive,' I explained, pointing at the healthy green leaves springing out from their graveyard of splintered crockery.

Ryu smiled at me and I blushed.

'Okay, everyone. Let's try to put together a picture of Felicia's life. Julian, what do we know?'

The younger baobhan sith looked up from where he'd plunked himself. His face was still attached to his laptop, as I imagine it had been since he'd left the squat a few hours previously.

'I've got quite a bit. Her parents died when she was eight; she's an only child. She was raised by a grandmother until she went to college.' Julian talked about her education, all of which I already knew from looking at her diplomas. So, instead, I bent down to try to find a good picture of Felicia. There were two or three of a plump, pretty biracial woman with various friends. Then there was what must have been a family photo of Felicia, as a child, with a mixed-race couple.

The man and woman had their arms around each other, squeezing their little girl between them. They looked so happy and in love. If they were Felicia's parents, as I figured it was safe to assume, the photo must have been taken just a few years before they died. Finally, there were a bunch of framed photos of Felicia with an older woman who had wild, untamed dreadlocks. They were shown together in fancy dress in front of a theater; in tourist clothes in front of that famous Roman fountain from *La Dolce Vita*; and in front of Shakespeare's Globe Theater in London.

'. . . did stints in Italy and London during college and grad school. She wrote a Facebook message to a friend about trying to find a job at a junior college, but they wanted her only as an adjunct, so she went back to work as an administrative assistant. She was really excited about her new job working for a doctor. Said the pay was great, her boss was a really nice lady, and she got to travel between Boston and Chicago all the time.'

Julian looked up, and I could see the pain in his eyes. The others were listening for clues, but I knew that Julian, like me, was building a picture of a person.

'Shit,' I heard Anyan swear. 'Let's find her. Safe.' I blinked at him, surprised at the raw fury in his voice. He obviously cared about finding the girl as well.

'Yes, let's,' replied Graeme in his beautiful, smooth, evil tenor, rather spoiling the moment and causing the base of my spine to shiver in horror. Graeme scared me even more than Jimmu had, something I would never have thought possible. The naga had been a killer, but the incubus would want to keep his victim alive. And screaming.

Wondering if my own, sadly underutilized English major skills could come in handy, I picked my way to the over- turned bookcase to look at what Felicia read. There were quite a few anthologies, a lot of the classics, and a lot of canonical stuff, all in the kinds of cheap paperbacks used in college classrooms. There wasn't really anything lowbrow or popular, and not much from after the 1900s. Except for a bunch of expensive hardcover books by Edie Thompson, a contemporary African-American writer who was very well respected in academic circles as both a critic and a novelist but who hadn't yet made a big splash in the popular market.

I picked up one of Thompson's books and found an autograph when I flipped it open. 'To Felicia, all best, Edie Thompson'. Each book had a similar autograph, although most were way more personal. 'To Felicia, with all my love', 'To Felicia, I'm so proud of your success', and 'To Felicia, You did it!' confirmed that Felicia was more than just Edie's fan; they knew one another, and probably well.

I couldn't remember too much about Edie Thompson, so I flipped back to her author bio, with its picture, and everything slid into place.

'Ryu,' I called quietly. I was hoping not to attract the attention of Phaedra's lot, but I might as well have hollered at the top of my lungs. Everyone stopped and stared at me.

I sighed as Ryu came toward me, and I decided I'd just show him what I'd found and let him choose what to reveal. I knew there were all sorts of Alfar power struggles going on here, and I had the feeling Ryu was fighting to stay dominant. He couldn't ignore Phaedra's orders to help him, but obviously neither could he trust her. So we all had to do a little tap dancing. With Ryu as our choreographer.

I pointed at the author's photo, which showed a very attractive older woman with long, thick dreadlocks pulled up into a bun. Her big hair accentuated the size of her large, dark eyes. There were laughter lines around her eyes and mouth, and – in her picture, at least – she looked like the perfect mother figure: approachable, intelligent, funny, and kind. Exactly the kind of person an orphaned girl might cling to – especially if the woman was Felicia's academic supervisor.

I then pointed from the photo to the other set of pictures, where Edie and Felicia smiled up at me from Boston, Italy, and London. Ryu grunted.

Then I traced my fingernail under the other pertinent bit of information. Edie was a professor at Harvard, and she made her home in Cambridge.

Ryu took the book from my hands and leaned over to kiss me on the cheek. I'd done good.

Now he had to figure out how we used the information without getting either of the two kindly looking women in the photos killed.

CHAPTER SIXTEEN

'You *bastard* . . .' I grunted. 'You pushed me in the *water*.'

'Learn how to drive, Toadstool,' was Anyan's only response. 'Learn how to drive.'

As soon as the little cloud had dropped me back on the track, I narrowed my eyes and pressed down on my accelerator button. It took me a wee bit to catch up, but when I did, I unleashed hell. First, I blew up Anyan's giant dragon/turtle character with a spare bomb I had, and then I shot past him to victory.

'Boo yah, motherfucker!' I shouted, rising to my feet to do a little victory dance. 'Who needs to learn to drive now, biatch?'

Anyan made a face at me from the other end of the sofa. 'Again.'

'You'll just get beat, *again*.' I grinned, causing Julian to chortle from the chair next to us.

Anyan laughed. 'Again. Again and again until I win,' he said. His iron-gray eyes, always intense, made his lighthearted words seem more serious, and for a second I was very aware of him, myself, and the space between us.

'I think I found another one,' Julian said from behind his computer screen.

Saved by the halfling, I thought. I dropped my game controller and wiped my suddenly damp palms on my jeans before moving to peer over Julian's shoulder.

It was the evening after we'd discovered the connection between Edie and Felicia. A couple of Stefan's deputies had been immediately dispatched to see if the women were there. There was no sign of them, so the deputies had secured the premises so that we could give the apartment a thorough search the next day, after we'd rested and regrouped.

Today, as soon as they were up, recharged, and ready, Ryu, Caleb, Daoud, and Camille, with Phaedra's lot in tow, had gone to check out Edie's Cambridge apartment for signs of either her or Felicia. Meanwhile, I'd volunteered to help Julian sort through the results of his search for recent fire-related deaths in the Chicago area. We were looking for people who might have something to do with the corporation that ran Conleth's laboratory, flagging any well-connected, wealthy people who'd been barbecued under suspicious circumstances. Despite a surprising number of possibilities to choose from, many had been easy to dismiss because they were the wrong type of victim, or the murderer was already caught, or they were obviously and genuinely accidents. But we'd put together another five names to add to the shortlist Dr Donovan had sent to her boyfriend.

Anyan also stayed behind with Julian and me. Most of the political and territorial machinations of the Alfar and their Court were still a mystery to me, but even I could see it was a really big deal that the barghest had contacts in the Borderlands. I could tell Anyan hadn't wanted to make his calls with Ryu around, no doubt because the baobhan sith's sharp hearing would pick up things to which Anyan didn't want him privy. So the barghest had stayed behind ostensibly to help us search, but really because I knew he wanted a modicum of privacy.

As soon as Ryu had left with the others, Anyan had called in Dr Donovan's original list. That had been hours ago, and we were still waiting to hear back from his contacts. Julian was still at work, but both Anyan and I had had enough of looking at police reports. He'd been teaching me silly little tricks to play with our power, before I'd found the old Nintendo.

'Victim's rich,' Julian continued, and I gave him my full attention. 'Had connections in both business and politics, and died in a house fire. Police figure he fell asleep, smoking, at around nine in the evening. But his ex-wife insisted to them that he never went to bed before midnight, ever. Also, that he'd quit smoking during the divorce, and I quote, "just to piss her off". They dismissed her claims, as forensics was unable to find any sort of accelerant or other signs of arson or murder. There may have been signs of trauma to the body, but it was so badly burned that the autopsy results were inconclusive and his death was eventually declared an accident.'

'Add the name to the list,' Anyan said after a second, and then he swore. I looked up to see he was still playing Mario Kart. The barghest had been unimpressed when I'd found the old game system inside a fancy trunk underneath Ryu's huge flat-screen. But once I'd switched it with the newest, state-of-the-art console already in place and had started playing, the big man had quickly changed his tune.

'Drinks, boys?' I called over my shoulder as I walked toward the kitchen. Both Julian and Anyan asked for water.

I had just gotten Julian and Anyan their waters when the troops returned. Alone, luckily, since I enjoyed being in the same room with Graeme about as much as I enjoyed someone randomly stabbing at my eyeballs with cocktail straws.

'Baby,' Ryu greeted me, adding a hug and a kiss to the mix. Then he eyed the glass in my hand and I gave it to him, before turning back to his cupboard for another.

I went to give Anyan and Julian their water only to find Daoud already playing against the barghest. They both wore the same intense yet paradoxically empty expression.

Who can resist the Mario Kart? I thought, smugly.

I'd just set down Anyan's drink when I felt a sparkle of strange power along my shields like nothing I'd ever felt. It was strong, but not elemental in any way. A pall of tense silence fell on the room, and I battened down my magical hatches. The tingle of magic intensified until, suddenly, a little creature poofed in right before me, knocking over the water glass I'd just set down and causing me to let out a very undignified shriek.

Anyan's hand touched my leg reassuringly, as both he and the creature threw up spheres of protective energy around it not a moment too soon. For, while I'd replied to the stranger's presence with a big girlie squeal, everyone else was ready to reply with mage balls to its face.

The little being chittered at us in a strange language, and Anyan laughed.

'No worries, people. Calm down. It's just a messenger.'

'Oh my gods,' I heard Camille breathe from across the room. 'Is that a . . . ?'

'Brownie?' Anyan replied. 'Yes, he's a brownie.'

Everyone in the room gathered closer to get a better look at the tiny creature standing on Ryu's glass-and-steel coffee table. It was only about a foot and a half tall, with brown fur so dense and fluffy it hid both features and figure. It actually looked a bit like an Ewok, if Kali had been the Ewok's paternal grandmother and a wolf spider its maternal grandfather. Six furry arms waved at us, almost all making some sort of obscene gesture, as six solid-black eyes glared while the creature continued its nonstop stream of tiny-voiced, incomprehensible invectives.

The creature was doing what I thought was a bizarre ritualistic dance. Then I realized its little feet were wet from the knocked-over glass of water.

'Oh!' I cried, running to the kitchen to grab a towel before rushing back to mop up the spill. The little creature eyed me as I dried up the puddle, backing away when I held out a dry corner of the towel. I kept still, until it finally approached. Balancing two of its six hands on my forearm, the brownie finally wiped dry its hairy feet. It took it a while to sop up the water from all that thick fur, but I held my arm still the whole time. When it was done, the wee creature patted my arm with two hands, while stroking a third down one of my fingers that held the towel.

I smiled and nodded my head in recognition of what was clearly a thank-you gesture, before carefully gathering up the wet towel so it wouldn't drip.

'Anyan, why is there a brownie in my living room? I thought they were extinct.' Ryu was carefully controlling his voice, but I could tell he was completely freaked out.

'Nope, not extinct. Just got tired of serving the Alfar's endless demands.' The barghest smiled down at the now much calmer little creature and then said something to it in that strange chittering language.

'And he speaks the old tongue,' Ryu said, throwing up his own hands in a gesture of surrender. 'Of course he does.' As he stalked toward the corner of the kitchen that held the liquor, I realized he meant Anyan, not the brownie.

I set the towel down on the floor next to me before turning to Caleb.

'What's going on?' I whispered.

The satyr blinked at me and then gave me a rueful smile. 'You take everything in such stride, Jane, that I forget this is all new to you.' Caleb was complimenting me, and I blushed. I wasn't a big fan of compliments.

'The Alfar are old, but they were not the first. The First Magics are a race utterly foreign to us, and very diverse in their origins and strengths. They are rare now. Some died naturally, but most died either by our hands or the encroachment of man into their lands. Brownies are of the First Magics, but they were happy to serve either Alfar or man for the price of a place to live and food to eat. Eventually, they were allowed to serve only the Alfar. But they disappeared, slowly, from our Territories, years and years ago. We figured they'd died out. Apparently, we were wrong.'

I had, of course, heard of brownies from my reading of human mythology. But I found it hard to believe that the little household sprites that one would placate with a saucer of cream not only existed, but also that they were of a magic and lineage older even than the Alfar.

'Does this mean they serve whoever rules the Borderlands?' I asked. Caleb only shrugged, his eloquent expression illustrating the depth of the mystery unfolding before our eyes.

'Wow,' I breathed as I watched Anyan and the brownie chitter at one another. Finally, the creature gathered together its six little fists and then flung out its arms with an equally explosive burst of that strange magic I'd felt when it had appeared.

We all ducked, throwing strength into our shields, but all that happened was that a file folder appeared, floating in front of Anyan's face.

The big man smiled as he took the folder in exchange for Julian's list of new names to be investigated. Anyan bowed his head at the brownie and then chittered what I imagined to be his thanks. The little creature reached out the hands on its left side, clutching the folded-up list with his right, in order to shake Anyan's finger. After which it gave me a little wave, the rest of the room two emphatic middle fingers, and disappeared with another audible *poof*.

Ryu wandered back, something tea-colored and sharp-smelling floating in his high-ball glass. He sat down heavily in the free chair across from where Julian sat. Scrubbing a hand over his face in his signature gesture of frustration, Ryu turned to the barghest.

'Please, Anyan. Please tell us what the fuck just happened. And how the fuck I'm going to explain any of this to Orin and Morrigan without them taking a strip out of both our hides?'

I studied the folder Anyan had passed to me as the boys argued. Basically, Ryu thought it was a really big deal that a brownie had popped in here moments ago. Anyan disagreed. No one had cared that much when the brownies had disappeared, so why would people care about their reappearance?

'You've always taken your position for granted, Anyan, as if you're untouchable—'

'And you care too much about what everyone thinks, Investigator . . .'

I shook my head, tuned the two men out, and opened the folder.

Besides what was written as part of the report, there was a sticky note to Anyan, signed 'Capitola', at the beginning of the folder. I knew I was being nosy, but I couldn't help it. The note read, '*This is all we could find. There is magic involved, but other than that we're as clueless as the human police. Good luck and keep in touch. We miss you.*'

I wondered about Capitola, and if she and the barghest were lovers. Then I wondered where that thought had come from as I flipped through the rest of the folder.

Whoever she was, Capitola and her team had done a thorough job. Each of our names had been checked out. Some were duds; the crime scenes and/or the bodies had not had any signs of magic on or around them. They'd died of normal fire, not magical fire.

A few, however, were different. Those victims had some indication of magic on or around them and their crime scenes. She wrote that even underground, in a coffin, one had stunk so powerfully of magic that you could feel it from the gates of the cemetery.

She also wrote that they were doing their own investigating, trying to find more recent deaths so that they could get their hands on an actual body. If she found anything, she'd be in touch by brownie.

I passed the file to Julian and then turned back to Ryu and Anyan.

'What could have induced them to leave the Alfar and go to the Borderlands? *That's* my question,' Ryu sniped.

'It's not about some powerful force seducing the brownies away, Ryu. They just got tired of being servants.'

'Brownies *like* serving. That's what they *do*.'

'Yes, but that doesn't mean they should be taken for granted or exploited . . .'

I sighed, watching them bicker. Now was not the time. So I said so.

'What?' they both said, turning to me.

'Now is not the time, guys. After we've found the women, then you can hash all of this out.' I kept my voice soft, but firm. They'd never know that what I really wanted to do was throw the wet towel I'd set at my feet directly into their faces.

Before Ryu could start arguing with me, I asked what they'd found at Edie's apartment.

'Nothing,' Camille said, stepping forward. She was obviously as ready to get back to work as I was. 'The apartment was empty and untouched. It did look as if someone had left in a hurry, and there seemed to be luggage missing.'

'Is she just on vacation?' I asked. 'Or on sabbatical or something?' Everyone looked at me and then at Julian, who nodded obligingly as he started typing on his laptop.

'Nope, she's scheduled for classes right now. But it does say she's taken a leave of absence.'

'So, let's go to her office. See what we can find,' I suggested.

Camille nodded. Julian told us he had the address. We all stood up to go, after figuring out who was riding with whom and whether anybody needed to call Phaedra.

In the meantime, I wondered when I'd become someone who made decisions.

And why it felt so good.

CHAPTER SEVENTEEN

An hour later we were standing next to Harvard Yard, near the T-stop at the Pit, waiting for Phaedra and her harpies. Apparently, she did want in on this action.

When the Alfar finally showed up, the harpies had their wings wrapped around them like sarongs. I would have thought them beautiful, but for the company they kept. And speaking of company, luckily Graeme and Fugwat were *not* in attendance.

As for our recent encounter with the First Magics, we'd already decided that Phaedra didn't need to know about the brownie, or the murders in Chicago, until more solid connections were made. We didn't trust her, and we didn't need her help. We just wanted to keep her and her entourage where we could see them; anything more could be dealt with as it became necessary.

The barghest herded everyone down Mass. Ave. toward the address we had for Edie's office. She was in one of the main buildings right off Harvard Yard, and walking through the campus was very impressive. The redbrick buildings gleamed in the night air, gently lit backdrops to the huge swathe of grass that was the yard. Cobblestone and concrete spirit paths

crisscrossed the winter-dead lawn, ushering students from
building to building. It was such a peaceful, pristine facade
that I could almost believe Harvard's aura of impermeability
could protect whoever lived there.

Almost.

When we got to the office, I stayed in back with Julian as
everyone else trooped up the stairs. They did some very
professional-looking fanning-out thing, with mage balls at the
ready. I felt like I was in a movie for just a second, until the
door clicked open and, once again, nothing happened.

I was beginning to realize that investigating crime actually
consisted of a lot of hurrying up and waiting, coupled with
hours of sitting and doing research.

Except for when you get stabbed through the hand, Jane,
my brain reminded me drily. *So stop looking for excitement.*

Edie's office was very empty and very neat. And *very* large.
There were two rooms: one a sort of lounge where she could
meet with students. Tons of books lined the walls, housed in
floor-to-ceiling bookcases, and there was a little seating area
complete with a sofa, a love seat, and a pair of wingback
leather chairs, all set around a lovely claw-footed, graceful-
legged coffee table. Next to the reception area was an office.
It was slightly more cluttered, with two desks covered in
papers and books. The towering bookcases were full in this
room as well.

'Okay, fan out and look for something, anything, that could
give us a clue about where Felicia and Edie could be. Their
lives depend on it,' Ryu said, and we all nodded solemnly.

I immediately went to the bookcases in Edie's office. Doing
so had worked the last time, in Felicia's apartment, so why
not here?

'Humans and their literature.' Phaedra yawned. 'So boring.
And so worthless as a form of immortality.'

I blinked at her, suddenly loathing her to the depths of my soul. Not only was she probably rather evil, and definitely thoroughly unpleasant, but she also didn't *read*.

'Of course you don't,' I said, accidentally letting loose my inner monologue.

'What, halfling?' the Alfar sneered, her voice sharp in my ears.

'Of course you don't read,' I replied, smiling at Phaedra sweetly to confuse her even more.

'Why should I? I care nothing for insight into humanity. I don't care how they deal with their psychological "issues", nor do I care how they come to terms with their history or the passing of their own lives. Human literature catalogs the flaws of an obscene species put on this earth only to serve and sustain their betters . . .'

Phaedra trailed off when she realized that I had totally stopped listening to her. I was too busy watching Julian, who looked like he had either figured something out or was about to have a seizure.

'History,' he said, staring at Phaedra. 'The passing of a human life . . . Edie Thompson is Edie's *married name*,' Julian announced to the room, beaming at me.

'Of course,' I breathed as I put together what he was saying.

'Sorry, what?' Ryu asked, still a supernatural step behind. They didn't do marriage, let alone married names. He was aware of the human tradition, obviously, but he didn't realize what Julian was trying to say. Hell, I was surprised Julian knew, but I guess his fascination with his human side extended to our marital practices.

'I read it about Edie when we were doing research, but it never clicked,' Julian told Ryu excitedly. 'There's very little biographical stuff on her; she's really private. But I did read that she goes by her married name for her professional stuff.

She was married for only, like, two years, to this asshole who tried to beat her, but in that time she published her first book. So she was stuck, professionally, with the name Thompson. Which is why I think that human women changing their names is silly, when you think about it, but that's neither here nor there . . .' Everyone in the room gave Julian the gimlet eye, till he got back on track. 'Anyway, I haven't yet searched for her under her maiden name. Whatever it is.'

Inspired by my fellow halfling's cleverness, I scanned the office till I saw what I was looking for. An ancient thesaurus, the kind that hadn't been published for eons, sat next to an equally ancient dictionary on the very corner of Edie's desk. *Bingo*. Every prof I've ever known had one: the dictionary/thesaurus set given to them as a graduation gift.

'I'm sure we could find it online, but if we're here . . .' I said, as I opened up the front cover to where people wrote their names in their books.

I grinned as I held up the book so everybody could see.

'Edie's not just Felicia's supervisor. She's her grandmother.'

I set the book down so Julian and I could give each other a loud, obnoxiously smacktastic high five before he charged for his computer. Everyone else still looked confused by what had just happened, but they went with it.

'Good work, Julian, Jane,' said Ryu. 'The rest of you, keep looking. Make sure we've found everything we can here. As long as those women are missing, they're in danger.'

As Julian typed, we all fanned out and Phaedra went to whisper something to her harpies. I put the thesaurus back where I'd found it.

Ryu was right. Real success would be finding the women alive.

Until then, we had work to do.

* * *

Julian wasn't yet finished with his Internet search, but we were done at the office. So we put everything to rights and locked up before heading back down to where we'd started. We wanted coffee and to give Julian some time to work.

So we commandeered a big group of tables on the elevated terrace at the Au Bon Pain across from Harvard Yard and right next to the T-stop at the Pit, where we'd started the evening. Daoud bought me something sweet and creamy and delicious, which I sucked away at like a child with a grape soda. Despite knowing we were still one step behind where we needed to be, the caffeine and the sugar immediately made me feel better, as did the lovely evening. The night air was crisp and cold, but the elevated terrace of the coffee shop was surprisingly full. At ground level, bundled-up chess players were still hunkered over games at the stone tables lining the other side of the wrought-iron fence encasing our patio. A few young couples, probably Harvardians, huddled down in their student togs of stupid knit caps, down jackets, Eskimo boots, and jeans. There were also quite a few very chilly looking Euro dudes dressed, too scantily for the cold weather, in thin leather jackets, button-down shirts, and shiny trousers. But they persevered, despite the cold, in smoking their unfiltered cigarettes and talking in the melodious grunts and sighs of their various homelands. The strong smoke of their black tobacco curled up into the naked limbs of the trees that grew out of holes in the concrete of the terrace. I breathed in a deep lungful of the cold, smoke-laced air and sighed happily.

I'd be even happier if we'd found Edie, but whatever.

I was watching Julian work, his glasses illuminated by the shine off of his laptop. I was also watching Phaedra and trying not to giggle.

The little woman was perched uncomfortably on the edge

of her chair, glaring balefully at the humans around her. She'd refused a drink when offered, as if we might poison her.

Not a bad idea, I thought, watching as she snapped at the remaining harpy. Kaya, or Kaori, had taken off after we left Edie's office, leaving only Kaori, or Kaya, behind to watch their mistress's back. The harpy was sipping at a coffee, making sure she showed no pleasure when Phaedra turned to her. But whenever the Alfar looked away, the harpy would take greedy sips from her cup before turning her face back to stoic mode before she got caught enjoying herself. I almost felt sorry for the harpy.

Almost.

I stood up, causing Ryu to look up at me questioningly.

'Just going to the bathroom, babe,' I said.

'Want me to come with?'

I laughed. 'Nah, I can handle this. You hold down the fort.'

Ryu smiled, turning back to continue his conversation with Camille.

Once inside, I had to wait in the ridiculously long line at the counter to get a stupid token thing that opened up the bathroom. It took forever, and the line hadn't gone down at all when I was finished. So I went out of the opposite side of the café, figuring I'd walk around the little terrace and hop over the fence to get to my seat.

I should have known better than to get fancy.

Just as I was at the far corner of the fence, something detonated in the Pit.

A large explosion took a knot of humans by surprise, sending the kids who were clustered – smoking grass and playing guitars – flying. All the humans at the café instinctively ducked, but the supes I was with were already in motion.

Anyan, Ryu, Camille, Phaedra, and Daoud were already leaping gracefully over the café's terrace, Caleb clip-clopping rather more cumbrously behind them. Julian, bless him, was furiously trying to get his laptop stowed away in his backpack. The harpy had launched herself in the air, pointing toward the Pit and shouting at Phaedra.

I was trying to decide whether to follow or stay put when another series of explosions rocked the ground, making my decision for me by spilling me onto my knees.

'Stay there, Jane!' Ryu shouted from where he and the others were already crossing the street. The humans were scrambling every which way, as blast after blast of energy erupted from the T-stop across the street. I could feel the power – Conleth's power – swirling from that spot, lifting my hair off my neck and sending the café detritus crashing about. The skeletal arms of the trees rattled a tardy warning.

I stayed crouched down, pushing power into my shields and using the fence to protect myself from the fleeing people. The Euro dudes didn't waste any time, vaulting over the rails of the terrace and hotfooting it away. The American college kids just looked scared, running this way and that before Julian, backpack now in place, directed them where to go.

The explosions were still coming from the T-stop, but the sheer *force* behind them illustrated just how much strength the ifrit halfling had at his disposal. Power rode the ground in waves that pushed over everything in their paths. The tables around me overturned, and I crouched lower, clinging to the concrete next to me so I didn't fall over or get hit by something from the terrace above.

I was so focused on watching my team forge a path to where Conleth was launching his attack from the center of the Pit that I felt only confusion when a hand touched my hair and Conleth's voice whispered in my ear.

'Jane,' he said.

Oh, shitballs, I thought, turning to face the inevitable.

Like the first time we'd met, Conleth had banked his fire. Crouching beside me, he would look, from a distance, like a scared human using the side of the terrace as a shield. But from up close, I could see his eyes. His utterly, totally, bat-caca-crazy eyes.

That wild gaze roamed over my face and I realized he was demanding to know whether I was hurt. I shook my head, unable to get my usually overactive tongue to form any words.

Conleth crouched in front of me, placing a hand on my cheek. I could hear the explosions still detonating, the fire behind us framing him like an eerie echo of his other, ifrit, form. He was keeping everyone well distracted and I had to give him props for his ability to multitask.

'Jane,' Con crooned again, shifting his fingers to cup my chin. My reflexes finally kicked in and I jerked my face away, but he tightened his grip, forcing me to meet his gaze with my own.

'There you are.' He giggled, and my heart went cold with terror. I responded with a heartfelt, if not particularly brave, whimper.

'Don't be shy, Jane!' Conleth said, grinning madly at me. 'I know it's hard to get to know new people. I understand that.' My fellow halfling's wackadoo blue eyes burned into mine. 'But we were meant to be together,' he added with an earnest nod.

I gulped, trying to overcome my panic so I could focus on surviving this little encounter. I had to humor the loony fire-man, or he'd kill me without a second thought. His hand was still firmly gripping my chin, and an occasional burst of flame skittered up and down his arm in alarmingly random bursts.

Despite all that power, he's got very little control, I realized, my fear sharpening acutely. Even if he *didn't* want to hurt me at the moment, I couldn't trust Conleth not to barbecue me by accident if he got too excited or angry. So I had to placate him, and fast.

Here goes nothing, I thought as I made myself smile, praying that someone – anyone – would turn around and notice that my face had been commandeered by the enemy.

'There you go. You're smiling! And you're so beautiful.' Conleth grinned, brushing my hair away from my face. I forced down the reflexive shudder that threatened to rack my frame. 'I know *he* only goes for pretty ones, but you are perfect.'

I felt a fresh wave of nausea, realizing that by 'pretty ones', Conleth meant the women Ryu must have fed on in my absence. I hated myself for the fact that Con's words bothered me as much as they did, given the circumstances.

'I followed you tonight. They were all so busy watching each other that I could have walked right up to you and said, "Boo!"' Conleth laughed, his hands moving over my cheeks and chin. It took everything I had in me not to pull away – I'd never realized just how invasive and personal someone touching my face could be.

'But I would never want to frighten you,' he continued. I'm not sure how he was oblivious to my terror, but I guess we all have our blind spots. 'I realized how special you were after your bravery that first night. Then you talked to me through those e-mails, and I knew we were meant to be together, so we need to trust one another. Because that's what relationships are all about. Trust.' Con nodded firmly, cupping my jaw in his hands and making me look into his eyes. 'I've never been able to trust anyone, Jane. But I know that we understand each other. We're like two sides of the same coin.'

My throat was dry; my lips felt like two desiccated crackers rubbing together. I licked them, trying to find my voice.

'How?' I croaked. I needed to engage him, keep him

distracted. *The others will be here soon. They have to be here soon . . .*

'We're so similar, Jane.' His hands were tightening convulsively on my jaw, and I struggled not to flinch. 'I know how hard you've had it, living among *humans*. And not being treated like an equal by the *others*.' He said both 'humans' and 'others' as if he were talking about 'shit' and 'crap'. Conleth had issues with both sides of his heritage, which I suppose was understandable. 'And I know how strong you are. I can feel you when you're near.' He stopped clutching my jaw and started stroking my neck, then my arms. His eyes got a faraway look I recognized: the slightly predatory, slightly desperate look of a horny man. 'Your power calls to mine. Fire and water.' He splayed the fingers of his stroking hands, so that his thumbs brushed the sides of my breasts. 'Water and fire,' he crooned, letting his gaze drop down to my body.

'Conleth,' I said, a little too sharply. I wanted to keep him distracted, yes, but not through sex. I needed to keep him talking.

'Conleth,' I repeated, more gently. 'Why me? I'm not special.'

'Jane, how can you say that? Look at us! Look at me!' His fire, which had begun to bank as he got distracted, flared up again, dangerously close to my hair. 'We *are* power. We have all the power of the others, but none of their weaknesses. None. We can do anything we want.'

I nodded, trying to keep my eyes wide, interested. He smiled at my reaction.

'They're corrupt, inbred. Their time is over. And humans are jokes. They wander around like sheep, being fed off of, used, bred like cattle.' He snorted, taking my hands in his. 'Both sides will fall. The purebreds are dying off, and the only way they can survive in any way is to keep breeding

with the humans. Creating more beings like us. We don't
need anyone else.'

He then raised my hands, palms outward, to his mouth.
His lips were thin and wet against my skin, and my gorge
rose as his tongue brushed against my right palm in a grotesque
parody of Ryu's favorite endearment. I also noticed that his
shields kept pulsing up and down, along with his fire. I was
right; he had no control. Conleth was entirely self-taught, and
his command of his magic was more than a little sketchy.

'Think of what our children will be like, Jane. Think of
their power. Your water, my fire, flowing through their blood.
They'll be able to stop the world spinning on its axis, recon-
figure society to their whims. Think of the world we would
create.' Conleth was tugging me closer, obviously intent on
kissing me, and his lower body was squirming in that telltale way that meant his trousers had just gotten tighter.

I put the brakes on my forward momentum, tugging back
sharply. His eyes narrowed, and his mouth hardened, and I
knew I had to distract him.

Luckily, I found my voice. Unfortunately, it didn't say what
it was supposed to. I meant to murmur something endearing
and soothing. Instead I said, 'I'd never be safe with you.
Silver practically *raised* you. And now he's missing.'

I'd expected Conleth to react with anger. I beefed up my
shields and put as much physical space as I could between
his body and mine. Which wasn't much, considering he was
still holding me by each forearm.

Instead of flaring up at me, however, Conleth merely looked
confused.

'Doc? Doc is missing?' he asked, his voice small.

'Don't act all innocent,' I snapped, without thinking. But
he still didn't react.

'Doc . . .' he whispered, and I would have sworn on my

Julia Child's cookbook that he was honestly horrified by the idea that Silver had disappeared. In fact, he was so surprised that his grip on my arms loosened. I'd been waiting for just such a moment, and I wrenched away from Conleth as hard as I could, just as the cavalry arrived. I'd gotten one arm free when Con was struck full in the face by two simultaneous balls of energy – one a bright white blue and the other a dark swirling green – that crashed against his faltering shields like two NFL linebackers.

Unfortunately, he still had a tight grip on one of my arms, and as the force of the strike catapulted him up and over and onto the terrace, he took me with him. We skittered to a stop against the far side of the iron fencing, just as I saw Ryu and Anyan vault over the fence where we'd been crouched a second earlier. *So close, yet so far away*, my brain sang, rather inappropriately, as Conleth hauled me up like a rag doll to hold me in front of him. I discovered there was nothing like being used as a human shield to give a girl serious doubts about the honesty of a boy's declarations of love.

We were at a stalemate. Balls of energy swirled in both Ryu's and Anyan's palms, but they were unable to let fly due to the fact that Conleth was crouched behind me. Ryu was obviously furious, but Anyan's rage palpably prickled off of his body. Conleth was in big trouble if the barghest ever caught up with him.

My two saviors exchanged glances, obviously communicating, and Anyan nodded as Ryu dropped his own little sphere of power. It fizzled on the ground before winking out of existence. Nell would not have approved of the waste of energy.

'Conleth, you've made your point. We know how powerful you are, how strong you are. But nobody wants Jane hurt, do we? She's shaking, Conleth. She's scared. Don't scare Jane. Let her go.'

I know Ryu was using my name, and Conleth's, on purpose, but I didn't think standard negotiating procedure was going to work with the halfling. Not at a moment like this. He was so angry, so crazy with rage and the excessive torments of his short life, that nothing would get through to him when he was threatened. All of his horrible experiences had combined to make him a survivor, in the worst sense of the word. He would do anything to keep alive, to keep going, no matter how many people got hurt doing so.

'Why?' Conleth snarled, his angry voice loud against my ear. 'So you can use her some more? Cheat on her? You don't deserve her, and she knows it as well as I do. She doesn't love you. She loves me.'

'You're right, Conleth. Jane does deserve more than I can give her. And we can talk about that. She can get a chance to know you, properly. Just let her go. Jane won't love you if you hurt her. You know that.'

Out of my peripheral vision, I could see Camille creeping up on one side, while Caleb and Daoud advanced from the other. I didn't know where Phaedra and her lot were, but for the first time ever I hoped they were nearby. Although the Alfar would have no qualms about blasting me away with Conleth, so perhaps I shouldn't have been quite so eager for the bald woman's intervention.

'Stop them!' Conleth was shouting, nearly taking out my eardrum. He'd noticed the others as well. 'Stop them! Tell them to come where I can see them! I don't want to, but I *will* hurt her,' he said, as I felt heat at my back and saw flames start to lick up the arms holding me tight. When Caleb and Camille didn't move, Con's hold on me tightened, and I felt the burn of his heat through my clothes. I whimpered and Ryu's face grew grimmer as he gestured for Camille, Caleb, and Daoud to come round toward him. So much for the sneak attack.

Obviously having had enough of playing negotiator, Anyan suddenly strode forward. 'Drop her, now,' the barghest growled menacingly. 'You *will* die here, boy. If you take Jane first, then you will die suffering. Let her go, give her to us, and you have a chance at survival.' The big man's hard gray eyes stared levelly into Con's, and I knew Anyan was serious. I got my first small glimpse of why the barghest was a legend. He wasn't *just* a killer, like Graeme. But Anyan was no stranger to violence.

Conleth swore softly. He was weighing his options, and he, too, had seen the promise in Anyan's eyes. I felt Con's body tense, and I shut my eyes, not sure if I was about to die. Instead, I felt a jolting pain as Conleth used a combination of his own physical strength and his supernatural power to launch me in the air toward the barghest. The ifrit halfling simultaneously unleashed four bolts of fire-tinged power that crashed into the terrace's four trees, sending them crashing down toward us. As the others swore and fought to catch the flaming trees with their shields, I hit Anyan. It was like hitting a brick wall. Only this brick wall caught and held me. My legs dangled as his arms wrapped around me, and he held me so tightly my vertebrae popped.

'Jane,' Anyan whispered hoarsely, his mouth pressed against my ear as he squeezed even tighter. His breathing was as ragged as mine, and I realized that hostage situations made for chaotic emotional reactions.

Then I was set down on my feet, gently, as Anyan took off after Conleth, who'd rocketed away as soon as I was out of his grip. I sat down, my shaking legs unable to support my weight, watching as everyone but those still holding the trees off of us with their shields either took part in the pursuit or began furiously glamouring the human witnesses. There was definitely going to be another 'gas leak' in Cambridge that night.

I sat down, cross-legged, as my adrenaline rush gave out, and my whole body sagged like a puppet whose strings had been cut.

Then I heard Julian swear.

He'd been holding one of the larger trees. Phaedra had finally reappeared and was helping Kaya (or Kaori) lift her flaming burdens up and away from the café. The harpy hovered, pulling with her power from above, while the Alfar pushed from below. Together, they were piling the still-burning trees up in the huge concrete expanse next to the terrace.

But Julian was losing his grip on the tree he held, quivering, above both of us. I didn't yet know how to make my shields solid against physical entities, just magical ones, so I genuinely thought my number was up as I watched the fiery tree sway and then break free of Julian's shields.

It stopped about a foot above me, held in a net of Alfar power. When I looked up through my fingers, Phaedra was staring at me as if she wasn't quite sure why she'd done what she did.

For a second, I wondered whether she'd changed her mind and was going to drop the tree on me. Instead, after a very long pause, she gave a negligent flick of her fingers and a second later the tree landed with a crash next to the others to smolder out of harm's way.

I couldn't believe the little Alfar had just saved my life.

But from the look on her face, I was a lot happier about it than she was.

CHAPTER EIGHTEEN

I came up out of the Atlantic, naked and dripping, and walked up to where Ryu sat waiting on the sandy beach with a towel. He held it outspread in his arms, enveloping me in both as I curled up between his thighs, resting my wet head on his chest.

Conleth was still being pursued, so Ryu had felt it was safe to take me for a wee swim. We were all knackered from our latest run-in with Con, but Carson Beach had, once again, come to my rescue.

'I can't believe we let Conleth get to you again,' Ryu's voice rumbled out from where I had my ear pressed against him.

'Don't worry, babe,' I replied, stroking a hand over his ribs. 'I totally thought he had to be at the center of that attack in the Pit. He may be crazy,' I conceded, raising my face to look up at Ryu, 'but he's wicked strong.'

Ryu inclined his head to kiss my forehead. 'Yes, he is.'

'What I can't get over is that Phaedra saved me.'

'Well, we may not like her, but she is a member of our team.'

I snorted. 'Yeah, right. That's why Jarl sent her. To be a member of our team.'

'The Alfar want this investigation wrapped up as much as any of us do, Jane. None of us are safe until Conleth is caught. Plus, we have to figure out how that laboratory of his was funded, and by whom. If we have a new enemy, we all need to know.'

I lowered my head back to Ryu's chest to hide my frown. I believed the Alfar did want Conleth caught, but I would've bet my life that Jarl's interest meant something more. We didn't know what yet, but it had to be *more*.

In the movies and in the books I read, everything about mysteries or investigations was all linear, and the plotlines progressed neatly from discovery to revelation to ultimate finale. So if you were smart and caring, you'd save the victims and catch the bad guys. But in reality, this 'investigation' was a giant clusterfuck where we were all stumbling about blind, being toyed with by Conleth. Either that, or by whoever was behind the Chicago killings. I still didn't believe those murders had been committed by Con. Whoever it was had to be strong and well connected, and aware of what was going on. I believed they'd sent the note to Conleth, telling him about Felicia Wethersby, in order to use Conleth as a decoy to hide his or her own machinations.

And, in the meantime, we were all dancing to this mystery piper's tune.

Is this what my new life will be like? I wondered. *Continually being shoved around by the Alfar or whoever else is more powerful and scarier than I am?*

'Cause if that were the case, I wondered if my new life would be worth the sacrifices. I hadn't had much all those months before, when I'd learned of my mother's supernatural legacy. But I'd been free to do what mattered to me. Even though I'd lived at home all my life, I was, in my weird way, really independent. I'd taken care of my father as much as he'd taken care of me. I'd been the major breadwinner for our family for the past few years. I had made the choices I wanted to make. Even if working at a local bookstore to care for my dad wasn't the most glamorous decision, it was *mine*.

And now? Nothing was mine. Ryu was paying for everything at this point, which I hated. Obviously, there was no salary going into my bank account. Somebody else was taking care of my father. I was being chased by a fiery lunatic who wanted to impregnate me with über-halflings.

I just want to go home, I thought, not for the first time but with a newfound urgency. *This is not how I want to live. The chasing, the running, the constant threat. This is not my life.*

Ryu shifted slightly, repositioning me so that I sat with my back against his chest.

'You okay, honey?'

'Not really. But I'm better than Edie and Felicia.'

'They may still be alive, honey.'

'Do you really think that?' I asked.

Ryu's heavy silence was answer enough.

'We still haven't talked about who wrote that note to Conleth telling him about Felicia. Either Phaedra's been around, or we've been chasing after Conleth, or being chased by Conleth. I think that note is the key to everything.'

Ryu shrugged. 'Maybe. But it could be something he found on one of his victims. It's not addressed to him.'

'I just don't think Conleth was ever in Chicago,' I argued. 'I think whoever killed the people in Chicago gave Conleth that note so that he'd finally murder someone who would serve as the missing link between the Boston victims and the Chicago victims.'

Ryu shrugged. 'If you *are* right, then we have another player in the mix.'

'It's gotta be whoever funded the laboratory. The new sponsor.'

'That would be logical *if* your theory is correct. But that's a big "if", baby.'

'I know it is. For me, though, it's like what you said when we were investigating Jimmu. I can see there's a pattern here somewhere; I just can't quite make it out. But I know who my money's on.'

'Jane,' Ryu said, using his most long-suffering tone. 'You can't keep blaming everything on Jarl.'

'Really?' I asked, raising my chin to meet his eyes. 'I still believe there was more to Jimmu's murders than we know, and I think that one of these days we're going to discover that it all traces back to Jarl.' Ryu made a noise as if to protest, but I didn't let him interrupt me. 'Don't you think it's strange that Jarl sent someone here to keep an eye on us? And why is Phaedra's lot always divided into two groups, one of which is with us and one of which is always missing? It's like one group is spying and the other is on call to act on whatever is uncovered.'

Ryu shook his head, as I knew he would.

'And why *haven't* we talked about the note in front of Phaedra? None of us trust her, Ryu. Not even you. How far does that distrust extend, if not to her boss?'

'There's a difference between not trusting Jarl or Phaedra, and thinking that they committed those murders in Chicago. We have nothing connecting them to anything. And yet, if I'm correct, what you're insinuating is that there's not only a connection between Jarl and these murders, but also a connection between Jimmu's murders and what's going on right now. You do realize how crazy that sounds?'

'Okay, so it's a stretch, but—'

'Jane, what part of "We investigated every aspect of

Jimmu's crimes" don't you understand? Do you think we're inept?'

'No, I don't think that at all. I just think that our enemies are *smart*, Ryu. Maybe smarter than we are.'

Ryu took a deep breath. I knew he was frustrated with me, but I wasn't going to back down.

'So how *do* you think Jarl is involved?'

I took a deep breath, carefully ordering my thoughts. I knew I had a tendency to spout off and sound like a conspiracy nut, so I had to choose my words carefully. 'Because I think Jarl is the mystery sponsor. You said yourself he's the spymaster. What if he was brought a rumor regarding Conleth, but he squashed it and took over the investigation himself? When he found Con already living in a lab, he took it over using magic and money. He's got an instant guinea pig, no muss, no fuss.'

Ryu looked at me like I'd just barfed cockroaches.

'That's so ridiculous I don't even know where to begin. No member of the Alfar would *ever* risk our discovery like that. We've guarded the secret of our existence with an avidity that has been entirely unscrupulous. Any human who discovered us, and attempted to share their discovery, was neutralized. Along with anyone he or she could have told. Back in the day, we wiped out entire villages protecting our secret.' I frowned but Ryu didn't let me interrupt. 'I'm not telling you this to debate the moral implications of our actions. I'm telling you because it's the truth. Besides which, what you're saying doesn't make sense. How could he have gotten involved in such an enterprise? And kept it hidden?'

I thought about Ryu's words. There'd been something Morrigan said to me months ago, when we were at the Compound, that had been really important at the time in terms of the murders we'd been investigating. I'd gone over and over everything that had happened, almost obsessively, because I still didn't get why Jimmu had done what he'd done. The other supes seemed happy to write the nagas off as mad racists who took advantage of an opportunity to kill halflings. But I knew there was more to their murders than just hate. I felt it in my little half-selkie bones.

Anyway, Morrigan's fateful words had obviously stuck with me because they helped me figure out that I'd seen a disguised Jimmu in Rockabill. But now they took on an entirely different connotation.

'Ryu,' I said, twisting my neck around to peer up at him. 'Remember how, way back when, Morrigan tipped me off about where I'd seen Jimmu by saying that thing about "teams of scientists"?'

'Yeah, 'course.'

'Well, think about it for a minute. I mean, even at the time I thought it was weird that she'd say *that*. We're talking about supe fertility, and she brings up the fact that they don't do things like humans with science. There's a million different things she could have said, so why that?'

Ryu thought about it a second and then nodded, albeit grudgingly, as he followed where I was leading.

'Like she had it on her mind,' he replied.

'Exactly. And now we're suddenly investigating a laboratory that tested on a halfling. What if it was something that had been brought up to her and Orin by Jarl? They would obviously dismiss the idea; she said "science" like it was the craziest thing she'd ever heard.'

'But she still had it on the brain.'

'So, what if Jarl brought up using human science to Orin and Morrigan, and they immediately pooh-poohed his idea? Jarl's not the type to let something go. What if he decided to do everything by himself? If he *was* trying to start up some fertility experiment using halflings, that would explain Peter Jakes's assignment . . .'

'But even if Jarl *did* want to experiment on halflings,' Ryu broke in, 'why kill them?'

'Oh.'

'Yeah.'

'Shit.' My brain shut down as it crashed headlong into the brick wall of reality. 'Yeah, that makes no sense. Why kill your lab rats?'

Ryu reached under my towel to stroke a hand over my belly. 'It was a clever idea, baby,' he murmured, his lips following his words, pressing into the soft lobe of my ear.

Which only reminded me of the bloodied ears Jimmu had collected, and I shuddered.

Ryu pulled away, frowning at me as I started to apologize. 'Sorry, Ryu. I was thinking of the ears Jimmu hacked off of those bodies . . .'

And with that, my brain leaped gracefully, like a gazelle, right over the top of that pesky old brick wall. I made a weird, low noise that sounded like a barn owl hooting. Ryu blinked at me and I blinked back, startled by my own noise before I remembered what I'd just thought.

It's a long shot, but worth looking into . . .

'Ryu, what happened to the bodies of Jimmu's victims?'

'Sorry?'

I sat up in Ryu's arms, feeling my towel slip but not caring.

'What happened to the bodies of Jimmu's victims? Were they buried, cremated, what?'

'No idea,' my vampire breathed, his eyes now focused on my bared breasts. I pulled up my towel and, hopefully, his attention.

'We need to find out what happened to the bodies. Can we find that out?'

Ryu's eyes flickered to mine before he reached out to tug at my towel. I held on to it, waiting for an answer.

He sighed. 'I'm sure we've got all of that information with each victim's file. We can check as soon as we get home . . .'

I stood, eager to check out my hunch. Ryu looked up at me and then reached out a hand as if he wanted help getting up. But when I took it, he pulled me down hard and we were again lying on the soft sand.

'Snack first,' he murmured, as he flipped me over effortlessly so that I was lying beneath him. His mouth found my nipple as his hand dove between my legs, causing me to yelp.

'Files later,' Ryu mumbled into the soft flesh of my breast.

I was about to protest when I remembered that this was as much about keeping Ryu's power topped up as it was about getting nookie. He'd been throwing a lot of mojo around this afternoon, so he was just as in need of a power fix as I'd been. And we needed every member of our team at top spec.

So I let the pleasure wash over me even as I tamped down my impatience to get home and look at those files, tightening my body around his fingers so that I would come more quickly. Ryu's tongue was already at my throat, preparing me for his bite.

I gotta admit, it felt really fucking good.

But I'd never felt so much like a goddamned granola bar in my entire life.

'Ryu,' I called, three and a half hours later. We were back in Boston and I was huddled over Ryu's desk with all of his files on Jimmu's halfling victims. He'd told me numerous times that he'd gone back and investigated each of the halfling murders, but I hadn't realized he'd been *this* thorough. Everything was in these files, including what happened with the corpses of the deceased . . .

'Ryu! This is important . . .'

Ryu came in from the kitchen, where he'd been ordering Thai food.

With another weird triumphant hoot that made both of us pause, I handed him the papers I'd pulled out of the files of each of Jimmu's victims. Ryu turned his body and leaned back on the edge of his desk while I avidly watched him read.

He went slowly through each piece of paper as my body thrummed with impatience. Finally, he looked up and shook his head ruefully.

'Jane, if I'd had any inclination you were such a genius, I would have gone right ahead and kidnapped you the first day we met.'

I blushed and then thought about what he'd just said. 'Wait, what *did* you think of me the first time you met me?'

He laughed. 'Honestly? I thought, "Nice rack," and then, "*Really* nice rack." In that exact order.'

I can live with that, I thought, perversely pleased that he hadn't been thinking about the essence in my blood. Him having a moment of mammary elation seemed more . . . satisfying than him thinking of me in terms of feeding.

'Seriously, though, you are amazing. We would *never* have thought to look for this connection.'

'Well, you don't do human science,' I said. 'Why would you think to look for what happened to the bodies?'

'It's so obvious, but so outside our frame of reference,' Ryu acknowledged.

What Ryu and the others had failed to notice was that every single one of Jimmu's victims had their bodies donated to science. And none of them had been signed up to do so, until *right before* they were murdered.

'Here's my scenario,' I said, pulling out the piece of paper

I'd been working on since we had gotten back to Ryu's and I'd seen 'body donated to science' at the bottom of the first and second victims' autopsies. 'We think, from what Morrigan said to me at the Compound, that someone floated to them the idea of using human science to figure out their fertility issues. It has to be someone close to the ruling pair, and who's closer than Jarl?'

'Jane—'

'Ryu, please just hear me out. You don't have to agree with everything I say, but hear me out.' After a few moments, he nodded. But he still looked unhappy.

'The next thing we know, we're discovering that Jarl's own second, Jimmu, has been murdering the halflings that Peter Jakes was sent out to catalog. Did you ever get an official reason for why Jakes was sent out?'

Ryu shrugged. 'Orin and Morrigan don't answer to me, obviously. They did tell me that they were cataloging halflings to try to understand just how many there were in the Territory, how powerful they were, and why they hadn't been brought into the fold, so to speak.'

I thought hard, chewing on a hangnail as I stared at my jumbled notes.

'Well, what if they didn't really *have* a point to sending out Jakes? What if they did it just to placate Jarl?' As I said it, it made sense. 'Maybe they promised to act depending on what they found.'

Ryu nodded slowly. I knew he didn't like where I was heading, but I also knew Ryu loved a challenge, loved figuring out the games his brethren played with one another. He might not entirely believe what I was saying, but he might be willing to join in the fun of speculation.

'I'm not saying I believe you, yet, but if Jarl *was* the sponsor of that lab, he might even have given our monarchs the idea of using Jakes so that Jarl could take advantage of the situation. He'd have Jakes wandering around the country, cataloging halflings who weren't integrated into the community – which means they'd be weak, vulnerable, and off our radar.'

I nodded. 'So Jimmu follows Jakes about until he leaves, and then Jimmu shows up and convinces the halflings to donate their bodies to science using his mojo. Once they've agreed, he later kills them. The bodies are funneled to a special laboratory. Either one Jarl's set up, or one that has some of his people on staff. Everything goes smoothly until Jakes realizes his catalog has become one of death, sees Jimmu hanging about, and puts two and two together. That's when Jimmu kills him.'

'How does Conleth fit in?'

I thought about that. 'I don't see how he could be directly involved . . . except,' I said, getting excited again, 'as an inspiration. Like I said, what if Jarl caught wind of some halfling rotting away in a human laboratory? He gets involved by taking over the lab. Later, he decides to expand operations.'

'Now you're just shooting yourself in the foot. If Conleth is the inspiration for Jarl, then why is he killing the halflings and using their bodies? Why not kidnap them and experiment on them like he's doing with Conleth?'

I frowned. That was a good point. But good points are like pencils: they wear down eventually.

'Well,' I replied, 'let's think this through. First of all, Jarl already has a live halfling in his clutches. There are tons of experiments you can do only on living beings, presumably, but there *also* have to be tons of experiments you can do only on dead ones. Plus, look at all the resources it took to keep Con prisoner. There was, like, a full roster of employees running that lab, which must have been really expensive.

Granted, Conleth is really powerful, but still. It's gotta be a pain in the ass to kidnap and hold people, right? Plus, most victims have friends or family or co-workers who notice when they go missing. But nobody notices a body funneled to a laboratory. They're already dead; you don't have to feed or guard them. As long as you don't get caught doing the murders – which you won't if you're a super-ninja magical snake-man trained to sneak and kill – it's sort of a perfect way to get test subjects, isn't it?'

'I've thought of something else,' Ryu said, after a second. I could tell he was nervous about voicing too much support of my idea, but, again, he liked playing the game. 'We only know of the murders because Jimmu got sloppy and was caught by Jakes. If he hadn't murdered Jakes, we would never have known what the nagas were doing. What if there have been other kidnappings, or deaths, but they've not been discovered or connected?'

I shuddered, horrified at that thought. And yet, at the same time, part of me was excited at everything we'd speculated on. It wasn't nice, or pretty, but I'd always thought there was more to Jimmu's murders. So we might not have every detail correct, but what we'd talked about made a lot of sense, on a lot of levels. That said, I could tell Ryu was about to try to throw down the old kibosh.

'It's a good theory,' he said, using his 'but' voice. 'But we've only got proof of *Jimmu's* involvement. And it all could *still* be a really freakish coincidence. I admit, what you're theorizing does have some . . . merit. But we would need real, concrete, irrefutable proof before accusing Jarl of anything.'

'I know,' I said, employing my *own* 'but' voice. 'But at least it's something. A connection. Even if we can't prove anything, *we* need to know who the real enemy is.'

What I left unsaid was my belief that the real enemy

was Jarl. And what Ryu left unsaid was that he was unconvinced I was right. So we were at another impasse.

'If you are right, then the question is, are there other laboratories? And where?' Ryu asked gently. My stomach dropped as he continued. 'And what are they working on now if they're no longer getting bodies from Jimmu?'

'Shit,' I murmured as I realized the implications of Ryu's words. If Jarl had lost Con, been foiled in his use of halfling cadavers for experiments, *and* he wasn't the type to give up, I didn't want to ponder the evils to which he'd graduated.

'Yup.'

'Not good.'

'No.'

I was beginning to realize that this investigation was bigger than Conleth – and probably bigger than anything Ryu and I could imagine.

And I so did *not* want to get caught up in it.

CHAPTER NINETEEN

When Anyan, Daoud, Camille, and Julian trooped in, Ryu got right down to business. He explained to everyone what we'd just found, but he didn't yet go into what we'd hypothesized. He probably wanted to see what conclusions they came up with on their own.

That's when I noticed the business-card holder. Supes didn't have last names; they just went by their factions, and so I was curious what Ryu used in his human incarnation. My eyes bulged when I read it.

'Ryu T. Tootie?' I demanded, but Ryu ignored me.

'Ryu T. Tootie?' I repeated, walking over to poke him in the stomach. 'Are you serious? Tell me these are a joke.'

Ryu glowered at Daoud. 'I lost a bet. For the next twenty years, I have to go by Ryu T. Tootie.'

'Seriously?'

'Seriously.'

I eyeballed Daoud, appraisingly. 'That was a good bet,' I said.

Daoud inclined his dark head toward me, his dimples winking as he grinned. 'Thank you. It *was* fairly inspired.'

'Ryu, this says you're a "private consultant".'

'Yeah,' Ryu responded. 'I always use "consultant". It's perfect: vaguely meaningless, yet redolent of money.'

'I tried to get him to put "privates consultant", plural, but it wasn't in the parameters of the original bet,' Daoud informed me, his voice serious, until we met each other's eyes and burst out laughing.

'Shit, is he gonna start charging me?' I started to joke with Daoud, but I was cut off by Anyan clearing his throat from where he was leaning against the doorway. He clearly wanted to put us back to the task at hand, but he also looked really grossed out by our banter.

Suddenly, I realized why. It explained why the barghest was always so gentle with me, why he'd done so much for me.

He'd known me all my life, seen me grow up. He'd probably been introduced to me as a baby, by my mother. I'd probably pulled his ears and drooled on his tail. When he was a dog, obviously. No wonder he looked uncomfortable.

He still saw me as a little girl.

And, to him, I *was* a child. I didn't know how old he was, but I knew he was older than Ryu, who was two hundred and seventy in human years. I don't know how the supes calculated their ages, but Ryu was *just* old enough to be taken seriously. In human years, he was probably the equivalent of, say, a thirty-year-old. Anyan was a whole different story. I had the impression he wasn't vastly older than Ryu, but that Anyan had lived just that much longer, during times that were just that much more interesting, to make a huge difference in terms of experience.

Not to mention, he was probably like a million and two in dog years.

So no wonder he didn't want to hear suggestions about my sex life with Ryu.

That said, I wasn't a little girl anymore, and I hadn't been since I held Jason's cold face in my hands and tried to kiss him back to life. And Anyan, along with all the other supes, needed to understand that I might be young by their standards, but I was no child.

Now I just had to figure out how to prove it to them. Partly so I could convince them that Jarl was a genuine threat, something no one but Anyan seemed to believe.

I came back to attention as Camille outlined what she thought our discovery meant.

'Either this is all coincidence, which I doubt, or Jimmu was murdering these halflings in order to stock laboratories.' Ryu nodded, clearly wanting more.

'But why?' she asked. 'And where are these labs, and who was running them?' she continued.

Julian spoke before either Ryu or I could.

'"Why" is relatively straightforward, Mother. Humans can do all sorts of experiments on tissues and organs. But they're tissues and organs you need to live, so . . .'

'Ah,' Camille said, nodding at her son. 'Of course.'

Ryu nodded. 'And as for your other questions, we have no idea. Julian can begin tracing those records as soon as possible. But something tells me we're going to find the same sort of shell organizations that ran Conleth's lab.'

'Basically, then, what you're saying is that there may be a connection between whoever took over the running of Conleth's lab and these other labs, if they exist,' Caleb rumbled in his bass voice from across the table.

Ryu nodded. I noticed that no one had yet said the name 'Jarl'. Interesting.

As if reading my mind, Anyan spoke from the half-shadows of the doorframe.

'The real question is, how much did Jarl know about his nagas' activities.'

'Exactly,' I said, as Ryu winced.

'We can't assume that Jarl is involved,' Ryu insisted. 'We do need to keep an eye on him, yes. But we can't assume he's this sponsor.'

Everyone at the table exchanged glances. I knew that all the supes didn't want Jarl involved. It made everything too big, too portentous. But I could also see the suspicion in their eyes. They trusted their king's second little more than I did.

'Phaedra and her group's presence here does seem . . . odd,' Julian said, as he cleaned his glasses nervously.

'But the Alfar did save Jane last night,' Daoud pointed out.

'There will be no love lost between Jane and Jarl, or Jarl's minions,' Anyan interrupted, touching on the secret he and I shared: that Jarl had attacked me and that he blamed me for his foster children's deaths. I looked to the barghest, but his eyes were shadowed. Was he intimating that we should tell Ryu what had happened?

'At this point, we need to trust Phaedra,' Ryu said. 'Capturing Conleth has to be our first priority. And Daoud's right; she did save Jane.'

I'd seen the look on Phaedra's face, like she'd been surprised to find me under the tree. I wasn't entirely convinced she'd saved *me* so much as she'd reflexively stopped the tree.

'We'd be fools to trust the Alfar,' Anyan said, moving into the light. 'Or any of their suggestions. And I've been told what she *has* suggested, Ryu, and the answer is no.'

Ryu straightened up, setting his shoulders. I had no idea what was going on, but I got the distinct impression that everybody else was suddenly studiously avoiding meeting my eyes.

'I wasn't going to bring that up until I could talk to Jane in private,' Ryu said to the barghest, his voice low and angry.

'Because you knew she would agree before anyone else

could talk sense into her. But I will not put her life in Phaedra's hands.'

The two men were facing one another, and the energy generated by their shields was so intense it was practically sparking. It was going to be like the showdown at the O.K. Corral in a minute.

'C'mon, both of you,' I said, standing up and putting myself between the barghest and baobhan sith. 'This obviously involves me, so spit it out. What did Phaedra suggest, and why don't you want me to know about it?'

Anyan raised an eyebrow at Ryu, who turned toward me with a sigh. 'Phaedra has suggested we use you to trap Conleth, Jane. That we take advantage of his obsession with you, and use you as bait.'

'Wow,' I replied, as Anyan growled. Like, really growled. I didn't realize he could still do that in human form.

'Okay,' I said, turning toward the barghest. 'This is complicated.'

'It's out of the question, Jane,' Anyan said. 'We can't allow this. You *know* we can't trust Phaedra—'

Ryu interrupted by rounding off on Anyan.

'There's nothing to *allow*, Anyan. Jane'll be up for it. I *know* her. Far better than you do.'

'Of *course* she'll do it; that's not the point.' Anyan was furious; he was snarling again. Meanwhile, I was getting tired of being discussed in the third person. 'The point is that she could get killed. She's strong but she has no offensive training. Yet you keep thrusting her into these situations where she can't defend herself.'

'She's got to learn, Anyan. You'd keep her in Rockabill playing with gnomes for the rest of her life.'

'I wouldn't "keep" her anywhere. She's living her life. Training. Learning. She'll be stronger than either of us one day.

But she's not going to live long enough to get there if you don't stop playing your stupid games.'

'Damn it, Anyan!' I shouted, fed up with their fighting. The fact was that they were having two different conversations. Anyan was talking with me about our Jarl secret, while Ryu thought we were talking about Phaedra and Conleth. We were getting nowhere fast, and I was tired of being argued *about* rather than *with*. 'Ryu, stop! Right now. This is pointless.'

I looked between the two men and shook my head. This was gonna suck.

But the truth will come out, my brain reminded me as I asked if we three could be left alone.

Everyone obligingly filed out of the office and then out the front door. Anyan, Ryu, and I followed them into the main room. After I'd locked the main door behind everyone, Anyan immediately started arguing.

'Jane, I know you want to help, but this is too dangerous.' If I didn't know better, I'd think the barghest was begging.

'I know you want us all safe, but this is not about me,' I replied, keeping my voice calm and collected. 'I know that, in terms of experience and ability, I'm the weakest link. But I'm also our best chance. I don't want to rule out the idea of using me to trap Conleth. As long as he's out there killing, then *we're* responsible for all those deaths.'

'I get that, Jane. I know.' The barghest was barely holding his frustration in check, and his long nose was twitching like crazy. 'But think about what you're saying. You're asking me to sit back while you walk into a trap set by *Phaedra*. Don't forget who she works for.'

Anyan and I stared at each other in a silence broken only by Ryu clearing his throat.

'I really don't understand why you're *so* opposed to this, Anyan,' he said.

I looked at my lover and then looked at the barghest. He nodded. We had to tell Ryu what had happened all those months ago.

'Ryu, we have to tell you something, but you can't freak out.'

Ryu blinked at me in surprise. He thought he knew all my secrets, and he did. Except for this one.

He was *so* going to freak out.

'What on earth could you have to tell me?'

I looked at Anyan. He shrugged his massive shoulders, letting me know he was willing to take one for the team. But this was definitely my cross to bear.

'Something happened when I was at the Compound last November. And I didn't tell you about it because if I'd told you, you would have gone loco and gotten yourself killed.'

Ryu's eyes narrowed, but he waited for me to continue. I took a deep breath.

'Remember when Jimmu killed that man Nyx had brought for supper, and was about to kill me, but you jumped on Jimmu?' I could barely follow what I had just said, but Ryu nodded.

'Well, I ran down this hallway.'

'And?'

'And Jarl caught me. He tried to kill me. He was saying all this stuff about how it was all my fault and I'd killed Jimmu. He was strangling me. Anyan hauled him off.'

Ryu's fists clenched, and he stared like I'd been caught shagging a football team and the photos would be in tomorrow's tabloids.

'I was pretty beat up. Anyan took me out to the pool to heal me, where you found us.'

'And you didn't tell me?'

'I couldn't, Ryu.' It was my turn to plead. He had to

understand. 'You're an investigator; you go after the bad guys. I know you would have tried to take on Jarl. And who am I to them? They would never have believed me.'

'They would have believed Anyan Barghest,' Ryu said, a bitter edge to his voice.

'Not in this,' Anyan responded gently. 'You know this would have been too big.'

Ryu sat quietly, while I fidgeted.

'*You* took on Jarl,' he said finally, but not to me.

Anyan shrugged. 'He wasn't expecting me. And he was distracted. He *really* wanted to see Jane dead. Which is why I think this is such a bad idea. Phaedra is Jarl's second, now that Jimmu's gone. You know how she resented the nagas, how she did whatever she could to gain Jarl's favor. Even if she wasn't ordered to get revenge, which I think she probably was, she's got to see killing Jane as a free ticket to Jarl's affections. So even if Jarl hasn't actually ordered her to try to kill Jane, Jane is *still* not safe around her.'

Ryu stayed silent. He was staring at me again. I flushed, squirming beneath the accusatory weight of his gaze.

'You're right, Anyan,' he said finally, in a heavy voice. 'We shouldn't risk Phaedra's trap except as an absolute last resort.'

Oh, gods, I thought. *Why does he have to be all reasonable about this?* I wanted Ryu angry, arguing, not sounding like . . .

Like I've just stuck a dagger in his heart, I realized.

'Babe,' I said, 'I'm willing to do it. I am. We can keep an eye on Phaedra. We can make sure she doesn't pull anything—'

'I know, Jane,' Ryu said, not meeting my eyes. 'I know you're willing. But only as a last resort. And in the meantime, we should keep you away from Phaedra—'

'And she needs more training. Have you worked with her

at all since she's been here?' I winced at Anyan's words. I hadn't trained, and Ryu and I had talked about the fact that I was getting behind.

'No,' Ryu said, gritting his teeth. 'We haven't been training.'

'Well, that changes now. Tomorrow I'll work with her. She needs to learn to use her shields for more than just defense. She needs—'

She needs to apologize to her boyfriend, I realized.

'Anyan, that's enough,' I interrupted, shooting the barghest a beseeching stare. After a second, he nodded, turning to leave.

'I'll, um, leave you two alone. But tomorrow, be ready to train, Jane.' I saluted, but his back was already turned.

'I saw that,' he rumbled. So I gave him the finger.

'That too,' he said, as I went to shut the door behind him.

I stood there, my hand on the doorknob, gathering the courage to turn around and face Ryu.

But he beat me to it.

His hands were gentle on my shoulders as he turned me around.

'Why didn't you tell me?'

'For the reasons I said, Ryu. I knew you'd do something. But I also knew there was nothing either of us could do.'

'It's me, Jane. How could you lie to me?'

I wrapped my arms around his trim hips, pulling myself into him. I hugged him hard, my cheek pressed into his chest.

'I didn't think of it like that. I promise. It's just, when it happened, Anyan thought it would be the best thing. And I understood why. I didn't know you well then, but I knew you wouldn't be able to let it go. All I could think of was that man the nagas had killed just to cover their own backs. They killed him, and chopped his body up, and dumped it out of a sack like it was a bunch of old clothes going to a garage sale.'

Ryu ran his fingers through my hair, and I nuzzled at his chest before raising my head to look into his eyes.

'I'm sorry, Ryu. I never meant to keep anything from you. I just didn't want you to end up in a sack,' I finished lamely.

He stared down at me, his gaze searching. Finally, he sighed and bent his head to kiss me.

'No ending up in sacks,' he agreed as his lips met mine.

'Well, not *all* sacks,' I said, after we'd shared one of Ryu's patented 'toenail scorching, ohmigod why are my eyeballs rolling in my head, and when did my hair curl?' kisses.

'*The* sack is still an option,' I murmured into his mouth as he carried me upstairs and to bed.

CHAPTER TWENTY

The river's energy flowed through me as I concentrated. The ropes around my wrists were just tight enough that I couldn't squeeze my hands through, but not tight enough to hurt. I probed at the knot with my power, but it resisted me. I switched tactics, imagining my power as a knitting needle rather than a finger. I slipped it through the knot finally, and I felt my bindings slacken. When I mentally, and magically, widened the circumference of the needle, I was free.

'Excellent, Jane,' the barghest rumbled as he leaned over to pick up the length of rope coiled on the cold ground behind me.

'Again,' he said, only this time he bound my ankles.

I wouldn't have thought we were at the place in our friendship where it was appropriate for Anyan to tie me up, but apparently desperate times called for a little bondage. This exercise was the first step in getting me to understand how I could physically manifest my power, and it was a helpful trick to know in case I ever did get captured.

It was also really difficult, and I'd wasted oodles of power learning the basics. So I'd also gotten a swim out of training with Anyan, and the experience of cavorting in the Charles

River had been awesome. Okay, a little gross, as it was a city river, but the water had its own distinctive force that felt really different from the ocean. I shivered, remembering how it spoke to me of earth and man and boats and the slice of oars and meandering . . .

'Too tight?' Anyan asked, slipping a thick finger under the rope at my ankles to loosen it. I shivered again, telling myself it was still the river's voice echoing through my body, whispering to me of all the places it had visited.

'No, it's fine.'

The barghest smiled at me, a little ruefully. 'Good. And no hands.'

I nodded, going in and finding my power and working on the knot at my feet. It was a different knot, I realized. I'd done a little sailing around Rockabill and knew there were many knot permutations. This was a clever one, and I wasn't going to be able to muscle through it like I could the others. I opened my eyes to shoot Anyan a withering look. He merely shrugged, as if to remind me that the cookie was already crumbled. I sighed, feeling martyred, and began to probe.

It was hard because my ankles felt farther away than my hands. That, coupled with a knot I had to pull rather than just poke at, meant I sat on the ground for a long time before I was finally free.

Anyan retrieved the rope and went to tie me up again, but I stopped him.

'My ass is frozen. Or asleep. Next time you decide to draw me into your sadomasochistic fantasies, can you at least bring a chair?'

He gave me the stink eye, but he took off his leather jacket and laid it on the ground.

'Thanks,' I said, settling myself on top of the jacket. It helped.

'Okay, now I'm going to truss you up. Like a pig.'

'Really? Like a pig?'

'It's what one trusses, Jane. I'm not calling you a pig.'

'Can't we just say that I get the knots and move on? Do we have to make like pigs and truss?'

'Pigs aren't the ones who truss. I truss; you get trussed.'

'Because I'm the pig.'

'In this exercise, yes. You're the pig.'

I lay down on my side, still grumbling. I'd lost my earlier enthusiasm about my chance to train with Anyan. It was like a workshop with Dominatrix Nell. I stuck my arms and legs in front of me, feeling less like a pig and more like an ass.

'Arms and legs behind you, please.'

'Pigs don't get trussed with their legs behind them,' I pointed out as I shifted so I could stick my arms out behind me, folding my legs up so they were near my arms. 'You'd break their piggy spines if you did that.'

'Well, this is how I truss when I truss people up,' Anyan said, as he commenced roping me.

'Do you truss people often?'

'You'd be surprised.'

For a second, I thought we were flirting but then I remembered that he was tying me up on the icy banks of the Boston University Beach. Cheerful banter had to be a prerequisite for such situations.

'You're lucky I'm flexible, dog breath,' I muttered as he tightened the bindings. They hurt a bit this time.

'I heard that. Now, out.'

'So commanding.'

'Yes. Out.'

It didn't take me long to undo these knots. Once I got the hang of it, I'd proven quite adept at getting out of things. That said, as usual when I learned something new, I was leaking power all over the place, so I had to swim again when we were finished. Anyan perched on the edge of the Charles River, his back toward me, glamouring the hell out of both of us as I stripped down and once again plunged into the Charles. Both the river and I could feel the ocean nearby, and we desperately wanted to go meet it. For a second, I let myself merge with the current, feeling everything it felt and only just managing to hold myself back from plunging madly toward the sea. When I finally emerged, admittedly rather oily and smelling slightly off, I was still happier than I'd been in days.

I rather regretfully dried myself with one of Ryu's expensive towels, certain that river water was not good for fine linens. I popped my clothes back on and returned to where Anyan sat waiting.

'All righty. What's up next?'

We'd already worked on my shields for quite a while, and Anyan had given me some really good tips on where I could strengthen them while at the same time conserve some energy. Eventually, I would build up my defenses to where I could use them to block or carry physical objects, as the others had with the trees at Au Bon Pain. But I wasn't there yet.

That said, the barghest was a good teacher. Anyan was like Nell, patiently building on skills. But he'd go in with me eventually and show me where I was doing something wrong or how I could do something faster or more efficiently. When it had become clear I wasn't getting the shields trick, he'd pulled out a rope, much to my evident consternation. It made sense, however, once I realized what he wanted to teach me. It did help me understand how power could manifest, and, if I did get captured, what Anyan was teaching me would work on most sorts of bindings. You just had to ante up the force to get out of handcuffs, or use a shitload of power if the bindings were magical. But the old probe and push/pull was all you really needed to get out of anything, as long as it was less powerful than you. The trick, however, was not to break your own bones if the binding was too strong.

'Now for something completely different,' the barghest rumbled. He put his hands on my shoulders and settled me squarely in front of him.

'Have you taken any self-defense courses?' he asked.

'Me? No. I've always been of the "turn tail and flee" persuasion.'

Anyan snorted. 'I've chased you. I'm sorry, Jane, but you couldn't outrun a sloth.'

I wrinkled my nose at him. 'Listen, buddy, just because you can go all hellhound doesn't mean you get to judge other people's running ability.'

'When we get back to Rockabill, I'm going to make you start jogging. You're slow as shit, no matter what form your pursuer. Your mother could probably outrun you as a seal.'

'You are *not* getting me to jog. There is not a force on earth that can make me *jog*. And I can outrun a seal, fercrissakes. And speaking of my mother, it's not my fault I inherited her build. I was engineered for comfort, not speed.'

Anyan laughed. 'Okay, fine. But now we live in times that do call for speed. So we're going to work on some basic self-defense.'

'Really? How is me trying to kick somebody like Jarl in the tchotchkes going to do anything? He'll just wallop me with his mojo and I'll be down for the count.'

'Why would you kick Jarl in the decorative knickknacks?'

I sighed. '"Tchotchkes" is too good a word to limit in meaning. It should be used often, as much as possible. And don't tell me you didn't know exactly what I meant when I said, "Kick Jarl in the tchotchkes".'

Anyan eyed me appraisingly. 'Okay, I'll give you "tchotchkes". If you give me "frabjous".'

'"Jabberwocky" frabjous?'

'Yes. Nice ID.'

'I'm good like that.'

'Well, "frabjous" is *my* favorite word. And I feel both ironic and less metrosexual when I say "frabjous" instead of "fabulous".'

'Do you say "fabulous" that often?'

'Again, you'd be surprised. I am an artist, remember. There is a lot of "fabulous" in the art world.'

I grunted, struck again by the fact that I didn't know shit about Anyan. I knew him as a dog, and I was getting a handle on him as a fierce warrior, but he was also this guy who lived in Rockabill and made art. He had a whole 'human' life I knew nothing about.

Anyan ignored my grunt, thank the gods. I really needed to stop grunting at handsome barghests.

'You'd also be surprised at how often a surprise physical attack works on our kind. Especially when they're powerful, like the Alfar.'

'Really?'

'Yeah. That's how I was able to take Jarl so easily when he was throttling you. If I'd thrown a mage ball at him, he'd have had shields up automatically. But he wasn't expecting a physical attack, and I got a chunk out of him before he could react. Then he was wounded, in pain, and never quite recovered his equilibrium. So I threw him at the wall. Another highly effective strategy, but probably not appropriate in your case . . . Anyway, the Alfar, especially – but this goes for any being with a lot of power and control – aren't used to getting thrown off balance. Pain can really unnerve them. They're used to sitting behind their shields and lobbing attacks that

never allow anyone to get close to them. If you can do something that hurts, like break their nose or get in a good bite,
you can really upset their control. Once that happens, they
find it hard to re-establish their calm because they're not used
to anything getting to them in the first place.'

'Huh,' I said. 'That makes sense. Although I'm not so adept
at either the nose breaking or the biting as barghests. You've
got bigger teeth.'

'All the better to eat you with, my dear.'

To my horror, I felt my cheeks flush hot and, most assuredly,
red. There was an awkward half-second pause before Anyan
cleared his throat.

'Right, well, what I'm going to show you is a pretty standard
technique to break a wrist hold. But you can also incorpo-
rate a knee to nut the guy in the forehead. Or nut him in the
. . . tchotchkes.'

With that, he made me grab his wrists and he showed me
his trick. It was all very absurd, since he towered over me
by more than a foot. But it was actually a really cool move,
not that I would ever admit that to him. Because I'm so flexible, like a halfling bendy straw, I was really good at the wrist
thing, as I could bend mine practically double. Of course, it
didn't matter with Anyan, because *he* could practically wrap
his fingers around my wrist twice. Barghests had extra-big
paws as dogs, and there was a direct correlation to their human
form's hands and feet.

I refused to allow my brain to conjecture about any other
legendary 'big hands' correlations.

When we were done, I was tired physically, but revved
magically. My dip in the river had been just what the doctor
ordered. But the swimming had also made me really hungry.
On our way back toward Commonwealth Avenue to catch the
T back to Ryu's, we stopped at a little food stand, which

looked like an old train trolley, to get something to eat. My stomach was yowling so loudly that Anyan could hear it over the traffic noise.

I got a falafel wrap, and he got the vegetarian chili. We eyeballed each other's food as we ate and ended up swapping – without speaking a word – when we'd eaten exactly half. After we finished our snack, we looked at each other, looked at the trolley, and then went and bought a rice and lentil wrap to share. It was delicious, and a mistake, at least on my part. I was bursting at the seams. Especially when the lentils and rice started to expand in my stomach.

I stretched out on the bench, groaning, when Anyan got up to throw away our garbage.

He came back, laughing at me. He picked my feet up, keeping them in his lap when he sat down. I was surprised at the close contact; we'd only ever touched when he was a dog. Except when he was carrying me. Or healing my numerous injuries. Or when he was teaching me to nut people in the forehead. Anyway, we almost never touched except under weird circumstances. So such casual physical proximity kinda threw me. And when I get thrown, I always use the same tried-and-True method to recover: I babble like an idiot.

'Why can I never stop eating? If I wasn't a swimming addict, I'd weigh eight hundred pounds. I'd be one of those people Jerry Springer has to remove a wall to get at. They'd have to take out my bedroom wall, load me on a flatbed, and haul me to Chicago on an eighteen-wheeler. And all so that Jerry could point out, over and over again, that I was really, really fat.'

Anyan listened to me rant, a smile on his face. He looked so relaxed, it made me relax. Which was stupid, since this would make a perfect moment for Conleth to attack. But I could also feel Anyan's power, strong and steady, beating around us. He might look like a lounging, if oversized, biker-grad student, but he was still on duty. So I went ahead and shut my eyes, soaking up the weak February sun falling on our little bench. And tried very hard not to belch garlic into the cold winter air.

We stayed like that for about ten minutes, until Anyan started fidgeting with the laces of my ancient, battered, green Converse.

'Jane?'

'Hmm?' I asked drowsily.

'Can I ask you something? If it's too personal, just tell me to shut—'

Before Anyan could finish his sentence, I felt that weird tingle in the air that had signaled the brownie's First Magic. I tensed, but before I could sit up, there was a soft *poofing* sound and a heavy weight flattened my stomach.

'Ooof,' I grunted, as the brownie peered down at me with its six solid black eyes. It waved at me with its right hands. When it noticed I was turning green, it shifted its weight around until I was no longer at risk of spewing hippie food all over it.

'Uh, hello,' I said to the little creature, who chittered back at me in a friendly voice. Then all six of its beady eyes roamed over my body, with at least three parking their gaze on my boobs.

Then it turned to Anyan and said something that made the very tip of the barghest's nose twitch hard.

When he replied in that strange language, there was laughter at the edges of his gruff voice.

'What did it say?' I demanded, giving the brownie the stink eye. From its face full of thick brown fur, it flashed me a Hollywood smile of alarmingly large, glaringly white teeth.

Before Anyan could make an excuse for the fuzzy little pervert, the brownie had thrown open his many arms, calling to him another file folder. This one was thicker than the last.

Then it winked at me with all three of its left eyes, said something that made the barghest's nose twitch again, and *poofed* back to wherever it had come from.

'Okay, first of all, what is that thing's deal, and second, can we do that?'

Anyan laughed. 'Nope, that's true First Magic, the ability to apparate. Gnomes can do it, but only inside their own territory. That's why they're so strong; their connection with their land gives them access to the First Magics. None of the rest of us can do it at all. As for Terk, he . . . he likes you, that's all. He thinks you're cute, for a hairless giant.'

'Eww, I can't believe you just called me a "hairless giant",' I said, sitting up on my elbows. I started to pull my legs off Anyan's lap, and he responded by pinching the fat of my calf.

'I didn't call you that; Terk did. You're never a giant to me, and you're only hairless when I'm a dog, but that's all relative.'

I frowned at Anyan. 'So, do you, like, think as a dog when you're a dog? Or are you always . . . you?'

He smiled at me and then reached out a hand to help me sit up.

'Always me, Jane. I'm always me.'

Sheepishly, I thought of all the times I'd rubbed his doggy belly, and the time or two I'd cried into his doggy neck. I met his steel-gray gaze and cocked my head querulously.

'Speaking of which, why do you spend so much time as a dog? You've been human this whole time, but I thought you always went around as a dog.'

Anyan frowned, and I wondered if I'd said something

wrong. I was about to tell him to forget about it when he finally spoke.

'It's just simpler that way, Jane,' he replied cryptically. Before I could ask him what he meant, he stood up. 'We should get going. We need to go see what's in this file, and the others are waiting. Ryu will be worried about you.'

I nodded, still mystified. But he was right.

Ryu would be waiting.

CHAPTER TWENTY-ONE

'Where the hell have you been?' Ryu demanded as soon as Anyan and I were in the door.

'Training,' I said. 'We're only a few minutes late—'

'Well, Julian just got a lead on a vacation home owned by Edie, under her maiden name, and when I tried to call, you didn't answer. I had to send Daoud and Caleb with Phaedra's lot. They just left, but why the hell did you turn off your phone?'

'Ryu, I never turned off my phone,' I said, fishing my cell out of my back pocket. To find out that it was, indeed, dead.

'What the hell?' I asked as Anyan pulled out his own phone and swore.

'Damn it, Terk,' he swore.

'Who the fuck is Terk?' Ryu asked as I turned my phone back on. Sure enough, there was a voicemail from right around the time the brownie had appeared on my stomach.

'Brownie,' Anyan grunted, brandishing the folder as he turned on his own phone. 'He apparated this to us.'

'Why would he turn off your phones?'

Anyan looked uncomfortable. 'Terk likes Jane. Thinks she's cute.'

For a hairless giant, I thought, still miffed.

'So why would he turn off both your phones?' Ryu's voice was increasingly impatient.

'He didn't want anyone to interrupt him while he was talking, probably,' Anyan replied, but he looked uncomfortable. Then it hit me.

He wanted to give Anyan and me some alone time, I realized, remembering the big man's reactions to the brownie's mystery words. Anyan looked horrified at the brownie's attempts at matchmaking, which made me unaccountably irritated.

'Uh-huh,' was Ryu's only response. He wasn't convinced.

'Guys,' I piped up. 'Let's not forget about the folder.'

Anyan had already flipped through the contents of the file to make sure that there was nothing so dire it needed immediate action, but we still needed to share the contents with Ryu.

Both men nodded, and Anyan quickly went over everything with Ryu. Basically, Capitola wrote that they'd connected another, more recent death to our investigation. The body was that of a Chicago man, but he'd been killed in a hotel room in New York. He had been burned, but not as badly as the others. The victim had bodyguards who smelled smoke and had been able to put the fire out before the corpse was too charred.

When the NYPD had finished with their autopsy, they'd sent the body back to the Chicago PD. The police, however, had kept the corpse, as this was one death *not* dismissed as an accident. So Anyan's contacts in the Borderlands had sent their own healer to the morgue, where she did her own magical autopsy. All the probes the supernatural healers sent in to fix a body could apparently be used to examine as well. What the healer found was extreme trauma. The man in question had been brutally, efficiently tortured.

Interestingly, this man's attack had occurred just before Conleth had attacked me, in Rockabill. Probably when Con was still in Boston becoming obsessed with me through reading my e-mails. Granted, New York City was much closer to Boston than Chicago, but still . . .

'Okay, I've got an idea,' I said. 'I think that Conleth discovered that note about the same time he was reading my e-mails. He stuck them all together because that's what people do – they use the envelope for their most recent electric bill as a bookmark, that sort of thing. Let's assume this man in New York was tortured for a reason, and not just for the hell of it. What's the most obvious thing he'd be tortured for?'

'More names,' said Anyan, nodding. 'I was thinking the same thing.'

'Technically, we can't rule Conleth out for killing this guy,' Ryu reminded us, and he was right. With the way Conleth could travel, he might be able to get from New York to Boston to Rockabill no problem.

'Well, actually, we can rule Conleth out, maybe,' Anyan interrupted. 'If Conleth was blasting off all over Boston, all the way to New York or Chicago, humans would have seen. They wouldn't have known what he was, but they would have reported something.'

'The infamous gas leak,' I said in agreement. 'Or a comet. Shooting star . . . something.'

'That's good. We'll have Julian get to work looking through the news agencies for reports of unexplained . . . fiery shit.'

I laughed. 'I can do it, too, when we get back. I'm not as good as Julian but I can work Google.'

'Cap also says that they have one more lead, so we'll wait and see what she says.' Anyan jerked his head toward the door. 'In the meantime, should we catch up with the others?'

We'd just stepped through Ryu's front door when his cell phone rang.

'Yeah?' he asked as he locked up with both keys and his magic.

He listened, his face darkening.

'Good work. We'll meet you at the bunker in ten. Thank you.'

Ryu held up his hand, and before we could ask any questions, he was dialing another number. He waited, swore, then dialed another. When that one didn't answer, he swore again, his expression as irritated as I'd ever seen it. This time, whoever he was calling answered immediately.

'Julian, where are you? I need you to head back the other way, to the address I'm going to text you. It's in Vermont. If you see Phaedra's Escalade on the way, get their attention. Caleb and Daoud have their phones off. Which seems to be a trend today,' he said, giving me the gimlet eye. 'Yes, we'll try to be right behind you. If you get to this address before we do, wait for us or for Phaedra. Do you hear me? I don't want you two getting yourselves killed. Wait for backup.'

Ryu flipped shut his phone and then turned toward where Anyan and I waited impatiently.

'That was Stefan. Silver's body's been found. They've got him at the bunker. In the meantime, Daoud's and Caleb's phones are shut off, so Julian and Camille are on their way to Edie's. I do think it's odd that four of my people had their phones taken out of commission when they *never* have their phones off. Are you sure you can trust this Terk creature, or the people he serves?'

Anyan snorted. 'I've known Cap her entire life. She's like a niece to me. Don't make accusations when you have no idea what you're saying.'

I felt a weird flash of relief when Anyan said Cap was like

a niece to him, but at the same time, it confirmed my own suspicions of how he saw me. I was another little girl under his care, and always would be.

I tried not to let any emotion play over my face as Anyan and Ryu argued. Ryu was accusing Anyan of keeping secrets; Anyan was accusing Ryu of being overdramatic. I was wondering whether or not I should invest in a black-and-white-striped shirt, since I spent so much time playing referee.

'Boys,' I interrupted wearily. 'Places to see, people to do . . .'

They both looked at me, confused, before sorting out my lame little joke. They both had the good sense to look sheepish for a second, before we left to visit this mysterious bunker.

The bunker wasn't really a bunker, just a big basement facility that Stefan's team used as a warehouse, lab, and morgue.

There was a blanketed form laid out on the table in the area they used for autopsies. A long, lean figure loomed above the body. The goblin was dressed in scrubs, the pale green of the material bringing out the yellow undertones in the creature's own green scales.

Ryu cleared his throat as we entered the lab.

'Ah, Investigator,' the goblin intoned, turning around only to blind us with the headlamp he wore strapped to his forehead.

We all put a hand over our eyes as he fumbled around with the straps around his head.

'Sorry, sorry . . . always forget about this damned thing . . . There,' he said as the glaring light shut off finally, leaving us blinking in the sudden darkness.

When our eyes adjusted, we moved toward the figure on the table. Ryu rested a comforting hand on the small of my back.

'Where was he found?' asked Anyan.

'Remote part of the state. He wouldn't have been found for months if it weren't for a U.S. Special Forces Combined Field Exercise Convention being held this weekend. They found the body while they were out placing dummy "victims" around a staged terrorist camp.' The goblin peered down at us, and I kept my eyes on his face so I didn't focus on all the person goop spattering his scrubs. 'One of the troops is a nahual and a bedmate of Stefan's. He recognized Silver from seeing him taped up over there . . .' The goblin pointed to a timeline thingie of photos, similar to the one we'd erected in Ryu's office, that had all of Conleth's known and suspected victims pinned up in chronological order of their deaths and/or the dates they went missing. 'He stole the body before the human police could be found, and he brought it straight back here.'

'And you're sure it's Silver?' Ryu asked.

'Oh, yes,' the goblin said as he ushered us forward to the sheeted figure. 'It's definitely your man,' he said as he twitched the sheet down off Silver's face.

My breath caught and my gorge rose as I caught sight of the dead man. Ryu's arms went firmly around my waist, and I went ahead and hid my face in his arm.

I'd seen death before, but not this sort of death. Not the kind of death enacted by someone who sought pain, who wanted to hear the victim scream.

Silver's poor face was ruined. One eye was gone, and the other was shut, swollen in a face deformed by bruising and what appeared to be burn scars.

For, yes, there was evidence of fire on Silver's body. But not Conleth's all-consuming, rage-induced fire. This was clever fire, used efficiently for maximum pain.

Anyan handed the goblin the file that Capitola had put together for him.

'There's an autopsy in there. A victim who might be connected to this one. See any similarities?'

The goblin coroner read the report, occasionally nodding his head.

'Yes, the two victims show nearly identical damage, including internal injuries. Some of a sexual nature,' the goblin added, averting his eyes from mine.

'Good gods,' I mumbled, my eyes filling with tears for the old man who, despite having kept Conleth a prisoner, never deserved to die in this manner.

Ryu kissed the top of my head as Anyan walked to the body to re-cover Silver's battered face.

'Thank you,' Ryu said to the goblin as he turned me toward the morgue door. 'Let us know if you find anything more.'

'Wait, Investigator. I have yet to show you the best part. Come, come,' the goblin said, taking up a position by Silver's feet and waving at us to return to the body.

I clutched Ryu's hand as we all gathered around the end of the table. I wasn't sure I wanted to see what the goblin considered 'the best part'. At the same time, I knew that I'd demanded to be a part of this investigation, and I didn't get to wimp out as soon as it got rough. So I commanded my stomach not to revolt and I stared forward toward the sheet.

Which the goblin flipped back to reveal something that made me gasp and made Ryu's hand convulse in mine as he swore. I looked up to see Anyan staring down at the legs, before turning to the goblin.

'Those look like—' he began to say.

'Claw marks,' the goblin finished for him. 'That's how Silver was carried to the site. By the legs, in something's claws. Something like—'

'Something like a harpy,' interrupted Anyan.

I let Anyan's words sink in, watching as Ryu made the same set of connections.

He hissed suddenly, scrubbing a hand through his hair. 'If it was Kaya or Kaori,' he said, 'it still doesn't mean they've turned on us.'

Anyan nodded. 'True. They could have tortured Silver for more information. Maybe they believed he was holding back. Neither they nor Phaedra would balk at harming a human.'

'But where are Stefan's deputies?' I asked. Both men gave me a grim look as Ryu let go of my hand and began shouting for Stefan to get Julian on the phone immediately.

After he'd barked a series of commands to Camille and Julian, we were off to find Phaedra.

And fast.

CHAPTER TWENTY-TWO

When we finally arrived at Edie's vacation home, two and a half hours away in Brattleboro, Vermont, the place was eerily quiet. We parked on the street at the end of the long driveway, across from Ryu's car. We had Caleb's SUV, since he was with Phaedra, and Camille and Julian had been sent ahead in Ryu's BMW. The whole way to Vermont, I'd sat in the backseat staring at where Caleb's horns had ripped up the roof's upholstery, praying for their safety.

As we climbed out, Julian and Camille came to greet us.

'We just got here about twenty minutes ago,' Camille reported, her usually calm voice tense. 'There was no sign of Phaedra on the way. We scouted from the outside of the house and it appears empty. But the door's been jimmied.'

'Damn it, I told you two not to engage!' Ryu snarled, his anxiety making him testy.

'I know, and we didn't go in,' Julian said, his mother putting a reassuring hand on his shoulder.

'All right, everyone fan out. Camille, Julian, with me. Jane . . .' Ryu's voice trailed off as he tried to come up with something for me to do. Probably something out of the way.

'Jane's with me,' Anyan said. 'We'll take the grounds; you take the house.'

Ryu gave Anyan a hard look. 'Keep her safe, Anyan Barghest,' he demanded, before turning in a flare of power that joined with that of Camille and Julian.

They stalked toward the house, where the door did, indeed, sit askew on its hinges. I prayed that Edie and Felicia weren't dead behind those broken doors.

'Shields up, Jane. Remember what we worked on yesterday,' Anyan said, his deep voice as comforting as the hand he laid on my shoulder. I did as he asked, feeling paradoxically safe out here with him, even though I knew that the shit was, once again, winding itself up to meet the fan.

As the others went inside, Anyan and I walked toward the garage that sat to the right of the house. I felt his power wrap around both of us like a protective cloak as he used his shields to raise the scissor door on the garage. The barghest had some serious abilities when it came to physically manifesting his power; he could almost use it like a second set of hands.

We both cursed when the door was finally raised and we saw that the garage did, indeed, contain a car with Massachusetts plates and a Cambridge parking sticker.

After peering around the otherwise-empty garage, we made our way to the back of the house.

I could see Ryu and the others framed in various windows. No one was being attacked, and they hadn't seemed to have found anything, either. There was no shouting or excitement or screams, just silence as their figures moved from window to window.

Anyan and I stalked about the backyard, his big nose twitching as he smelled the air.

'Seems clean,' he rumbled as we walked the borderline

between the mown lawn and the high grass that constituted the rest of the country property.

I nodded my agreement, peering out into where the grass gave way to trees. I could have sworn I saw something—

'There,' I said, pointing. 'Anyan, there's a path.'

And so there was, cutting through the brush. It appeared to loop back into the trees behind the house.

The barghest took the lead, using both magical probes and scents carried on the wind to scout our way down the slender trail.

'Water,' he muttered, aware of things I couldn't yet see that made sense only when we rounded a corner and suddenly, in front of us, there was another small, mown glade encircling a pond. It was obviously a swimming hole, as there was a small wooden dock jutting out of the water strewn with pool noodles and two fancy floaties. It was a beautiful spot, unmarred, luckily, by the bodies of the two humans.

Or any sign of our friends.

We sighed and I walked toward the dock. I was starting to realize that I really, really wasn't brave. I was the girl who always sat in the back of the theater, eyes hidden under her coat, thinking at the heroine of the horror film, *Don't open that door! Don't you dare open that door! Why would you? Ohmigod, she's opening the door* . . .

And yet, there I was, creeping out onto the wood of the dock, waiting for something to jump out at me from the water, thinking, *Why am I walking out on this dock? Why would I do this? Who walks out on the dock?!*

But nothing happened, and I was safe. Not least because Anyan watched me the whole time, sending his own strength into my shields, his nose twitching.

He could probably smell my fear. So much for playing the warrior.

I finally crept out to the end of the dock and slowly, carefully peered over the edge. There was nothing: no bodies, no Conleth, no nothing. Just a wayward floatie, half inflated.

'You're doing great, Jane,' Anyan's voice rumbled from behind me suddenly, causing me to jump.

I held my hand over my racing heart as I turned to find him studiously not laughing.

'Don't *do* that! You nearly gave me a coronary!'

The barghest's control broke and he chuckled. 'Sorry. Can't help it. Used to walking quietly.'

'Yes, well, Mr McCreeperson, let's not sneak up on Jane. Or Jane might pee in her pants.'

'Why are you referring to yourself in the third person? That's weird.'

'You're weird.'

We paused, and then smiled at each other, satisfied with our exchange. I liked the way the skin around his eyes crinkled into crow's feet when he smiled.

'There's more path,' Anyan said, interrupting my reverie.

'Hmm?'

'There's more path,' he repeated, nodding his head toward the opposite side of the little glade.

'Crap,' I said, making my way toward solid ground. But before I could get there, Anyan grabbed my arm.

'Jane, I just want to tell you that I'm serious. You really are doing great. I know you're scared, but you're fighting it. That's all any of us can do.'

I blushed, ducking my face. 'Thanks, Anyan,' I replied, as we set off toward the other end of the path.

I had little time to bask in the barghest's affections, however, for as soon as we neared our destination, Anyan tensed.

'Behind me, Jane,' he muttered. If I thought his power had been blanketing me before, it was now almost a physical weight on my shoulders as we walked down the trail. Eventually, we came across another little track branching off from ours. Anyan turned to peer down that trail, his nose twitching furiously. He finally started to walk forward, with me practically treading on his heels as I concentrated on keeping my own defenses up to supplement his. When he stopped dead in his tracks, I was so close behind him that I crashed into him with an 'Oof.' He reached behind himself, steadying me on my feet and holding me still. My nose was pressed into the leather of his jacket, my breasts into the small of his back. I also recalled he had stuffed quite a big can in those ragged-looking jeans. *Barghest got back*, I thought, feeling a powerful – and entirely inappropriate – urge to spank him. Then I remembered biting that same derriere all those months ago, and my cheeks flushed.

We moved forward again, Anyan's hand still on my waist, keeping me pressed against him. My cheeks grew even hotter, and I couldn't believe I was reacting like this, considering the circumstances. I didn't know what Anyan had smelled, what was going on, but it couldn't be good. And yet all I could think of was the feel of Anyan's body against mine as we strode forward.

'What's going on?' I whispered, trying to refocus my energy, just like I'd been told.

'Blood,' he whispered, and my libido fizzled away as if it had never awakened to begin with.

'Shit,' I replied.

'That too,' he murmured, distracted by everything the wind was carrying to him.

We stopped again, and I peered around his big frame to see that in front of us was a little house. It looked like an oversized children's playhouse or a small artist's studio. *Or a writer's retreat*, I realized, my heart falling into my boots.

'Stay here, Jane,' he murmured, but I kept on his heels as we walked forward. I wasn't going to let him face whatever was in there alone.

The door to the little studio was locked, but Anyan didn't bother with mojo. He just raised a big-booted foot and kicked in the door. It swung open, banging against the wall. Two bodies lay splayed, drenched in blood that looked fresh. Anyan swore, trying to pull me behind him before I saw too much. But it was too late. I screamed once: a short, sharp burst that took all my lung capacity. I clapped my own hand over my mouth a second before Anyan did.

He turned me around and pulled me to him to shield my eyes from the sight of Edie's and Felicia's bodies. For they were definitely dead. Very definitely dead. And, from the amount of blood on the floor, walls, and the ceiling, and the haunting expressions on their shattered faces, they hadn't died easily.

'Shh,' he said, but it wasn't to comfort me. It was a sharp shush, meant to stop my horrified bleating. He pulled me out of the doorframe and onto the studio's little porch. Pulsing with power, his shields held me still behind him as he sniffed, raising a hand that suddenly held a swirling-green mage ball.

Anyan pivoted just as Fugwat broke cover and ran toward us from the trees to our left. Still unsure of his intentions, we waited until he fired a mage ball directly at us, not breaking stride. The spriggan was surprisingly fast for something so bulky, but he was no match for Anyan's own aim or power. The barghest blasted Fugwat square in the chest with a crushing wave of force, and even though his shields absorbed most of the blow, it was still powerful enough to send the spriggan skidding over the ground.

We heard a shout from our right, and suddenly Graeme was running at us, his beautiful face contorted in rage.

Anyan was still holding down the struggling spriggan with his power, and I knew if the barghest came to my aid, it would be at the expense of unleashing Fugwat. So I concentrated, putting all the power I had into making my shield not just a barrier for magic, but on making it a wall.

And with a satisfying *thump*, the incubus bounced off my shields like he was a giant rubber ball. Landing on his back in an undignified sprawl, he shot me a look of pure venom. But before he could rise, Ryu was there, summoned by my scream. Graeme crab-crawled backward to where his compatriot lay, as the three baobhan sith approached, wicked-looking mage balls sizzling in their upraised hands. Graeme knew he was bested, and his body sagged where he sat.

Meanwhile, Anyan concentrated his power on holding down the spriggan, so I shifted my own shields to encompass both of us. He smiled at me, funneling everything he had into pinning down the small giant, leaving me in charge of protecting us.

Part of me thought he was nuts, but another part of me appreciated the faith he had in me.

Ryu walked around to the studio, poking his head inside. His free hand clenched into a fist, and when he turned back to face the culprits, I could tell he was barely containing his fury.

'What the hell have you done?' Ryu demanded of our two prisoners, his voice cold with rage.

Both males stared up at him mutinously, silent.

'Who are you working for? Phaedra? Jarl? Yourselves?'

Neither Graeme nor Fugwat spoke. Ryu nodded to Anyan, and I felt the barghest's power *squeeze* around Fugwat. The spriggan endured for a while, before he gasped. But before he could break, Graeme interrupted.

'Torture us all you want, baobhan sith. You'll get nothing. We serve a greater cause than ourselves.'

There was an iron intractability in the incubus's voice that seemed to boost Fugwat's own resolve. The spriggan pressed his meaty face into the earth, as if to gag himself.

'Fine,' Ryu said, glancing in my direction. I wondered what he would have done had I not been there. 'Maybe Orin and Morrigan can loosen your tongues.'

Ryu straightened, his voice taking on a crisp tone of authority. 'Graeme Incubus and Fugwat Spriggan,' he said, 'You are hereby charged with endangering the secrets of our race and violating our code of human-Alfar relations. You are stripped of all rights as of this moment, including the right to fair combat. With these words I commend you to the tender mercy of our king and queen. Let their judgment—'

'As the humans say, "Not so fast, Investigator . . ."' chimed a voice from above our heads.

Phaedra.

A harpy set the Alfar down on the roof of the studio. She peered down at us, her face calm as Kaya, or Kaori, fluttered away. She was making a point: Alfar didn't need any backup.

'We have your people, Phaedra. And we know what they've done,' Ryu shouted. He was losing control of his temper, fast.

'You have nothing,' the little woman replied, 'except for dead humans and theories. You have also forgotten that I, too, have *your* people.' From behind us, both harpies prodded our friends out into the little clearing around the studio. Caleb and Daoud were battered and bruised, but they were alive.

'You are interfering with an official Court investigation, Phaedra, and your minions have committed crimes that will end in their execution,' Anyan growled, not letting up his hold on the spriggan.

'Interfering? How? My people have committed no crime,' Phaedra purred. 'You attacked them for no reason. They were merely investigating the murder of these two *unfortunate* women, just like you . . .'

I looked to where Graeme and Fugwat lay, covered in blood that wasn't their own. Was she serious? They *had* to have killed those women. They *had* to—

'You *lie*, Alfar,' Ryu roared, and the shields around him ignited in an eerie blue light. My boyfriend did have some mad skills at his disposal.

'Enough,' Phaedra hissed as we heard a gasp behind us. The harpies had raised a wickedly sharp, hooked claw to the throats of both Caleb and Daoud. The harpy holding Daoud either Kaori or Kaya, had already pierced deep into the djinn's neck.

'We are at an impasse. We have your men; you have ours. You believe one story . . . I think that the Court will believe another. So I suggest we make an exchange . . . your men's lives in exchange for a race. Whoever makes it to the Compound first gets to tell their version of events. And then we can let our king and our queen decide.' Phaedra's smile was cold, calculated, and confident. She knew who Jarl would side with and that Orin and Morrigan would follow his lead, at least publicly.

'Never,' Ryu snarled, but his protestations were cut short by a strangled gasp from Daoud as the harpy's claw slashed across the djinn's throat. I'd seen Daoud's uncle, Wally, seamlessly replace his own amputated arm, and Daoud was doing something similar with his own torn flesh. But every time he healed himself, the harpy cut deep again. Blood was everywhere, and Daoud's face grew unhealthily pale as the harpy who held him slashed at his throat again and again—

'You have a choice, Investigator. Eventually your man will bleed out, and not even a djinn can recover from a true death. Do we have a deal?'

Ryu's shoulders were so tense with anger he was already quivering. He glanced at Anyan, who, after a brief moment, nodded.

'Fine,' Ryu barked, his voice brittle with resentment. 'Let my men go. And we *will* see you back at Court—'

Before he could finish his sentence, Kaya (or Kaori) slashed once more across Daoud's throat. To our horror, her sister Kaori, or Kaya, did the same to Caleb. The satyr's hands found his throat, holding shut the wound and beginning to heal himself, but the djinn dropped to the ground like a stone.

Anyan turned with a shout to Caleb, letting up on the spriggan as he did so. Fugwat, his brute face awash in anger, made as if to follow him. I threw up another of my springy, physical shields at the barghest's back, feeling my power eaten up by the unfamiliar exercise. But my shield held, and the spriggan bounced back, to be grabbed by the incubus and dragged toward the harpies. Phaedra's gang hightailed it out of there, leaving us to attend to our wounded.

Anyan was already healing Caleb, while Ryu worked on Daoud. We all cooled our heels, waiting. If Camille, Julian, or I ran after the Alfar, we were toast. So we watched as Anyan finished with Caleb, and then both men immediately turned their attention to Daoud. For our part, we funneled power to the satyr so that his exhausted body could still pump healing energy into the ragged wounds in his friend's neck.

After what felt like hours, but could have been only about twenty minutes, Caleb looked up.

'He'll live. But he needs a blood transfusion as soon as possible.'

The satyr stood, swaying a bit before Julian ran up to charge the big man with elemental force until Caleb could draw his own power from the earth.

Anyan gathered Daoud up in his arms, cradling him as Ryu barked orders.

'Julian, hot-wire Edie's car and get Daoud and Caleb to the nearest healer in the area. Camille, you and Anyan take the SUV. Jane, with me. Phaedra can't have gotten too far . . .'

I'd never taken part in a chase, but I panted alongside the others as we raced back to our cars, and I belted myself in as quickly as I could when Ryu practically threw me in his car.

Then we were off, peeling away down the dirt road, away from where Edie and Felicia lay, cooling in their own blood. I closed my eyes at that thought, knowing that I would have to deal with the deaths of those two women sometime, but all that grief and remorse would have to come later.

I took a deep breath as Ryu shouted at Anyan over his phone; they were trying to figure out the best way to the Compound from where we were. Anyan thought they should try to catch up with Phaedra; Ryu thought we should try to beat them back to the Compound. And even though one was a vampire and one was a shape-shifter, they were both male. So both had to be right and neither could stop and ask for directions.

It's funny, in the movies, everyone in a chase scene always seems to know where they're going. They never run into dead ends, or trains, or—

I was just starting to enjoy my musings when, as if on cue, came the attack.

One minute Ryu was arguing and I was pondering the unrealities of action blockbusters; the next everything was awash in fire and the car was spinning like a top. Ryu was swearing, trying to get the BMW back under control when another blast of heat and energy hit us. Everything went upside down, confusingly, until I realized *we* were upside down. The car flipped once, twice, and then landed on Ryu's side on the edge of the road.

Everything was bleary, not least because of the blood that was dripping from a cut on my forehead down into my eyes. I shook my head, trying to clear it, while I called out Ryu's name.

He lay unmoving against the smashed glass of the side window. His body was twisted up in his seat belt, his eyes closed. I tried to reach for him, but my own arms were trapped in a tangle that I realized was my deflated air bag.

I finally unwound myself and touched his shoulder, just as his eyes fluttered open. Relief washed through my system but it was short-lived. My lover's eyes had barely focused on me when they widened. He called my name as I heard a loud wrenching sound behind me. Suddenly, there was a hand on my shoulder and a sharp pain in my neck. My mouth went slack as my limbs went numb. I felt myself pulled upward into the waiting arms of our attacker.

Conleth's insane blue eyes met mine as I sank into his gaze. I struggled, my vision starting to blur, until I felt my muscles fall slack against him. He caressed my cheek with one hand while the other held me close. As everything went dark, I heard him murmuring my name over and over, like a prayer, while I was swallowed by darkness.

CHAPTER TWENTY-THREE

The fog clouding my brain dispersed slowly, leaving a dull ache in its place. I tried to raise my head but it wasn't responding. I tried again, with more force, and my head lolled backward on my neck like an egg on a string.

I knew two things. The first was that I was completely fucking terrified. I was terrified that Con had killed Ryu, terrified that I was in Con's clutches, and even more terrified that I knew exactly what Con wanted from me. It involved making super-babies, and it did *not* involve clothes. Which, except for my jacket, I was pretty sure I was still wearing, thank the gods, since he could have done anything to me while I was unconscious.

Not that you would know if he raped you, since you still can't feel your legs, my brain reminded me unhelpfully. I swore at my brain for making me, on top of everything else, suddenly terrified of not feeling my legs.

Besides my multiplicity of terrors, however, I knew one good thing. I was near water. And not just water, but the ocean . . . *my* ocean. I could feel the Atlantic beckoning. She was seething, enraged at my predicament, demanding I return to her. Either that or there was a storm front passing.

I kept my eyes shut, feigning unconsciousness, and did my best to hear something, anything, that would tell me where Con was or where I was. Meanwhile, my extremities were starting to get a pins-and-needles feeling that really hurt, but also informed me that I seemed to be sitting, and that my hands – but not my feet – were definitely bound.

One for the barghest, I thought.

I couldn't hear anything, so I cracked my eyelids. No one was standing above me, and my neck was finally in my own control so I raised my head slowly.

'There you are, Jane,' Conleth cooed lovingly from somewhere to my left.

Fuck, I thought, shuddering at the sound of his voice.

The ifrit halfling was sitting cross-legged on the floor. His fire was totally banked, and he looked like any tall, skinny, middle-class white guy on the street.

I couldn't tell what he was doing for a moment. Then I realized he had his finger jammed in a long-dead electrical outlet. I felt a strange pull from him, as if his power were calling to something, and suddenly I saw electricity surge up his arm.

Conleth's face slackened in pleasure, and I realized he was recharging.

I always wondered how ifrits got their power, I thought. Despite the circumstances, I was also fascinated by how Conleth called the power he needed to him. But I also needed to figure out where the fuck I was, so I stopped staring at Con and started looking around the room. It was a big empty space that looked like it could have been an office. It was familiar, though, in a weird way, and after a second I realized why.

It's got the same kind of crap he had at his squat, I realized, looking around. There was a battered old desk that probably belonged to the chair upon which I was currently tied. A stained mattress lay in one corner, and junk-food wrappers were strewn about everywhere. *Con must have been living here since we found his place in Southie . . .*

After a few more minutes at the plug, Conleth stood, wiping down his bedraggled jeans before coming toward me.

'Sorry I had to drug you, Jane, but I knew I didn't have time to explain. So I figured this was easiest.' Conleth sounded genuinely apologetic, and I realized that he thought, given a chance to talk, that I would have agreed to come with him. Which meant that he still thought I was on his side.

I cleared my throat, trying to find my voice. My tongue was dry and wooden.

'Need a drink?' Con asked, and I nodded. He walked away and came back with a bottle of water.

'I know, I know,' he soothed as he uncapped the bottle and raised it to my lips. I greedily drank nearly half the liter. 'The drug I used makes you thirsty. It does make you sleep, but I still always hated that one, for the thirst.'

His words hit me like a fist. I hated this creature, but hearing him talk so nonchalantly about the fact that he'd had his entire life *stripped* from him made me shudder with pity. I closed my eyes to blink back tears as Con crouched in front of me again.

He started rubbing my legs gently, but he might as well have been branding me with his hands. As the feeling returned to my limbs, it felt like little knives were dancing over my flesh. I whined, and the tears broke free, rolling down my cheeks.

'I know, it hurts. I'm sorry,' Con said, stricken.

I gritted my teeth against the pain and nodded.

'Not your fault,' I managed to croak.

He smiled beatifically. 'No, it's the drugs. But it'll wear off soon.'

Keep him talking, keep him distracted, I thought, as his massaging hands started to wander up toward my knees.

'How?' I mumbled, fighting my still-dry throat. 'How do you know these things?'

'Like what?'

'Drugs. Computers.'

Conleth laughed, but there was no real mirth in his tone. 'What else did I have to do, trapped in that lab all my life? When I was younger, they let me play outside, but by the end, I wasn't even allowed to leave my cell. Except to go for testing.'

His voice was grim, and I felt another surge of sympathy, even as my skin crawled as his hands made their way up over my knees toward my thighs.

'You're smart,' I said, trying to distract him.

'Yeah, well, it was either learn stuff like that or go crazy.'

His strategy wasn't entirely effective, I thought, still forcing myself to meet his mad blue eyes.

'More water?' I asked. I was still really thirsty, but he was also groping my inner thighs.

'Of course,' he said, his voice suddenly deeper.

Not good, I thought as my still-loopy brain scrambled to think of a way to distract him.

He gave me another long drink and then tossed away the now empty bottle. He stood in front of me, staring down and letting his eyes rove over my body. The sight was more terrifying than if he'd raised a fist.

'Can you untie my arms?' I hazarded. 'They hurt.'

'No, sorry. I know it's just because you don't know me yet, but until we're friends, I can't let you go.'

I watched him, noting how his own power flared up and down erratically. Every once in a while, his fire burst free, and I couldn't believe just how much mojo he had at his disposal while having so little control. He crouched down in front of me again, reaching for me—

'What was it like?' I asked, my voice overly loud. Con paused, his eyes snapping back to my face.

'What was what like?'

'Growing up the way you did.'

Conleth sat back on his heels and gave me a hard look. He obviously didn't like my line of questioning, but I persevered.

'You don't have to talk about it if you don't want to. But I want to know. If we're going to be friends, we should be able to talk . . .'

He shook his head and sat backward onto his bottom, crossing his long legs, indian-style. He looked so young sitting like that, and so vulnerable. I wondered what it was inside of him that switched on, or off, when he killed.

'Okay, okay. You're right.'

I waited for him to begin, glad for the respite from his touch but dreading what I was about to hear.

'It wasn't that bad, really. For a long time.'

I cocked my head, giving the ifrit halfling my best 'listening' face.

'I mean, I didn't know any better. I wasn't born in the lab, but I might as well have been. I got there when I was really young.' He stopped talking to stare at his feet, lost in thought.

'How'd you get there? Into the lab?' I prompted, even though I knew the basic facts already.

Con shivered and started wringing his hands nervously. 'It's pretty fucked up,' he said.

'It's okay, Con,' I said. 'What happened?'

'I was just a baby. Probably only a few months old. My mother was human. Bitch abandoned me at a convent. I know that a nun called the police around midnight, reporting tha a baby had been left on the doorstep. She said she was only awake because she'd had a bad dream. Cops said they were busy and couldn't get there right away. The nun said she was enjoying taking care of me. Then there was crying in the background, and all of a sudden the nun was screaming. I must have gotten upset and burned the place down. Everyone in the convent died.'

'My god,' I breathed.

'I was born a killer, I guess,' he said. Shame laced his voice, along with a strange, fierce pride. Conleth was a whole hot mess of crazy.

'How do you remember what happened? What the nuns said?'

Con shook his head. 'No, someone played me the nine-one-one recording. Someone . . . who came later.'

'Later?'

'Yeah, when the lab . . . changed.'

'Oh,' I said. Then we sat in silence. He was probably thinking about what had been done to him under the new regime, but I was wondering how much he knew about the power structure behind his lab. And how to get him to tell me what I wanted to know.

'It was okay before that,' he said eventually.

'The lab?'

'Yeah. Like I said, I didn't know any better. And they treated me pretty well. I mean, some of the tests hurt or were scary, but the nurses were nice and the doctors, especially Dr Silver, seemed to care.'

'They probably did care, Con. They'd raised you.'

He snorted. Unlike my snorts, his was made up of fire. 'Whatever. I thought they cared because I didn't know any better. But none of them did. I was just a job for them, an experiment. They kept me happy because it made the testing easier. And because, although I didn't know it at the time, I could blow them all to hell.'

I nodded. He'd certainly illustrated his 'blowing to hell' abilities.

'So what happened when the lab changed?'

He fell silent for a while, gathering himself. I waited, entertaining myself by crinkling my forehead to watch the dried blood flake onto my jeans.

'It was slow. Happened over time,' he answered finally. 'The nurses began to change. Then the doctors. Finally it was all different. Even Silver was fired. That's when I realized how lucky I'd been.'

'What did they do?' I prompted gently.

He looked up to meet my eyes, and his were haunted. If he'd looked vulnerable before, now he looked . . . devastated.

'What didn't they do? Some of it was sort of like what they'd always done but some of it . . . I think it was just to hurt me. There was one doctor . . . he was the first to come to the lab that wasn't . . . human. Not the last, but the first. He's how I learned I wasn't alone. He called himself "the healer", and that was it. I don't know what he was, and the humans all thought he looked normal. But he was using his magic, because he was anything *but* normal. He looked like he was part . . . lizard.'

Goblin? I thought, even as I asked Conleth for more details.

'Like I said, he looked half lizard. His nose was sort of flat and snakelike, and he was mostly sort of scaly. But his face had human flesh and his eyes were human. And his hands looked human . . . but for his claws . . .' Con's voice trailed off, and he wiped his palms on his jeans, as if trying to wipe away a bad memory. He had totally retreated inward at this point, and he was talking as much to himself as to me. In the meantime, I was still trying to figure out what this healer could have been. What had I met that looked half lizard?

Maybe a nahual trying to scare him? And then my brain hit on the obvious. *Or a goblin halfling . . .*

'He was even worse than the woman and her pet psycho.'

'Well,' I said soothingly, for Con was getting agitated. And his agitation took the form of tiny fireballs that flew out of him, landing willy-nilly around the room. I swiftly pulled a bit of water out of the air to dampen one that had landed on my jeans. I figured he was talking about people he'd killed while he was escaping, so I said, 'You took care of them, right, when you escaped?'

Con looked at me darkly. 'No. The woman wasn't there that day and neither was the healer. He was there a lot to begin with, but I think he got promoted.' Con's voice grew even colder to match his eyes. 'He was good at his job, after all. Really into pain. He did things . . .' Conleth fell silent again, and I knew this silence wasn't to be broken.

'He did bad things,' I said, trying to let him off the hook and let him know he didn't have to continue if he didn't want to.

But that's not how Con took it. He looked up sharply, his power flaring in a white-hot burst of flame.

'What the fuck do you know about it, Jane?'

I blinked, confused by his sudden anger. My kidnapper and I had been getting along so well up till then.

'Your life has been a fucking cake walk. What do you know about pain? About humiliation?' Conleth stood up, advancing on me.

'Con, I didn't mean—'

'No, fuck you, Jane. You had a boyfriend die. Your loving mother left you with your loving father. So you did some time in a *real* hospital, watched over by your family

and friends. What the fuck do you know about suffering?'
Conleth's voice was steadily rising, as was the heat pulsing
off of him.

'You're right,' I said soothingly. 'I'm sorry—'

'The shit they did to me toward the end, Jane . . .' His voice
broke and his fire died, revealing shoulders slumped in an
agony of recollection. But it was only a momentary lapse,
and soon enough his fire sprang back to life and he advanced
on me another step.

'I thought we could be friends, Jane, but maybe you can't
understand me. Maybe you're just like everyone else. What
the fuck do you know?' he repeated, reaching out a flaming
hand toward me.

I flinched backward, throwing up a strong shield and pulling
some water out of the ocean-laden air that doused his fire as
his hand penetrated my hastily erected barrier. I didn't want
to piss him off by not letting him touch me, but I also didn't
want my cheek barbecued.

'You're right. I'm sorry!' I cried, letting the tears I'd been
holding back fall free. 'I'm sorry! I can't understand. I *have*
been lucky. But I want to try, Conleth. I want to get to know
you.'

His hand gripped my jaw as he searched my eyes, trying
to discern whether or not I was lying. Which I was, by the
way – like a fucking rug. There had been a minute, early on,
when I wondered if I wouldn't be able to get through to him,
maybe coax him in to get the help he needed. And to see
some justice done.

Now I realized that was a total pipe dream. Yes, he was a
victim. But Con was too much of a loose cannon for me to
handle. I needed to get the fuck out of Dodge, not attempt
to play counselor.

But I didn't let my eyes say any of those things. I just

made my already big, black eyes look extra baby seal. He seemed to like what he saw, for he nodded, finally, and took a step back, trying to regain his self-control. What there was of it.

'I'm sorry, Con. Really, I'm so sorry. You're right. I don't know you yet, but give me a chance.'

'You should be sorry.'

'I am, Con. I am. So sorry.'

'What happened to me . . .' His voice trailed off, as did his power, leaving only sadness in its wake.

'What happened to you was monstrous, Conleth. What you had to endure is beyond horrible.'

Con hung his head, then sat down heavily at my feet. He laid his cheek against my knee. His back shook and, after a stunned moment, I realized he was crying.

'I hoped you'd understand,' he snuffled. 'I thought, when I read your writing, that you could know me. Really *know* me.'

I made soothing noises, all the time using the cover of my still-erect shields to start poking at the knots at my wrists. Con might be a computer whiz, but he obviously had never done any sailing. I was pretty sure he'd tied me up with a bow, double knotted.

'You know what I find most ridiculous, Jane? The word "halfling". I couldn't believe when that woman told me we were called "halflings".' Con snorted after he'd gotten his tears under control. 'As if we're "half" of anything.' He rubbed his cheek against the outer thigh of my jeans, and I could feel his heat through the material. I pushed harder at the knot, doing my best to maintain both shields and my probing knitting needle of power, despite the fact that Con had shifted around to kneel in front of me and was making very free with the leg touching.

'Tell me about it,' I improvised. 'I'm so tired of having to deal with the purebreds. And the humans.'

Luckily, Conleth stopped staring at my crotch to grin at me.

'I knew it! I knew you didn't mean that stuff you'd written to that investigator. I knew you were just telling him those things so he wouldn't understand how much you really hated him.'

'Erm, yes. Obviously. Totally lied to him,' I agreed, as I probed more desperately at my bindings. I'd have to advise Anyan that double-knotted bows were bizarrely effective as trussing mechanisms.

'That's great, Jane. Great. I'm so glad to hear you say it.'

Con was beaming at me, so I beamed back at him as I changed tactics, trying to remember what I did when I untied my beloved green Converse. I began plucking at my bindings with my power, trying to get the right angle.

'There were a few times I thought you really did love him,' he admitted, as he leaned toward me. Visualizing my power as my favorite kitchen tongs, I had a good grip on the rope at my wrists and I pulled sharply. My bindings slackened and fell, my shields absorbing and camouflaging the surge of power I'd expended. I clasped my hands behind my back to keep from revealing my newfound freedom.

'But I knew you couldn't really be into somebody flashy, like him. I mean, you two have nothing in common . . .'

I let Con babble at me as I flexed my wrists, trying to get some feeling back into my arms. I had an idea, but I didn't know if it would work or not. And if it did work, it'd probably use up the majority of my stored energy.

I was, however, running out of options. A point driven home by Con's face slowly descending toward mine. He kissed me, his lips wet and surprisingly cold. He moaned in ecstasy, and I only barely controlled my overpowering urge to jerk away from him. When his hands went to my breasts and he started murmuring my name again, I knew that all other options had left the building. I had to act.

I braced myself and started kissing him back, hard. He had to believe that I wanted him, and I needed to distract him so I could gain some leverage. I stood up, but he was so busy with my mouth that all he did was grunt when he felt me stand. Before he could open his eyes, I flicked my tongue over his lips, making him whimper. At the same time, I pulled back with both my fist and with my own elemental force.

I totally hit like a girl, so the punch I threw at Conleth's jaw was hardly impressive. But what *was* impressive was the burst of energy I channeled through my arm and out of my knuckles. The effect was admirable.

Was it a good long-term strategy to blow my magical wad in one go? Probably not. But as I slid down to plop bonelessly into the chair Con had tied me to, the ifrit halfling was still flying through the air. That was totally worth it. As was the sound of him smashing against the wall. And the feeling I got when I realized he wasn't getting back up?

Priceless.

CHAPTER TWENTY-FOUR

My legs were still rubbery, and my need for the ocean was overwhelming. I felt like a tube of toothpaste that had been squeezed dry. Check that: I felt like a dry tube of toothpaste that was trying to run on spaghetti legs.

I had tottered through a series of small rooms into an enormous warehouse. It was full of huge shipping containers, all rusted and empty. They were lying around, higgledy-piggledy, some stacked two or three containers high, making a veritable labyrinth of the large space. I could also feel the ocean directly underneath me. My sluggish brain put together the clues and decided I was in some kind of dockyard.

Having the ocean so close and not being able to reach her was torturous. If the windows weren't ten feet off the ground, I would have just crawled out of one and swum to safety. And if I hadn't been so drained, I would have attempted to blast a hole in the floor. Unfortunately, the only option I had left was my rather unsteady little feet.

I had no idea where I was or where I was going. I hoped I was moving forward; that I wouldn't trap myself; that Con wasn't following. But there was nothing I could do to guarantee any of those things except to keep my numb legs pumping, which went against every instinct I had. My entire being was telling me to find a hole and crawl in it, mostly because I recognized this scene I was currently enacting. Countless novels and untold movies had drilled into me what happens when defenseless women ran through dark, creepy places. None of them were good. Meanwhile, the containers offered enemies a thousand places to hide; hands could erupt from dark corners to grab me or spring out from underneath containers to trip me. What I wanted to do was buck the trend by finding somewhere relatively out of the way and lie down until I heard the credit music rolling.

And I really *need to powder my nose*, my bladder chimed, much to my annoyance. I was distracted enough by my need to pee that I shuffled right around a container corner without pausing to look first.

My progress was halted by a well-known wall o' man.

'We need to stop running into each other like this,' I croaked, my nose smushed into Anyan's leather jacket. As the familiar scent of lemon wax and cardamom washed over me, my knees gave and I started sliding to the ground. The barghest caught me, swearing softly as he steadied me on my feet. At the touch of his big hands, I felt a powerful, if inappropriate, desire to jump into his arms. I knew he'd carry me to safety, and I wanted safety – at that moment – more than I'd ever wanted anything else in my life. I was so not cut out for the role of action-adventure heroine.

I managed to control my urge to fling myself on him, but I did lean forward, settling myself against his solid bulk with a sigh. Anyan stiffened, obviously surprised. But then he softened, crouching down to wrap his arms around me in a rib-cracking hug. His power followed his arms, until I was blanketed in Anyan.

'By the gods, Jane, are you all right? You scared me sense-
less.'

Anyan's voice was rough but his hands were gentle as he
eased them over my arms, down my waist, and then up and
over my back. I knew he was just checking me for injury,
but I reacted to his touch like a startled horse. My labored
breathing eased, my still-frantically beating heart calmed beat
by beat.

'I've lived for nearly three hundred and fifty years, woman.
I've survived two wars. And yet *you* are going to be the death
of me. Did Conleth hurt you?'

'No,' I mumbled into the barghest's shoulder before raising
my face to meet his eyes. 'But I think I hurt him.'

Anyan smiled at that, his aura of power pulsing around us,
rubbing against me like giant affectionate cats.

'What did you do? You're totally drained.'

'I pulled out a can of whoopass, Anyan. Big, strong
whoopass.' My knees buckled again, and Anyan swore.

'Next time, use half the whoopass,' he chided, holding me
steady.

'I don't know how to use half,' I whined, trying to get my
limbs to stop trembling. 'It was either use a whole can of
whoopass, or make sweet love to Conleth. I chose the
whoopass.'

My bravado was short-lived, however, as my legs totally
gave way. Anyan's face, which had gone from concerned to
horrified when I'd said 'make sweet love' and 'Conleth' in
the same sentence, went back to concerned as he held me on
my feet till I'd recovered.

'At least I got away,' I reminded his worried frown. I didn't
really want to be the death of him.

'That you did, Jane. Good girl,' he said, a hint of a smile
peeking from behind that big, crooked nose.

I peered up at the barghest, my forehead wrinkling in consternation. I was about to remind him that, while I was a zygote by the standards of his people, by human standards I was no 'girl'. But I lifted my chin, belligerently, at the very same time that he crouched down to run his hands over my legs. We were suddenly nose to nose, and his gray eyes were as wide as mine at our predicament.

I cleared my throat, pushing myself back from him.

'Is Ryu all right?'

'Yes,' Anyan said, crouching down the rest of the way to finish playing doctor. When he was satisfied I wasn't hurt, he stood back up to tower over me. 'But he'll be a lot better when he knows you're safe. Let's go find the others.'

He took my hand to lead me away and I followed, trying to keep my legs steady. We walked and walked, meandering to and fro between the walls made by all the various containers. But Anyan's nose was twitching the whole time as he sniffed out our route. There was one pressing issue, however, that I couldn't wait any longer to address.

'Um, Anyan?'

'Yes?'

'Is there a bathroom?'

The barghest stopped. 'What?'

'Is there a bathroom? I really have to pee.'

'You have *got* to be kidding me,' Anyan said, swinging around to stare at me like I was crazy.

'No, I'm not. I really have to pee. I drank, like, a whole liter of water, and when I get stressed, I always need to pee. Getting kidnapped is stressful. Really, really stressful.'

Anyan shook his head. 'Jane, I don't even know where to begin. I'm trying to rescue you from a psychotic serial killer who is apparently intent on impregnating you. And you want to take a potty break.'

'I really have to go.'

The barghest closed his eyes, mumbling something to himself. I think he was counting to ten.

'Okay. There's no bathroom. Just go in one of the containers. Or behind one. Whatever.'

'Um, I'm really not very good at that.'

'At peeing?'

'At popping a squat. I tend to pee on myself. It's embarrassing.'

'Either pee, or don't pee. But make a decision. Before I fucking freak out.'

'Fine, jeez. What, do you never have to pee? Do they teach extreme bladder control at obedience school?' I shot back as I crept behind one of the containers and undid my pants.

'Jane, I am *this* close to returning you to Conleth.'

'Whatever,' I mumbled as I squatted down.

'I heard that.'

'Ew, don't listen, you pervert.'

All I got in response to that was a strangled sound. I rolled my eyes, finishing up behind the container, then stood up and put my clothes back to rights. 'I was kidding, Anyan,' I said as I stepped out from where I had hidden myself . . .

. . . to see my savior dangling from the thick fist of Phaedra's spriggan.

'Oh, fuck,' I groaned, fear flooding my system with adrenaline.

'Yes, "fuck",' murmured a silky voice in my ear. '"Fuck" is exactly the word I was looking for.'

'Graeme,' I said, squeezing my eyes shut to try to control the panic that threatened to send me gibbering to the floor.

Hands grabbed my shoulders to pull me back, despite my desperate struggling, against the incubus's muscular chest.

'Little Jane,' he said, holding me against him with one

viselike arm as he ran his other hand across my hips. 'I knew I'd find some time alone with you.'

Graeme's fingers found their way between my legs, and I froze, my heart beating frantically. Anyan, meanwhile, wasn't faring much better. The huge man was being shaken by the neck like a rag doll by the nubbly gray giant. Fugwat was grinning like a little kid with a new toy. The kind of little kid who would soon be torturing the neighborhood pets.

I tried to pull on my power, but between my fear and my already depleted resources, it was completely unresponsive.

'None of that, little Jane,' my captor said, reaching up to squeeze my breast painfully. I hissed as he found my nipple to twist it with a vicious pinch. When my hiss became a whimper, he finally stopped, pulling me around to stare down into my face.

I tried to look brave, but the sight of his beautiful, soulless eyes totally freaked me out. I started struggling again, and I reached, desperately, for my depleted mojo. Graeme's reaction was swift and resolute.

His fist smashed into my left cheekbone, sending my head flying back, and with it any chance of me mounting an offensive. Graeme did *not* hit like a girl, and the pain was excruciating. I groaned as he hit me again, and then a third time, this time catching me right in the eye. Graeme paused for a second to smile at his handiwork and to watch as blood dripped from my previously split eyebrow down my face. He kissed me roughly, before sinking his teeth through my bottom lip. I squealed, crying salty tears that burned down my raw cheeks.

'I am going to love breaking you, little Jane,' the incubus purred, unleashing his emotional glamour. I felt his lust, and his rage, and his desire for my pain. And it was all tied up together in the big, sick package that was Graeme.

'I just adore your eyes,' he said, nuzzling my now bloody

lips with his own. 'They're so selkie . . . puts me in the mood for a good clubbing.'

I heard something crash behind me, and I prayed Anyan had gotten free of the spriggan. But before I could crane my neck to peer around, Graeme had lowered his mouth to sink his teeth into my neck. I cried out, pain coursing through me.

'I thought you'd appreciate my love bites,' the incubus chuckled after his teeth released me. 'Since you *are* fucking a sith,' he explained, turning to throw me, with all his strength, against the hard wall of a steel container. I went flying, my breath knocked out of me as I landed smack dab in the middle of the container's wall. I slid down, struggling to gasp in air, till I was lying at the base of the container. Then something deep inside my chest really started to hurt.

My left eye was swelling shut, but I could still see out of my right. Graeme was unbuckling his studded Ed Hardy belt and advancing toward me. I rolled into a fetal position, covering my face with my hands. The first blow caught me on the forearms, and the upraised studs tore through the delicate skin. The second was aimed at my thigh, bruising me through the thick denim of my jeans. I waited, crying in pain, for him to land a third.

It never came. Just as Graeme raised his arm, ready to strike, he was broadsided by a blinding torrent of rage and fire.

It was Graeme's turn to smash into the side of a container, and smash he did. Before he could get up, Conleth was there, holding him up by his chin so that the incubus was on his tiptoes. Con then went totally nuclear, and I'd never heard anything like Graeme's screams as Con applied himself to what I can only describe as melting the incubus's face.

'I told you I'd see you again, motherfucker,' Conleth cried in triumph, even as he burned brighter. Graeme's screams echoed through the warehouse, bouncing eerily off the metal containers.

That's when the spriggan came reeling into my peripheral vision, a very angry barghest clinging to his back like a leather-clad burr. Anyan was clubbing at Fugwat's head with both his fists and all of his power, but, unlike me, Anyan wasn't losing any strength. His barrage was ceaseless, which was a good thing, as the spriggan obviously had an incredibly hard noggin. But eventually even Fugwat's cranium gave way, and he shuddered to his knobby gray knees before keeling forward onto his face.

Anyan looked from where Conleth was still torturing Graeme to where I lay prone against the container's wall, before darting toward me. But before he could make it, Con threw Graeme straight at the barghest. Anyan was bowled over by the incubus, whose shuddering whimpers testified to the fact that he was still alive, if terribly burned. Con was instantly at my side, where he tried to haul me up. I cried out at his touch, since I'd not only just gotten the shit kicked out of me but also because he'd forgotten to bank his fire and was searing my already sliced-up forearms.

'Oh, Jane, what did he do to you?' Conleth hissed, his eyes wide as he pulled his fire inward.

I went ahead and kept crying. At this point, after being rescued by my kidnapper, I'd lost all sense of who was the good guy and who was the bad guy. I don't think I even cared anymore. I just wanted the pain – all of my various pains – to go away. Whatever injury was causing the dull ache inside of me, however, was also making it difficult to breathe, so my sobs sounded more like a series of tear-strangled gasps.

The ifrit halfling picked me up, cradling me to his chest. He started to walk away but hesitated at Anyan's harsh cry.

'Conleth, stop!' the barghest commanded. 'Stop and look at her. She's badly hurt. What can you do for her?'

My one good eye made out Conleth's face peering down at me. I licked my swollen bitten lip and whimpered piteously.

'Please, Conleth,' I wheezed, my voice breathy and unnatural.

Conleth stood there, studying my face. So I really turned on the waterworks, which only made me cry even harder as the tears brought fresh agony to my swollen, bloody eye.

'I can heal her, Conleth, and we have an even better healer coming. I can smell him; he's near. He'll fix her, and I swear to the gods I won't let anyone hurt you or capture you. You saved Jane, and I owe you. I'll guarantee your safety, and she'll get the help she needs.'

Conleth didn't respond, but his arms around me tightened.

'Please,' the barghest pleaded. 'I'm begging you.'

Con gave me one long, last look and then turned around toward Anyan.

'You heal her and you let me go?'

'I promise.'

'How can I trust you?'

'You can't, Conleth. You don't know me. But look at Jane. She needs to be seen to; that you can trust.'

Conleth's bright blue eyes met my good one and he nodded sharply.

'Fine. I set her down; you come get her. But when you're done with her, you give her back to me.'

'Of course,' the barghest lied smoothly. 'Just give us the chance to take care of her.'

Con stalked forward a few paces before setting me down on the cold, damp floor of the warehouse. Then he scuttled backward, raising his flames. Anyan gave the ifrit just enough time to return to his corner before the big man was at my side.

'Jesus, Jane,' he whispered, gathering me to him. 'Caleb!' he shouted. 'Here!'

While we waited for the clip-clops of the satyr to get nearer, Anyan began to heal me himself. He didn't seem to know where to begin, and I felt his right hand touching me all over as the healing warmth of his power shifted from my eye to my cheek to my mouth to my neck and then to my forearms before returning to my eye. I gritted my teeth against the pain of the injuries and the occasional pain of the healing and concentrated on Anyan's other hand. It was clutching my hip, holding me close, but I found it with my own. I wrapped my fingers around his, needing the comfort of his strength, and he responded by shifting his hold on me so his big hand engulfed mine. He was trembling.

'I'm so sorry, Jane,' he whispered, stroking his healing fingers down my cheek again and again. I shook my head.

'My fault. Get diapers next time,' I croaked out between my swollen lips. 'No more potty breaks. Ever.'

'No more "next times",' the barghest responded grimly. 'Ever. You're not allowed to leave Rockabill again until I say so.'

I might have argued with that if I hadn't started coughing up blood.

'Caleb!' Anyan shouted again, turning his attention to my chest and sides. 'Hurry the fuck up!'

Just as I was starting to feel distinctly woozy, I felt another set of hands on me and Caleb's powerful healing magics flood through my body. Although unsure of exactly how long I'd been held unconscious by Conleth, I knew it had to have been quite some time for Caleb to be fully operational and for everyone to have found me.

Suddenly, Ryu's voice was there, then Julian's and Camille's. People were yelling but I couldn't see why, mostly because Caleb had given up trying to heal me one injury at a time and just went ahead and enveloped me with his shaggy body, blasting me with wave after wave of healing magic.

When Caleb finally unwrapped himself from me, I understood why there was so much drama. Anyan was standing between an extra-fiery Conleth and a very pissed-off wall of baobhan sith. Camille, Julian, and Ryu were all poised to strike, but Anyan wouldn't let them. Meanwhile, Conleth couldn't seem to choose between staring at the barghest in surprise and glowering at Ryu.

Caleb wasn't done healing me, and his magics were still whizzing around my body as I watched Anyan negotiate with the others. I heard something about how Con had saved Jane. The barghest was pointing at the motionless lumps that were Graeme and Fugwat. When Julian walked over to prod the spriggan with the toe of his Vans, he noticed I was awake. So he wandered over to give me a boost.

Lying there in Caleb's arms, soaking up his healing energies while Julian began to recharge me, I let myself believe, for a split second, that everything was going to be okay. I imagined Conleth getting the help he needed. I imagined Graeme and Fugwat brought to justice for killing Edie and Felicia. Maybe they'd even squeal on Phaedra, and then Phaedra would turn on Jarl. The good guys would win, and we'd all ride off into the sunset, safe and whole.

Which was why Phaedra chose that exact moment to show up, Kaya and Kaori in tow.

Sometimes I felt like Murphy's Law incarnate.

CHAPTER TWENTY-FIVE

The harpies came first, both their power and their wings beating the air around us. One of them cried out when she saw Graeme, rushing to his side to crouch above him and murmur endearments. Kaya, or Kaori, began weeping when she saw his face, before we felt all of her power shift toward healing him. Kaori, or Kaya, went to poke at the spriggan with one dun wing, before sending her own blast of healing magic at Fugwat.

We were so distracted by the harpies, and especially by the fact that Graeme, the sadistic rapist, appeared to have a girlfriend, that none of us noticed Phaedra's entrance. Except for Conleth.

'You!' we heard him shout, and we all turned first toward him and then toward where he was pointing.

The little Alfar emerged from the shadows, still clad in her leathers and knives.

'Me,' she said drily.

Suddenly, I remembered Con whispering to himself. *'The woman and her pet psycho,'* I recalled him saying as I looked from Phaedra to Graeme. *'I told you I'd see you again . . .'* Suddenly, Con's ramblings made sense.

Everything fell into place.

When we'd seen those claw marks on Silver's legs, we'd feared Kaya and Kaori's involvement in his death, but we hadn't known their motivation. Or the motivation of their mistress, Phaedra, or her master, Jarl. But now I knew.

'She's been behind everything the whole time,' I whispered. I'd had my suspicions, but now, to me at least, it was all as clear as day. Jarl had to be the sponsor; Phaedra wouldn't have the resources to run an operation like that. When Con escaped, she and her team wiped out everyone who could have known of Jarl's involvement in those laboratories. In case anyone was watching, she'd burned the bodies to make it look like Conleth had done it.

And she'd known where Conleth was the entire time; after all, she must have sent that note about Felicia to Conleth. Donovan must have tipped the girl off, like she did Silver and her boyfriend. Told Felicia to hide. The young woman did a good job, and so Phaedra used Con as she'd used him this whole time: to camouflage her own crimes.

Which meant that, at any point, Phaedra could have stopped the ifrit's murders, but she hadn't. She needed him out there, killing, as her scapegoat. Felicia, meanwhile, was supposed to be the link that bound Conleth to the Chicago murders, even though he had nothing to do with them . . .

Then my frantic mind caught onto another stray thought.

If Phaedra knew where Conleth lived in Southie, did she know about this place?

Because it was one thing if she'd followed as Anyan and Ryu had tracked Conleth and me back to this place. It was another thing entirely if Phaedra had known of the existence of this warehouse the entire time.

This could be a trap, I realized, my blood freezing in my veins.

My thoughts were interrupted as everyone responded to Phaedra's entrance. Caleb's arms tightened protectively around me and he retreated backward. Julian, Camille, and Ryu fanned out, keeping an eye on the Alfar. Anyan strode forward, his power exploding forth in a blunt, bullying wave.

I was so busy watching Conleth's reaction to Phaedra that I didn't see Ryu had made his way to my side.

'Jane, are you all right?' he whispered, taking me from the satyr. I felt Caleb's power shift away from healing and toward offensive magics.

'Are *you* all right? I was so worried . . .'

'I'm fine,' he murmured, leaning down to kiss my face all over. 'What did Conleth do to you?'

'Not Conleth, Graeme.'

'Oh gods. What did he do?'

'Beat me up. Conleth saved me.'

Ryu started to say something else, but I shushed him. 'Listen, Con knows Phaedra.'

'That's impossible—' Ryu began, just as Conleth yelled, 'Phaedra, you bitch!'

I raised my stiff, but now healed, eyebrow at Ryu.

'What the . . . ?' Ryu's voice trailed off as we all turned to watch the circus.

Phaedra and the ifrit halfling were circling one another. Con's power was flaring out in brutal waves that would have incapacitated most other beings. But the Alfar's shields deflected it without strain.

'You lied to me, you bitch! You said "my people" were coming for me. You told me about your world. You gave me hope, and then you let me rot in that lab with that monster!'

The little Alfar's blood-red eyes were wide. 'I promised you nothing, halfling. I explained to you the truth of your heritage. If you chose to misinterpret my words, it is through no fault of mine.'

Conleth's power flared stronger, his fire burning so hot it was tinged with blue.

'Goddamn you, stop *lying*! You gave me hope!' he cried, as he shot off a fireball at Phaedra. It ricocheted off the Alfar's shields and flew to the left, nearly taking the ear off Graeme's harpy girlfriend as she cradled him in her lap, crooning sweet nothings at his ruined face. She looked up, surprised, and then went back to her beloved sexual deviant. And I thought Linda Allen had issues.

Phaedra retaliated with her own wave of power that met Conleth's shields dead-on. He staggered under the force of the blow, but his defenses held.

They battered at each other like this for a while. To protect ourselves against the magic flying about, my group had gathered together around where Ryu and I were standing, feeding our own power into Anyan's shields, as he was the strongest.

'We have to help him, Anyan,' I shouted, as Con nearly went to his knees under a particularly fierce barrage by Phaedra. The barghest either couldn't hear me over the din, or he ignored me. He was busy distributing our combined power about his own shields as energy boomed out like cartoon sound waves from where Con and Phaedra's attacks met each other in the middle.

'Ryu, please,' I cried. 'He saved me! Help him!'

Ryu looked at me like I was nuts. 'Jane, it's Conleth. He's a monster.'

'Maybe, but he never had a chance! We can give him one! Phaedra is the *real* monster—' My voice was cut off as a container came toppling off a stack behind us to smash down directly where we were standing. It landed with a bone-rattling crash just as Ryu flung us to safety.

The toppling container gave Phaedra her opportunity. Conleth, distracted by the noise of the falling steel, lost his control for a split second. Nobody's fool, Phaedra had been waiting for just such a moment. The instant his shields wavered, she hit him hard, with two simultaneous blasts of pure Alfar elemental force. The combined elements hit him full in the chest, and he collapsed to his knees. He stared down at the smoking ruin of his torso before looking to where Ryu held me. Conleth raised his hand in supplication, and I strained forward, but Ryu's arms were like a vise around my waist.

Phaedra strode toward the ifrit halfling, pulling at one of the two hilts that peeked out from behind her shoulder. A machete flowed into her hands, the steel cold and deadly in the weak glow of our few, forgotten mage lights. I screamed, fighting against Ryu's grasp, as Anyan shouted as well. But before the barghest could stop her, the little Alfar had raised her gleaming blade to hack downward at Conleth's neck. With a single sickening chop, she held his head in her hands. I tasted bile as I collapsed in Ryu's hold.

The Alfar scanned over her prize dispassionately before she dropped Con's head next to his still-twitching body.

'Kaya, Kaori, away,' she commanded, advancing on us. The harpy who'd been healing the spriggan grabbed him firmly under the armpits and, using a massive amount of power, launched herself and her giant burden up and out of the warehouse, crashing through a skylight to escape. The other did the same with Graeme. They hovered, just over the roof, and we felt their power grow.

'While it has been entertaining playing with you, I am afraid that our time together is at an end. The boy is dead, and with him his secrets. Except that you have all become what humans call "loose ends". You know too much, and

I regret that you must follow your halfling friend into oblivion.'

Phaedra's little mouth was upturned in a small smile as she sprang her trap. Using the power of the harpies' element, air, as a catalyst, she unleashed her own imitation of Conleth's fire. But she also bound us, at the same time, in a tight web of Alfar force that pushed us together into the center of the room and kept us from moving. With every beat of the harpies' wings far overhead, the fire raged higher, until even the metal containers seemed to be burning.

Phaedra paused, and I felt a shift in her mojo as she locked her web into place. We were trapped, coughing, in the maelstrom of her power as her artificial inferno swiftly advanced. Then she turned tail and fled before she could get caught in her own trap.

Everyone around me was furiously trying to staunch a section of the flames surrounding us, but their struggles only seemed to make the Alfar's trap grow tighter. I tried to keep out of the way, but my eyes were streaming and I was coughing like crazy.

Nevertheless, through my rising panic, and the Alfar's net, the Atlantic beckoned. *Water, water, everywhere, and not a drop to drink*, my brain cackled unhelpfully. Particles of seawater hung in the air, droplets of moisture connecting me, like an invisible string of beads, to the water directly below our feet. The ocean would take care of the fire, obviously. But I'd been probing at Phaedra's web with my own severely weakened power, and I thought I understood how she'd made it. I knew that I could bring it down if I only had the resources.

I stared down at the floor and remembered Conleth and his electricity.

'Bring the mountain to Mohammed,' I murmured as I closed my stinging eyes, centered myself, and *pulled*.

I had only a little bit of power left from Julian's abbreviated attempt to recharge me. And for a second, I thought it wouldn't be enough. When I reached and nothing happened, I nearly panicked. But I pulled myself up sharply and reached again, hard. This time, it was enough to make contact. Using the dregs of my force, I called to my ocean, and much to my surprise, she answered with all the passion of a long-lost lover.

None of the others were aware of what I was doing, and they were so busy battling the fire they didn't hear what I heard. They didn't hear the ocean still, as if drawing in a breath. They didn't hear the suck of the waves receding, gathering themselves. But they did hear what came next, as crashing waves broke through the tall windows on all four sides of the warehouse, soaking us and putting out Phaedra's fires. And with every drop of water that touched me, more of the Atlantic's power forced its way into my body.

We were still caught in Phaedra's net, but most of the fires were out as torrents of water crashed through the thin, rusted walls of the warehouse. Then the sea was actually rising through the floorboards as unnatural waves rose up directly underneath us to meet me. As the water pooled around my ankles, I felt myself both reinvigorated and consumed by the power of the ocean, and I began to understand my devil's bargain.

For the sea always takes as much as she gives, and I had just asked for one hell of a favor.

The water was up to our knees now, and the ocean's power arced through me like electricity. The force was so strong that it lifted me, causing me to float, my arms and legs spread like Michelangelo's famous drawing, a few feet above my friends' heads. Ryu blinked up at me, stunned, his wet hair plastered to his head like a slick, dark cap. But I was brought back to the business at hand as another, increasingly painful, surge of power shot through my body, blasting out of me willy-nilly. I knew, at that moment, what a forty-watt light-bulb must feel like when it gets plugged into a hundred-watt socket. I was going to get that damned web down, but the ocean was going to burn me up doing it.

I closed my eyes and concentrated, trying to dampen down the pain as I focused the Atlantic's power on a particular section of Phaedra's trap. It felt complicated and solid, but it was really just like one of Anyan's knots. It had a seam where it joined, and if I could force the seam apart, we could escape. And while I wasn't confident I was going to survive my bright idea, I did know my only chance was to get the job done quickly.

I opened myself even wider, and the ocean responded by flooding me with more of her power. The influx was too much, and the pain was turning into agony; it felt like the power was building to a point where it would explode out from my skin. Meanwhile, as if to reiterate her claim on me, tendrils of seawater rose from the floor to wrap around my wrists, ankles, and my waist. The water caressed me, gentle as a lover, as it made its way under my top to writhe between my breasts and wrap itself around my neck. The ocean's elemental force surged through my watery bonds, and I screamed as my system was taken to its breaking point.

The pain was too much, making it hard to concentrate. But then I felt something warm, solid, and decidedly nonaqueous wrap around my ankle. I looked down to see Anyan's hand grasping me as the barghest countered the force of the ocean with his own elements of earth and air. He grounded me, siphoning off the excess energy that would otherwise have torn me apart. My pain lessened, allowing my mind to focus – once again – on Phaedra's Alfar web.

Thin edge of the wedge, I chanted to myself as I imagined slipping a slender needle of power into the seam of our trap. When it was in, I widened it, feeling the ocean respond like an eager lapdog to my beckoning. Power flooded through me, most of it directed toward the web's seam and the excess flowing out of me and through the barghest, where it dissipated into the wooden floor of the building.

Finally, the seam was wide enough for us to squeeze through. Camille and Julian were first, Ryu and Caleb second, and then Anyan pulled me forward by my ankle. I floated above the big man like a bizarre human-shaped helium balloon, trailing tendrils of writhing water as he tugged me to safety. When we were free, he pulled me down, hard, by my legs, till we were face-to-face. Then he did his power-cloak trick, only ten times stronger than before. It squeezed us together as close as Siamese twins, but it also severed me neatly from the ocean's grasp.

Without the Atlantic's force flooding through me, I drooped like a rag doll. My whole body ached, and my magical 'nerves' – whatever the hell it was that let me feel my power – felt like they were on fire. I moaned piteously as Anyan passed me wordlessly to Caleb.

'. . . you were sick . . .' I mumbled to the satyr, who smiled grimly as he held me tight. We were walking *and* healing, no doubt in case Phaedra was waiting somewhere off in the wings.

'There was a healer right in the area, for Daoud. Then we could come help find you,' he said. 'Brave lady Jane,' Caleb rumbled, stooping down to kiss me lightly on the forehead. It was the kiss of a proud parent, and it made me blush.

The warehouse was also beginning to creak ominously, and we picked up our pace when it started to sway. The ocean, as if pissed off that she didn't get to claim me as her reward, was still clawing at the walls and floor around us.

Ryu led the way, issuing commands to Camille and Julian as they sent out all sorts of probes and shields to check for more traps. But Phaedra must have had complete faith in her web, or she was busy tending to her wounded, for there was nothing between us and freedom. As we cleared the building, we heard an awful ripping sound, and we hotfooted it for the cars. We clustered around them, safe on solid land, watching as the entire dockyard slid groaning into the sea.

I blinked, wide-eyed, at the space where the huge warehouse had just stood. Until I realized that everyone else was looking at me. Everyone except for Anyan, who'd sat down on the hood of Ryu's little car as he stared out into the ocean.

'Jane, what did you *do*?' Ryu asked, frowning at me.

'I dunno,' I said, suddenly feeling woozy. I started to slide forward, but Ryu caught me and held me close.

'Take me home,' I murmured to my lover.

'Of course,' he said, as he kissed me. Then he picked me up and carried me to the passenger's seat of his car. Anyan was gone from the hood, and I craned my head around to look for him. But there was no sign of the barghest.

I felt dazed, empty, and annihilated as Ryu got in the car and we turned toward the city. Dawn was just breaking over the skyline. When I'd said 'home', I'd meant Rockabill. Although, right now, I'd take anywhere that had a bed. I was exhausted, physically and mentally, but I also felt unfinished somehow. Conleth was dead, yet there was no justice to be found in his murder. Meanwhile, Phaedra and her lot were still running free, despite all the atrocities they'd committed. It felt like everything was resolved, and nothing. I also felt about two decades older than when I'd stepped off that plane at Logan Airport. I curled up in my seat, facing my window, and tried to concentrate on the city lights flashing past my face. But the memory of Con's white face as he reached for me superimposed itself over the busy life of Boston.

So I squeezed my eyes shut and prayed for an oblivion that never came.

CHAPTER TWENTY-SIX

Ryu yawned as I lolled against his chest. It was about five o'clock the following evening. After everything that had happened at the pier, none of us had been in any shape to chase after Phaedra. All of us were battered, bruised, and in need of both physical and magical recuperation.

Despite my exhaustion, I'd slept fitfully, finally giving up after I woke shouting, having dreamed something particularly horrible involving Graeme. I'd removed my traumatized ass to Ryu's wet room, using up most of the city's hot water before my lover awoke from his coma and came to join me. That's when I discovered that good sex with someone you trusted was the best cure for icky dreams involving rapist incubi. Not that I ever hoped to need such a remedy again.

'You were amazing,' Ryu said, nuzzling my neck.

'Thanks, but I gotta give credit to Iris. She's the one who told me the trick was to use two fingers *and* your big toe, unless you have a Gummi Worm handy. Or a Twizzler. Then you can just go ahead and—'

'Jane!' Ryu interrupted me, laughing. 'I meant you were amazing yesterday.'

I snorted. 'Yeah, amazingly stupid.'

'What?'

'Ryu, I drained myself escaping Conleth, which meant I was a sitting duck for Graeme. Then I nearly fried myself channeling the ocean, or whatever the hell I did. I'm lucky I survived. If it hadn't been for Anyan, I'd be dead ten times over.'

'You were the one who rescued *us*, Jane.'

'Anyway,' I said, changing the subject. What he called heroism, I called dumb luck, and we weren't going to see eye-to-eye on this one. 'Where did Anyan go, anyway?'

Ryu frowned at me. 'Who knows? He does whatever he wants. Always has. Why do you care so much?'

'I want to know he's okay.'

'Don't worry about the barghest. He takes care of himself. I'm here now.'

'I know, honey. I just want to make sure everyone is safe. I take it Phaedra went back to the Compound?'

'Yes. I talked to Wally first thing when I woke up, while you were boiling yourself in the shower. He sends his love. I wouldn't accept it, though, just to be on the safe side. Anyway, Wally told me Phaedra's already back at the Compound, covering her tracks and telling everyone we're heroes, killed in the line of duty. Won't she be excited to find out we all survived "Conleth's" attack.' Ryu chuckled, his eyes lighting up. 'I told Wally to keep our survival to himself, for now. To let me tell her in person. It almost makes me look forward to seeing Phaedra again.'

I sighed. Ryu loved intrigue, and I knew that all the shit we'd experienced over the past week was just another roll of the dice in the game he called his life. But I wasn't like Ryu. I wasn't used to casual displays of violence or to watching lives thrown away as if they were holey socks. Okay, I'd survived and, because of Caleb, I didn't even have a scratch on me to testify to what I'd endured. But I still felt scarred, and I had a funny feeling I was going to need quite a bit of time to pick at the mental scabs I'd formed over the last few days.

The big thing haunting me was my feelings regarding the ifrit halfling. I still couldn't believe Con was dead, and I also couldn't believe how much it bothered me. He'd caused so much pain, committed so many barbarous acts. But I knew the terrible pity I felt for him would never go away, not after the way he'd died. Conleth would stay with me, for many reasons. Not least because I realized now that I was so lucky to have the life I'd been given. My mother had left, but I had finally realized she hadn't *abandoned* me. I could never compare my own experiences to Con's.

'So what happens now?' I asked.

'What do you mean?'

'What happens to Phaedra? And to the others? We know damned well that she and her lot were committing the other murders. What Graeme and Fugwat did to Edie and Felicia . . .' I shivered, suddenly cold despite Ryu's generously shared body heat.

'Nothing happens. At least not right away.'

I sat upright when I heard that. I knew it was the case, but hearing it totally pissed me off. 'What do you mean, Ryu? How can *nothing* happen?'

Ryu shrugged. 'Phaedra's Alfar, and she's Jarl's second. To accuse her would be to accuse Jarl. And we have no proof besides our own testimony. Meanwhile, she's blaming everything on Conleth and she'll be believed.'

'But when you show up at the Compound, alive . . .'

'Jarl will throw us a party, apologize for assuming we were dead, and reward us for our heroism.'

I shook my head, mute with anger.

'Jane, nothing is going to happen. Accept that.'

We stared at each other for what felt like forever.

'I think I hate your world,' I snapped, leaning back against Ryu's black-leather headboard.

'I know, baby. I'm not any happier about it than you are. But look at it this way: now we know for sure that Jarl is up to something, and we know who else is involved.'

'I knew Jarl was up to no good when he tried to fucking strangle me.'

Ryu went quiet at that, and I realized my mistake.

'Well, I didn't know he tried to strangle you until a few days ago. So I guess I'm playing catch-up.'

I swore at my own idiocy before turning my body toward Ryu.

'I'm sorry, Ryu. I was trying to protect you. It was stupid.'

Ryu cuddled me closer. 'Yes, it was. I protect you, not vice versa.'

I almost made a joke about how letting me get kidnapped wasn't exactly my idea of protection, but I figured if I said that, I might as well go ahead and castrate him at the same time. So I held my tongue.

'Fine. Nothing happens, for now. But someday, I'm totally kicking Phaedra's ass for everything she did.'

'Brave Jane,' Ryu murmured, his hand stroking down my side as he found my mouth with his. Then his hand was between my legs, and we made love again, as if we were the last two people on earth. Afterward, we cleaned up, got dressed, and then went downstairs and ordered pizza.

It was so bizarre, after everything that had happened the night before, to be arguing with Ryu over whether to order the meat supreme or the regular supreme that I couldn't deal.

I let him decide and then went upstairs to do what I'd been dying to do since I'd woken up.

I started packing.

I was just finished sorting through what was clean and what was dirty when Ryu came to investigate where I'd disappeared to.

'Jane, what are you doing?'

'I'm packing. Should I go online to order my ticket? Or should I call the airline directly? Is tomorrow too short notice? I don't want you to have to pay more for me to get home.'

'Jane, honey—'

'I just hope I can get a ticket for tomorrow. Otherwise I might rent a car. I can pay for it, though—'

'Jane, wait a second.'

'Sure . . .' I mumbled, mentally organizing my stuff. I'd already packed my makeup and most of my toiletries, except for what I needed the next morning. So I started shoving all of my dirty clothes into a clean garbage bag I'd brought from the kitchen, until I realized Ryu was trying to get my attention.

'Sorry, what is it?' I asked, as I finished shoving my stankies in the bag.

'Honey, we need to talk.'

'About what?'

'About us. About this week. About everything.'

I paused, my tired mind scrambling. Then I forced myself to throw my last pair of dirty socks in the bag and to tie it off before turning to face Ryu.

'Is this the talk where you tell me that it's been fun, but you're running off with the satyr?' I joked, not at all happy with this turn of events. I didn't want to have 'talks', not about anything serious. I felt so mixed up, and so tired, that any sort of 'talk' would be a bad idea.

'No, it's not that talk,' Ryu said, smiling. 'It's the talk where we cut to the chase and admit how we feel. Where we talk about our future. I want us to be together.'

'Ryu, we are together. If this is about being exclusive, I can assure you that I'm not running around behind your back with Stuart when I'm in Rockabill.'

'That's the whole point, honey. Exclusivity.'

'Huh?'

'I need you with me.'

'I *am* with you—'

'Baby, please. If this week has proven anything to me, it's how much I want you in my life. So I want you to give moving to Boston serious consideration. It doesn't have to be right this minute. But I want you to think about it.'

'Oh,' I said, staring down at my hands. My mind was racing. I couldn't even follow my own thoughts, but they centered around one giant negative emotion: *no*. There was no way I could move to Boston anytime soon. There was my training and my dad and my life in Rockabill and the fact that I didn't even know if I wanted to . . .

'Is that all you have to say?'

'No, I just don't know where to begin . . . I don't think I'm ready for this.'

'That's not good enough. I think we *are* ready. I love you, Jane.'

I winced. Did he? Really?

'Ryu, we barely know each other—'

'What are you talking about? I've known you for months now. I know you're strong and smart and brave. I know you fit with me. We look good together, and we like the same things. We'd make each other even stronger.'

I thought about his words. We had gone through so much together and were so close in some ways. But, in other ways, we didn't know each other at all. And did I *really* fit with him?

I looked around the pristine, cold, expensive expanse of his bedroom and, again, unbidden came the thought: *no*.

'Okay, why?' I replied, trying to distract myself from that word. 'Why now? Why can't we just stay as we are?'

'Do I really need to spell it out?'

'Considering that moving would mean leaving my life, my family and friends, and also my training, then yes. I don't see why we have to push this.'

Ryu knelt down next to where I sat by my suitcase.

'Jane, I want you here for so many reasons. But most of all, baby, I need you here because otherwise *I* can't be faithful. Don't tell me you haven't figured that out. And I hate it as much as you must hate it. I'm tired of random humans and having to worry about whom I'll be with to feed. I love you, Jane. I've never felt this way about someone, and you can be *everything* to me. I hate myself for being what I am, if it means I have to betray you.'

'Wow,' I grunted, taking deep breaths. I hadn't expected quite *that* much honesty.

'Yeah. It sucks.'

'It sucks to suck, says the vampire,' I quipped weakly. I was so not ready for this conversation.

Ryu harumphed humorlessly.

I turned back to my suitcase, fitting my dirty clothes bag over my shoes at the bottom. Then I started stacking the clean clothes at the top, shifting around what had never gotten unpacked to make room.

What he said was true, but I didn't know if it was entirely honest. I didn't know how much of his desire for me to be a bigger part of his life was because he didn't like cheating on me or because my being with him meant he had a constant food source handy. I'd wondered more than once if that hadn't been why he'd taken me to the Compound with him all that time ago. The other baobhan sith, Nyx, that we'd met had also brought a pet human, or a 'sack lunch', as she called him. Don't get me wrong, it's not that I thought Ryu was consciously using me, but at the same time he'd organized his life, as everyone does, around his needs. And imbibing essence was a huge need for him. So where did Ryu the man end and Ryu the baobhan sith begin?

And who liked me more? Man or vampire?

'Ryu, I really don't see how this can happen anytime soon. I've got my father and my job and my training. I'm not ready to move to Boston, especially when I have almost no offensive magics.'

'I can train you, baby. And we can get your father a nurse. Money isn't an issue.'

I snorted. 'It's an issue for me, Ryu. I can't just live off of you. I would need a job and . . .' I shook my head, focusing myself on the real issues. 'And I don't want some random person taking care of my father. *I* want to take care of him. He's my dad and I don't know how long he's got left.'

'Well, maybe we can move him here—'

'To Boston? Where he knows no one? Where he can't get around? That's not feasible.'

'I'm not saying it has to be right now, Jane. I'm just saying . . . I'm telling you that I love you.'

'Ryu . . .'

'Do you love me, or not? It's that simple.'

First of all, it wasn't that simple. I knew he was switching tactics, trying to make me admit I loved him so that he could use that in his negotiations with me. It also wasn't that simple because I couldn't answer the fucking question. I closed my eyes.

Do I love Ryu?

I adored him on so many levels. He made me laugh. I admired his bravery and his panache. He did things to my body that left me sobbing with pleasure. But did I *love* him?

No . . . came that whispering voice in my head.

I realized that Ryu was waiting for me to agree with him. I also realized I was holding an enormous, purple dildo. *Damn it, Iris*, I thought as I stashed it in my suitcase, hurriedly covering it with the few remaining clothes still sitting next to me.

All of a sudden, I was packed. Which meant I'd lost 'packing' as a diversionary tactic. So I zipped up my suitcase and walked it to the top of the staircase before coming back to kneel in front of Ryu.

'Ryu—' I pleaded, but he didn't let me start.

'No, Jane. I *know* you. I know you love me. Fine, it's not the same as what you felt for Jason. But you were *children*. Of course it's not the same. We're adults, living with all the compromises and bullshit and worries that adults have to deal with.'

I sat stunned at the mention of Jason.

'Ryu,' I said finally. 'This isn't about Jason—'

'Is it about Anyan, then?'

'What the hell does Anyan have to do with anything?'

'Don't be stupid.'

I blinked at Ryu, having gone from stunned to shocked. He was so pissed off suddenly, and I didn't understand why. Was he jealous of the barghest? Who I'd seen, what, a handful of times in the past four months before this week? And the only reason I even saw him this week was because of Ryu and his irritating inability to keep business and pleasure separate.

I remembered Anyan saying something to that effect to

Ryu, all those months ago, and I flushed. Was I just one more example of Ryu's boundary issues?

'Ryu, I don't know where any of this is coming from. I don't compare you to Jason, and I certainly don't compare you to Anyan. But you're asking so much from me, and you can't expect me to make decisions this big, this quickly.'

I watched as Ryu scrubbed a hand through his rich, chestnut hair. I ached to touch him, to erase everything that had just been said, to go back in time and start over from when we'd lain in bed, curled around each other, just a few hours ago.

'I'm only asking if you love me, Jane. That shouldn't be hard to answer.'

Fuck this, I thought, suddenly tired of diplomacy.

'Well it *is* difficult to answer. We don't see each other often, and when we do, everything is cushioned by the fact that we're on vacation, in some B and B, where nothing is real. I don't know that I *know* you, Ryu. And, to be honest, I doubt that you really know me any better.'

His face fell, and I sighed. 'Look, I'm not saying I don't want to get to know you. Or that I don't think we have a future together. I just don't *know*. And I don't want to find out by giving up everything that is important to me on the off chance that we will work out. How would you feel if I asked you to move to Rockabill?'

He gave me a contemptuous look. 'Jane, please . . .'

I nodded my head sharply. 'Exactly. Why should a deal breaker for *you* be an acceptable compromise for *me*?'

'But we can't just continue like this, Jane.'

'Why can't we? Relationships take time. We've given ours four months.'

'Well, then *I* can't continue this way,' he replied mulishly, staring down at his hands.

Oh, shit, I thought, realizing this argument had, for him, become about pride.

This time, when he looked up at me, my heart froze. I knew the look on his face because I'd seen it before. Ryu was a gambling man, a poker player, and I recognized when he was about to put everything he had on the line.

'Jane,' he began, but I interrupted him.

'Ryu,' I begged. 'Don't do this. Don't make me choose.'

But Ryu hadn't listened to anything I'd said. He thought I was a safe bet. He was so convinced he knew me, so convinced he held all the good cards.

'Honey, I know you want this. You're scared, and it's a big step. But it's *right*, and you know it.'

'Ryu—'

'No, Jane. I can't live like this. You can't live like this. We are either together, or we're not. That's all there is to it.'

'Please. Do *not* do this.'

'No, that's it. You either love me or you don't. It's that simple.'

'You're giving me an ultimatum. That's what we've come down to.'

'Yes,' Ryu said, but I knew he was lying. He didn't think it *was* an ultimatum. He thought he was just giving me an out, making this whole process easier for me. If he 'made' me move to Boston, I didn't have to feel guilty about leaving my father or Rockabill or Nell and the others.

He was so sure he knew me. That he knew my desires, my ambitions, what made me content and what made me proud. What made me Jane.

I sat staring into his eyes. There was a woman there, reflected back at me, whom I didn't even begin to recognize. And I suddenly realized that he knew nothing.

That said, I was as surprised as he was when I got up and left.

Surprised, and heartbroken, and entirely certain I was doing the right thing.

CHAPTER TWENTY-SEVEN

'So you broke up with Ryu?' Iris asked, her beautiful blue eyes huge.

'No, not really. Kind of. I don't know. I walked out.'

'You walked out?'

'I did, indeed. I believe I did what is known as "hotfooting" it. Or "scarpered", as they say in Britain. I made like a refrigerator and ran . . . Rob Roys are delicious, did you know that?'

'Yes, you told me that. Two Rob Roys ago.'

'Bullshit. I've had only one. *This* is my second.'

'No, that's your third. You, Jane True, are schnockered.'

'That is so not true, succubus. I am merely . . . well lubricated.'

'You know what happens when you say that word around me. So be good. And tell me what *happened*, for Pete's sake.'

I sighed, then took a very large gulp of my second Rob Roy. Or was it my third? Sarah had taken one look at my disheveled appearance and she'd gone straight for the Sty's secret stash. She and Marcus were Scotch drinkers, and they kept a little collection of *very* good stuff hidden behind the bar for special friends. She'd pulled out a bottle of Balvenie Signature, as she already knew I liked bourbon, and whipped

e up a Rob Roy. After one sip, I knew Rob was my new
est friend.

If you asked me to move to Boston, things might be different,
told the charming Mr Roy, even as my lovely Scotch concoc-
on whispered to me that it might be a good idea to start my
tory at how I got home, because it was pretty durn funny.
o I told Iris about how the pizza-delivery guy had just been
etting out of his car when I walked out of Ryu's front door.
le'd agreed, once I promised to pay for the pizza and give
im an extra twenty, to drive me down Commonwealth Avenue
o where I remembered seeing an Enterprise Rent-A-Car. That
aid, the delivery guy wasn't quite so keen when Ryu came
hasing us down the street after he figured out I hadn't just
arried my suitcase downstairs to pout.

Unfortunately, the rental car company had been closed. I'd
alled Julian for a ride to a hotel, but he'd shown up with
Caleb, and they'd insisted on driving me back, all the way
o Maine.

'I told them, "He's going to be *soooo* pissed at you when
e finds out you drove me home." But they didn't care.'

In fact, Caleb had responded to my warning by saying,
Fuck it,' his mahogany baritone making the obscenity sound
trangely dignified.

'Yeah, fuck it!' Julian had chortled, like a little kid. My
ellow halfling had gotten an enormous kick out of sticking
t to the man. Or vampire. Whatever.

'And so they drove me home,' I concluded. 'And even
hough I haven't slept in, like, forty-eight hours, I *still* couldn't
ucking sleep. So I called you, and you took me out to get
drunk. Because you, Iris, are a good friend.' I sighed and
eaned back in my seat. In reality, the tiny part of me that
was still curiously sober couldn't believe I'd walked out on
Ryu.

'So is it, like, *over* over?' Iris asked.

'Pshaw. No. I do really care for him. But he had to kno
that I'm not a pushover. Okay, fine, you can physically pus
me over, as that fucking incubus demonstrated. But I'm n
about to be bullied into moving to Boston.'

'Nor should you be, Jane,' Iris said emphatically, and
raised my now-half-empty – or was it half-full? – glass
toast with her.

'So what, exactly, did he do? Was it just the ultimatu
that pissed you off?'

At Iris's question, I stopped and really tried to break dow
what it was about Ryu's demands that had bothered me s
much. Obviously there was the drama-queen aspect of landin
that ultimatum on me, especially after everything we'd ju
been through. Everything *I* had been through. You didn
demand someone make major life changes when they'd bee
beaten to a pulp the night before. And why did *I* have t
move? That would be one stonkingly big compromise on m
part.

But is compromise such a bad thing? the maraschino cherr
in my drink inquired philosophically. *It's the first thing you'r
taught in kindergarten, after all. How to share each other
toys.* I groaned softly, rubbing my palms into my eyes. The
I ate the damned cherry.

'The thing is, Iris, I've never liked the idea of compromise
In films and in stories, people who love each other – reall
love each other – make horrendous sacrifices. They giv
kidneys, they move across the world, they *die*. Or become th
undead, because you know I like that sort of book. Basically
the heroine's lover calls, and she answers. Which is stupid
You know why?'

Iris shook her head.

'Because he's always fucking calling.'

Iris nodded, pushing my water toward me. I ignored it and took another drink of my delicious, golden-brown, new best friend.

'So I've never liked that idea, Iris. You know why?' Iris again shook her head. 'Because I think that sometimes, when you really love somebody, you don't ask them for the kind of compromise that is actually a sacrifice. The kind where one person gives up everything they have, everything they are, just so they can be with the other person. And you certainly don't *expect* that shit. You don't *expect* someone to prove their love. To love you that little bit more than you love them.'

I took another long draught of my drink. Pontificating was thirsty work, and I needed to wet the old whistle. Then I could wax poetic. *Or babble like a drunken lunatic*, the cherry mumbled, vengefully, from the pit of my stomach. I went right ahead and digested it into submission.

'What Ryu wants from me,' I warned, waggling my finger emphatically in the air, 'I can't give him. Not now, and maybe not ever. I don't know whether it's because I don't love him, or because I can't love him for *demanding* something like that from me. Or because he doesn't know me for squat. But I couldn't give him my whole life. And that's what he wanted from me. He wanted everything, and I wanted him to love me for what I had already offered.' I paused, suddenly worried. And because I had to hiccough.

'Iris, am I a bad person?'

'No, honey, you're not a bad person,' my friend responded, leaning over to grab my hand.

I blinked for two reasons when she touched me. The first was that I realized, suddenly, that I was completely shitfaced. The second, however, was because I also realized that despite the fact that I was schlitzed, and still a basket case from everything that had happened over the last week, my shields had gone up, totally reflexively, the minute Iris reached for me.

'I think I learned a lot on vacation,' I whispered at my friend, leaning conspiratorially across the table toward her.

'I think you did too, honey,' Iris said, laughing.

'And I figured out that thing with the two fingers and the Twizzlers you told me about . . .'

Iris began laughing almost immediately, and I felt good, sitting there with my friend. Then again, it might just have been the booze. I knew I still had to deal with Ryu like an adult, but we – me and the three Rob Roys floating around in my stomach – were secretly thrilled that I'd walked out like that. I felt . . . sassy. Like I should be in a rock video.

Then it was my turn to bust my guts laughing when Iris told me about everything that had gone down in the bookstore while I was away. I'd had a long talk with Grizzie and Tracy as soon as I got back to Rockabill. They had been amazingly understanding. Basically, Grizzie had said she didn't have a leg to stand on, since she was constantly disappearing herself. And Tracy said that she understood life sometimes got the better of us. I still felt guilty, however, and I had promised to open the store – off the clock, single-handedly, and even when I wasn't working that day – for the next month so they could sleep in.

But they'd also been sketchy about what had happened while I was away. I think they didn't want to make me feel guilty. So Iris spilled the beans.

Apparently, Miss Carol had taken Linda on as her cause célèbre. Don't get me wrong, Miss Carol was one lecherous gnome. But she firmly believed in *consensual* lechery. So she'd refused to let Linda purchase any of her pulp-fiction rape fantasies. Instead, Miss Carol had started Linda on an

itial course of feminist antibiotics: Wollstonecraft, Millett,
d Greer. When Linda hadn't responded to treatment, Miss
arol had switched to something more aggressive. If Linda
anted violence, Miss Carol would give her pain tempered
ith philosophy. So poor Linda left Read It and Weep buried
nder a stack of Henry Miller, D. H. Lawrence, and the
larquis de Sade. She'd returned, two days later, clutching a
py of *Justine* and crying her eyes out. Before Miss Carol
uld slip Linda *Philosophy in the Bedroom*, Amy had inter-
ened. She'd sent Linda home with Danielle Steele and a
upcake, before firmly lecturing Miss Carol about tampering
ith the humans.

I was nearly snorting Rob Roy out of my nose when Iris's
hone rang. I recovered fast when she said, 'Hold on,' and
eld the phone out toward me.

'It's Ryu. Should I tell him to bugger off?'

I took a deep breath, then a sip of my water, then shook
ly head.

'No, I'll talk to him.'

She passed me the phone and slipped out of our booth to
o chat with Marcus at the bar.

'Jane?'

'I'm here.'

'You made it home okay.'

'Yes, I'm fine.'

There was an awkward silence.

'I tried your cell—'

'I have it on silent,' I cut in.

Crickets chirped.

'Why did you leave like that?'

I shrugged, and then remembered he couldn't see me.

'I dunno. I just didn't feel like you left me with any options.'

'So you walked out.'

'You weren't listening. You were making declarations. Y
are not George Bush.'

'What?'

'I'm not with you or against you, Ryu. I care about yo
but I can't just up and leave my life here. It was unfair
you to ask me to do that, and especially unfair right then.

There was silence from the other end of the line. I w
just about to up my bitchiness ante by pressing End when I
finally spoke.

'You're right. I'm sorry. I was a dick.'

'Yup.'

'I'm sorry. Really, I am. I was just so afraid when we lo
you . . . I never took the idea of losing you seriously till the
I can't lose you, Jane. I can't.' Ryu's voice nearly brok
sending me over the edge.

'Oh, Ryu . . .' I sniffled as tears formed in my eyes.

'Are we all right?'

I thought about that, scrubbing my shirt over my face t
wipe up any tears. Then I looked to my Rob Roy for mora
support. When none was forthcoming, I drank it.

'Jane?'

'I don't know, Ryu.' I hated having to tell him this, but
had to. 'Because you were right, too. We can't just go o
like this, I guess. Especially now. Maybe we need a breal
Or a rain check. I've got so much going on, and I really nee
to be . . . *stronger* to be with you.'

'Baby, I would never hurt you.'

I snorted. 'Ryu, I don't mean stronger for you. I mea
stronger so I can *go* anywhere with you. I got *creamed* las
week. The floor was mopped with me. I never want to be i
that position again.'

'You were fine, Jane. You did well. You saved *us*.'

'You only saw me post-Caleb, Ryu. You didn't see th

unches. I got *punched*. A lot. Then bit, and not one of your
exy bites. I mean *bitten*. I probably need a rabies shot. Oh,
nd whipped. Let's not forget the whipping. And that's just
hat Graeme had on for starters.'

Ryu was silent for a moment before he swore softly.

'Jane, I'm so sorry. I didn't realize.'

For a second, I considered harping on the fact that he *didn't
realize* – didn't realize how fucked up I was from everything
hat had happened. That I still had a weird ache, which I
new damned well was purely psychological, where Graeme
ad bitten clean through my lip. That I was hoping alcohol
would grant me sleep, finally, despite the dreams that plagued
ne. How, when I closed my eyes, Conleth was there waiting . . .
f I was lucky. Because Graeme was there if I wasn't.

In the end, however, I didn't bother. Instead, I told him
hat it was okay, that we'd talk soon. That I needed a few
ays to rest and get my head round everything. That I'd call
when I was ready.

I knew Ryu wasn't happy, and he wanted something more
oncrete. But he was shit out of luck.

When I got off the phone, I sat for a second, feeling a bit
umb. Not least because I'd managed to imbibe the remaining
regs of my Rob Roy. I was more booze than Jane at that
oint.

'Are you all right?'

'Iris, your voice is like honeysuckles and stars. With a
unicorn in it.'

'Hmm. I think it's time to go home.'

'No, let's go dancing. You know, I've *never* gone dancing?
've lived a sheltered life.'

'I know, honey. C'mon, we can talk about it in the car.'

'Or we can go to Mexico. "You boys like Mex-eee-ko?"'
quoted, laughing. 'I love *Super Troopers*.'

'I know you do, Jane. It's a classic. Now, just hold on my arm . . .'

Iris managed to pull me out into the parking lot, wavin Marcus away when he tried to help. 'She's got me,' explained to the ice chest that stood outdoors next to tl Sty's entrance.

'I sure do, Jane. I'm just going to prop you up right . here . . . while I find my keys . . .'

Iris was digging through her voluminous purse, her golde hair flowing down around her like a nimbus of light ar butterflies, when I realized something.

'Iris, I love you.'

The succubus laughed. 'I know you do, Jane.'

'No, really. I love you.'

'I know, babycakes.'

'No, *seriously*. I really love you. And I know you alway try to make out with me but that you don't mean it becaus you're a sex demon and whatnot. So we're cool.'

'We're not demons, Jane. And where the hell did I pi my . . . There they are. C'mon, honey.'

'Did I tell you I loved you?'

'Yeah, you did. I love you, too.'

I shook my head, pulling us up short. 'No, Iris. I reall like my life now, and you're part of that. Thank you.'

Iris laughed and brushed the hair from my face.

'You're welcome, pookie,' she said as she pressed a gentl kiss to my lips.

'Did I tell you I loved you?' I mumbled against her mouth

She was laughing, still kissing me, when we wer ambushed. An all-too-familiar voice rang out from the Sty' parking lot.

'I always knew you were a fucking dyke, Jane. What witl all your dyke friends.'

Stuart, bless him, always had a knack for bad timing. But this time it almost got him blasted to smithereens.

I whirled around, a swirling orb of iron-gray power aloft in my hand. I only just managed to keep from blasting it at Stu when I realized he wasn't one of my other more dangerous enemies.

'What the fuck?' Stuart stammered, his face white as he backpedaled to where his SUV was parked.

Yeah, what the fuck? the Balvenie burbled in my veins. I had no idea where I'd pulled the mage ball from.

'. . . fucking freak,' Stu garbled, just as he tripped in a pothole, falling on his back.

Fry the sucker, the part of me that was bloodthirsty and frazzled and sick of being pushed around advised. *And you'll never have to deal with his shit again . . .*

I looked at Stuart and I looked at the ball of light. Then I let it fizzle and die, reabsorbing its power like a good little girl.

'Make him forget, please,' I asked Iris as I lurched toward her little pink car.

Her already big eyes were huge in her face as she turned to glamour Stuart. I leaned my suddenly heated forehead against the cool steel frame of her car door, and I let myself shake it out. I'd been *this* close to killing Stu, and the thought horrified me. Despite the fact that he was a complete and utter butt munch.

Then Iris drove me home, and we sat in her car in my driveway for a bit to talk.

'I totally thought the human was toast.'

'Yeah, well, he sucks. But he doesn't deserve to die.'

'That's debatable. Did you see his shoes? They involved *velcro*.'

I couldn't help but laugh. Iris definitely had her own, very particular, priorities.

'G'night, Iris.'

'Good night, Jane.'

As I was getting out of the car, Iris stopped me.

'Jane? When you said that you learned a lot last week, you were right. I'm really proud of you.'

'Thanks, Iris.'

'No, I'm serious.'

'Okay. Well, thank you.'

'If you need me, call.'

I was still mumbling my thanks to Iris for being such a good friend as I let myself into the house. Then, after listening for my dad's snores to make sure he was asleep, I left him a note and grabbed my sleeping bag.

The sand in my little cove was soft as a bed, and I lay down with a happy sigh. I stared up at the stars through heavy eyelids and thought about the coming weeks.

I think part of me had still thought of my new life as a game, despite everything that had happened at the Compound so many months ago. But now I knew it was no game. Or, if it was, it was one of Russian roulette.

So I knew I had to be ready for whatever came next. No more joking around. Tomorrow, I'd find Nell, and we'd *really* train. I wouldn't fantasize about tossing her about by the bun. Or about riding away on her little pony. I'd work my tail off till I could divvy out the whoopass like a *real* action-adventure heroine.

But first I needed some rest.

Between the familiar comfort of my cove and the strangely soothing sucking sounds of the Old Sow, I finally felt safe enough to sleep. At one point during the night, I did start to dream about Graeme. But my nightmare was dispelled by a warm pant of cardamom breath on my cheek, followed by the caress of a dog's soft tongue. I shifted automatically as a big, soft, and very furry form nestled in the sand next to me. Snuggling against the huge dog and mumbling my thanks against his hairy side for saving me from dream-Graeme, my exhausted brain was pulled deeper into sleep as, after what felt like weeks, I finally felt safe.

Now graced with peaceful slumber, in my dreams Graeme exited stage left as Anyan entered stage right. In reality, while I slept, the real Anyan was curled up next to me in his doggy form. But in my dream world, my subconscious had grown tired of indulging my conscious mind's usual repression tactics. So dream-Jane watched as dream-Anyan shifted from doggy to man. Then dream-Jane's eyes bulged as she realized her sleeping brain had dressed the barghest in that big smile of his. And nothing else.

The dream that followed was definitely not a nightmare. Except it did leave me sweating and wide-eyed and more than a little disconcerted upon waking. At least I was alone, but for a long, black dog hair that I pulled out of my mouth.

I laid the hair down on the sand next to me and stared at it for a bit before I pulled my sleeping bag back over my head.

Ryu was going to be so pissed.

Acknowledgments

My family, as always, comes first. A million thanks to Rella, Dennis, Chris, Lisa, Wyatt, and Abby Peeler for their limitless support, love, and enthusiasm.

I would like to thank Devi Pillai and Rebecca Strauss, my editrix and my agent, for giving me this amazing opportunity. Thanks to everyone else at McIntosh and Otis and at Orbit for their hard work, as well – especially Ian Polonsky, Alex Lencicki, Jack Womack, Lauren Panepinto, and Jenn Flax. You've all made me feel like part of this amazing extended family. Granted, it's an extended family with Orc heads in the closets, but that suits me just fine.

Thank you, Sharon Tancredi, for another brilliant cover. You've given Jane such beautiful and vivid life.

I extend huge amounts of gratitude to my Alpha Readers, Christie Ko and Dr James Clawson, and to my new critique partner, Diana Rowland. You helped me whip a flabby rough draft into shape, and I owe you many a beer.

I also have to thank the illustrious Dr and Mrs Whisky and their wee dram. You two couldn't be more amazing friends. Thank you for the drinks, the laughter, the love, and the party.

Finally, I'd like to thank all of my friends, colleagues, and students here in Shreveport. A special shout-out goes to Dr Mary Lois White, for being My One Friend for so many months as well as the newest member of my Alpha Team. But thanks to all of you for putting up with my constant crabbiness and deadline stress. And thanks to everyone at LSUS for being ridiculously supportive to an academic turned urban fantasist. It's been a wild ride, but y'all have been marvelous.

extras

www.orbitbooks.net

about the author

Nicole D. Peeler is off on another adventure! This time, she's moving to Pittsburgh to teach in Seton Hill's MFA in Popular Fiction. Yes, folks, she'll be mentoring up and coming urban fantasists as they try to break into the publishing world. Or, as she likes to call it, 'infecting them with her madness'. In the meantime, she's still taking pleasure in what means most to her: family, friends, food, and travel.

Find out more about Nicole Peeler and other Orbit authors by registering for the free monthly newsletter at www.orbitbooks.net

if you enjoyed
TRACKING THE TEMPEST

look out for

SOULLESS

book one of the Parasol Protectorate
by
Gail Carriger

1.

In Which Parasols Prove Useful

Miss Alexia Tarabotti was not enjoying her evening. Private balls were never more than middling amusements for spinsters, and Miss Tarabotti was not the kind of spinster who could garner even that much pleasure from the event. To put the pudding in the puff: she had retreated to the library, her favorite sanctuary in any house, only to happen upon an unexpected vampire.

She glared at the vampire.

For his part, the vampire seemed to feel that their encounter had improved his ball experience immeasurably. For there she sat, without escort, in a low-necked ball gown.

In this particular case, what he did not know could hurt him. For Miss Alexia had been born without a soul, which, as any decent vampire of good blooding knew, made her a lady to avoid most assiduously.

Yet he moved toward her, darkly shimmering out of the library shadows with feeding fangs ready. However, the moment he touched Miss Tarabotti, he was suddenly no longer darkly doing anything at all. He was simply standing there, the faint sounds of a string quartet in the background as he foolishly fished about with his tongue for fangs unaccountably mislaid.

Miss Tarabotti was not in the least surprised; soulless-ness always neutralized supernatural abilities. She issued the vampire a very dour look. Certainly, most daylight folk wouldn't peg her as anything less than a standard English prig, but had this man not even bothered to read the vampire's official abnormality roster for London and its greater environs?

The vampire recovered his equanimity quickly enough. He reared away from Alexia, knocking over a nearby tea trolley. Physical contact broken, his fangs reappeared. Clearly not the sharpest of prongs, he then darted forward from the neck like a serpent, diving in for another chomp.

'I say!' said Alexia to the vampire. 'We have not even been introduced!'

Miss Tarabotti had never actually had a vampire try to bite her. She knew one or two by reputation, of course, and was friendly with Lord Akeldama. Who was not friendly with Lord Akeldama? But no vampire had ever actually attempted to feed on her before!

So Alexia, who abhorred violence, was forced to grab the miscreant by his nostrils, a delicate and therefore painful area, and shove him away. He stumbled over the fallen tea trolley, lost his balance in a manner astonishingly graceless for a vampire, and fell to the floor. He landed right on top of a plate of treacle tart.

Miss Tarabotti was most distressed by this. She was particularly fond of treacle tart and had been looking forward to consuming that precise plateful. She picked up her parasol. It was terribly tasteless for her to be carrying a parasol at an evening ball, but Miss Tarabotti rarely went anywhere without it. It was of a style entirely of her own devising: a black frilly confection with purple satin pansies sewn about, brass hardware, and buckshot in its silver tip.

She whacked the vampire right on top of the head with it as he tried to extract himself from his newly intimate relations with the tea trolley. The buckshot gave the brass parasol just enough heft to make a deliciously satisfying thunk.

'Manners!' instructed Miss Tarabotti.

The vampire howled in pain and sat back down on the treacle tart.

Alexia followed up her advantage with a vicious prod between the vampire's legs. His howl went quite a bit higher in pitch, and he crumpled into a fetal position. While Miss Tarabotti was a proper English young lady, aside from not having a soul and being half Italian, she did spend quite a bit more time than most other young ladies riding and walking and was therefore unexpectedly strong.

Miss Tarabotti leaped forward – as much as one could leap in full triple-layered underskirts, draped bustle, and ruffled taffeta top-skirt – and bent over the vampire. He was clutching at his indelicate bits and writhing about. The pain would not last long given his supernatural healing ability, but it hurt most decidedly in the interim.

Alexia pulled a long wooden hair stick out of her elaborate coiffure. Blushing at her own temerity, she ripped open his shirtfront, which was cheap and overly starched, and poked at his chest, right over the heart. Miss Tarabotti sported a particularly large and sharp hair stick. With her free hand, she made certain to touch his chest, as only physical contact would nullify his supernatural abilities.

'Desist that horrible noise immediately,' she instructed the creature.

The vampire quit his squealing and lay perfectly still. His beautiful blue eyes watered slightly as he stared fixedly at the wooden hair stick. Or, as Alexia liked to call it, hair stake.

'Explain yourself!' Miss Tarabotti demanded, increasing the pressure.

'A thousand apologies.' The vampire looked confused. 'Who are you?' Tentatively he reached for his fangs. Gone.

To make her position perfectly clear, Alexia stopped

touching him (though she kept her sharp hair stick in place). His fangs grew back.

He gasped in amazement. 'What are you? I thought you were a lady, alone. It would be my right to feed, if you were left this carelethly unattended. Pleathe, I did not mean to prethume,' he lisped around his fangs, real panic in his eyes.

Alexia, finding it hard not to laugh at the lisp, said, 'There is no cause for you to be so overly dramatic. Your hive queen will have told you of my kind.' She returned her hand to his chest once more. The vampire's fangs retracted.

He looked at her as though she had suddenly sprouted whiskers and hissed at him.

Miss Tarabotti was surprised. Supernatural creatures, be they vampires, werewolves, or ghosts, owed their existence to an overabundance of soul, an excess that refused to die. Most knew that others like Miss Tarabotti existed, born without any soul at all. The estimable Bureau of Unnatural Registry (BUR), a division of Her Majesty's Civil Service, called her ilk preternatural. Alexia thought the term nicely dignified. What vampires called her was far less complimentary. After all, preternaturals had once hunted them, and vampires had long memories. Natural, daylight persons were kept in the dark, so to speak, but any vampire worth his blood should know a preternatural's touch. This one's ignorance was untenable. Alexia said, as though to a very small child, 'I am a preternatural.'

The vampire looked embarrassed. 'Of course you are,' he agreed, obviously still not quite comprehending. 'Again, my apologies, lovely one. I am overwhelmed to meet you. You are my first' – he stumbled over the word – 'preternatural.' He frowned. 'Not supernatural, not natural, of course! How foolish of me not to see the dichotomy.' His eyes narrowed into craftiness. He was now studiously ignoring the hair stick and looking tenderly up into Alexia's face.

Miss Tarabotti knew full well her own feminine appeal. The kindest compliment her face could ever hope to garner was 'exotic', never 'lovely'. Not that it had ever received either. Alexia figured that vampires, like all predators, were at their most charming when cornered.

The vampire's hands shot forward, going for her neck. Apparently, he had decided if he could not suck her blood, strangulation was an acceptable alternative. Alexia jerked back, at the same time pressing her hair stick into the creature's white flesh. It slid in about half an inch. The vampire reacted with a desperate wriggle that, even without super-human strength, unbalanced Alexia in her heeled velvet dancing shoes. She fell back. He stood, roaring in pain, with her hair stick half in and half out of his chest.

Miss Tarabotti scrabbled for her parasol, rolling about inelegantly among the tea things, hoping her new dress would miss the fallen foodstuffs. She found the parasol and came upright, swinging it in a wide arc. Purely by chance, the heavy tip struck the end of her wooden hair stick, driving it straight into the vampire's heart.

The creature stood stock-still, a look of intense surprise on his handsome face. Then he fell backward onto the much-abused plate of treacle tart, flopping in a limp overcooked-asparagus kind of way. His alabaster face turned a yellowish gray, as though he were afflicted with the jaundice, and he went still. Alexia's books called this end of the vampire life cycle dissanimation. Alexia, who thought the action astoundingly similar to a soufflé going flat, decided at that moment to call it the Grand Collapse.

She intended to waltz directly out of the library without anyone the wiser to her presence there. This would have resulted in the loss of her best hair stick and her well-deserved tea, as well as a good deal of drama. Unfortunately, a small group of young dandies came traipsing in at that precise moment. What young men of such dress were doing in a library was anyone's guess. Alexia felt the most likely explanation was that they had become lost while looking for the card room. Regardless, their presence forced her to pretend that she, too, had just discovered the dead vampire. With a resigned shrug, she screamed and collapsed into a faint.

She stayed resolutely fainted, despite the liberal application of smelling salts, which made her eyes water most tremendously, a cramp in the back of one knee, and the fact that her new ball gown was getting most awfully wrinkled. All its many layers of green trim, picked to the height of fashion in lightening shades to complement the cuirasse bodice, were being crushed into oblivion under her weight. The expected noises ensued: a good deal of yelling, much bustling about, and several loud clatters as one of the housemaids cleared away the fallen tea.

Then came the sound she had half anticipated, half dreaded. An authoritative voice cleared the library of both young dandies and all other interested parties who had flowed into the room upon discovery of the tableau. The voice instructed everyone to 'get out!' while he 'gained the particulars from the young lady' in tones that brooked no refusal.

Silence descended.

'Mark my words, I will use something much, much stronger than smelling salts,' came a growl in Miss Tarabotti's left ear. The voice was low and tinged with a hint of Scotland. It would have caused Alexia to shiver and think primal monkey thoughts about moons and running far and fast, if she'd had a soul. Instead it caused her to sigh in exasperation and sit up.

'And a good evening to you, too, Lord Maccon. Lovely weather we are having for this time of year, is it not?' She patted at her hair, which was threatening to fall down without the hair stick in its proper place. Surreptitiously, she looked about for Lord Conall Maccon's second in command, Professor Lyall. Lord Maccon tended to maintain a much calmer temper when his Beta was present. But, then, as Alexia had come to comprehend, that appeared to be the main role of a Beta – especially one attached to Lord Maccon.

'Ah, Professor Lyall, how nice to see you again.' She smiled in relief.

Professor Lyall, the Beta in question, was a slight, sandy-haired gentleman of indeterminate age and pleasant disposition, as agreeable, in fact, as his Alpha was sour. He grinned at her and doffed his hat, which was of first-class design and sensible material. His cravat was similarly subtle, for, while it was tied expertly, the knot was a humble one.

'Miss Tarabotti, how delicious to find ourselves in your company once more.' His voice was soft and mild-mannered.

'Stop humoring her, Randolph,' barked Lord Maccon. The fourth Earl of Woolsey was much larger than Professor Lyall and in possession of a near-permanent frown. Or at least he always seemed to be frowning when he was in the presence of Miss Alexia Tarabotti, ever since the hedgehog incident (which really, honestly, had not been her fault). He also had unreasonably pretty tawny eyes, mahogany-colored hair, and a particularly nice nose. The eyes were currently glaring at Alexia from a shockingly intimate distance.

'Why is it, Miss Tarabotti, every time I have to clean up a mess in a library, you just happen to be in the middle of it?' the earl demanded of her.

Alexia gave him a withering look and brushed down the front of her green taffeta gown, checking for bloodstains.

Lord Maccon appreciatively watched her do it. Miss Tarabotti might examine her face in the mirror each morning with a large degree of censure, but there was nothing at all wrong with her figure. He would have to have had far less soul and a good fewer urges not to notice that appetizing fact. Of course, she always went and spoiled the appeal by opening her mouth. In his humble experience, the world had yet to produce a more vexingly verbose female.

'Lovely but unnecessary,' he said, indicating her efforts to brush away nonexistent blood drops.

Alexia reminded herself that Lord Maccon and his kind were only just civilized. One simply could not expect too much from them, especially under delicate circumstances such as these. Of course, that failed to explain Professor Lyall, who was always utterly urbane. She glanced with appreciation in the professor's direction.

Lord Maccon's frown intensified.

Miss Tarabotti considered that the lack of civilized behavior might be the sole provenance of Lord Maccon. Rumor had it, he had only lived in London a comparatively short while – and he had relocated from Scotland of all barbaric places.

The professor coughed delicately to get his Alpha's attention. The earl's yellow gaze focused on him with such intensity it should have actually burned. 'Aye?'

'Very little mess, actually. Almost complete lack of blood spatter.' He leaned forward and sniffed. 'Definitely Westminster,' he stated.

The Earl of Woolsey seemed to understand. He turned his piercing gaze onto the dead vampire. 'He must have been very hungry.'

Professor Lyall turned the body over. 'What happened here?' He took out a small set of wooden tweezers from the pocket of his waistcoat and picked at the back of the vampire's trousers. He paused, rummaged about in his coat pockets, and produced a diminutive leather case. He clicked it open and removed a most bizarre pair of gogglelike things. They were gold in color with multiple lenses on one side, between which there appeared to be some kind of liquid. The contraption was also riddled with small knobs and dials. Professor Lyall propped the ridiculous things onto his nose and bent back over the vampire, twiddling at the dials expertly.

'Goodness gracious me,' exclaimed Alexia, 'what are you wearing? It looks like the unfortunate progeny of an illicit union between a pair of binoculars and some opera glasses. What on earth are they called, binocticals, spectoculars?'

The earl snorted his amusement and then tried to pretend he hadn't. 'How about glassicals?' he suggested, apparently unable to resist a contribution. There was a twinkle in his eye as he said it that Alexia found rather unsettling.

Professor Lyall looked up from his examination and glared at the both of them. His right eye was hideously magnified. It was quite gruesome and made Alexia start involuntarily.

'These are my monocular cross-magnification lenses with spectra-modifier attachment, and they are invaluable. I will thank you not to mock them so openly.' He turned once more to the task at hand.

'Oh.' Miss Tarabotti was suitably impressed. 'How do they work?' she inquired.

Professor Lyall looked back up at her, suddenly animated. 'Well, you see, it is really quite interesting. By turning this little knob here, you can change the distance between the two panes of glass here, allowing the liquid to—'

The earl's groan interrupted him. 'Don't get him started, Miss Tarabotti, or we will be here all night.'

Looking slightly crestfallen, Professor Lyall turned back to the dead vampire. 'Now, what is this substance all over his clothing?'

His boss, preferring the direct approach, resumed his frown and looked accusingly at Alexia. 'What on God's green earth is that muck?'

Miss Tarabotti said, 'Ah. Sadly, treacle tart. A tragic loss, I daresay.' Her stomach chose that moment to growl in agreement. She would have colored gracefully with embarrassment had she not possessed the complexion of one of those 'heathen Italians', as her mother said, who never colored, gracefully or otherwise. (Convincing her mother that Christianity had, to all intents and purposes, originated with the Italians, thus making them the exact opposite of heathen, was a waste of time and breath.) Alexia refused to apologize for the boisterousness of her stomach and favored Lord Maccon with a defiant glare. Her stomach was the reason she had sneaked away in the first place. Her mama had assured her there would be food at the ball. Yet all that appeared on offer when they arrived was a bowl of punch and some sadly wilted watercress. Never one to let her stomach get the better of her, Alexia had ordered tea from the butler and retreated to the library. Since she normally spent any ball lurking on the outskirts of the dance floor trying to look as though she did not want to be asked to waltz, tea was a welcome alternative. It was rude to order refreshments from someone else's staff, but when one was promised sandwiches and there was nothing but watercress, well, one must simply take matters into one's own hands!

Professor Lyall, kindhearted soul that he was, prattled on to no one in particular, pretending not to notice the rumbling of her stomach. Though of course he heard it. He had excellent hearing. They all did. He looked up from his examinations, his face all catawampus from the glassicals. 'Starvation would explain why the vampire was desperate enough to try for Miss Tarabotti at a ball, rather than taking to the slums like the smart ones do when they get this bad.'

Alexia grimaced. 'No associated hive either.'

Lord Maccon arched one black eyebrow, professing not to be impressed. 'How could you possibly know that?'

Professor Lyall explained for both of them. 'No need to be so direct with the young lady. A hive queen would never have let one of her brood get into such a famished condition. We must have a rove on our hands, one completely without ties to the local hive.'

Alexia stood up, revealing to Lord Maccon that she had arranged her faint to rest comfortably against a fallen settee pillow. He grinned and then quickly hid it behind a frown when she looked at him suspiciously.

'I have a different theory.' She gestured to the vampire's

clothing. 'Badly tied cravat and a cheap shirt? No hive worth its salt would let a larva like that out without dressing him properly for public appearance. I am surprised he was not stopped at the front entrance. The duchess's footman really ought to have spotted a cravat like that prior to the reception line and forcibly ejected the wearer. I suppose good staff is hard to come by with all the best ones becoming drones these days, but such a shirt!'

The Earl of Woolsey glared at her. 'Cheap clothing is no excuse for killing a man.'

'Mmm, that's what you say.' Alexia evaluated Lord Maccon's perfectly tailored shirtfront and exquisitely tied cravat. His dark hair was a bit too long and shaggy to be de mode, and his face was not entirely clean-shaven, but he possessed enough hauteur to carry this lower-class roughness off without seeming scruffy. She was certain that his silver and black paisley cravat must be tied under sufferance. He probably preferred to wander about barechested at home. The idea made her shiver oddly. It must take a lot of effort to keep a man like him tidy. Not to mention well tailored. He was bigger than most. She had to give credit to his valet, who must be a particularly tolerant claviger.

Lord Maccon was normally quite patient. Like most of his kind, he had learned to be such in polite society. But Miss Tarabotti seemed to bring out the worst of his animal urges. 'Stop trying to change the subject,' he snapped, squirming under her calculated scrutiny. 'Tell me what happened.' He put on his BUR face and pulled out a small metal tube, stylus, and pot of clear liquid. He unrolled the tube with a small cranking device, clicked the top off the liquid, and dipped the stylus into it. It sizzled ominously.

Alexia bristled at his autocratic tone. 'Do not give me instructions in that tone of voice, you –' she searched for a particularly insulting word – 'puppy! I am jolly well not one of your pack.'

Lord Conall Maccon, Earl of Woolsey, was Alpha of the local werewolves, and as a result, he had access to a wide array of truly vicious methods of dealing with Miss Alexia Tarabotti. Instead of briding at her insult (puppy, indeed!), he brought out his best offensive weapon, the result of decades of personal experience with more than one Alpha she-wolf. Scottish he may be by birth, but that only made him better equipped to deal with strong-willed females. 'Stop playing verbal games with me, madam, or I shall go out into that ballroom, find your mother, and bring her here.'